Praise for *New York Times* bestselling author Nalini Singh

'Nalini Singh is a major new talent'
#1 *New York Times* bestselling author Christine Feehan

'Her books are gems, true treasures . . . that just get better and better'
Romance Reviews Today

'A writer that will no doubt shine for some time'
Romance Reader at Heart

'This book is a must even for those uninitiated in the paranormal genre. The story ends much too quickly, and the author's magical writing conjures up sensual images and intense emotions that linger long after the last word is read'
Romantic Times

'Sexy, crisp, hard-edged and intelligent, Slave to Sensation is a terrific book . . .'
Bookpage

Also by Nalini Singh

SLAVE TO SENSATION

NALINI SINGH

The right of Nalini Singh to be identified as the author of this work
has been asserted by her in accordance with the
Copyright, Designs and Patents Act 1988.

First published in Great Britain in 2010 by
Gollancz
An imprint of the Orion Publishing Group
Orion House, 5 Upper St Martin's Lane, London WC2H 9EA
An Hachette UK Company

A CIP catalogue record for this book is available
from the British Library

Printed in Great Britain by Clays Ltd, St Ives plc

www.nalinisingh.com

www.orionbooks.co.uk

The Orion Publishing Group's policy is to use papers that are
natural, renewable and recyclable products and made from wood
grown in sustainable forests. The logging and manufacturing
processes are expected to conform to the environmental regulations
of the country of origin.

SLAVE TO SENSATION

This one is for my wonderful editor, Cindy Hwang, and my awesome agent, Nephele Tempest, for being so enthusiastic about this book from the start, and as always for my family, for being there no matter what.

PROLOGUE

Silence

In an effort to reduce the overwhelming incidence of insanity and serial killing in the Psy population, the Psy Council decided, in the year 1969, to instigate a rigorous program called Silence. The aim of Silence was to condition young Psy from birth. The aim of the conditioning was to teach them not to feel rage.

However, the Council soon discovered that it was impossible to isolate that one emotion. In 1979, after a ten-year debate over the millions of minds in the PsyNet, it was decided to change the aim of Silence. Its new mission was to condition young Psy to feel nothing. Not rage, not jealousy, not envy, not happiness, and certainly not love.

Silence was a resounding success.

By the year 2079, when the fifth or sixth generation of Psy are being conditioned, everyone has forgotten that they had ever been any other way. The Psy are known to be icily controlled, inhumanly practical, and impossible to push to violence.

They are the leaders of government and business,

eclipsing both humans and changelings, races that allow their animal natures to rule them. With mental capabilities running from telepathy to foresight, telekinesis to psychometry, the Psy consider themselves a step up the evolutionary ladder.

In keeping with their nature, they base all their decisions on logic and efficiency. According to the PsyNet, their mistake rate is close to nil.

The Psy are perfect in their Silence.

CHAPTER 1

Sascha Duncan couldn't read a single line of the report flickering across the screen of her handheld organizer. A haze of fear clouded her vision, insulating her from the cold efficiency of her mother's office. Even the sound of Nikita wrapping up a call barely penetrated her numbed mind.

She was terrified.

This morning, she'd woken to find herself curled up in bed, whimpering. Normal Psy did not whimper, did not show any emotion, did not feel. But Sascha had known since childhood that she wasn't normal. She'd successfully hidden her flaw for twenty-six years but now things were going wrong. Very, very wrong.

Her mind was deteriorating at such an accelerating rate that she'd begun experiencing physical side effects—muscle spasms, tremors, an abnormal heart rhythm, and those ragged tears after dreams she never recalled. It would soon become impossible to conceal her fractured psyche.

The result of exposure would be incarceration at the Center. Of course no one called it a prison. Termed a "rehabilitation facility," it provided a brutally efficient way for the Psy to cull the weak from the herd.

After they were through with her, if she was lucky she'd end up a drooling mess with no mind to speak of. If she wasn't so fortunate, she'd retain enough of her thinking processes to become a drone in the vast business networks of the Psy, a robot with just enough neurons functioning to file the mail or sweep the floors.

The feel of her hand tightening on the organizer jolted her back to reality. If there was one place she couldn't break down, it was here, sitting across from her mother. Nikita Duncan might be her blood but she was also a member of the Psy Council. Sascha wasn't sure that if it came down to it, Nikita wouldn't sacrifice her daughter to keep her place on the most powerful body in the world.

With grim determination, she began to reinforce the psychic shields that protected the secret corridors of her mind. It was the one thing she excelled at and by the time her mother finished her call, Sascha exhibited as much emotion as a sculpture carved from arctic ice.

"We have a meeting with Lucas Hunter in ten minutes. Are you ready?" Nikita's almond-shaped eyes held nothing but cool interest.

"Of course, Mother." She forced herself to meet that direct gaze without flinching, trying not to wonder if her own was as unrevealing. It helped that, unlike Nikita, she had the night-sky eyes of a cardinal Psy—an endless field of black scattered with pinpricks of cold white fire.

"Hunter is an alpha changeling so don't underestimate him. He thinks like a Psy." Nikita turned to bring up her computer screen, a flat panel that slid up and out from the surface of her desk.

Sascha called up the relevant data on her organizer. The

miniature computer held all the notes she could possibly need for the meeting and was compact enough to slip into her pocket. If Lucas Hunter stuck true to type, he'd turn up with paper hard copies of everything.

According to her information, Hunter had become the only ruling alpha in the DarkRiver leopard pack at twenty-three years of age. In the ten years since, DarkRiver had consolidated its hold over San Francisco and surrounding regions to the extent that they were now the dominant predators in the area. Outside changelings who wanted to work, live, or play in DarkRiver territory had to receive their permission. If they didn't, changeling territorial law went into force and the outcome was savage.

What had made Sascha's eyes open wide in her first reading of this material was that DarkRiver had negotiated a mutual nonaggression pact with the SnowDancers, the wolf pack that controlled the rest of California. Since the Snow-Dancers were known to be vicious and unforgiving to anyone who dared rise to power in their territory, it made her wonder at DarkRiver's civilized image. No one survived the wolves by playing nice.

A soft chime sounded.

"Shall we go, Mother?" Nothing about Nikita's relationship to Sascha was, or had ever been, maternal, but protocol stated she was to be addressed by her family designation.

Nikita nodded and stood to her full height, a graceful five eight. Dressed in a black pantsuit teamed with a white shirt, she looked every inch the successful woman she was, her hair cut to just below her ears in a blunt style that suited her. She was beautiful. And she was lethal.

Sascha knew that when they walked side by side as they were doing now, no one would place them for mother and daughter. They were the same height but the resemblance ended there. Nikita had inherited her Asiatic eyes, arrow-straight hair, and porcelain skin from her half-Japanese mother. By the time the genes had been passed on to Sascha, all that had survived was the slightest tilt to the eyes.

Instead of Nikita's sheet of shimmering blue-black, she had rich ebony hair that absorbed light like ink and curled so wildly she was forced to pull it back into a severe plait every morning. Her skin was a dark honey rather than ivory, evidence of her unknown father's genes. Sascha's birth records had listed him as being of Anglo-Indian descent.

She dropped back a little as the door to the meeting room drew closer. She hated encounters with changelings and not because of the general Psy revulsion to their open emotionalism. It seemed to her that they *knew*. Somehow they could sense that she wasn't like the others, that she was flawed.

"Mr. Hunter."

She looked up at the sound of her mother's voice. And found herself within touching distance of the most dangerous male she'd ever seen. There was no other word to describe him. Well over six feet tall, he was built like the fighting machine he was in the wild, pure lean muscle and tensile strength.

His black hair brushed his shoulders but there was nothing soft about it. Instead, it hinted at unrestrained passion and the dark hunger of the leopard below the skin. She had no doubt she was in the presence of a predator.

Then he turned his head and she saw the right side of his face. Four jagged lines, reminiscent of the claw marks of some great beast, scored the muted gold of his skin. His eyes were a hypnotic green but it was those slashing markings that grabbed her attention. She'd never been this close to one of the changeling Hunters before.

"Ms. Duncan." His voice was low and a little rough, as if caught on the edge of a growl.

"This is my daughter, Sascha. She'll be the liaison for this project."

"A pleasure, Sascha." He tipped his head toward her, eyes lingering for a second longer than necessary.

"Likewise." Could he hear the jagged beat of her pulse? Was it true that changeling senses were far superior to those of any other race?

"Please." He gestured for them to take seats at the glass-topped table and remained standing until they'd done so. Then he chose a chair exactly opposite Sascha.

She forced herself to return his gaze, not fooled by the chivalry into dropping her guard. Hunters were trained to sniff out vulnerable prey. "We've looked at your offer," she began.

"What do you think?" His eyes were remarkably clear, as calm as the deepest ocean. But there was nothing cold or practical about him, nothing that belied her first impression of him as something wild barely leashed.

"You must know that Psy-changeling business alliances rarely work. Competing priorities." Nikita's voice sounded utterly toneless in comparison to Lucas's.

His responsive smile was so wicked, Sascha couldn't look away. "In this case, I think we have the same ones. You need help to plan and execute housing that'll appeal to changelings. I want an inside track on new Psy projects."

Sascha knew that that couldn't be all of it. They needed him but he didn't need them, not when DarkRiver's business interests were extensive enough to rival their own. The world was changing under the noses of the Psy, the human and changeling races no longer content to be second best. It was a measure of their arrogance that most of her people continued to ignore the slow shift in power.

Sitting so close to the contained fury that was Lucas Hunter, she wondered at the blindness of her brethren. "If we deal with you, we'll expect the same level of reliability that we'd get if we went with a Psy construction and design firm."

Lucas looked across at the icy perfection of Sascha Duncan and wished he knew what it was about her that was bugging the hell out of him. His beast was snarling and pacing the cage of his mind, ready to pounce out and sniff at her sedate dark gray pantsuit. "Of course," he said, fascinated by the tiny flickers of white light that came and went in the darkness of her eyes.

He'd seldom been this close to a cardinal Psy. They were rare enough that they didn't mingle with the masses, being given high posts in the Psy Council as soon as they reached any kind of mature age. Sascha was young but there was nothing untried about her. She looked as ruthless as the rest of her race, as unfeeling and as cold.

She could be abetting killer.

Any one of them could be. It was why DarkRiver had been stalking high-level Psy for months, looking for a way to penetrate their defenses. The Duncan project was an unbelievable chance. Not only was Nikita powerful in her own right, she was a member of the innermost circle—the Psy Council. Once Lucas was in, it would be his job to find out the identity of the sadistic Psy who'd stolen the life of one of DarkRiver's women . . . and execute him.

No mercy. No forgiveness.

In front of him, Sascha glanced at the slim organizer she held. "We're willing to offer seven million."

He'd take a penny if it would get him inside the secretive corridors of the Psy world but he couldn't afford to make them suspicious. "Ladies." He filled the single word with the sensuality that was as much a part of him as his beast.

Most changelings and humans would've reacted to the promise of pleasure implicit in his tones, but these two remained unmoved. "We both know the contract is worth nothing less than ten million. Let's not waste time." He could've sworn a light sparked in Sascha's night-sky eyes, a light that spoke of a challenge accepted. The panther inside him growled softly in response.

"Eight. And we want rights to approve each stage of the work from concept to construction."

"Ten." He kept his tone silky smooth. "Your request will cause considerable delay. I can't work efficiently if I have to traipse up here every time I want to make a minor change." Perhaps multiple visits might allow him to glean some information on the murderer's cold trail, but it was doubtful. Nikita was hardly likely to leave sensitive Council documents lying around.

"Give us a moment." The older woman looked at the younger.

The tiny hairs on the back of his neck rose. They always did that in the presence of Psy who were actively using their powers. Telepathy was just one of their many talents and one that he admitted came in very handy during business negotiations. But their abilities also blinded them. Changelings had long ago learned to take advantage of the Psy sense of superiority.

Almost a minute later, Sascha spoke to him. "It's important for us to have control at every stage."

"Your money, your time." He put his hands on the table and steepled his fingers, noting how her eyes went to them. Interesting. In his experience, the Psy never displayed any awareness of body language. It was as if they were completely cerebral, shut into the world of their minds. "But if you insist on that much involvement, I can't promise we'll hold to the timetable. In fact I'll guarantee we won't."

"We have a proposal to counter that." Night-sky eyes met his.

He raised a brow. "I'm listening." And so was the panther inside him. Both man and beast found Sascha Duncan captivating in a way that neither could understand. Part of him wanted to stroke her . . . and part of him wanted to bite.

"We'd like to work side by side with DarkRiver. To facilitate this, I request that you provide me with an office at your building."

Every nerve he had went taut. He'd just been granted access to a cardinal Psy almost twenty-four seven. "You want to be joined at the hip with me, darling? That's fine." His senses picked up a change in the atmosphere, but it was so subtle that it was gone before he could identify it. "Do you have authority to sign off on changes?"

"Yes. Even if I have to consult with Mother, I won't need to leave the site." It was a reminder that she was Psy, a member of a race that had sacrificed its humanity long ago.

"How far can a cardinal send?"

"Far enough." She pressed at something on her tiny screen. "So we'll settle at eight?"

He grinned at her attempt to catch him unawares, amused at the almost feline cunning. "Ten, or I walk out and you get something lower quality."

"You're not the only expert on changeling likes and dislikes out there." She leaned forward a fraction.

"Yes." Intrigued by this Psy who appeared to use her body as much as her mind, he deliberately echoed the movement. "But I'm the best."

"Nine."

He couldn't afford to let the Psy think of him as weak—they respected only the coldest, cruelest kind of strength. "Nine and a promise of another million if all the homes are presold by the time of the opening."

Another silence. The hairs on his nape lifted again. Inside his mind the beast batted at the air as if trying to catch the sparks of energy. Most changelings couldn't feel the electrical storms generated by the Psy, but it was a talent that had its uses.

"We agree," Sascha said. "I assume you have hard-copy contracts?"

"Of course." He flipped open a binder and slid across copies of the same document they undoubtedly had on their screens.

Sascha picked them up and passed one to her mother. "Electronic would be much more convenient."

He'd heard it a hundred times from a hundred different Psy. Part of the reason changelings hadn't followed the technological wave was sheer stubbornness; the other part was security—his race had been hacking into Psy databases for decades. "I like something I can hold, touch, and smell, something that pleases all my senses."

It was an innuendo he had no doubt she understood, but it was her reaction he was looking for. Nothing. Sascha Duncan was as cold a Psy as he'd ever met—he'd have to thaw her out enough to gain information about whether the Psy were harboring a serial killer.

He found himself oddly attracted by the thought of tangling with this particular Psy, though until that moment, he'd considered them nothing but unfeeling machines. Then she looked up to meet his gaze and the panther in him opened its mouth in a wordless growl.

The hunt had begun. And Sascha Duncan was the prey.

Two hours later, Sascha closed the door to her apartment and did a mental sweep of the premises. Nothing. Located in the same building as her office, the apartment had excellent security, but she'd used her skills at shielding to ring the rooms with another level of protection. It took a lot of her meager psychic strength but she needed to feel safe somewhere.

Satisfied that the apartment hadn't been breached, she systematically checked every one of her inner locks against the vastness of the PsyNet. Functioning. No one could get into her mind without her knowing about it.

Only then did she allow herself to collapse into a heap on the ice-blue carpet, the cool color making her shiver. "Computer. Raise temperature five degrees."

"Complying." The voice was without inflection but that was to be expected. It was nothing more than the mechanical response of the powerful computer that ran this building. The houses she'd be building with Lucas Hunter would have no such computer systems.

Lucas.

Her breath came out in a gasp as she allowed her mind to cascade with all the emotions she'd had to bury during the meeting.

Fear.

Amusement.

Hunger.

Lust.

Desire.

Need.

Unclipping the barrette at the end of her plait, she shoved her hands into the unfurling curls before tugging off her jacket and throwing it aside. Her breasts ached, straining against the cups of her bra. She wanted nothing more than to strip herself naked and rub up against something hot, hard, and male.

A whimper escaped her throat as she closed her eyes and rocked back and forth, trying to control the images pounding at her. This shouldn't be happening. No matter how far out of control she'd gone before, it had never been this bad, this sexual. The second she admitted it, the avalanche seemed to slow and she found enough strength to push her way out of the clawing grip of hunger.

Getting up off the floor, she walked to the kitchenette and poured herself a glass of water. As she swallowed, she caught her reflection in the ornamental mirror that hung beside her built-in cooler. It had been a gift from a changeling advisor on another project and she'd kept it despite her mother's raised brow. Her excuse had been that she was trying to understand the other race. In truth, she'd just liked the wildly colorful frame.

However, right now she wished she hadn't held on to it. It showed too clearly what she didn't want to see. The tangle of darkness that was her hair spoke of animal passion and desire, things no Psy should know about. Her face was flushed as if with fever, her cheeks streaked red, and her eyes . . . Lord have mercy, her eyes were pure midnight.

She put down the glass and pushed back her hair, searching. But she hadn't made a mistake. There was no light in the darkness of her pupils. This was only supposed to happen when a Psy was expending a large amount of psychic power.

It had never happened to her.

Her eyes might've marked her as a cardinal but her accessible powers were humiliatingly weak. So weak that she still hadn't been co-opted into the ranks of those who worked directly for the Council.

Her lack of any real psychic power had mystified the instructors who'd trained her. Everyone had always said that there was incredible raw potential inside her mind—more than enough for a cardinal—but that it had never manifested.

Until now.

She shook her head. No. She hadn't expended any psychic energy so it had to be something else that had caused the darkness, something other Psy didn't know about because they didn't feel. Her eyes drifted to the communication console set into the wall beside the kitchenette. One thing was clear—she couldn't go out looking like this. Anyone who saw her would have her sent in for rehabilitation in a heartbeat.

Fear gripped her tight.

As long as she was on the outside, she might one day figure out a way to escape, a way to cut her link to the PsyNet without throwing her body into paralysis and death. Or she might even discover a way to fix the flaw that marked her. But the second she was admitted into the Center, her world would become darkness. Endless, silent darkness.

With careful hands, she pulled off the cover of the communication console and fiddled with the circuits. Only after she'd replaced the cover did she press in Nikita's code. Her mother lived in the penthouse several floors above.

The answer came seconds later. "Sascha, your screen is turned off."

"I didn't realize," Sascha lied. "Hold on." Pausing for effect, she took a careful breath. "I think it's a malfunction. I'll have a technician check it out."

"Why did you call?"

"I'm afraid I'll have to cancel our dinner. I've received some documents from Lucas Hunter that I'd like to start going through before I meet with him again."

"Prompt for a changeling. I'll see you tomorrow afternoon for a briefing. Good night."

"Good night, Mother." She was talking to dead air. Regardless of the fact that Nikita had been no more a mother to her than the computer that controlled this apartment, it hurt. But tonight that hurt was buried under far more dangerous emotions.

She'd barely started to relax when the console chimed an incoming call. Since the caller identification function had been disabled along with the screen, she had no way of knowing who it was. "Sascha Duncan," she said, trying not to panic that Nikita had changed her mind.

"Hello, Sascha."

Her knees almost buckled at the sound of that honey-smooth voice, more purr than growl now. "Mr. Hunter."

"Lucas. We're colleagues, after all."

"Why are you calling?" Harsh practicality was the only way she could deal with her roller-coaster emotions.

"I can't see you, Sascha."

"It's a screen malfunction."

"Not very efficient." Was that amusement she could hear?

"I assume you didn't call to chat."

"I wanted to invite you to a breakfast meeting with the design team tomorrow." His tone was pure silk.

Sascha didn't know if Lucas always sounded like an invitation to sin or whether he was doing it to unsettle her. *That* thought unsettled her. If he even suspected that there was something not quite right about her, then she might as well sign her death warrant. Internment at the Center was nothing less than a living death anyway.

"Time?" She wrapped her arms tight around her ribs and forced her voice to even out. The Psy were very, very careful that the world never saw their mistakes, their flawed ones. No one had ever successfully fought the Council after being slated for rehabilitation.

"Seven thirty. Is that good for you?"

How could he make the most businesslike of invitations sound like purest temptation? Maybe it was all in her mind—she was finally cracking. "Location?"

"My office. You know where that is?"

"Of course." DarkRiver had set up business camp near the chaotic bustle of Chinatown, taking over a medium-sized office building. "I'll be there."

"I'll be waiting."

To her heightened senses, that sounded more like a threat than a promise.

CHAPTER 2

Lucas prowled to the edge of his office and stared down at the narrow streets that led into the sensory explosion that was Chinatown, his mind on Sascha Duncan's night-sky eyes. His animal nature had sniffed something in her that didn't quite fit, wasn't quite . . . right. And yet, she didn't have the sickly smell of insanity but a delectably enticing scent that was at odds with the metallic stink of most Psy.

"Lucas?"

He had no need to turn around to identify his visitor. "What is it, Dorian?"

Dorian came to stand beside him. With his blond hair and blue eyes, he could've passed for a surfer hanging out, waiting for the right wave. Except for the feral edge in those eyes. Dorian was a latent leopard. Something had gone wrong in the womb and he'd been born changeling in all ways except one—he lacked the ability to shift forms. "How did it go?"

"I have a Psy shadow." He watched a car glide by on the darkening street, the energy cells that powered it leaving no trace of their passage. The cells had been created by changelings. Without their race, the world would've sunk into a quagmire of pollution by now.

The Psy thought themselves the leaders of the planet, but it was the changelings who were attuned to the Earth's heartbeat, the changelings who saw the intertwined streams of life. Changelings and the occasional human.

"Think you can pump her?"

Lucas shrugged. "She's like the rest of them. But I'm in. And she's a cardinal."

Dorian rocked back on his heels. "If one of them knows about the killer, they all do. Their web keeps every single one of them in contact."

"They call it the PsyNet." Lucas leaned forward and pressed his palms to the glass, luxuriating in the cool kiss. "I'm not so sure that's how it works."

"It's a damn hive mind. How else could it work?"

"They're very hierarchical—it doesn't track that the masses would be allowed access to everything. Democratic is the one thing they're not." The Psy world of cold, calm survival of the fittest was as cruel as anything he'd ever seen.

"But your cardinal would know."

As the daughter of a Councilor and a powerful mind in her own right, it was almost certain that Sascha was a member of the inner circle. "Yes." And he had every intention of finding out what she knew.

"Ever slept with a Psy?"

Lucas finally turned to glance at Dorian, amused. "You're saying I should seduce the information out of her?" The idea should've revolted him but both man and beast were intrigued.

Dorian laughed. "Yeah right, your cock'd probably freeze off." Something bright and angry glittered in those blue eyes. "I was going to say that they really don't feel anything. I went to bed with one back when I was young and stupid. I was drunk and she invited me to her dorm room."

"Unusual." The Psy liked to keep to themselves.

"I think I was some kind of experiment to her. She was a science major. We had sex but I swear it was like being with a block of concrete. No life, no emotion."

Lucas let the image of Sascha Duncan run through his mind. His panther senses stilled, sniffing at the echo of her memory. She was ice but she was also something more. "We can only pity them."

"They deserve our claws, not our pity."

Lucas looked back at the city. He hid it better but his anger was as deep as Dorian's. He'd been with the other man when they'd discovered Dorian's sister's body six months ago. Kylie had been butchered. Coldly. Clinically. Mercilessly. Her blood had been spilled with no thought to the beautiful, vibrant woman she'd been.

There had been no animal scent at the scene but Lucas had picked up the metallic stink of the Psy. The other changelings had seen the brutal efficiency of the kill and known exactly what type of monster had done this. But the Psy Council had claimed to know nothing, and the authorities in Enforcement had done so little, it was almost as if they didn't *want* to find the murderer.

After DarkRiver had started digging, they'd discovered several other murders with the same signature. All buried so deep that only one organization could've been behind it. The Psy Council was like a spider and every Enforcement station in the country was caught in its web.

The changelings had had enough. Enough of Psy arrogance. Enough of Psy politics. Enough of Psy manipulation. Decades of resentment and fury had built up into a powder keg that the Psy had unknowingly ignited with their latest atrocity.

Now it was war.

And one very unusual Psy was about to be trapped in the middle.

When Sascha arrived at the DarkRiver building at seven thirty sharp, it was to find Lucas waiting for her by the entrance. Dressed in jeans, white T-shirt, and black leather-synth jacket, he looked nothing like the businessman she'd faced yesterday. "Good morning, Sascha." His slow smile invited a similar response.

This time she was prepared for him. "Good morning. Shall we proceed to the meeting?" Nothing but the coldest practicality would serve to keep this male at a distance—she didn't have to be a genius to understand that he was used to getting what he wanted.

"I'm afraid there's been a change in plans." He raised his hands in a placatory gesture but there was nothing submissive about him. "One of my team couldn't get into the city in time so I postponed the meeting until three."

She smelled deception. What she couldn't figure out was whether it was because he was trying to charm her or because he was lying. "Why didn't you call me?"

"I thought that since you were already on your way, we might as well go check out the site I've scouted." He smiled. "A very efficient use of our time."

She knew he was laughing at her. "Let's go."

"In my car."

She didn't protest. No real Psy would. He knew the way so it made sense for him to drive. But she wasn't a normal Psy and she wanted to tell him to keep his autocratic commands to himself.

"Have you had breakfast?" he asked when they were both in the car and he'd brought up the manual controls.

She'd been too nervous to eat. Something about Lucas

Hunter was accelerating her descent into madness but she couldn't stop the tumble, couldn't stop herself from continuing to tangle with him. "Yes," she lied, not quite sure why.

"Good. Wouldn't want you to faint on me."

"I've never fainted in my life so you're safe." She watched the city flash by as they neared the Bay Bridge. San Francisco was a glittering jewel by the sea but she preferred the areas beyond, where nature held full sway. In some cases the forests stretched all the way to the border with Nevada and kept going.

Yosemite National Park was one of the bigger wilderness areas. At one stage a couple of centuries in the past, it had been mooted that the park be limited to an area east of Mariposa. The changelings had won that war and Yosemite had been left to sprawl to the extent that it had merged into several other forested areas, including the El Dorado and Tahoe forests, though the lake city of Tahoe continued to thrive.

It now covered half of Sacramento and curved around the lucrative wine-growing region of Napa to hug Santa Rosa to the north. To the southeast of San Francisco, it had almost swallowed Modesto. Because of its ongoing sprawl, only part of Yosemite was now a national park. The rest was protected from general development but habitation was allowed under certain circumstances.

As far as she knew, no Psy had ever sought permission to live so close to the wild. It made her wonder what their green, wooded land would've looked like had the Psy had total control of it. Somehow, she doubted that most of California would've been a series of giant national parks and forests.

Suddenly aware of Lucas sending her a questioning glance, she realized she'd been silent for over forty minutes. Luckily for her, lack of small talk was a Psy trait. "If we agree to buy the site you've chosen, how long will it take to close the deal?"

He looked back at the road. "A day. The land is in Dark-River territory but owned by the SnowDancers through an accident of history. They're happy to sell for the right price."

"Are you an impartial party?" She took the chance afforded by his concentration on driving to look her fill of the markings on his face. Savage and primitive, they tugged at something hidden inside of her. She couldn't help thinking that they likely told the true story of his nature, the smooth business persona merely a mask.

"No. But they're not going to deal with anyone else so you'll just have to hope I don't screw you over."

She wasn't sure whether to take him seriously. "We're well aware of property values. No one has yet managed to 'screw' us."

His lips curved. "It's the best location for what you want. The thought of living in that area gives most changelings wet dreams."

Sascha wondered if he was being crude in an effort to rattle her. Had this far too intelligent leopard figured out that she was flawed in the most basic way? Hoping to throw him off the scent, she made her next words completely toneless. "Very colorful, but I don't care about their dreams. I simply want them to buy the properties."

"They will." Of that Lucas had no doubt. "We're almost there." He pulled off the side road they were on and headed down another before parking the car beside a huge open space dotted with trees. Situated near Manteca, the area wasn't heavily forested but it was definitely wooded.

He slid open his door and stepped out, frustrated by his inability to penetrate the layer of ice Sascha had wrapped around herself like steel. He'd engineered this drive and site-visit in order to start probing her for information. But getting a Psy to open up was like trying to get a Snow-Dancer to turn into a leopard.

The worst part was, he found himself fascinated by everything about his quarry. Like how the rich silk of her hair turned impossibly darker in the sun as she moved to stretch out her legs. Or how her skin gleamed a dark honey. "May I ask you a question?" The hunger came from the panther inside but the man saw the possibilities in this line of questioning.

Sascha glanced up. "By all means."

"Your mother's ancestry is clearly Asiatic but your first names are Slavic and your last, Scottish. I'm curious." He walked beside her as she started to explore the site.

"That's not a question."

Lucas narrowed his eyes. He had the feeling she was teasing him but of course the Psy never teased. "How did you end up with such an interesting mixture?" he asked, far from convinced about this Psy.

To his surprise, she answered without hesitation. "Depending on the family structure, we take the names of either our maternal or paternal line. In our family, the last name has been maternal for the last three generations. However, my great-grandmother, Ai Kumamoto, took her husband's name. He was Andrew Duncan."

"She was Japanese?"

She nodded. "Their daughter was Reina Duncan, my grandmother. Reina had a child with Dmitri Kukovich and he chose the first name of their child—Nikita. My mother continued that naming tradition, as our psychologists believe a sense of history better enables a child to adapt to society."

"Your mother looks very Japanese, while you don't." Her features were so unique that they defied definition. Nothing about her said she'd been manufactured in the same machine as the rest of the bloodless, robotic Psy.

"The paternal genes appear to have held sway in my case, while in hers, the maternal ones prevailed."

He couldn't imagine ever speaking of his parents in such a cool fashion. They'd loved him, raised him, and died for him. Their memory deserved to be honored with the most powerful depths of emotion. "And your father? What did he add into the exotic mix?"

"He was of Anglo-Indian descent."

Something in her voice set off the protective instincts of his beast. "He's not in your life any longer?"

"He never was." Sascha continued walking along the pathway, trying not to feel the pain of this oldest of wounds. It was nothing that would ever change. Her father was as Psy as her mother.

"I don't understand."

This time she didn't tease him about it not being a question. "My mother chose a scientific method of conception."

Lucas stopped so suddenly, she almost betrayed surprise. "What? She went to a sperm bank and picked out a donor with good genes?" He appeared astounded.

"Very crudely put, but yes. It's now the most widely used form of conception among the Psy." Sascha knew Nikita expected her to follow the same path. Not many of their race chose the old-fashioned method any longer. It was apparently messy, wasted time that could be put to more cost-effective use, and had no advantages over medico-psychic selection.

"The process is both safe and practical." But she was never going to undergo it. There was no way she'd ever chance condemning a child to the flaw already pushing her to the brink of insanity. "We can weed out sperm and eggs that are damaged in any way. It's why the Psy have a negligible rate of childhood diseases." Yet mistakes were made—she was living proof.

Lucas shook his head and it was such a feline movement, her heart jumped. Sometimes he was so smooth, so charming, she forgot his animal nature. And then he looked at her with that naked heat in his eyes and she knew that what prowled behind the civilized facade was nothing tame.

"You don't know what you're missing out on," he said, standing just a little too close.

She didn't move. He might be an alpha used to obedience but she wasn't one of his pack. "On the contrary. I was taught animal reproduction at an early age."

He chuckled and she felt the stroke of his laughter deep inside where no one should've been able to reach. "Animal reproduction? That's one way to put it. Have you ever tried it?"

She was having trouble concentrating on his words with him so near . . . so touchable. He smelled of danger and wildness and passion, all the things she could never allow herself to feel. It was the ultimate temptation. "No. Why would I?"

He leaned infinitesimally closer. "Because, darling, you might find that the animal in you likes it."

"I'm not your darling." As soon as the words were out, her soul froze. No Psy would've ever risen to the bait.

Lucas's eyes blazed with challenge. "Maybe I can change your mind."

Despite the teasing words, she knew he'd picked up her lapse and was even now considering what it meant. There was nothing she could do to retract the slip but she could bring the conversation back to purely business. "What did you want to show me?"

His wicked smile shot to pieces her hopes of getting this meeting under control. "Lots of things, darling. Lots of things."

Lucas watched Sascha move around the lot and savored the lingering taste of her, as warm and exotic as her history.

The panther prowling the cage of his mind was intrigued by her, intent on licking at her to see if she tasted as good as he imagined. Her golden skin enticed the tactile nature of his changeling soul, while the lushness of her lips made him want to bite . . . in the most erotic way. Everything about her invited the senses.

What had him fighting the urge was the knowledge that it had to be some kind of Psy trick. Had they finally figured out a way to exert psychic control over changelings? His people had always been safe because the Psy were too cold to figure out what made them tick. Life, hunger, sensation, touch, sex. Not cold, ascetic sex like Dorian had described, but passionate, sweaty, low-down and dirty sex.

Lucas loved the scent of both human and changeling women, adored their soft skin and cries of pleasure, but never before had he been drawn to one of the enemy. He fought the attraction even as he traced the shape of Sascha's body with his eyes.

She was tall but there was nothing willowy about her. The woman's body had more dangerous curves than should be legal on one of her race. In spite of the black pantsuit and stiff white shirt she wore like corporate armor, he could tell her breasts would overflow his hands. When she bent to examine something on the ground, he almost gave in to the urgings of his beast. The curve of her hip was sensually female, her bottom a heart-shaped enticement.

Her head turned as if in response to his intent gaze, and, despite the distance separating them, he could almost taste the earthy sensuality she tried to bury. Frowning at his own thoughts, he began to walk toward her. The Psy weren't sensual. They were about as close to mechanical as you could get and still remain human. But there was something different about this one, something he wanted to sink his teeth into.

"Why did you choose these sections?" she asked as he approached. Her night-sky eyes watched him without blinking.

"It's rumored that the sparks of white light in a cardinal's eyes can turn into a thousand colors under certain circumstances." He searched her face for an answer to the puzzle of her. "Is that true?"

"No. Cardinal eyes can go pure black but that's about it." She looked away from him and he wanted to believe it was because she found him disturbing to her senses. It annoyed the panther that he was mesmerized by her while she remained unmoved. "Tell me about this lot."

"It's prime changeling real estate—just over an hour out of the city, in an area that's forested enough to feed the soul." He looked down at her sedate plait. The compulsion to reach over and tug at it was so strong, he didn't bother to resist.

She jerked away. "What are you doing?"

"I wanted to feel what your hair was like." Sensation was as necessary to him as breathing.

"Why?"

No other Psy he'd ever met had asked that question. "It feels good. I like touching soft, silky things."

"I see."

Was that a tremor he heard in her response? "Try it."

"What?"

He bent a little in invitation. "Go on. Changelings don't mind touch like the Psy."

"It's well known that you're territorial," she said. "You don't let just anyone touch you."

"No. Only Pack, mates, and lovers have skin privileges. But we don't go crazy like the Psy if someone unknown touches us." For some inexplicable reason, he wanted her to touch him. And it had nothing to do with learning about a killer. That should've given him pause but it was the panther who was in charge at this moment and he wanted to be stroked.

She lifted her hand and then paused. "There's no reason to do this."

He wondered which one of them she was trying to convince. "Think of it as research. Ever touched a changeling before?"

Shaking her head, she bridged the remaining distance and ran her fingers through his hair in a wave that made him want to purr. He'd expected her to back off after a single stroke but she surprised him by doing it again. And again.

"It's an unusual sensation." Her hand seemed to linger before dropping. "Your hair is cool and heavy and the texture is similar to a satin-silk I once touched."

Trust a Psy to analyze something as simple as touch. "May I?"

"What?"

He touched her plait. This time she didn't react. "Can I undo it?"

"No."

The panther in him froze, sniffing a hint of panic in her tone. "Why?"

CHAPTER 3

"You don't have those privileges."

Chuckling, he let the plait run through his hand. She stepped away the second it hit her back. Playtime was over. "I chose this land," he said, answering her earlier question, "because of its closeness to nature. Though most changelings live a civilized life, we're as animal as we are human—the need to roam the wild is in our blood."

"What do you think of yourself as?" she asked. "Human or animal?"

"We're both."

"One must dominate." A frown of concentration marred the perfection of her face.

A frown? On a Psy? It was gone a second later but he'd seen. "No. We're one. I'm as panther as I am human."

"I thought you were a leopard."

"Black panthers exist in several feline families. It's the color of our fur that makes us panthers, not our species." He wasn't surprised she didn't know that. To the Psy the changelings were all animals, all the same. That was their mistake. A wolf was not the same as a leopard, an eagle nothing like a swan.

And a stalking panther was danger and fury combined.

Sascha watched Lucas return to the car to pick up his phone in order to call the SnowDancers. Protected by his turned back, she allowed herself to appreciate his sheer male beauty. He was quite simply . . . luscious. She'd never used that word before, had never found anyone or anything worth using it for. But Lucas Hunter definitely fit the definition.

Unlike the cold formality of Psy men, he was playful and approachable. That only made him all the more dangerous. She'd glimpsed the predator lurking beneath the surface—Lucas might play nice but when it was time to bite, he'd go for the throat. No one made alpha of a predatory pack at such a young age by being anything less than the top of the food chain.

That didn't scare her. Maybe because she'd seen true terror in the labyrinth of the PsyNet, things so vicious and vile that Lucas's openly predatorial nature was as welcome as a breath of fresh air. He might've tried to charm her, but he'd never pretended to be anything other than what he was—a hunter to the core, a predator inside and out, a sensual male well aware of the effect of his sexuality.

He made her hunger, made her feel raw and wild things that threatened to crack the ever more fragile mask of Psy coldness she wore to survive. She should be running as far from him as possible. Instead, she found herself walking toward him as he headed back, a sleek silver device held to his ear that was light-years advanced from Bell's original invention.

"They'll sell for twelve million." He stood a couple of feet from her and indicated that the connection was live.

"That's double what this land is worth on the open market." She wasn't going to be bullied. "I'm offering six and a half."

Lucas held the phone to his ear and when he didn't repeat her offer, she realized the SnowDancer on the other end had to have heard her. It was a reminder that despite her race's egotistical view of themselves as the supreme leaders of the Earth, changelings had some remarkable powers.

"They said they're not interested in enriching the Psy. It's no skin off their back if you don't buy it. They'll happily sell it to your competitor."

Sascha had done her homework. "They can't. The Rika-Smythe family group has already sunk all available funds into a venture in San Diego."

"Then they'll leave it empty. Twelve million or they walk." Lucas watched her with an intent look in those incredible green eyes and she wondered if he was trying to see into her soul. She could've told him it was a futile effort. She was Psy—she had no soul.

"We can't afford to put that much into the development. We'll never recoup the cost. Find me another site," she said, attempting to sound cool and in control despite the unsettling effect of Lucas's presence.

This time he did repeat her words into the phone. After listening for a moment, he said, "They're not backing down. But they have a counteroffer for you."

"I'm listening."

"They'll give you the land in exchange for fifty percent of the profits and a signed agreement that none of the houses be sold to the Psy. They also want covenants placed on all the deeds ensuring future owners can't sell to the

Psy either." He shrugged. "The land has to remain in changeling or human hands."

It was the last thing she'd expected but Lucas's eyes said he'd known. And he hadn't warned her. It made her wary. Was he trying to provoke a reaction from her? "Give me a moment. This isn't a decision I'm authorized to make."

Walking a distance away, though it wasn't strictly necessary, she connected to her mother through the PsyNet. Usually they used a simple telepathic link, but Sascha wasn't strong enough to send over such a long distance. The blunt illustration of her weakness served to remind her to stay on guard. Unlike other cardinals, she was disposable.

Nikita answered at once. "What is it?" Part of her consciousness faced part of Sascha's in a closed mental room in the vastness of the PsyNet.

Sascha repeated the offer and added, "It's definitely a prime location in terms of changeling needs. With the SnowDancers putting up the land, our investment is halved so sharing profits isn't going to cut into our bottom line. We might even do better in the end."

Nikita paused before answering and Sascha knew she was doing a data search. "Those wolves have a bad habit of trying to take over anything they have a hand in."

Sascha had a feeling that most predatory changelings had a habit of doing that. Look at Lucas—he'd been trying to take her over since the moment he'd laid eyes on her. "They're not known for property investments. I think this may be an emotional reaction against letting control of their land fall into Psy hands."

"You could be right." Another pause. "Draft an agreement stating we have control over everything from design to construction and marketing. They have to be a silent partner. We'll share profits but nothing else."

"What about their demand that no plots be sold to us?" Us. The Psy. The people to whom she'd never really belonged. But they were all she had. "It's legal under the Private Development laws."

"You're the head on this project. What do you think?"

"No Psy is going to want to live out here." This much space scared most of her race. They preferred to live in nice square boxes with defined limits. "It's not worth fighting over and we don't have to pay Lucas his million if he doesn't sell all the units."

"Make sure he understands that."

"I will." Her gut said that the panther was way ahead of them. Lucas didn't strike her as anybody's fool.

"Call me if you have any problems."

Nikita's presence winked out. When Sascha returned to Lucas, she found him rubbing the back of his neck as if something had irritated it. Her eyes followed the motion of his arm, fascinated by the sleek lines of muscle obvious even under the leather-synth jacket. Every move he made was fluid, graceful, like a big cat on the prowl.

It was only when he raised a brow that she realized she'd been staring. Fighting a blush, she said, "We'll agree to their demands if they agree to be a silent party. And that means not a sound out of them."

He dropped his hand from the back of his neck and put the phone to his ear. "They agree—I'll draft the contract." He closed the small flat communicator.

"We're not going to forget that you have to sell all the residences to receive that final million."

There was something distinctly smug about his slow smile. "Not a problem, darling."

It was as they were getting back into the car that she realized this was the first Psy-changeling fifty-fifty business deal she'd ever heard of. That didn't bother her—her instincts said they'd do very well out of this. Too bad that mentioning the word "instincts" would get her chemically lobotomized.

* * *

Lucas was utterly frustrated. Not only was Sascha refusing to reveal anything useful, she kept picking up on small changeling traits no Psy should've been able to sense. Even worse, he was having to fight the urge to educate her rather than subtly interrogating her for answers.

"How about this?" He showed her another line of the proposed contract. They were sitting in his office at the top of the DarkRiver building. He'd found her an office right next door. It was the perfect setup. If she'd talk.

She looked at the piece of paper and slid it back across the dark wood of the desk. "If you change the word 'at' to 'in,' it's fine with me."

He thought over the change. "All right. The Snow-Dancers aren't going to fight you over that."

"But they will fight me?"

"Not if the contract is fair." He wondered if a Psy even understood the meaning of integrity. "They trust me and I'll tell them the truth. So long as you don't try anything underhanded, they'll stick to their word."

"A changeling's word can be trusted?"

"Probably far more than a Psy's." He felt his jaw tighten as he thought of the self-righteous way the Psy claimed to be without anger and violence, when it was becoming damn clear they were anything but.

"You're right. Subtle prevarication is considered an efficient bargaining tool in my world."

He was more than surprised by her acceptance of his point. "Just subtle?"

"Perhaps some take it too far."

There was a stillness to her that made him want to cover the space between them and stroke his hand over her body. Perhaps touch would achieve what words hadn't. "Who punishes the ones who take it too far?"

"The Council." The statement was absolute.

"What if the Council is wrong?"

Her eyes met his, unflinching and eerily beautiful. "They know everything that goes on in the PsyNet. How could they be wrong?"

Which meant, he deduced, that not everyone was privy to the secrets of the Net. "But if no one else has access to all the information, how can they be held accountable?"

"Who holds you accountable?" she asked instead of answering. "Who punishes the alpha?"

He wished he were on the other side of the desk so he could touch her and find out if she was fighting fire with fire, or simply being practical. "If I break Pack law, the sentinels will take me down. Who takes down your Council?"

He almost thought she wouldn't answer. Then she said, "They are Council. They are above the law."

Lucas wondered if she understood what she'd just admitted. More than that, he wanted to know if she *cared*. That was truly madness, because the only thing the Psy cared about was the cold sterility of their lives. Except every instinct he had said that Sascha was different.

He had to uncover the truth about her before he did something he regretted. And the best way to crack that impenetrable Psy shell might be to yank her from the safety of the world she knew and throw her into the flames. "How about lunch?"

"I can meet you back here in an hour," she began.

"That was an invitation, darling." He added the endearment as a tease. She'd reacted last time and he wanted to see if she'd slip again. "Or do you have a date?"

"We don't date. And I accept your invitation." No obvious reaction but he felt the spike of temper.

He stood, satisfaction thrumming in his veins—the trap had sprung. "Let's go feed the hunger."

Those slightly uptilted eyes seemed to widen but then she blinked and it was gone. Was he fooling himself, imagining emotion on one of the merciless Psy because he found himself drawn to her? Sleeping with the enemy was not part of the plan. Unfortunately, his panther half had a way of destroying the best-laid plans once it began craving a taste of something . . . or someone.

Almost forty minutes later, Sascha got out of Lucas's car in front of what he'd told her was a packmate's home. Located in the wide zone where urban dwellings gradually started giving way to the trailing edges of the forests, the house was isolated at the end of a long drive and appeared to back on to a wooded reserve.

She felt uncertain and out of place. No one had ever taught her how to deal with the situation she was in . . . because Psy weren't usually invited into changeling homes. "Are you sure your packmate won't mind?"

"Tammy'll love the company," Lucas assured her. His quick knock was answered by a call from inside the house and he walked in without hesitation.

Following him down the hallway, she found herself at the entrance to a large room that appeared to be a kitchen and dining area combined. A rectangular wooden table with six chairs sat to her right. It bore a number of scratches that she thought might've come from careless claws. The thick legs were similarly scarred.

The table and chairs sat on a shiny wooden floor covered by a colorful rug that couldn't disguise the number of scratches in the wood. For the most part, the scratches were thin and closely spaced, far too narrow to have come from leopard paws. They puzzled her analytical Psy mind.

"Lucas!" A beautiful woman with rich brown hair walked out from behind a counter.

Lucas met her in the middle of the room. "Tamsyn." Leaning down, he brushed her lips with his. The woman held him for a second before stepping back.

Sascha was shocked at the sick feeling that invaded the pit of her stomach at witnessing the casual intimacy. Trained to recognize emotion so she could destroy it, she identified this one as jealousy. It was characterized by anger and possessiveness and made people extremely vulnerable. The aim of the training had been to teach her how to exploit changeling and human weaknesses, but she'd used the information to mask her own flaw.

"Who have you brought to visit?" The brunette walked over. "Hello. I'm Tamsyn." She went to stretch out a hand and then dropped it as if remembering the Psy aversion to touch.

"I'm Sascha Duncan." Glancing over Tamsyn's shoulder, she met Lucas's gaze. He was looking at her in a way that unsettled her with its directness. She had to force her attention back to Tamsyn.

"Come on," the woman said. "I've just made the most divine chocolate chip cookies. You two can have first pick before the rest of the pack sniffs them out. I swear Kit and the juveniles always know when I'm baking cookies." She headed back to the other side of the counter. As she passed Lucas, he ran the knuckles of one hand down her cheek and she rubbed back gently against him.

Skin privileges.

Mates, lovers, and Pack.

"Is she your mate?" Sascha walked to stand beside Lucas, trying not to grit her teeth against the jealousy churning in her gut.

Tamsyn laughed, startling Sascha. She'd forgotten that changelings had far better hearing than the Psy. "Good Lord, no. Don't say that around Nate—he might decide to challenge Lucas to a duel or something else equally archaic and testosterone driven."

"I apologize," she said to Tamsyn, far too aware of the acute interest in Lucas's eyes. "I misunderstood."

The other woman frowned. "What?"

It was Lucas who answered. "We kissed. We touched."

"Oh that!" Tamsyn lifted up a plate from behind the counter and put it on the top. "That was just saying hello to a packmate."

Sascha wondered if they knew how lucky they were. They could show such extreme emotion without fear that they'd be locked away and rehabilitated. Part of her wanted to tell them that she, too, hungered for touch, that her hunger was so great she was starving. But she knew that was the madness talking. Changelings despised the Psy. Even if they somehow sympathized, what could they do? Nothing. No one had ever withstood the might of the PsyNet—the only way to leave it was death.

"Come on." Tamsyn beckoned her over. "These are decadent."

Sascha had never thought of food as decadent. Curious, she walked over to pick up a warm cookie. Chocolate. It was a sweet substance coveted by humans and changelings. The Psy meal plan didn't include it as it had no nutritional value that couldn't be provided by other, more efficient means.

"You're looking at it as if you've never tasted chocolate before." Lucas leaned on the counter beside her. There was no mistaking the amusement on his face.

Her hands itched to trace his markings, to find out if they were soft or hard, sensitive or not. "I haven't." She concentrated on the cookie instead of the heat coming off Lucas's skin. Now that he'd taken off his jacket, she could see far too much sun-golden male flesh.

Tamsyn's eyes went wide. "You poor thing. You've been deprived."

"I've been given balanced nutrition every day of my life." She felt compelled to defend her people, though she knew they'd discard her without a thought the second they discovered her defect.

"Nutrition?" Lucas shook his head, sending dark hair sliding across muscular shoulders. "You eat so you'll function?" He disposed of a cookie in two bites. "Darling, that's no way to live." Laughter flickered in his eyes but there was also something hotter, something that whispered that he could show her how to really live.

She swallowed the flare of desire threatening to shatter her control. Lucas Hunter was potent. And a crazy part of her wanted to take a sip of him to see if he tasted as good as he sounded.

"Go on," Tamsyn said, snapping her back to reality none too soon. "Try one before Lucas demolishes the whole lot. It won't poison you."

Sascha took a careful bite. Sensation flooded her. It was all she could do to stop herself from crying out. No wonder the church had once termed chocolate an enticement of the devil. Pacing herself, when she wanted to gulp it down and snatch the whole plate for herself, she finished it off. "It has an unusual taste."

"But did you like it?" Tamsyn asked.

Before she could answer, Lucas did. "The Psy don't like or dislike, do they, Sascha?"

"No." Not if they were normal. She wondered if anyone would notice if she took one more cookie. "Something is either useful or it isn't. Liking doesn't come into it."

"Here." Lucas lifted another cookie to her lips. "Maybe chocolate will change your mind." Temptation lingered in the playful curve of his lips.

Sascha wasn't strong enough to resist. "Since we haven't yet had lunch, this'll provide needed calories."

"Lucas! You worked through lunch again? Both of you, sit!" Tamsyn pointed to the table. "Nobody walks out of my kitchen hungry."

Sascha was confused by the hierarchy in the room. "I thought Lucas was your alpha."

Lucas chuckled. "Yeah, but this is Tamsyn's kitchen. We might as well sit before she throws a pot at us." He headed over to the table. "Tammy, I confess. I came here so you'd feed me. Nobody cooks like you."

"Cut the sweet talk, Lucas Hunter." In spite of the sharp words, the brunette was smiling.

Sascha tried to finish her cookie in sedate bites instead of inhaling it. She was going to have to smuggle some chocolate into her quarters. For the first time, she'd found something relatively safe with which to indulge her senses. One more sin would make no difference to a life she'd lived in secret since before she could remember.

They'd just taken their seats when two small leopard cubs barreled into the room. Eyes wide, Sascha watched the pair slide across the shiny wood of the floor before being caught on the rug. Several long, thin scratches marked their passage.

"Roman! Julian!" Tamsyn walked out from behind the counter and picked up both cubs by the scruff of their necks. "What do you think you're doing?" Two sheepish leopard faces turned to look at her. Sascha was riveted by the kittenish mewls coming from their throats.

Tamsyn laughed. "You two charmers. You know you're not supposed to run in the house. I've already lost two vases this week."

The cubs wiggled.

"Here." Tamsyn walked over and dumped them on the table. "Explain yourselves to your uncle Lucas."

The cubs put their heads down on their paws and looked up at Lucas as if awaiting judgment. Sascha wanted nothing more than to stroke her fingers through the silky-soft pelt of the one nearest her. They were so beautiful, their eyes a lively green-gold that had her spellbound.

She almost jumped out of her chair when Lucas growled beside her, a low rumble that came from a human throat but sounded completely feral. The cubs sprang up and growled back. Lucas laughed. "Scary, aren't they?" His eyes invited her to join in the fun.

She couldn't resist. "Fierce."

One of the cubs suddenly skidded to stand in front of her, so close they were almost nose to nose. Sascha stared in fascination at those eyes. Then he opened his mouth and growled a baby growl at her. Laughter bubbled in her throat. How could anyone remain unmoved around such mischief? But she was Psy and she wasn't allowed to laugh. Yet there was no way she wasn't going to indulge at least one more sense. She might never get this chance again.

Reaching out, she mimicked Tamsyn's hold and lifted the cub up by the ruff of his neck. His fur was soft, his body warm. He wiggled and growled, batting at her hands with sheathed claws, and she realized he was playing with her. At that moment, the other cub jumped to land on her lap and began to climb up her body.

Lost, she turned to Lucas. His amusement was obvious. "Don't look at me, darling."

She narrowed her eyes at her two little playmates. "I'm Psy. I can turn you into rats." The cubs stopped wiggling. Picking up the one in her lap, she put them both on the table in front of her and leaned down to their level. "Be very careful of people like me." It was a soft, sincere warning. "We don't know how to play nice."

Scooting forward on little baby paws, one of the cubs licked the tip of her nose in a quick movement. She was so startled that she blurted out, "What does that mean?"

"It means he likes you." Lucas tugged at her plait. "But that doesn't matter to you, does it?"

"No." She wished he'd stop touching her. Not because she didn't like it but because she liked it far too much. It made her hunger for things that could never be hers. And if someone went hungry for too long, they started to starve. Started to hurt.

CHAPTER 4

"Gotcha!" Tamsyn reached out and scooped up the cubs in her arms. They turned to nip playfully at her skin. "I love you, too, babies. But Uncle Lucas and your new friend have to eat so you have to stay on the floor." She put them down after a cuddle.

The cubs scooted under the table, one of them curling himself up on Sascha's leather-synth boots. The heavy warmth brought tears to her eyes. In an effort to hide her reaction, she looked down at the table and focused on the way Lucas continued to hold her plait.

He was sliding his fingers up and down, as though he liked the feel of the strands against his fingertips. The smooth, repetitive motion was oddly arousing—would he stroke other body parts with such exquisite care?

Her thoughts could get her interned at the Center but she didn't care. She'd experienced more sensations in the space of the last few hours than she had in the rest of her lifetime combined. It terrified her and yet she knew she'd be back tomorrow. She'd be back until someone found out.

And then she'd fight to the death. She would not be rehabilitated, would not allow her mind to be turned into a
mockery of who she was.

"Here you go." Tamsyn laid plates in front of them.
"Nothing special but it'll keep you going."

Sascha looked at her plate. "Pita pockets." She knew the
names of many things. Like most, she used mental exer-
cises to keep herself strong. One exercise involved memo-
rizing items—it had been one of her guilty pleasures to
choose lists that spoke to her senses. Food was one. Her
other favorite list had been compiled by the computer from
an ancient book of sexual positions.

"It's my special 'Hot Lips' type." Tamsyn winked. "A
little chili never hurt anybody."

Lucas tugged on the plait he had yet to release.

"Yes?" What would he do if she threw caution to the
winds and started touching him in return? Male that he
was, he'd probably ask for more.

"It might hurt if you're not used to it."

Stubbornness had always been her Achilles' heal. "I'll
survive. Thank you, Tamsyn."

"You're welcome." The other woman pulled up a chair.
"Eat!"

Sascha picked up her pita pocket and took a bite. It
nearly took off her skull. However, thanks to her training,
nobody looking at her would've guessed at her discomfort.
Lucas had finally stopped playing with her hair and was
demolishing his own meal in short order.

"So," Tamsyn asked, "could you really turn my cubs
into rats?"

Sascha thought Tamsyn was being serious until she
caught the twinkle in those caramel-colored eyes. "I could've
made them think they were rats."

"Really?" The brunette leaned forward. "I thought Psy
found changeling minds too hard to work with."

Too hard to manipulate was the right statement. "Your thought patterns are so unusual that yes, they're difficult to work with. Difficult, not impossible. But the amount of energy required to control you generally isn't worth the outcome." At least that was what she'd heard, having never been in a situation where she was trying to handle a changeling mind.

"Good thing we're so hard to take under or the Psy would be ruling the planet." Lucas's tone was lazily satisfied as he leaned back, one arm stretched over the back of her chair. Territorial didn't begin to describe him.

"We do rule the world."

"You might be high up in politics and business but that's not the world."

She took another bite of the pita, having discovered she quite liked the feeling of having her head taken off. "No," she agreed after swallowing.

At the same moment, she became aware of baby leopard teeth nibbling at the toe of her boot.

Sascha knew she should reach down and dislodge the cub but she didn't want to. Drowning in sensation was far preferable to being conditioned to numbness. A discreet chime interrupted her in midthought.

It took a second for her to realize it was her organizer. Reaching into the inner pocket of her jacket, she checked the caller ID and then linked to the other Psy, who was close enough for simple telepathic contact.

"Aren't you going to answer it?" Tamsyn asked when she put the slim electronic tablet back into her pocket.

"I am answering it." Answering in such a way took less than 10 percent of her concentration. If she'd been a true cardinal, it would've taken less than a tenth of a percent.

"I don't get it." Tamsyn frowned. "If you can communicate mentally anyway, why the actual call in the first place?"

"Boundaries." She finished her meal. "It's like knocking before you enter a house. Only certain people have the right to initiate mental contact with me." People like her mother and the Council.

Lucas touched her shoulder with the fingers of the hand he had across the back of her chair. "I thought the PsyNet meant you were all in constant contact."

The PsyNet wasn't a secret but neither was it to be talked about in detail. She'd failed part of her conditioning but this had held. Her mouth opened and she said, "Perhaps we should be leaving for our meeting."

She felt his entire body go so motionless, it was like he'd turned into the lethal beast he carried within. Lucas Hunter wasn't used to being told no. "Of course."

She should've feared this side of his nature, but found herself fascinated. "Thank you for lunch," she said to Tamsyn, wriggling her foot so the cub would let go. She didn't want to hurt him or get him in trouble. He clung.

Lucas pushed back his chair and stood. "Tell Nate I dropped by."

Tamsyn began to stand. Aware that she couldn't remain sitting, Sascha decided to take a risk. Sending out a narrow telepathic beam, she *spoke* to the cub. *Let go, baby, or you'll get in trouble.* She'd expected to have difficulty contacting him but the link was made in an instant, as if she were talking to a child Psy. The find was something she should've immediately fed into the PsyNet but she didn't. It felt like betrayal.

The cub—Julian—couldn't answer, but he let go. He was pleased she hadn't told on him because he wasn't supposed to be chewing on shoes anymore. He was a big boy. Trying not to smile, she rose to her feet. It was difficult to keep her boot out of sight as she walked to the door but she maneuvered so that Lucas's big frame was between her and Tamsyn.

"Drop by anytime," Tamsyn said. Putting her hands on Sascha's arms, the other woman kissed her cheek.

Sascha had frozen the instant Tamsyn touched her, feeling such overwhelming kindness from the brunette that she could do nothing else. She'd always imagined she could read the emotions of others but her delusions had never been this bad—there was simply no raw material in the Psy world to feed the fantasies of her fractured mind.

"Thank you." The second Tamsyn let go, she stepped back and walked out the door to the waiting vehicle. It was too difficult to be in that room full of laughter and touch, warmth and temptation, and not hunger for more . . . for everything.

"Oh dear," Tamsyn said, watching Sascha retreat. "I shouldn't have touched her."

Lucas hugged her to him. "Of course you should have. Just because she's Psy doesn't mean we are."

Tamsyn laughed. "Did you see her boot?"

"Yes." Lucas was the alpha of DarkRiver—he'd known exactly what was going on with Julian. What he couldn't understand was why Sascha had let it happen. And there had been that moment when Psy energy had flared extra bright. Perhaps her telepathic call had gotten heated, or perhaps she'd been doing something else. Like talking to a cub.

"I never expected a Psy to be so good with children." Tamsyn laid her head against his chest.

"Neither did I." Quite simply, she shouldn't have been. The Psy would never allow a child to nibble on their shoes. There was no reason behind it, no efficiency. Yet this Psy had. "Tell me if the cubs say anything interesting."

The healer of DarkRiver was no fool. "Still nothing?"

"Not yet." Dropping a kiss on her hair, he said good-bye and headed out.

Sascha was already in the vehicle when he took the driver's seat. "Your first time with changeling children?"

"Yes." She tucked the chewed toe behind her leg and right then and there, Lucas knew he was in trouble. "Are you always in animal form as children?"

"No." Backing slowly out of Tamsyn's long driveway, he turned onto the street, the passage of air smooth and swift under the vehicle. "We gain the ability to shift forms a year or so after birth. It's as simple as breathing to us."

She was silent for the next stretch of road, as if thinking over what he'd said. "What about clothing? What happens to it when you change?"

"It disintegrates. We prefer to change while naked." He paid close attention to the energy in the air as he spoke and detected a definite spike—Sascha Duncan reacted to the thought of him naked.

Both sides of his nature liked the idea of disturbing this intriguing female on a sensual level, but as alpha, he had to consider the deeper ramifications of what he'd learned . . . and how it could be used against her.

"Tamsyn—what role does she occupy in your pack?" she said, changing the subject so quickly that he knew he'd been right. "I know you're hierarchical."

"Exactly like the Psy. You show me yours and I'll show you mine." If she clammed up to such a simple request, then he was going to have to rethink his strategy. He needed to get inside a Psy mind to get into the PsyNet. There was no other way to track the killer, not if the Psy Council was covering for him.

"Our overall leadership is in the Council."

He tried to keep his exhilaration under control. "We have no overall leadership. Each pack is autonomous."

"Within the overall structure we're organized by family groups."

They hadn't known that for sure because to the outside world, the Psy concept of family looked like any other business relationship. "Family ties exist within the pack but ultimate loyalty is to the pack itself."

"What about mated pairs?" she asked, displaying an insight into the changeling mind that startled him. "Surely their loyalty is to each other first."

"That's the one caveat. Leopard changelings mate for life so no other option is workable." He wondered what she'd make of that, this woman who'd been created by medicine not passion. "What about the Psy? Where is your loyalty?"

"The good of our people," she said. "We're allowed to compete with other families for business, but that's on the inside. Against outsiders we have only one loyalty."

"To ensure the continuation of the Psy race."

"Yes." Shifting in her seat, she asked him another question he wasn't expecting. "Mating for life? Is that a choice like human marriage?"

"Actually, changelings and humans can mate. Several of my pack are mated to humans." Children from such matches always had the ability to change forms.

"I've heard that Psy-changeling unions occurred in the past."

"My great-great-grandmother was Psy." He glanced at her. "Do you think I would've made a good Psy?"

She stared at him for a second before saying, "Perhaps you should watch the road." Cool, practical, and without feeling. Except for the fact that the toe of her boot had been chewed by baby leopard teeth.

He obeyed her this once. "To answer your question, no, it's not a choice like marriage—at least not for the leopards.

Once we find our mate, the only choice we have is whether or not to take the final step. There's no walking away after that's done."

"What's the final step?"

"Tell me about the PsyNet."

She paused. "It is secret?"

"It is private."

"How do you find your mate? How do you know that he or she is the one?" Her tone was neutral but her questions held hints of the deepest curiosity.

He wondered if she'd be this inquisitive in all aspects of life. A curious lover was the ultimate lure to his panther soul. "I can't answer that—I'm not mated." He'd seen his father's heart shredded by his mother's death. Part of him didn't want to be that vulnerable to anyone.

It was one of the reasons he'd never nurtured a long-term relationship with any female, human or changeling. Mating couldn't be so easily influenced, but he'd done his damnedest to limit the chances of his mate finding him.

If she did hunt him down despite that, he'd accept her and then he'd never let her out of his sight. Forget about freedom—his mate was going to be protected every moment of her life. Pulling to a stop in the parking lot of the DarkRiver building, he switched off the engine and slid up the door of the car.

"Do you want to be?"

The question had him turning to face those night-sky eyes. No Psy should've ever asked that. No Psy should've ever heard the ambivalence in his voice. "Do *you*?"

"Is it private?" She tipped her head slightly to the side. It was a tiny movement but it wasn't in the nature of her race to make such movements.

He reached out and stroked a finger down her face, wanting to see what she'd do. "I'll tell you the answer to that once you have skin privileges."

She froze at his touch and then jerked away to exit the car. When he joined her on the other side, she kept at least a foot of distance between them. He wanted to close that distance badly enough to scare himself. The enemy was starting to look far too enticing. The feel of her skin had been a jolt to the senses, the dark honey like warm gold brushed with velvet, sensuous and luscious.

The panther in him craved more, while the man . . . the man was starting to think that Sascha Duncan was unique, a Psy unlike any other. Whether that made her less dangerous or more remained to be seen. What *was* clear was that both panther and man were captivated by her.

Kit was waiting for them in the meeting room. "Hi, Lucas." At a fraction under six feet, the boy was tall but hadn't yet filled out. Not that it mattered at his age. With his rich auburn hair and dark blue eyes, he was never short of female company. But Lucas knew the juvenile was more than good looks—he had the scent of a future alpha.

"Sascha Duncan, meet Kit Monaghan."

Kit smiled in that way he'd already learned brought most women to their knees, all slow burn and promises of delight. "A pleasure."

Sascha nodded. "Do you have the designs?"

Lucas wanted to laugh at the crestfallen look on the boy's face. "Kit works part-time as a general assistant. Zara is the designer." He shrugged out of his jacket.

As he spoke her name, a small female with mocha skin and cloud gray eyes walked in through the door behind them. Sascha immediately shifted to avoid contact but the move was so unobtrusive that neither Zara nor Kit noticed.

"I'm sorry I'm late," Zara said. "The copying machine got stuck." She was holding rolled-up copies of several designs in her arms. Lucas helped her put them on the circular table and gestured for everyone to be seated.

Sascha took a seat to his left, with Zara to her left and Kit beside the designer. Lucas had noticed Sascha glance at Zara several times since she'd entered the room and so, apparently, had Zara. "If you have a problem working with me, tell me now." The petite woman wasn't one to keep silent.

Sascha didn't react in any physical way but he was sure he smelled confusion. "Why would I have trouble working with you? Are you unable to do your job?"

"I can do my job fine," Zara bit out. "Some people just don't like the fact that I'm a darker shade of brown."

"That reaction is based on nothing but human emotion. I'm not human." Sascha pushed up her jacket sleeve. "If it soothes you then please see that I'm also a . . . darker shade of brown." The beautiful rich honey of her skin seemed to glow even in the artificial light.

Lucas felt Kit's beast buck at the reins and couldn't blame the boy for wanting to touch. Sascha's skin was an invitation to the senses and now that he'd stroked it once, he found himself starving for more.

Zara laughed. "If you're not bothered by color, then why are you staring at me?"

"I'm not sure, but you don't appear to be a leopard."

Lucas froze. There was no way a Psy should've picked up on that. *No way.* Scenting another animal was a changeling trait. Precisely what the hell kind of Psy was Sascha? Had he brought a spy into his world while trying to infiltrate hers?

Zara didn't answer until he gave her a subtle nod. "I'm not. I'm a distant cousin—wildcat."

"Then why are you working in a leopard business?"

"Because she's the best there is." Lucas drew Sascha's attention back to him. Part of it was because he thought her far too dangerous to leave to anyone else. But part of it was because he didn't like her being fascinated by anyone or anything except him. Given his possessive nature, that could turn out to be a problem. A big one.

"Did you have to give her permission to work here?"

There was a reason changelings didn't give away information to the Psy—it had to do with survival. However, this tidbit was common knowledge. "Once I'd enticed her to join us, I had to ensure her safety." To guarantee that, he'd "adopted" her into DarkRiver for the duration of her stay. She was marked by the scent of him and his sentinels so that enemies and friends alike knew who she belonged to.

If she hadn't been . . . There was a reason predatory changelings were very careful about straying into areas controlled by other predators. Enforcement officers had no jurisdiction in intrachangeling disputes, and the changeling way of settling things could be savage.

It occasionally put them on the back foot in terms of business because the Psy could move much faster. But it balanced out in the end—unlike the Psy, they had an open-and-shut friend-enemy line. There was no backstabbing. His race preferred to go straight for the throat.

"Let's see the designs, Zara," he said, wanting Sascha off this topic. Most of her race thought of changelings as lesser beings who'd somehow clawed their way to enough power to hold back the Psy. He'd never before met one who seemed to respect their ways enough to want to learn them. Was she merely curious by nature or was she the advance guard of a subtle invasion, feeding everything she learned into the PsyNet?

Zara rolled out one plan. "This is the design for the first home."

"The first?" Sascha asked. "They aren't all going to be the same?"

Kit stared. "Of course not. Who'd want to live in something that sterile? It'd be like a stack of those coffins the Psy live—" Suddenly appearing to realize who he was talking to, he turned bright red.

"Take your foot out of your mouth." Lucas tried not grin. "Changelings are different from the Psy, Sascha. We like things that are ours alone, things that are unique." His eyes met the night-sky glimmer of hers and he wondered if she felt what he did. It was as if a thin wire connected them, vibrating with their unacknowledged awareness of each other. "We don't share well." Lucas was the worst of the lot. What was his, was *his*.

"I see." She paused for a moment. "Will this delay the completion date?"

"No. We've factored that into account." He nodded at Zara to continue.

"Since this area is controlled by leopards and wolves, I've designed the houses mostly for them." Zara pointed out the wide-open living spaces and the easy access whether on human or animal feet. "But I've got a few plans for the nonpredatory species."

"How likely are they to want to settle in with the cats and the wolves?" Once again, her question displayed disturbing insight.

"That's the thing," Zara said. "They're not very likely to. I mean, we don't attack nonpredatory changelings without provocation, but if you were a deer, would you want to live next door to a leopard who might get peckish one night?" It was the blackest of changeling humor.

Kit grinned. "Yum, yum. I love deer shish kebab."

Sascha looked at him as if examining a bug. To his credit the juvenile didn't fidget and even tried out his smile again. Sascha's response was to shut her eyes for three seconds. When she opened them, she said, "I've been given the authority to veto or accept designs. Please show me the ones you think will work the best."

Before Zara could speak, Sascha asked another question. "How likely are the wolves and the leopards to coexist peacefully? I don't want to waste money building for the wolves if they're not going to go near the leopards and vice versa."

This was beyond unusual. Lucas knew he had to start looking *very* carefully at this slender Psy who thought disturbingly like a changeling. He said, "We've declared a truce that allows us to live together without major bloodshed. The bulk of the residents will be leopards but there'll be enough wolves for it to be worth planning for them. There's a shortage of homes for both species."

This was because the Psy owned a lot of building enterprises and they built the coffins Kit had mentioned—small, compact homes no self-respecting predator would go for. The Duncan family had been the first to grasp the need for changeling involvement in the initial phases of a development. In order to lure the hunters, the beasts of prey, you had to think like them.

Zara chose that moment to speak. "This is the design I like for the cats and this for the wolves." She put two fairly basic plans on the table. "I'm going to customize from there to take the land, the views, and the available runs into account. For a few homes, I'll begin from scratch in order to match the client's personality."

Sascha studied the designs. "To do that you'd have to know who was going to be the purchaser."

"We've already got a waiting list of prospective buyers. Their money is sitting in our trust account." Lucas watched Sascha's eyes as she looked up and caught the momentary flicker in the stars that lit them from within. Surprise, baby, he felt like saying.

"What?"

"It's the first new development that's being designed and built by changelings." He shrugged, fully aware it made the musculature of his shoulders stand out under his T-shirt. Like any cat, he liked to be admired, but this time it was a deliberate attempt to make Sascha react.

She looked away. "So you already knew you'd fulfill your part of the bargain when you negotiated the bonus."

"Of course."

"I consider myself bested." But when she glanced at him, he saw anything but meek acceptance.

Good thing he'd never liked easy prey.

CHAPTER 5

Sascha returned to the Duncan building and made a quick visit to her apartment before heading up to her mother's office. She'd begun repairing the fissures in her inner shields the moment she'd left DarkRiver and by the time she walked into the office, her heart was locked behind so many layers of power that she betrayed nothing, even when she found Santano Enrique ensconced with Nikita.

"Come in, Sascha." Nikita looked up from the computer screen where she was showing Enrique something.

"Hello, Sascha. I haven't seen you for a while."

"Councilor Enrique." Sascha bowed her head in a respectful nod. Night-sky eyes met hers.

Belying his Latin name, the other cardinal was a tall blond with almost too-pale skin. Nothing about him said he was sixty years of age but Sascha was well aware of the time he'd had to hone his considerable powers.

"Nikita tells me you're running your own project."

Sascha wasn't surprised that her mother had shared the

information with the other Councilor. Enrique was an academic, not a business rival. That made him no less deadly. None of the Council were people you'd turn your back on. "Yes, sir."

She'd always been uneasy around Enrique. Maybe it was because he was an off-the-scale Tk-Psy with so much telekinetic power that he could crush her without blinking. Or maybe it was because he had a way of looking at her as if he could see inside her skull. She wanted nobody in the confines of her mind.

"I have every confidence in you—you are Nikita's daughter, after all." Walking out from behind the desk, he looked her up and down. "Though the genetics seem to have taken an unexpected direction."

"She has no genetic deficiencies," Nikita stated. "I chose her father with great care to the mixing of our genes. And I produced a cardinal."

Sascha tried to understand the conversational undercurrents between them without success—the Psy were great at keeping secrets and she was talking to two masters of the art.

"Of course." Enrique smiled the cold smile of the Psy. "I have a lecture to prepare so I'd better be going. I look forward to seeing more of you, Sascha."

"Yes, sir." She kept her tone robotically flat, not saying another word until he'd walked out and she'd closed the door behind him. "It's not like Councilor Enrique to visit you here."

"He wanted to talk away from prying eyes." Nikita's tone said that that was the end of the discussion.

"I need to know, if I'm going to start taking on more responsibility."

"You don't need to know this." Her mother put her arms on the desk. "Tell me about the changeling."

Sascha knew it would do no good to push. The woman

who was sitting in front of her was part of the most closed and secret society in the world, the Psy Council.

They are Council. They are above the law.

It had taken a changeling to make her see the truth. The Council were a law unto themselves. When they spoke, the PsyNet trembled. And when they sentenced an individual to rehabilitation, there was no Court of Appeal.

Looking into her mother's cool brown eyes, Sascha accepted that if the moment came, Nikita would vote to put her own daughter in the Center rather than lose her position of power.

Those who felt emotion were the enemy . . . and enemies were to be shown no pity.

"He's extremely intelligent," she said, amazed at her own understatement. Lucas was one of the smartest, coolest negotiators she'd ever met. "Each and every unit has been presold."

"So he gets his ten million."

"Our profits will be substantial despite that—there's a huge shortage in the market."

"Are you suggesting we do another deal with them?"

"I'd wait a while. We don't know if we can work with them in the long term." All she knew was that she'd betray herself if she dealt with Lucas and his people for any length of time. Today she'd had to change her boots. Tomorrow she might have to change her entire personality. It was impossible to be around the vibrant *life* of the leopards and not hunger to live like them.

Then there was Lucas.

He was the first male she'd ever met who sent her hormones into complete overdrive. Her years of Psy training felt like nothing when she was with him. The worst thing was, she didn't care.

"I agree," Nikita said. "Let's see if they deliver."

"I have little doubt they will. Mr. Hunter doesn't strike

me as the kind of man who leaves things unfinished."

"I found out something very interesting about our new partners while you were gone." Nikita's slender fingers pulled up some data using the computer's touch screen. "It appears that the DarkRiver-SnowDancer pact goes much deeper than is common knowledge. The SnowDancers have a twenty percent stake in a lot of DarkRiver projects."

Sascha wasn't surprised. In spite of his lazy charm, Lucas was iron-willed enough to impress even the most ruthless. "Is it reciprocal?"

"Yes. DarkRiver owns twenty percent in a commensurate number of SnowDancer projects."

"An alliance based on shared territory and shared business profits." It was a unique situation for the predatory changelings, notorious for their turf wars. That weakness made it easy for the Psy to manipulate them. All they had to do to create conflict was manufacture a territorial transgression. But Sascha had a feeling that things were changing—and most of her people were just too caught up in their sense of superiority to notice.

"Don't let your guard down around Hunter."

"Yes, Mother." Sascha had every intention of following Nikita's advice. Lucas was not simply an alpha leopard, he was a highly sensual male. It was the latter that terrified her. Something in her flawed psyche reacted to him on the most visceral level.

After much thought, she'd decided that the only way to get rid of the voracious need pushing at her shields was to indulge it in a safe environment. The actual event couldn't be that difficult—she'd done her research, memorized several books of positions and skills.

Her heartbeat staggered at the thought of what she was considering, throwing doubt on her certainties. What if it didn't work? What if a taste made her crave more?

Impossible, she told herself. She wasn't that far gone,

not yet completely lost. She was still Psy, still cardinal. It was all she knew how to be.

Lucas met with his sentinels late that night. Sprawled around his lair, Nate, Vaughn, Clay, Mercy, and Dorian were the toughest members of the pack. In a one-on-one fight, every one of them would lose to him. But together they were formidable. As he'd told Sascha, if he broke vital Pack laws they'd take him down. Until then, they were his absolutely.

Not all pack alphas commanded such pure loyalty, but he'd earned his, earned it in the bloodiest, most terrible of ways. A fist squeezed his heart as memories of his parents awakened. It was always worse at this time of year, the ghosts of the past constant whispers in his mind.

They'd been cut down before they'd had a chance to live, and he'd been forced to watch. Like all children, he'd grown. Unlike most other young men, he'd grown into an alpha Hunter with the capacity to track down murderers and the brutal strength to demand justice. For some crimes forgiveness was impossible and vengeance the only cure.

"Nate, you first." He nodded to the most experienced member of the team. Nate had already been a sentinel for five years when Lucas had been confirmed as alpha a decade ago. But Nate hadn't waited for that official recognition of Lucas's status to give him his loyalty—he'd chosen to walk into hell beside Lucas years before, when Lucas was only eighteen, earning his absolute trust.

"We've confirmed our suspicions about the seven kills in Nevada, Oregon, and Arizona beyond any doubt." Nate's blue eyes were cold with withheld fury. "It's definitely the same killer."

"Bad news is, we have no new leads," Mercy picked up. The female sentinel was a tall, shapely redhead who could fight like the most lethal of blades. At twenty-eight she'd been a sentinel for a short two years but she'd earned the respect of all five males. "The cops are worse than useless as an information source—they refuse to call this a serial. It's like they can't even think the idea."

None of them had to voice what that might mean. The Psy were more than capable of clouding human thinking and changing the course of an investigation if they were determined to do so. There were Psy scattered through every level of Enforcement, probably for that very purpose.

"From what Sascha let drop, I'm certain that the PsyNet isn't equal opportunity," Lucas told them. "Democracy bypassed their Council a few centuries ago." He thought of his personal Psy shadow and wondered whether she had access to the core, whether she was guilty of covering up after a killer. Somehow, it didn't fit with the image of the woman who'd let a baby leopard gnaw on her boot. Nothing about Sascha Duncan fit the Psy mold and that made her unique. A unique Psy was a contradiction in terms.

"I can't find out any more information about that damn hive mind," Dorian muttered from his seated position on the floor. "Not even the dope fiends are willing to talk and, Psy or not, they'd sell their mother if it would get them another fix."

Lucas agreed. The Psy had the biggest drug problem on the planet. As long as they didn't try to addict his people, he didn't care how many of them killed themselves.

"I tracked your Psy's mother." Vaughn crossed the room and leaned against the wall by the door, his thick amber-gold hair gathered in a tie at the back of his neck. It was clear that he was a predator. What most people never guessed was that he wasn't leopard but jaguar.

Adopted into DarkRiver over twenty years ago at barely ten years of age, he was Lucas's closest friend and quite possibly the only male capable of holding the pack together if Lucas were killed, in spite of the fact that, to the leopards, he didn't have the scent of an alpha.

The jaguar changelings had remained truer to their animal roots—they were solitary wanderers for the most part and didn't need a hierarchy. But Vaughn had been raised as a leopard and Lucas thought of him as another alpha, one who'd given him his loyalty by choice. He was also one of the three sentinels who'd been there the night Lucas had turned the moon blood-red with vengeance. The jaguar had been seventeen at the time.

"I wouldn't want to meet Nikita Duncan on a dark street." The look in Vaughn's cycs said he wasn't joking.

Lucas raised a brow. "What did you find out?"

"She's held on to her Council seat for more than a decade because other Psy, even cardinals, are terrified of her. The woman's a seriously powerful telepath." He folded his arms across his chest, the small tattoo on his right biceps clearly visible. An echo of the markings on Lucas's face, it was a quiet statement of where his loyalty lay. All of the sentinels had followed the jaguar's lead, though Lucas hadn't asked it of them. Lucas's own upper arm bore the image of a hunting leapard, the promise of an alpha to his pack.

"That's not unusual enough to scare people," Dorian pointed out. Nothing about him indicated that he was latent and people had learned not to taunt him, because when Dorian bit, you didn't survive.

"No," Vaughn agreed. "But her talent has a little twist. She can infect other minds with viruses."

"Run that by me again?" Mercy sat up on one of the huge flat cushions that served as Lucas's sofas and pushed back her thick waist-length hair. "A virus?"

"Apparently it's like a computer virus but affects the mind of the person it's directed at. The rumor on the street is that Nikita rose to the Council by quietly getting rid of the competition." Steel lay beneath Vaughn's deceptive drawl.

"Several cardinals suffered mysterious breakdowns or deaths around the time of her ascension. Nothing could be traced to her and the general consensus is that that only increased her cachet with the then sitting Councilors. Murder is an accepted part of Nikita's arsenal."

Lucas prowled around the room. "We've always assumed the entire Council was in on it, but even if we're wrong and some members don't know, Vaughn's information makes it highly unlikely that Nikita doesn't."

And if Nikita knew, then it was almost impossible that Sascha, her *cardinal* heir, didn't. He was having trouble accepting her complicity in the cover-up—the panther in him was captivated by her, and he didn't want to be captivated by cruelty. "Sascha is our way in."

Clay, who'd been sitting silently on a window ledge, finally spoke. "Can we break her?"

Lucas knew what the sentinel was asking. Nobody on the changeling side was willing to play nice anymore, not after eight of their women had been butchered in the most brutal way.

"We don't torture women." He made his voice a whip.

"I was talking about sex." At thirty-four years of age, the dark-skinned sentinel was the only other packmate, aside from Nate and Vaughn, who knew the full details of that blood-soaked night that had turned Lucas from juvenile to alpha in everything but name. "Women are drawn to you. Can you use that against her?"

Dorian laughed. "You don't know the Psy, Clay. They're about as vulnerable to sex as I am to mating with a Snow-Dancer."

Lucas let the idea wash over him. Seducing Sascha was a strangely compelling idea. His body recognized hers in a way that made not touching her an exercise in restraint. The panther wanted to lay her down and luxuriate in the essence of her femininity, while the man wanted to shatter the shell she lived inside and discover the real woman. What made him wary was the possibility of learning that she was rotten to the core, daughter to a woman who'd killed with cold brilliance.

"We go in slow. Don't tip them off," he told the sentinels. "Let them think we're just animals."

Too bad if the Psy had forgotten that animals had teeth . . . and claws.

Lucas shifted into panther form after the sentinels had disbanded, and went for a run. A second after he set out, he knew that one of them was following him. The sentinels existed to protect him but they weren't his bodyguards—no leopard liked to be babysat. Clay was good enough to have hidden his scent if he'd wanted to. The fact that he hadn't meant he was asking permission to join his alpha.

Circling back, Lucas came close to sneaking up on the sentinel, but he moved out of reach a bare instant before Lucas dropped down from the tree limb he'd been padding along. They greeted each other with throaty rumbles and then set off. It was something beyond price to run like this, to let the night air whisper along his fur, to blend into the darkness until he was only a shadow and Clay an orange-black blur.

Running with his sentinels was one of the things every alpha did to strengthen the bonds of loyalty. Lucas had no need to do that with Clay. Like Vaughn and Nate, the sentinel had been tied to him since the night they'd hunted down and savagely ripped every single male member of a roaming leopard clan into tiny little pieces. It had been changeling justice. An eye for an eye. Vengeance to lay his parents' souls to rest.

Now he ran with the sentinels because they were tough, fast, and dangerous enough to test him to the limit. No alpha could afford to let his skills slip. Though they were more civilized than their wild brethren, an alpha's rule would only be accepted as long as he was strong enough to lead the pack. And such strength wasn't always of the body.

The Psy thought the changelings stupid because they sacrificed the wisdom of their elders in favor of young blood. The Psy didn't know anything. The sentinels withdrew from frontline positions as they grew older because *they* had to be physically invulnerable—Nate was already on the lookout for his replacement. Upon retirement as a sentinel, he would become one of Lucas's advisors, his rank undiminished.

If Lucas retained the incoming sentinels' respect as he aged, they'd take over the physical role he played in the pack—meting out Pack justice and keeping Pack discipline. During such times, those who didn't understand their ways often came to believe that the strongest of the sentinels had become the new alpha. Changelings saw no need to educate them otherwise.

But that was in the unknown future. Right now he had to be the most lethal of them all, savage and brilliant. Because not only was the pack watching but so were the SnowDancers. One hint of weakness in DarkRiver and the wolves would come down on them in a hail of teeth and claws.

He couldn't allow his inexplicable attraction to one of the Psy sway him from his goal. More depended on this than merely the sating of vengeance. After DarkRiver had realized the existence of a serial killer preying on changeling women, they'd warned all other changeling groups in the killer's hunting grounds. Every single alpha had wanted to go for the jugular—none more so than the wolves.

Lucas had insisted on taking on the job of hunting the killer because in spite of losing Kylie, he was the lone alpha who could still think. It was as if the blood that had christened him had also given him the ability to see beyond the dark-red glimmer of fury and retribution.

The SnowDancers had reluctantly handed him the reins because his pack had lost a member while theirs hadn't. But their patience was limited. The wolves knew that sooner or later, the killer would strike them too. The second that happened, all bets were off—the SnowDancers would begin to hunt down the Psy and the Psy would retaliate, leading to war on a catastrophic scale.

Lucas slept deeply after the exertion of a run that had left even Clay exhausted. He'd expected only darkness but the most exquisite pleasure welcomed him into his dreams.

Slender fingers traveled down his front as he lay sprawled on his back, exploring him so carefully that he felt owned. No woman had ever come close to owning Lucas Hunter, but in this dreamworld he allowed her to play. After endless moments, the fingers stopped their stroking and he felt the brush of wet heat against his nipple. His dream-lover was taking her time licking circles around it, arousing him to fever pitch. Opening his eyes, he tangled a hand in the silky curls cascading over his chest.

Her head rose and night-sky eyes met his.

He wasn't surprised. The panther in him had found Sascha Duncan enticing from the start and in this dreamworld, it was okay to let that fascination free, to indulge his feline curiosity about this most unusual woman. Here there was no possibility of war and she was no longer an emissary of the enemy.

"What do you think you're doing, kitten?" He let his gaze wander over the dark honey of her bare skin.

Those eyes widened in shock. "This is my dream."

He chuckled. Even in his dreams, she was as willful as she was in life. He'd begun to suspect that not everything was efficiency with Sascha. No, sometimes she just liked sharpening her claws on him. "I'm at your mercy."

She made an annoyed sound and sat up on her knees. "Why are you talking?"

He folded his arms behind his head, delighted by the sight of her lush breasts displayed so beautifully for him. He liked this dream. Even the panther was pleased. "Don't you want me to?" He made it a temptation.

"Well . . ." She frowned. "The whole point is to taste you . . . I guess you'd never be silent in bed."

"You're right." He watched her watch him. Her eyes held such pure heat that he felt branded. The alpha in him wanted to reach out and tangle his fingers in the shadowed triangle of curls exposed by her kneeling position, but he was wary of shattering this strange dream.

"Can I?" She ran her fingers along the markings on his face, her lower lip caught between her teeth. "Do you feel my touch?"

He wanted to bite down on that sexy mouth she was teasing him with. "Every stroke." The markings were highly sensitive and he was very, very choosy about who he let touch them.

"I've been wanting to stroke them since we first met." With a sigh, she leaned down to place a row of kisses along the jagged lines. The deep rumble of his purr seemed to startle her but it wasn't a bad kind of startlement—he felt her nipples harden against his chest. After exploring his face to her satisfaction, she sat back up, raking her nails gently down his chest.

"Harder, kitten. I won't break."

She took a shaky breath and did as he'd asked. "Cats like to be petted." It was a soft murmur.

"I told you we're picky about who we allow to pet us."
He ran a hand up the outside of her thigh.

She shivered. "Why would I dream of you touching me?
I want to touch you."

"But if you're dreaming of me, wouldn't I be touching
you?" He was delighted by this odd dream, which felt almost like reality, except of course the real Sascha would
never display her emotions so openly.

"Yes . . . you're very territorial." A frown line appeared
on her forehead. "You'd want to mark me. My subconscious must be filling in the gaps."

He tried not to grin. "Who do you let pet you?"

"Psy don't get petted." A hint of sadness flickered in
those eyes he was starting to be able to read.

"Maybe you've been hanging around with the wrong
people." He stroked his hand to the curve of her buttock
and stopped. "I'd take great pleasure in petting you."

Her breath came out in a gasp. "Me first," she whispered, leaning down. "It's my dream. Just a taste," she said
again. "That's all, just a taste."

He would never say no to being petted by this exotic female who fascinated him. Not when she looked at him with
fire not ice in her gaze. His hand clenched on her bottom as
she nibbled, licked, and sucked at his nipple with the utmost attention to detail. She didn't stop him when he ran
his fingers down her thigh, luxuriating in that honeyed skin
he wanted to lick all over.

Her mouth moved to his neglected nipple, one hand
reaching down to scrape the nails up his thigh. He growled
softly in the back of his throat. She looked up. "What does
that mean?" Her hand had dropped to lay against his inner
thigh, excruciatingly close to his rock-hard erection.

Her head tilted slightly to one side and he remembered
her questions in the car. Odd that his subconscious would
remember that small giveaway gesture, but then again, this

whole dream was odd. Not that he was complaining.

"It means keep doing exactly what you were doing." He moved his hand around her bottom and slid down to lightly rub at the wet heat of her entrance, sending the scent of her desire flaring into the air.

She gasped and pulled away. "Not yet."

He was used to taking control but there was something in her eyes that told him she'd disappear if he pushed any harder. He put his hands back under his head, telling her without words that he was hers to play with. For now. As if she'd heard the unspoken caveat, she moved down the bed and straddled his thighs midway up his legs.

He looked his fill of that lush female body and knew he was going to mark her when he took her. Nothing hurtful. Just a bite or two, a playful nip here and there in places where no one could mistake their meaning. Sascha Duncan was going to be Lucas Hunter's woman.

Night-sky eyes wide, she wrapped one slender hand around his jutting erection. He shuddered. "Tighter."

She squeezed and then began to move her hand up and down. "Why does this make me feel good?" Her voice was heavy with sexual heat, her breath coming out in soft pants. "There was nothing about this in the manuals."

Moving his hands from behind his head, he reached down and pulled her forward by gripping her thighs. She came only so far and not far enough. "What?"

"I'm caressing you and yet I'm the one who feels . . . pleasure." The last word was a moan as he grew even harder in her hands.

Lucas was used to sex, used to sensual women who knew what they were doing, but this Psy with her questions and her strange innocence had him so desperately hungry, he was starting to lose the ability to think. "Suck me, kitten. Taste me." The raw demand came from the animal heart of him.

She didn't scare. And he was pleased. "Taste you? Yes . . . I have to taste you . . . have to satisfy the craving." Scooting down his body, she knelt on all fours, knees between his legs, hands on his hip bones. Then she dipped her head and began to taste him as he'd asked.

He clenched his hand in her hair, telling himself not to buck as his body demanded. The sweet suction of her mouth was the most intense pleasure he'd ever experienced. When he saw lights flicker behind his eyes, he knew they were shifting from human to cat, cat to human. Only the most extreme edge of arousal could make him lose that much control.

Using his other hand to push her hair back, he watched her as she moved her head up and down the hard length of his erection, the sight serving to arouse him almost to madness. The need to pound into the silky heat between her legs was a driving rhythm in his brain, but tonight, he was at her mercy . . . and she wanted him in her mouth. He came with a growl that reverberated around the room, the thick richness of her hair in his fists.

"Thank you, kitten," he said.

There was no answer.

With a frown, he opened his eyes. And found himself in his lair, spent, pleasured, and alone.

CHAPTER 6

Sascha was having trouble meeting Lucas's gaze, scared he'd be able to see the erotic images flashing through her mind like a full-motion picture. What was happening to her? She'd spent last night lost in the most seductive dreams of her life, had woken gasping for release, her skin wet with perspiration.

And Lucas had been the star figure in her fantasies.

The plan had been to get him out of her system by programming her brain to dream about him. She'd intended to let her senses run wild in the safety of her mind and indulge until she was sated. It had backfired horribly. She'd had her taste and now found she wanted even more. Like an addict, she craved the sensations he'd shown her.

"I'll be taking you to meet Clay Bennett, our construction supervisor, in about twenty minutes. After that I want to show you the materials we'll be using for construction, since you want to double-check every nut and bolt." Those piercing green eyes were tinted with hints of mocking amusement.

She couldn't help but remember how those same eyes had looked as she'd used her mouth to suck him to orgasm. That word brought her to her senses. Her shields were cracking again and he was the catalyst.

"Thank you for telling me." She tried to note down the details on her organizer but could barely see through the buzzing in her head. This was bad, very bad. Instead of containing them, the dreams appeared to have strengthened the creeping fingers of insanity.

"You don't look like you slept well."

Was there a subtle innuendo in that sentence? No, she told herself. How could there be? *She* was the one who'd had the dreams. Lucas surely had no need for release found in fantasy—she'd seen the way women looked at him. And why not? He was a man who made no bones about his sexuality and even she understood the kind of primal heat a male like that could produce.

Once again, her mind threatened to run away with her sanity. Shoving up shield after mental shield, she said, "My rest was disturbed but I'm perfectly capable of functioning." As soon as she got control of her runaway thoughts.

"Bad dreams?" He watched her with the concentration of a hunter stalking prey.

"The Psy don't dream." It was the accepted wisdom. If that was a lie, she thought, what other lies had she been fed? Or was it true for all other Psy? Did they not live even in their dreams?

"A pity," Lucas said, that rough-edged voice smoothing into a drawl. "Dreams can be very . . . pleasurable."

Wet heat flared. She pressed her thighs tight, terrifyingly aware that her body had reacted in a way a changeling might detect. Panic had her shoving everything deep into the secret compartments of her mind.

The panther inside Lucas crouched low, tracking Sascha's every movement. Man and beast were both puzzled—what was it about her that had triggered the sensual eroticism of that dream? In life she was as cold as ice, as touchable as a hunk of metal. Aside from the hint of fire in those cardinal eyes that he refused to believe was a figment of his imagination.

He froze as he picked up the faintest traces of female arousal. The panther lunged at the walls of his mind, telling him to take her, that she was ready. The man wasn't so certain. What if it was a Psy trick—the ultimate back door into his mind? Until he knew for sure, he wouldn't be stroking Sascha except in his dreams.

"The Psy know nothing about pleasure," she commented, looking down at her little computerized tablet. "And we intend to keep it that way. Shall we be on our way to see your construction supervisor?"

"After you." He stood and waved toward the doorway. "How's your mother?" It was time to start digging. The reason for this charade could never be forgotten.

"Fine." Sascha reached the glass-enclosed elevator and waited for it to rise up to their level.

"She's an extraordinary woman," he commented. "I heard that she became a Councilor at forty. Isn't that very young to reach such a high post?"

She nodded. "But Tatiana Rika-Smythe was younger at the time of her ascension. She's only thirty-five now."

"The Rika-Smythes are your primary business rivals?"

"You know that already."

He shrugged and gestured for her to enter the elevator ahead of him. "Never hurts to make sure."

In the closed atmosphere, the scent of her was intoxicating to his animal senses. She was pure woman, lush and barely awakened, and he was very interested, the panther in him arrogantly convinced that her reaction was without trickery. He had to force down the low growl that gathered at the back of his throat. Now was not the time to stalk this particular prey.

"It's well known that the Rika-Smythes and the Duncans have some of the same business interests."

"How can your mother work with Tatiana when they're rivals?" The doors opened on the first floor.

Sascha walked out beside him, graceful and eerily beautiful with those eyes that kept startling people who came up on them. Cardinals were not often seen outside the rarefied walls of the Psy headquarters. It was critical he find out why he'd been honored with Sascha Duncan.

"Their responsibilities in the Council are separate from their business loyalties."

"Some of it must bleed over. Every administration has its cliques." Which might mean that the Councilors could be keeping secrets from each other.

Sascha gave him a sharp glance. "You're very interested in the Council."

"Do you blame me?" He pushed open a manual glass door. "I'm hardly likely to get another chance to talk to a Psy so high up in the hierarchy."

She walked through the doorway before speaking. "I may be a cardinal but I'm not as high up as you seem to believe. Simply because my mother is Council doesn't mean I'm in the inner circle. I'm just another Psy."

"No cardinal is ever ordinary." Why was she protesting so much? What was it that she was hiding? Blood and death or something else?

"There is an exception to every rule." It struck Sascha that the intensity with which Lucas was pursuing this line of inquiry probably wasn't due to simple curiosity. Wariness kicked in but it was too late—she'd already betrayed her abnormal status within the Psy.

She had to start remembering that Lucas's last name wasn't merely a name—it was a designation. "May I ask you a question?" she said before she could talk herself out of it. Notwithstanding her awareness of his nature, her interest in him continued to heighten. And each time she gave in to the need, it created another chip in the already fragile wall of her sanity. Yet, she couldn't stop herself.

He paused in front of the door that likely led to the construction supervisor's workspace. "Ask."

"What does a Hunter do?" She'd heard rumors on the PsyNet but changelings were very closemouthed about some things.

"I'm afraid you're going to have to barter something special to get that information."

The slow curve of his smile shot her composure to pieces. "What would you like to know?"

He answered almost on top of her words. "What's the incidence of violence in the Psy population?"

She hadn't expected the question but the answer was easy and well known. "Close to zero."

"Are you sure?" The question echoed in the air. "As for what Hunters do, we hunt down rogues."

"Rogues?"

"Sorry, darling. You only paid for one answer." He pushed open the door.

Frustrated, she walked in and found herself standing a heartbeat away from a dark-skinned man with eyes a deeper shade of green than Lucas's. Something about him made her want to take a step back . . . and run.

"Meet Clay Bennett, our construction supervisor."

Sascha knew the changeling in front of her was much more than that. "Mr. Bennett." The man's eyes were so calm that she should've felt at home with him. Instead he reminded her of a cobra lulling his prey into a false sense of security—the second she lowered her guard, he'd instigate a deadly strike.

"Ms. Duncan. I'm the man you come to if you have any problems with the materials used during construction, the workers, anything like that."

"I've noted that." She looked around the huge office space, which housed a number of desks. Glass doors made up the facing wall but she could see Zara to the left and an unknown blond male at a desk to the right. He wasn't looking at her, but somehow she knew that he was completely attuned to their conversation. "Do those doors open?"

"Of course," Lucas drawled. "We're animals under the skin—we can't stand being caged." She knew he was mocking the simplistic Psy view of changelings, mocking her. The urge to give back as good as she got was a devil on her shoulder—a mad part of her thought it might almost be worth it simply to see the look on his face.

"What about the higher floors?" She answered her own question the second she looked outside. "The trees. Leopards are excellent climbers."

Lucas went unnaturally still beside her. "You've done your research."

"Of course. I'm Psy."

A few minutes later, Sascha closed the door of the lavatory, put down the lid, and sat. Her whole body shuddered. What a joke. She was no Psy. She was a woman close to the edge of insanity, reduced to hiding in toilets in order to repair the fractured walls of her mind.

Her organizer chimed before she'd done more than gather together the ragged edges of her psyche. It was Santano Enrique, requesting a conference on the PsyNet. The inside of her mouth suddenly felt like it had been stuffed full of cotton wool.

Enrique was too powerful a Psy, had had too many years of experience at spotting mistakes. She didn't want him connected to her in any way. None of the other Councilors had ever approached her telepathically or on the PsyNet—they preferred to talk face-to-face if necessary. She knew why, of course. They weren't sure that she hadn't inherited her mother's deadly little ability.

Refusing Enrique's call wasn't an option. Hurriedly completing the repairs on her shields, she closed her eyes and took a step into darkness. The glittering plane of the PsyNet opened before her, filled with the endless stars, bright and faded, large and small, that represented the minds of the Psy. Enrique blazed and so did she. They were both cardinals. The crucial difference was, she had no real power, while he could pulverize her with a thought.

His consciousness was waiting for her. "Thank you for coming, Sascha."

"I can't stay long, sir. I'm in the midst of a delicate situation for which I need my full attention." While in the Net, she couldn't even allow herself to think that what she was saying was a lie. She had to believe absolutely.

"The deal with the changelings."

It wasn't a question so she didn't answer.

"An interesting choice. Unusual. Why did you decide to do what the rest of the families haven't?"

"I'm sorry, sir. I'm not permitted to discuss our business practices. Please speak to my mother—she's the head of our household." Nikita had officially achieved that pinnacle in 2075 when Sascha's grandmother, Reina, had died. In truth, Nikita had been the power behind the throne for almost ten years prior to that.

"I had the impression you'd been granted more independence."

If they'd come from anyone but a Psy, she would've said that the words were meant to prick her pride and make her speak without thinking. Unless, of course, that was his plan. Was that why he was paying her so much attention suddenly—because he suspected she was flawed?

All these frantic thoughts buzzed in a small, secret part of her. It was the same place where she hid the core of her self—the shining rainbow of her mind. Layered in multiple shields she continually reinforced, it couldn't be breached by anyone without using such brutal force that it would kill her.

"Would you like me to link you to my mother?"

"No, Sascha. I wanted to ask you a favor."

Fear spiked in that small, secret heart. "What, sir?" This had to be a trap. Why would a Councilor, a cardinal with off-the-scale Tk powers, be asking her for a favor?

"You'll be coming into a lot of contact with changelings during this project. I'd like you to pass me any new information you discover about them."

It was the last thing she'd expected. "I'd be happy to do so, sir, but—"

"Think carefully, Sascha. There could be . . . benefits for you. Some of us are starting to think it's past time we utilized you properly."

It was a bribe, pure and simple. Her hunger to finally be accepted and valued as a cardinal urged her to accept the offer and not look back. Conversely, that very hunger also made her aware that no matter how much she tried, she'd never be normal. Getting closer to the Council would only increase her chances of being exposed.

The ashes of lost dreams floated to her feet and in the deepest, most hidden core of her soul, she cried. Only years of Psy training and a desperate desire to hide the truth of her broken mind had her answering logically. "They're understandably cautious around me. I'm not sure I'll discover anything." It was a lie. Already she knew so much no Psy had ever known, but she found herself unable to give up their secrets . . . Lucas's secrets.

"They're animals. Treat them well and they'll start to trust you." It was evident he thought trust a weakness.

Sascha saw it as a gift. "I'd be happy to cooperate but first I have to—"

"I've already cleared this with Nikita." Enrique neatly cut her off.

"Then I'll get the information to you."

"I'd like to meet you once a day for briefings."

Sascha was beyond scared now. She didn't want Enrique evaluating her daily. "I'm sorry, sir. That could interfere with my work and I'm sure Mother wouldn't like that. I'll contact you as soon as I have anything worth sharing." It was a daring statement and if she'd allowed herself to feel, she would've been trembling.

Enrique's presence on the PsyNet was a pure white star, so cold that she wanted to shiver. "Don't wait too long."

"Is that all, sir?"

"For now."

Sascha dropped out of the PsyNet and immediately contacted the head of her household as any good Psy would do. She could telepath without problem at this range, which at least gave her relief from keeping constant vigilance over her consciousness. During telepathic communications, neither party could "see" the other.

As soon as Nikita answered, she outlined Enrique's requests, hugging her arms so tight around her body that she almost bruised her own ribs. If her mother told her to keep those daily meetings . . .

Enrique has overstepped his bounds. Nikita's mental voice was frigid. *I gave him permission to solicit information, not tie you to a schedule.*

Relief threatened to turn her limbs to jelly. *Mother, I think it would be preferable if I gave you any pertinent information and you . . . shared it with Enrique.* The pause was calculated. Nikita enjoyed being in a position of power. *You're the head of the household—I should be reporting to you first in any case.*

Nikita was silent for a couple of seconds. *I'd already considered that. Unfortunately, Enrique is too strong to defy without consequences. And he wants to talk to you.*

Perhaps, Sascha said, thinking desperately, *you could imply to him that I find dealing with his powerful presence too much on top of my first independent project.*

Now you're thinking like a Duncan. Nikita was clearly pleased. *He can't argue with me for trying to protect the deal.*

The deal, Sascha thought, not her daughter. Even though she should've been used to the heartlessness of the Psy after a lifetime of living with them, she felt a sharp stab of hurt. *Then I'm free to concentrate on the development and keep you up to speed?*

Yes.

With that, Nikita was gone. Sascha allowed herself a huge sigh of relief and dropped her head into her hands. Something was wrong. It wasn't paranoia. Why was Enrique suddenly so concerned with a failed cardinal most of the Psy ignored? Doubly troubling was the extent of Nikita's cooperation with the other Councilor.

Her gut twisted. She had a feeling she was being used as a pawn in a game for which she didn't know the rules. What worried her even more was that she didn't know the consequences of checkmate . . . or how to stop it.

Suddenly realizing she'd been sitting there staring into nothingness, she stood up and only then did the ridiculousness of her situation strike her. She'd just had conversations with two members of the Council while sitting on the closed lid of a toilet. The thought had her stifling giggles as she lifted the lid and opened the door.

When she checked her appearance in the mirror above the basin, she was surprised to find that nothing betrayed her slight case of hysteria. Her physical masks were holding, even as the mental ones broke down piece by piece. Glancing at her timepiece, she saw that she'd been in here for almost thirty minutes. The changelings would be full of questions and she'd better have answers for them.

Before heading out, she ensured that she looked exactly as she should—every hair on her head smoothed into a tight braid, the cuffs of her dark gray suit perfectly aligned, and her face so calm that she almost convinced herself her stomach wasn't tied up in knots.

Nobody was in the corridor but heads turned the instant she walked back into the room used by Clay Bennett and the others. One particular pair of green eyes tracked her every move. "I apologize for keeping you waiting," she said, before anyone could speak. "I was called into conference."

Lucas tapped at the side of his head with a finger. "That kind of conference?" His lips curved.

She wanted to tease him back so badly. "Yes."

"Strange place for one," Kit remarked, tongue in cheek. It was a measure of her distraction that it took the comment for her to notice the young male who'd entered the room in her absence.

She couldn't help herself. "In what way?"

Kit stopped looking through some papers on Clay's desk and stared at her. When she calmly stared back, he started to turn red, looking as young and adorable as the two cubs she'd been allowed to touch. "Um, well . . . d-don't you . . . I have to get these upstairs." He grabbed what looked like a random pile of papers and almost ran from the room.

"You should be more merciful—he's only recently grown out of being a cub." Lucas's chuckle held real amusement.

She fought not to let her lips twitch. "I was merely asking a question."

His eyes narrowed. "Sure you were."

"When do you consider your children full grown?" she asked, trying to get him to stop thinking about her impulsive decision to tease Kit.

An odd tension seemed to infiltrate the room.

"Sugar for sugar, darling." The Hunter marks were starkly beautiful against the stillness of his expression.

"We're considered adults when we turn twenty." Conditioning was officially complete at eighteen, though in reality, most Psy were fully conditioned by sixteen. Two more years were given to allow any slipups to come to light.

"There's quite a difference between being considered adult and being adult."

"You don't think twenty is old enough?"

"Our juveniles have to prove their maturity before they're accorded adult status." Lucas was convinced Sascha had meant to tease Kit. Her expression betrayed nothing, but he wasn't Psy and he didn't disregard his feelings.

As he'd suspected from the start, this Psy was different, very different. Different enough to be dangerous . . . unless her own people hadn't picked up on her uniqueness. It wasn't impossible—in some matters the Psy were quite blind, blinkered by their belief in their own superiority.

Lucas's gut said that Sascha was the key to everything. If he solved the mystery of her, he might come close to shattering the closed walls of the most inhuman of races.

"A harsh law," she said.

"Our world is harsh." Especially with the Psy in charge. Without changeling heart and human spirit, the world would've been hell.

Lucas called Clay into his office after Sascha had returned to Duncan headquarters. "What did you think?"

"She's smart. Those eyes miss nothing."

"That's a given with cardinals."

To his surprise, Clay shook his head. "Some of them are so cerebral that they barely notice anything physical."

"You've had contact with them." It was a statement, not

a request for information. Clay's past was shrouded in mystery but Lucas trusted the leopard to tell him anything he needed to know.

"Some," Clay confirmed. "I'm no expert but the one thing I can tell you for sure is that something about Sascha doesn't fit."

The confirmation of his own instincts added impetus to his determination to solve the mystery that was Sascha. "What did the background check turn up?"

"She's what she seems—a cardinal Psy who hasn't been co-opted into their power structure." Clay rubbed at the stubble on his jaw. "That in itself's weird enough to make her stand out. Every other adult cardinal we've tracked works for the Council in some way."

Lucas rocked back on his heels, thinking. "Which means it's either all a front and she's a Council spy . . ."

". . . or there's something wrong with her," Clay finished, verbalizing what Lucas didn't want to admit. "If she's been shoved out of the inner circle, she's of no use to us."

The panther inside Lucas flexed its claws—there was nothing wrong with the female who'd caught its attention. "Let's give it a few more days," he said, fighting the animal. "We don't have any other option at this point. The other Psy won't even talk deals with us."

"We could let the SnowDancers do what they want."

"If they start taking out high-level Psy, any hope of ending this without massive loss of life goes out the window." The SnowDancers wanted to torture information out of those they blamed for condoning the killings, including Nikita Duncan. "The Psy will retaliate against all of us and they won't spare the cubs."

Clay nodded. They'd been through this before and the same thing had swayed them back then. DarkRiver was a powerful but young pack. They had a lot of cubs and juveniles under their protection. If the Psy struck back after a

SnowDancer attack, the entire next generation could be wiped out in one bloody wave. Even Dorian's thirst for vengeance had been overpowered by his deep-rooted need to keep their young safe.

"Setting the wolves loose has to be our last choice."

It was a choice he hoped he never had to make but he wasn't naïve enough to believe that it wouldn't end in violence. Too many changeling women had died and they were all out for blood. Psy blood.

CHAPTER 7

That night, when he finally went to bed after a lengthy meeting with his sentinels, his mind was full of images of death. His desire to find justice for their women warred with his unexpected need to protect Sascha from harm. It was baffling but he was beginning to feel as if she had a prior claim on his loyalty.

It only seemed fitting that his dreams should echo his very real hunger. When he "woke" inside the dreamworld, it was to find himself sprawled on his front as a feminine hand stroked the back of his thigh. The touch was familiar and as acceptable to the panther who was his other half as it was to the human male. She had skin privileges. He looked over his shoulder. "You're back."

Sascha jerked away. "You're talking."

"I thought we figured this out last time around," he teased. "Why are you wearing clothes?" Not that she didn't look delectable in the white bra and panties she had on, but he preferred seeing her naked, skin gleaming and flushed.

In his dreams she was the woman he needed her to be—hot and needy and wild enough to tantalize.

"I thought it might help slow matters down." Calm words but her cheeks were flushed, her body taut in expectation.

He chuckled. "I'm sorry, kitten. Was I too fast for you last time?"

"Why are you remembering the other dream?" Tiny lines appeared on her forehead.

"Why shouldn't I?" He turned onto his side and curved one hand over her waist as she knelt beside him.

"Because it was my dream, my fantasy." Breathy and soft, her voice was a stroke to his senses.

"Maybe me remembering is part of your fantasy. Otherwise how would things progress?" he said, playing along. Was this how Sascha would've acted had she not been born one of the Psy? If he'd met this sensual, stubborn creature in reality, he would've made it his goal to seduce her until she belonged to him without compromise.

Tapping at her lower lip with a finger, she nodded. "That makes sense."

He reached out and pulled her down beside him without warning. Night-sky eyes went huge in surprise. When he rose so that he was braced over her, she couldn't hold back her gasp. His erection was hot and hard between them. Given that "she" had imagined him naked on a large bed, it was difficult to ignore, especially since it was nudging at her navel.

Before she could tell him that this was *her* dream and he shouldn't be interfering, he leaned down and nuzzled at her neck, taking her scent into his bloodstream. "I'm never going to be an easily controllable lover, in your dreams or out of them."

Her hands clenched on his biceps. "But—"

"Shh." He nipped gently at her chin. Her hands gripped

him tighter. "If you want to fantasize about me, don't try and turn me into someone else. Take me as I am, rough edges, dominance, and all." Trailing his lips across her jaw and back, he kissed her. Hard. Fast. His way. "I love your mouth," he murmured. "So, how about it?"

She took a ragged breath. "I don't want to fantasize about anyone else."

The panther let out an almost subvocal growl. Running his hand down her side, he said, "I'm possessive and I'm territorial. Can you handle that?" Under his palm, the supple skin of her bottom felt beautifully bitable.

"I can always wake up if I can't." Fire glittered in her eyes. "Don't try to intimidate me."

He smiled and began to kiss and suck at the side of her neck. "I'll always try but it would be no fun if you didn't push back." He liked her spirit, her stubborn will, her refusal to bend to his every demand.

Her hands slid to his shoulders, then tunneled into his hair, her body moving restlessly against his. He let her feel more of his weight, bracing himself on one arm so he could move the other up and down her body. On the upward stroke, he cupped her breast, shaping and petting.

"Stop." It was a sharp cry.

He froze at the sound of real distress. "Did I hurt you?" Looking up, he searched her face.

She shook her head. "I can't feel so much so soon." Panic shimmered in the dark skies he was getting used to seeing in his dreams.

"Pleasure is nothing to fear." He kept his hand on her breast. "Stop fighting it."

"I'm afraid." It was a husky whisper.

"Afraid enough to let it control you?"

A short pause and then she shook her head, the defiant nature of her personality asserting itself. "If I'm going to go down, at least I'll know what I died for."

His hackles rose. "Who are you frightened of?"

"No." She touched his lips with a finger. "This dream is about pleasure. We can talk about death in the real world. Show me pleasure, Lucas. Show me the things I've never known."

Protective instincts vied with arousal. In the end they both won. If pleasure was what it would take to banish the fear from her eyes, then he'd drown her in it. Claiming her mouth in a kiss that was just this side of savage, he let the leopard out to play. The growl at the back of his throat poured into her mouth and he felt her entire body vibrate in response.

The sound she made fed the hunger but it also fed the protectiveness. He let her catch her breath before taking her lips in another kiss, but this time he gentled himself. This time, he used his tongue to tangle with hers. The surprised jerk of her body gave way to enthusiastic participation only seconds later.

Certain that she was ready to embrace the next step of their dance, he bit her lower lip as he broke the kiss and moved down the slender vulnerability of her neck. Half covered by the lace of her bra, the tender upper curves of her breasts teased at his every male instinct. She was more than a handful and he was delighted.

"Purr for me, kitten." He kissed his way across the bared expanse of skin.

She shuddered. "I'm n-not a cat."

Chuckling, he let his thumb and forefinger play with the taut bud of one nipple. Her fingers dug into his skull. He arched into the caress and she understood, raking her hands through his hair hard enough for him to feel the pressure against his scalp. Just like he'd taught her last time. "You remember, too." He replaced his fingers with his mouth, sucking the nipple hard and tight through the lace.

"Oh! Please! Please." Her hands gripped frantically at

his shoulders, but he had no intention of rushing this. He intended for the waves of pleasure to lap at her before consuming her, before turning her into passion and heat, surrender and demand.

Releasing the suction, he returned to steal another kiss while her chest heaved up and down under him. She tasted tarter than last time, as if the spice in her nature had risen to the top. "Did you like that?" he asked against her lips, not waiting for an answer before moving down to repeat the teasing caress on her neglected breast.

Her body almost bowed as sensation shot through her. The pressure of his weight kept her from arching all the way up but he couldn't keep her completely immobile. Suddenly, his erection was cradled in the vee of her thighs, snug against the place it wanted to be. All he had to do was push aside the gusset of her panties and he could have her. Claim her. Brand her.

Claws pushed against the skin of his humanity.

Gritting his teeth, he tried to move away. Slender feminine limbs wrapped around his hips, holding him tight. "Let go." He was so close to the edge that he was starting to see the world through the panther's eyes.

"I can't take any more."

"Sure you can." It took every ounce of willpower he had to chain the beast more than willing to take Sascha—she wasn't ready yet. Using the leverage he had, he began to rock against her vulnerably parted flesh.

"Lucas!" It was a scream. Her hands fell to the sheets, clutching wildly as she tried to ride the pleasure.

"Shh," he gentled, stopping to give her a little tenderness. "I like hearing you scream my name." He kissed her brow, her eyelids, the tip of her nose, her cheeks, and finally her lips. Soft, slow, undemanding. Until her breathing was easier and those night-sky eyes were no longer blind with desire. Then he started moving again.

Her eyes fluttered shut and reopened as if by force of will, her exotic skin shimmering with a layer of perspiration. Rich and heady, the musky scent of her was a carnal invitation. She lasted a couple of minutes this time before he had to stop and bring her back down until she could handle it again.

Each time she lasted longer and his control grew more fragile. He wanted this female with a hunger he'd never before felt. He wanted to ravage her, adore her, mark her. But even the panther knew she had to come to him willingly. There could be no doubt between them, no boundaries and no hesitation, because when the panther shattered its bonds and animal hunger took over, she had to trust him absolutely. Otherwise they'd both break.

Somewhere during the teasing, he got off her bra and feasted his eyes on the beauty of her breasts. She was too dazed by pleasure to protest the kisses he dropped on the upper slopes or the caresses he bestowed with one of his hands. He kept everything easy, getting her used to her own sensuality.

It threatened to drive him to madness.

He *could* be like this in bed but it was usually after he'd sated himself in his partner's body and drunk deep of her screams of pleasure. The panther wasn't selfish—it merely liked to quench the edge of its thirst before it started to play. But today Lucas was with a woman who needed the play before anything else.

"Don't you stop this time!" she snapped, when he started to slow the rocking motion. Her hands rose to lock around his neck as she tried to pull him down.

"I'm too heavy." He leaned down far enough that his chest rubbed against her breasts, far enough that they could tangle their tongues in a heated mating of mouths. "And," he said as the kiss broke, "you still have on these." He ran the fingers of one hand along the bottom edge of her panties, stroking at the tender skin he found.

Her tongue flicked out to wet her lips. "I don't know if I can handle skin to skin."

It was his nature to push. "Then we finish it this way." But it wasn't his nature to force. He could show her pleasure without feeling the silky softness of the tight, wet heat between her legs. Pressing hard against her, he started grinding in slow circles.

She screamed out scant moments after he'd begun, her neck muscles standing out in sharp relief. He felt the pleasure ripple through her and it was enough to have him fighting his own release. Barely capable of rational thought, he slipped one hand under her nape to hold her in place for his kiss . . . and froze.

Her eyes were no longer night-sky. Sparks of color fountained where the white stars usually resided, spectacular fireworks on the most miniature of scales. Neither man nor panther had ever seen anything more beautiful.

Lucas woke up feeling supremely sated. He wondered what his efficient Psy would say if he told her she'd brought him to orgasm twice now. He grinned. She'd probably ask him the technical details and note them down on that slim computer she carried everywhere. Why did he find that image cute as hell?

Whistling as he exited the shower, he headed into the bedroom and glanced up at the wall calendar. Suddenly there was no more music in his soul.

How could he have forgotten?

Never before in two decades had he failed to remember— never before had anything or anyone distracted him badly enough to wipe this day from his mind.

After pulling on a pair of jeans and a white T-shirt, he drove to the office, glad to find that Sascha hadn't yet arrived. He couldn't deal with his puzzling reaction to her today. On this day he needed every one of his faculties to patch up a scar that refused to stop bleeding.

"I'll be back after nightfall," he told Clay. "If Sascha turns up, take care of her."

Clay nodded and didn't ask any other questions, well aware why he was taking off during such a critical time. Some loyalties had prior rights over Lucas.

Leaving the sentinel in charge, Lucas got in his car to make the same trip he made once every year. His first stop was a florist.

"Hello, Lucas." A small, bespectacled brunette smiled at him from the other side of the shop as he entered.

"Hi, Callie. Is it ready?"

"Of course. Stay here. I put it out back."

He watched Callie go to fetch his standing yearly order and wondered at the difference between them. The florist was near his age but she was so innocent that he felt a thousand years older. He knew it wasn't because she was human and he was changeling. No, it had been blood and death that had aged him.

A minute later, she emerged, a huge wildflower bouquet in her arms. "Special order for someone special."

He'd never shared who the flowers were for, the wounds too deep to subject to casual scrutiny. "Thanks."

"I charged it to your account."

"See you next year."

"Take care, Lucas."

The second he got in his car he felt cold, chilled, alone. It was always this way on this one shadowed day, as if his childhood desolation resonated through time to torment him.

It took him over three hours to head out of the city and deep into the forests. Leaving the car on a hidden track, he traversed the remaining distance on foot. Nothing marked the spot where his mother and father had been buried, but he found their graves as if they'd been flashing welcoming beacons. He'd chosen a hidden grove surrounded by trees for their last resting place.

"Hey, Mom." He laid the flowers on the thick grass. He never tidied here, never stopped the forest's advance. His parents had both been leopards at home in the wild. "I bought you the flowers that always got Dad out of trouble." In this place he was a child again, watching the two people who mattered more to him than any others, laugh and live. He should've never had to watch them die. A fist clenched around his heart as memories cascaded through his mind.

His mother's scream.

His own helpless, tortured shouts.

His father's cry of black despair as his mate's life was stolen right in front of him.

Something in Carlo had broken at that instant, but he'd stubbornly held on to life until his son was safe. Only then had he taken the step that would reunite him with his slaughtered mate. A black panther like her son, Shayla had been the reason for Carlo's heartbeat.

"I miss you, Dad." He put his palm on the earth on the other side of the flowers. His mother had been found and buried first but when the time had come to bury Carlo, Lucas had insisted on a reburial. They'd been put to rest in each other's arms. In his heart, he hoped that that meant they'd found each other again.

"I need you to guide me." He should've never become alpha at barely twenty-three years of age but it had been inevitable. When the previous alpha, Lachlan, had died unexpectedly two years after stepping down, Lucas had lost even that source of support. "I need to know if what I'm doing is right. What if this leads to more death? The Psy aren't going to stand back and let us tell the world they've been running interference for the worst kind of killer."

The tree branches whispered in the wind as he spoke

and he liked to think it a sign that his parents were listening. They were the only ones. None of his sentinels ever followed him here. No one asked him where he was going. No one asked him where he'd been.

He stayed for hours, speaking to two extraordinary people who'd been deprived of their love and their lives in the most brutal fashion but hadn't broken. Carlo and Shayla had fought to the end like the courageous changelings they'd been. They'd fought not for themselves but for the life of their son. For him.

"I won't let you down." He wiped away tears that came from the heart of the boy who'd almost died with his parents. Only his hunger for vengeance had kept him going when no one thought he'd survive.

That bloody day and the ones that followed had shaped him, scarred him, and strengthened him. No one hurt the people Lucas cared about. No one took those who were his. He'd proven that he'd kill anybody who tried. *Anybody*.

Sascha had been feeling odd since the moment she'd woken. Worried that the changelings would pick up on the strange sadness weighing her down, she'd canceled her meetings with DarkRiver and occupied herself at Duncan headquarters, trying to keep under the radar so that Enrique wouldn't track her down.

It was a relief to come home and shut out the probing eyes of the other Psy. The heavy darkness in her had increased through the day until it was a sharp pain in her heart. Not sure if it was an effect of her rapidly deteriorating mental state or something physical, she considered going to Medical.

A second later, she ruled that out. She didn't know what the M-Psy saw when they looked inside a body. What if her mental patterns were so aberrant that they showed up and the medics demanded further tests? Sleep seemed the best option. If she wasn't feeling better by tomorrow, she'd try to find some way of getting treatment without exposing herself to deep scans.

Another wave of thudding pain rocked through her body. She winced and rubbed her temples. Her eyes went to the communication panel. Maybe Lucas would know a medical person who would be discreet. Almost immediately, she shook her head. What was she thinking? Lucas clearly considered the Psy to be heartless automatons—why would he help her?

And why couldn't she stop thinking about him?

Lucas met no one on his way home. Parking his vehicle in a distant spot, he ran the rest of the way on panther feet, feeling the pounding earth like an extra heartbeat. The climb up the tree to his lair was as easy as breathing.

What wasn't easy was coming back from the animal. He wanted to retreat into the panther's mind and wipe away the human's pain. The temptation was dangerous, a lethal seduction that could turn him rogue, unable to remember his humanity but retaining enough human intelligence to do far more damage than a normal leopard. That was why rogues were hunted down—they were far too dangerous to be left to roam. Often it was their former packmates who became their targets, as if some broken part of them knew what they'd once been . . . and could never be again.

Driven by his instinctive need to keep his people safe from harm, he pushed past the enticing voice of decades-old despair and gave his body the command to change.

Ecstasy and agony.

Part pure pleasure and part ripping pain, the change took only seconds but seemed to last forever. He knew that from the outside it looked like his body was turning into a thousand particles of brilliant light and re-forming itself into another shape. It was quite beautiful.

But from the inside it felt as if his skin was being torn from him as a new form tried to emerge. Melting heat sizzled through every part of him from fingertips to toes. When he opened his eyes, he was human again, his beast caged behind the walls of his mind.

Naked, he padded to the shower and turned it to cold. The brutality of the sharp needles succeeded in removing the last vestiges of temptation from his mind. Usually, he had no trouble switching between the animal and human parts of his psyche but today wasn't a good day.

Today, he could almost understand the Psy need to banish emotion. If he didn't feel, he wouldn't remember. If he didn't feel, he wouldn't mourn. And if he didn't feel, he wouldn't hurt with every beat of his very human heart.

CHAPTER 8

He was beginning to expect her in his dreams. When she touched his shoulder, he rolled away to look up at her. His intention had been to tell her that he had no heart to play with her tonight, but when he saw her, he stopped. Wearing what looked like old cotton pajamas, her hair in two simple braids, she appeared about sixteen.

That was when he realized that he was dressed in a pair of dark gray sweatpants identical to his favorite pair. "What's the matter, kitten?"

A kind of confused vulnerability swirled in her eyes. "I don't know." She wrapped her arms around herself.

Opening his own arms, he said, "Come here."

After a small hesitation, she laid her head down on his chest and stretched her legs out along his side. "I feel so . . . heavy." One fine-boned hand rested beside her head, palm-down on his skin.

"Me, too." The rock that sat on his heart would be gone by morning but its memory would linger.

Her hand stroked over his heartbeat. "Why are you sad?"

"Sometimes I remember that I can't always protect those I love." Under his fingers, her hair was soft and silky.

She didn't try to tell him that he wasn't God, that he couldn't protect everyone. He knew that. But knowing and believing were two different things. What she did say succeeded in stopping his heart. "I wish you'd love me."

"Why?"

"Because then maybe you could protect me, too." Haunting sorrow whispered through her tone.

"Why do you need protecting?" His male instincts were rising past the dark burden of memory.

She cuddled closer and he wrapped his arms tight. "Because I'm broken." Her hand kept smoothing over his heart and he could feel a melting warmth invade his body. "And the Psy don't allow broken creatures to live."

"You feel perfect to me."

No answer. Only that smoothing hand over his chest. With each stroke he felt more at peace. A different form of heaviness infiltrated his bones. It felt strangely as if he was going to sleep again. As darkness closed over him, her quiet statement circled his mind like an endless river.

Because I'm broken.

And the Psy don't allow broken creatures to live.

Sascha was waiting for him when he arrived at the office the next day. Troubled by the disquieting intensity of the dream, he tried to draw her into conversation but hit a brick wall. It was as if she'd retreated deep within herself, so deep that she'd almost ceased to exist.

"Are you all right?" He could feel the shadows around her, feel *her* . . . as if she were Pack.

"I'd like to suggest some alternatives to the materials you're planning to use," she said, instead of answering. "My research tells me this type of wood will weather better in the site environment." She slid across a sample and an accompanying inch-thick report.

Frustrated by her intransigence, he fingered the sample. "This stuff is cheaper."

"That doesn't mean it's no good. Please read the report."

"I will." He put it aside. "You look like hell, Sascha darling." No way was he going to let her push him away, not after last night. She was Psy and he'd been dreaming some pretty odd dreams. He could do the math.

Her hands tightened on her organizer before she got herself under control. "I've been having trouble sleeping."

Every instinct he had told him it was time to press hard. "Dreams keeping you awake?"

"I've told you, the Psy don't dream." She refused to meet his gaze.

"But you do, don't you, Sascha?" he said softly. "What does that make you?"

Her head jerked up and he glimpsed something very lost in her eyes in the second's window before her computerized security-blanket chimed. "Excuse me." She walked out of the room and he knew it was because of him, not the call. He'd finally reached her. If that call hadn't interrupted them . . .

"Damn it." His claws sliced out of his hands, an indication of just how much control he'd lost. Forcing them back in, he went to hunt down his elusive prey.

She was gone.

Ria, his administrative assistant, gave him the message. "Said she had to leave to take care of something but that she'd be back for the two o'clock with Zara."

Lucas took the message with an ill-hidden frown. "Thanks." His tone said otherwise.

"Sorry. I didn't know I wasn't supposed to let her go." Ria screwed up her pretty human face into a scowl. "You're supposed to warn me about things like that." Mated to a DarkRiver leopard for the past seven years, she had no problem talking her mind with Lucas.

"Don't worry about it. She'll be back." Where else could she go? If he was right about her, then her very uniqueness might get her rejected by her own people.

What worried him was that rather than calculating how he could use her weakness to further his own goals, he was concerned for her. The unexpected development was enough to disturb both man and beast—how had one of the enemy gained a slice of his loyalty?

She didn't turn up for the meeting until a minute before two. "Shall we go in?" were her first words to him. Her suit was black, her shirt white, and her tone as chilling as the most brittle of frost.

In spite of his concern at what she made him feel, he wanted to reach out and kiss her until she purred. He'd seen beneath the shell and he was never going help her bury the woman he'd glimpsed. Sascha Duncan might be Psy, but he was a Hunter.

"By all means." He waved his arm, willing to let her believe she'd defeated him. Sometimes an unexpected ambush worked better than a full frontal attack. "Zara should be in there with Dorian, one of the other architects. Kit's asked to sit in. Fine with you?"

"Of course. I learned business the same way."

The second they walked into the meeting room, he knew there was going to be trouble. Dorian was standing with his back to the window, the lines around his mouth white with strain, his shoulders so taut that the muscles were almost vibrating.

"Kit." Lucas chose to greet the juvenile next to Dorian, giving the sentinel time to get himself under control.

"Hey, Lucas. I have the designs." Kit pointed to the pile of document tubes on the table, his gaze shifting to Sascha and then skating away.

"Where's Zara?" Lucas didn't take his eyes off Dorian—the other male hadn't stopped staring at Sascha since the moment they'd entered the room. Beside him, Sascha had gone preternaturally silent, as though she knew how precarious the situation was.

Kit pulled at the cuffs of his brown cable-knit sweater and shoved a hand through his hair. "She got delayed." His tone held a subtle appeal—he didn't want to discuss Pack business with an outsider in the room.

Lucas spoke without looking away from the lethal fury that was Dorian. "Would you give us a moment, Sascha?"

"I'll wait outside." She turned and walked out the door, pulling it shut behind her.

"What happened?" he asked.

The other man bared his teeth. "SnowDancer lost a female today."

Lucas felt rage arc through his bloodstream. "When?"

"Dorian said two hours ago." It was Kit who answered. "One of Hawke's lieutenants just called him."

"Which means we have a week before a body turns up." Dorian's voice was raw, his fists clenched so tight that the tendons in his neck stood out. "He'll keep her for that week and when he's finished doing whatever it is he does to them, he'll slice her up and leave her someplace that was once a safe haven."

Lucas didn't even try to soothe the other man. "Do they know anything?" Despite his rejection of torture as a way to find the killer's identity, a fury as cold as Dorian's had burned in Lucas's heart since Kylie's murder. She'd been under his protection, a juvenile not much older than Kit. What had been done to her had been inhuman and the panther in him craved justice.

"No." Dorian shoved both hands through his hair. "Why don't you drag your pet Psy in here and force her to tell us who he is?" His eyes held such pure menace that Lucas knew he couldn't be allowed anywhere near Sascha.

"She might not know anything," he pointed out. "Kit?"

"Yes."

"Go tell Zara we need her." His eyes held a different message. It wasn't the wildcat they needed, but their healer. Many of the other juveniles wouldn't have understood. However, Kit was already being trained for soldier duties—it was the only way to keep a future alpha out of trouble.

The boy nodded. "I'll get on it." He ran from the room.

It was lucky for them that the healer had come into the city proper to take the cubs shopping. Her presence here was vital—Dorian was almost at breaking point. Until this moment, Lucas hadn't known just how fragile the sentinel's control was. He could almost see the rage clawing behind those surfer-blue eyes, ready to maim, torture, kill.

"Kidnapping one Psy will give us nothing. They aren't like us—they'll cut family dead without a thought." He walked over to stand in front of Dorian, keeping his body between him and the exit.

Suddenly Dorian's head snapped up to focus on something behind Lucas. "She's part of their damn hive mind! Get her to tell us where the SnowDancer is before it's too fucking late!" His voice vibrated with anger but he wasn't completely out of control. Yet.

Lucas didn't have to turn to know that Sascha was in the doorway—he could smell her. "Leave, Sascha." The panther wanted to grip her by the nape and haul her out of harm's way.

"No." Dorian pushed at his chest hard enough to have cracked a human's ribs. His latency had robbed him purely of the ability to change, nothing else. "Tell her what this freak's been doing. Tell her what her precious Council is hiding from her."

Sascha took a step into the room and closed the door. "What's he talking about?" There was steel in that icy tone, resolve in the way she walked around to stand less than a foot away. No fear clouded those night-sky eyes.

Lucas continued to keep himself between her and Dorian. "A serial killer has been preying on changeling women for several years." The time for subterfuge was over—a life hung in the balance.

Sascha's expression didn't change. "We don't have serial killers in our population."

"Bullshit!" Dorian spit out. "The killer is Psy and your Council knows it. You're a race of psychopaths!"

"No, we're not."

"No conscience, no heart, no feelings! How else do you define psychopath?"

"How do you know that it's one of us?" She tried to get around Lucas.

He pushed her back with a single hand. "Don't get too close. Right now, Dorian would settle for ripping out your throat in lieu of the murderer's. His sister was one of the victims." He made sure she saw truth in his expression.

After a short silence, she took a step back and allowed him to hold Dorian at bay. "How do you know it's a Psy?" she repeated.

"We detected the scent of a Psy at the site of Kylie's murder." Lucas would remember the pervading ugliness of that scent to the day he died. "You have a very distinctive smell to us. Unlike humans or changelings, you give off only coldness, a metallic stink that repels." It was why so many changelings refused to work with the Psy or live in buildings created by them. The taint, some felt, could never be erased.

He thought he saw hurt shadow Sascha's face but when

she spoke, her voice was calm. "If this is a serial, why hasn't it been reported? I haven't heard a single thing about it on the Net or through the human-changeling media."

Dorian turned to bang his palms flat against the window. The glass cracked. "Your Council killed the reports like they killed the investigations. Changelings and a couple of humans have tried to get the cases marked as the work of a serial, but they've been blocked over and over."

Lucas met Sascha's intent gaze and decided to take a step that could be a mistake. They had no more time to go softly, softly. Either his instincts about Sascha were right or he'd never had a chance. "Detectives are working underground on their own time and changeling packs are sharing information across the affected areas.

"Given enough time, we *will* hunt down the killer." He had no doubt about that. All the predatory changelings had one thing in common—if one of their own was hurt, they'd track the perpetrator with grim determination even if it took years.

"What's changed? Why are you so angry?" she asked Dorian and there was something almost like pain in her tone.

The sentinel didn't speak, his head bowed, palms pressed against the glass. Lucas knew that rather than striking out, he was withdrawing into himself and that couldn't be allowed. He was Pack. He would never be left to suffer on his own.

He put one hand on Dorian's shoulder. It was enough to hold him to the bonds of Pack until Tamsyn arrived. "SnowDancer lost a female two hours ago. If we don't find her within seven days, she'll be discovered mutilated in a way that would make even a Psy throw up."

There was a flurry at the door and Tamsyn ran into the room alongside Kit and his older sister, Rina, a curvaceous, sensual female with the rank of soldier. Lucas turned to Sascha. "Wait for me outside." This was Pack business. And no matter how much he craved her, she was an outsider. In spite of the chance he'd taken in telling her the truth, she might even be the enemy.

She looked at Dorian for a long time then silently turned and walked away. Rina closed the door behind her, shutting her out.

Sascha went down to the public lounge at the bottom floor of the building, Dorian's anguish continuing to pound at her. She'd never felt such excruciating agony. It took everything she had not to scream in unison with him. It was almost as if the pain was drawn to her, as if she were sucking it inside, where it could mingle with her own unbearable hurt.

. . . you give off only coldness, a metallic stink that repels . . .

She couldn't forget either Lucas's words or the hatred she'd felt directed at her. Dorian, Kit, that beautiful blonde female, and even Tamsyn. They'd all looked at her as if she were the embodiment of evil. Perhaps she was. If they were right, she belonged to a race which would allow murder in order to protect their code of Silence.

A stab of pain slashed across her heart. She gasped and tried to stifle it but it only grew worse. She had to stop it, had to find some way of helping Dorian before he killed her. Locating the leopard was easy. He pulsated with anger and rage, the air around him pure darkness churning with endless echoes of pain.

Psychically, she didn't know what she was doing. No one had ever trained her in this. She didn't even know what it was that she was trying to do. Reaching into the darkness enclosing him, she gathered up his pain into her arms. There was so much of it that it overflowed. Determined, she kept gathering until the shadows around him softened and the agony in her heart became easier to endure.

Her arms were full of sorrow and she could think of only one way to destroy it, an instinctive understanding that came from a buried part of her mind. But she couldn't do it here. Barely able to see, she walked out of the building, still holding her incomprehensible harvest.

Getting into her vehicle, she programmed in the destination and set the car to automatic. The sorrow was getting heavier and heavier. She had to get to the safety of her apartment before her mind cracked wide open under the pressure. Already her flaw was obvious in the tremble in her fingertips, in the hollow beat of her heart.

With most of her remaining energy, she reinforced her mental shields against the PsyNet. The energy that kept her alive was tied into those shields. If they failed, it would be because she'd died and there was nothing left to sustain them. She only hoped she made it inside the walls of her apartment before the darkness became too much, before it destroyed her from the inside out.

Lucas felt the pain being drawn away out of Dorian. From his position cradling the other man's body against his chest, he said, "Tamsyn, what did you do?"

The healer ran her hands over Dorian's face. "I've barely started. This wasn't me. Dorian, what did you feel?"

"Like someone took the pain and left . . . peace behind." He shook his head and sat up. There was no shame in him at having leaned on Pack. That was what they were there for—if Lucas fell, Dorian would do the same for him.

Rina linked her fingers to Dorian's. "You feel . . ." Lost for words, the soldier turned to Tamsyn.

"Balanced," Tamsyn said, as Lucas got to his feet.

Dorian frowned and pushed back his hair. "It was the

damnedest thing. If felt like warmth spreading inside me, shoving out the rage. I can think again. For the first time since Kylie was taken, I can think." He let Rina wrap her arms around him and lay her head against his chest.

Dorian ran his hand over Rina's bare arm and Lucas knew he was grounding himself in the feel of her skin, in the way she smelled of Pack. This had nothing to do with male-female sharing and everything to do with Pack healing.

"If it wasn't you, then who?" Lucas's heart was thumping with a suspicion so outlandish, he could barely bring himself to believe it. But his instincts had never lied about this one thing and he'd felt the flare of power.

"I don't know anyone who could do what Dorian's described." Tamsyn paused. "I've heard rumors but they're just that—rumors."

Dorian looked at Lucas. "It doesn't matter. Not now. We have to find the SnowDancer female before the wolves go berserk. At this point they're in shock but that's going to turn into rage."

"We'll find her." It was an alpha's promise. "I'm going to ask Sascha to help us."

"A Psy?" Rina's voice was harsh. "They don't even help their own children."

"We don't have a choice." There was no other way to infiltrate the PsyNet.

Sascha was gone. According to the ground-floor receptionist, she hadn't looked so good.

"Got in her car and took off." The woman shrugged. "I was going to ask if she was okay but you know, she's one of *them* so I figured she wouldn't want to be bothered."

"Thanks." Lucas shoved both his hands into his pockets.

Rina, who'd come down with him, said, "Think she's gone back to report to the Council?"

It was a valid suspicion but something in Lucas rebelled against accepting it. Pulling out his phone, he pressed her code and waited. No answer. "I guess we'll know soon enough. Tell the sentinels to alert the pack." If the Council discovered that DarkRiver was working to bring them down, they'd launch a preemptive strike.

The Psy might not be able to manipulate the minds of changelings without a huge expenditure of power, but they could kill if they were determined enough. The most vulnerable were the cubs, who hadn't yet finished developing the natural shields which made older changelings that much harder to hurt.

He watched Rina take off as he pushed in another code. Within ten minutes, every member of DarkRiver would be contacted. The weaker ones would head to the safe houses, where Pack soldiers could protect them. The one advantage changelings had was that the Psy had to come very close to attack them through psychic means. No Psy had ever killed a changeling from afar.

But today, someone had reached Dorian from afar.

CHAPTER 9

The call was answered. "Hawke."

"We might've had a leak to the Council about the hunt. Protect your pack."

"Anyone touches another one of my people, I'll gut them." The ruthless alpha of the SnowDancers wasn't kidding. "I'm declaring open season on the Psy."

An image of Sascha's bloodied body flashed into Lucas's mind. His hand squeezed the phone. "We might be able to find your packmate in time."

"How sure are you?"

"The probability is low but there *is* a chance. If you move now, we'll lose the opportunity and large numbers of both our packs." The SnowDancers were merciless killers but so were the Psy. Both sides would suffer massive casualties.

A pause that hummed with anger. "I won't be able to control my people once the body is found."

"I wouldn't want you to." Lucas had barely managed to restrain DarkRiver after Kylie's murder. The only reason they'd listened to him was that three of their females had recently birthed cubs. No one had wanted to leave the babies vulnerable. Because once the alphas and soldiers were gone, the cubs and their mothers would simply be exterminated. The Psy had no sense of mercy.

"If you go to war, we'll go with you." It was a promise that Lucas had made to his pack. In the months since burying Kylie, they'd made arrangements to hide the cubs with other packs, packs which had seeded from DarkRiver and would raise the children as their own if everything went to hell.

A short silence. The SnowDancers didn't play well with others but Lucas hoped that Hawke would listen to the voice of reason, that he'd trust in the strength of their alliance. The alternative was carnage on a scale the world hadn't seen in centuries.

"You're asking me to wait while Brenna dies."

"Seven days, Hawke. Time enough to track her." He trusted his gut. Sascha wouldn't betray them . . . betray him. "You know I'm right. Once the Psy realize we're hunting them, she *will* die. They'll do anything to cover their trail."

Hawke spit out a curse. "You'd better be right, cat. *Seven days.* Find my female alive and you'll never have to worry about territorial threats again. If her body turns up, we go for blood."

"For blood."

Sascha woke to the chime of the communication console. She was collapsed in the entry of her apartment, slumped against the closed door with her legs spread out in front of her. She had no memory of anything after exiting the elevator that had brought her to this floor.

Forcing herself to her feet, she clutched the door and

walls for support as she somehow made her way to the console. Nikita's name flashed up. Too exhausted to do anything but stand there, she let her mother leave a message and then glanced at her watch.

It was ten at night. That meant she'd lost in excess of seven hours to unconsciousness. Frantic, she checked her shields. They'd held. Her relief made her aware of something else—the pain of the grief and rage that had been crushing her was gone. She couldn't remember how she'd defused it and she didn't want to think about it either. Didn't want to think about anything.

A long shower took her mind off matters for a few minutes. She followed that by sitting still and trying to meditate herself into a trancelike state, unwilling to face up to what she'd learned that day. It had been one straw too many. Her brain was in danger of overloading. She did mental calisthenic after mental calisthenic.

By the time she made herself return Nikita's call, she'd achieved a measure of outward calm. Her mother's face flashed up on the screen. "Sascha. You got my message."

"I'm sorry I was out of touch, Mother." She didn't explain where she'd been. As an adult Psy, she had the right to her own life.

"I wanted an update on the changeling situation."

"I have nothing to report but I'm sure that'll change." Right now she was hanging on to her sanity by a thread and didn't know what to believe.

"Don't let me down, Sascha." Nikita's brown eyes probed her face. "Enrique isn't happy with you—we need to give him something."

"Why do we need to give him anything?"

Nikita paused and then nodded as if she'd decided something. "Come up to my suite."

* * *

Ten minutes later, Sascha found herself standing beside her mother, looking out at the glimmering darkness of a city going to sleep.

"What does it remind you of?" Nikita asked.

"The PsyNet." It was a very crude approximation.

"Weak lights. Strong lights. Flickering lights. Dead lights." Nikita linked her hands loosely in front of her.

"Yes." Sascha felt a slight pounding at the back of her neck, more irritating than painful. A leftover from whatever had happened this afternoon? If anything had happened. What if she'd imagined the entire psychic scenario? Perhaps it was a sign of her accelerating insanity. What proof did she have that she'd done anything other than collapse? Nothing.

The more she thought about it, the more convinced she became that she'd constructed the entire episode in an attempt to explain the fragmentation of her psyche. There was no other viable explanation. What she'd imagined doing was like no psychic power she'd ever heard of.

"Enrique is a very bright light."

She forced herself to pay attention. "So are you. You're both Council." Just like Enrique, Nikita was dangerous, the poison of her mind as lethal as the deadliest biological virus.

"Several other Councilors would gladly see me dead."

"More than Councilors alone."

"Yes. There are always aspirants." Nikita continued to stare out at the night. "Allies are necessary."

"Enrique is yours?"

"In a way. He has his own agenda but he watches my back and I watch his."

"So we can't afford to alienate him?"

"It would make things difficult."

Sascha read between the lines. If Enrique didn't get what he wanted, Nikita's life might well be forfeit. "I'll find some information for him. But tell him if I push, we might get nothing."

"You sound very sure."

"The first thing you can share with him is that contrary to popular Psy belief, changelings aren't stupid." No one who'd met the hard blaze of intelligence in Lucas's eyes could ever believe anything that asinine. "They're not going to open up to a Psy who's clearly out to gather data. If I go softly, we'll get more. We have months."

But she didn't. As today had demonstrated far too clearly, she was coming apart at the seams, breaking into a thousand pieces. She no longer understood her own actions. Right at that instant, she was standing there lying to her mother through her teeth, keeping everything she'd learned to herself. Why?

"I'll tell him. Good night, Sascha."

"Good night, Mother."

Sascha couldn't sleep. She'd tried every trick she could think of to put herself under and failed. After the lush dreams of the past few days, it was a rude awakening to reality. Ever since she'd met Lucas, the physical symptoms of her accelerating mental disintegration had leveled off. She'd become used to a good night's sleep, free of night terrors or muscle spasms.

She finally gave up and began to pace up and down the confines of her room, back wall to front wall, front wall to back wall, side to side, left to right. And back again.

A serial killer . . . changeling women . . . metallic stink . . . the Council . . . psychopath . . .

In the hours since she'd spoken to Nikita, she'd used every electronic means at her disposal to secretly surf the human-changeling Internet. The murders had been reported. However, instead of being front-page items in major newspapers and magazines, they'd only gotten serious attention on fringe sites nobody really took seriously. That didn't change the fact that the killings had occurred and been noticed.

Before mysteriously disappearing.

The killer is Psy and your Council knows it.

Dorian's angry words reverberated in her head.

"No," she whispered aloud. He had to be wrong, had to be driven by emotion rather than logic. The Psy didn't feel rage, jealousy, murderous fury. The Psy didn't feel. Period.

Except that she was a living, breathing rebuttal to that statement.

"No," she said again. Yes, she felt, but a serial killer? Nobody could've hidden such a huge flaw in the Silence Protocol. Nobody had that much power.

They are Council. They are above the law.

Her own words returned to haunt her. Was it possible . . . ? "No." She stared at the blank wall in front of her, unwilling to believe so quickly that her mother was guilty of aiding and abetting a murderer.

Nikita might not feel maternal emotions but Sascha felt a child's. Her mother was the sole constant presence in her life. She'd never met her father, her grandmother had been distant, and she had no cousins or siblings. Not that it would've meant much if she had had them. They would've been as cold as the woman who'd borne her.

She had to find out more information.

Decision made, she began to code in a call from the communication console. Then she cut it off. Enrique's too-focused interest in her had made her wary of being monitored. Picking up a black leather-synth jacket to throw over her jeans and black shirt, she headed out to her car.

It was only when she'd almost reached the DarkRiver building that she started thinking.

It was two in the morning. No one would be there.

Certainly not the man she wanted to talk to. Her hands clenched on the wheel as she parked the car in the deserted lot and dropped her head back against the seat. She'd come here acting on instinct, seeking Lucas.

Lucas.

Sitting there staring at the darkness, she kept thinking about the way his eyes had gone cold as he'd told her that the Psy had a "metallic stink." Tears rose perilously close to the surface. Why had she indulged herself with those dreams? They were impossible, even if she didn't have the threat of rehabilitation hanging over her head. And they had been a conscious indulgence.

She'd given herself those moments hidden deep in her subconscious to explore her needs, her hunger, and had been fully aware of what was happening. Aware of the way Lucas felt under her fingertips, his skin so hot, so alive. Aware of every sound he'd made, every flash of those amazing eyes. Aware of his every demand, his every need.

Lies. All of them. She'd made up his reactions as she'd made up everything else. It had been *her* fantasies that had driven those dreams. How pathetic was it that she'd imagined him holding her, imagined him *caring*. She slammed her palm against the manual steering wheel and opened the door. It slid smoothly back, allowing her to swing her legs out and take a breath of night air.

Getting out, she leaned against the part of the hood closest to the driver's-side door and stared up at the sky. Diamonds on velvet, that's what it looked like. She knew the clarity wasn't thanks to the Psy. It was humans and changelings, particularly changelings, who'd fought pollution, fought to keep their world beautiful.

She owed them a portion of her sanity.

Even when she was forced to lock herself into the cage of the Psy world, the shimmering night sky gave her beauty that no one could take from her. No one could damn her for staring up at the sky.

Something moved to her left.

Sascha spun around but all was silent darkness, the hedge lining the side of the parking lot blocking her line of sight. Heart thudding so hard she could feel every vibration, she sent out a cautious psychic probe.

And brushed up against something so hot and alive that she felt burned.

She withdrew immediately. A few seconds later, a hand touched her shoulder. If she hadn't felt his emotional shadow before he'd reached her, she would've jumped sky high and blown her cover to smithereens.

When she turned, it was to find herself face-to-face with the very male she'd been searching for. "You're wearing clothes" were the first words that popped out of her mouth.

Not much but it was clothing. A pair of low-slung jeans and a faded white T-shirt that defined every muscle on his impressive upper body. Her hormones flickered awake, her body aroused in spite of the terrible matters that lay heavy on her mind.

He chuckled. "I always have clothes accessible in places where I might often change."

"What are you doing here?" Silence blanketed the night, creating a dangerous kind of intimacy.

"Don't you ever undo this?" He tugged at the end of the braid hanging over her breast.

"Sometimes when I sleep." She didn't pull away, almost convinced herself that she was merely pandering to his changeling need for touch, that it had nothing to do with her own desires.

A slow smile spread over that savagely beautiful face. "I'd like to see that."

"I thought you said we stink?" She was still hurting from the blow.

"Most Psy do. You, however, don't." Leaning close, he sniffed at the curve of her neck. "In fact, I find your scent quite . . . luscious."

It took every ounce of her concentration not to betray her reaction to his disturbing nearness. "That should make it easier for us to continue working together."

"Darling, it'll make all sorts of things easier." The heat coming off his body was a physical caress, intimate and exquisite.

She was intelligent enough to know that he was sexually flirting with her. She'd watched him with Tamsyn, with Zara. He didn't touch either of those women the way he touched her. But what was his agenda? Did he suspect she wasn't what she seemed, or was he merely amusing himself at her expense? "You didn't answer my question."

"I think it should be mine, don't you?" Dropping her braid, he braced himself against the car by placing one arm across the roof. The position put him to her left, standing as she was with the car at her back. He was far too close for comfort but she couldn't move way. "What're you doing in my territory, Sascha?"

The words threatened to get stuck in her throat. "I wanted to talk to you about what you told me this afternoon."

He ran a hand through his hair and her eyes followed the graceful movement. Something told her that he'd be just as graceful while stalking and taking down prey. "You picked an odd time for it."

She could hardly say that she'd been driven by emotions run amuck. "I wasn't actually expecting anyone to be here, but decided to come on the off chance that someone was."

"Someone?" He raised a brow.

"You," she admitted, knowing it was useless to lie. "What *are* you doing here?"

"I couldn't sleep."

"Bad dreams?"

"No dreams." It was a husky whisper. "That was the problem."

Something throbbed between them, an awareness that shouldn't have existed. They'd never really touched, never really spoken about anything other than business. Yet it was there, a growing, beautiful thing. "Why come here?"

"Instinct," he said. "Maybe you drew me to you."

"I don't have those abilities." It was just another one of her flaws. She was a cardinal without power, a cosmic joke. "Even if I did have them, I'd never use them to summon someone against their will."

"Who said it was against my will?" The arm on the roof of the car reached out to toy with a strand of her hair. "Why don't we go somewhere else to talk? It's unlikely anyone will see us here but if they do, I don't think your mother will understand."

She nodded. "Yes, you're right. Where?"

He held out his hand. "Keys."

"No." There was only so much she'd take and Lucas Hunter was pushing it to the limit. "I'll drive."

"Stubborn." He laughed and walked around to the passenger side. "You're in charge, Sascha darling."

After she'd got in and started up the car, he said, "Take a left on the street."

"Where are we going?"

"Somewhere safe."

He directed her across the Bay Bridge and through Oakland. They hit the trailing edges of the wilderness that pressed against Stockton and kept going. The trees grew ever more dense, telling her that she'd entered some part of the massive Yosemite forests. Even with the considerable speed of her car, she'd been driving almost two hours when he told her to stop.

"Are you sure you want me to stop here?" Nothing but trees met the eye.

"Yes." He got out.

Having no other choice, she followed. "We're going to talk here? We might as well sit in the car."

"Scared?" It was a whisper in her ear.

His speed was frightening. He'd moved around the back of the car and to her in the space of a sentence. "Hardly. I'm Psy, remember? I'm simply confused by the logic of this."

"Maybe I've brought you here to do dastardly deeds." His hand rested on the curve of her hip.

"If you'd wanted to hurt me, you could've easily done so in the parking lot." She wondered whether or not to make an issue over the hand on her hip. What would a normal Psy do? Would a normal Psy ever get herself in such a position in the first place? She didn't know!

That hand slid up until it lay against the curve of her waist. "Stop."

"Why?"

"Such behavior isn't acceptable." She coated each word with deliberate calm—it was the only way she could fight what he was doing to her. Unused to sensation, she was close to becoming a slave to it, the fantasies she'd indulged in during sleep leeching into her waking life.

He moved away at once. "You sound just like a Psy."

"What else do you expect me to sound like?"

Looking into Sascha's night-sky eyes, eerie in the darkness, Lucas found himself saying, "More. I expect you to be more." Before she could respond, he began walking. "Follow me."

Already, he was debating the wisdom of his decision in bringing her to his lair. It was a stupid thing to do by any standard. Yet, he hadn't been able to stop himself, driven by instincts far older than human thought. The panther wanted her in its territory.

When he'd found her in the lot, where he'd been drawn by impulses he barely understood, he'd thought that he was starting to see the real Sascha at last. Except that if he were to believe the way she was acting, the real Sascha existed nowhere but in his mind.

Had he been wrong about her right from the outset?

He took her through the hidden pathway that exited beneath his lair—most people never watched for danger from above. "How high can you jump?"

She glanced up. "An aerie."

"I'm a leopard. I climb." Even in human form, he could jump higher and farther, climb faster than any human and most other changelings. It was part of what made him alpha, what made him Hunter-born.

"Your home is very far from your business premises."

"I have a city apartment I use when I'm pressed for time. Let's go."

"Is there any other way up?" She was looking at the smooth trunk of the huge tree that supported his home among its branches. Like the other mostly coniferous trees in the forest, it shot up straight as a ruler. But this particular species had an impressive canopy that stretched in every direction, blocking out the starlit night.

"Afraid not. You'll have to hold on." He gave her his back.

After a minute's silence, he felt two tentative hands on his shoulders and almost laughed in relief. Her actions spoke far louder than her frosty tones—his poor kitten was scared and dealing with it the only way she knew how.

He'd been around her race a lot more than she knew, though, for the most part, they'd been low-level Psy the Council would never bother with. Still, they'd all had one thing in common—a complete and utter lack of reaction to most stimuli.

In contrast, he'd caught Sascha looking up at the night sky as if it held a thousand dreams. He'd watched her playing with cubs with what most would term affection. And he'd felt her touch him as if he disturbed her on the most intimate of levels.

"Harder, darling," he drawled, the cat in him giving in to the impulse to tease. "Press close."

"Perhaps it would be easier to speak in the car."

His instincts were going crazy. His personal Psy was definitely disconcerted by his body. Good. He smiled where she couldn't see it. "I have food up there and I, for one, am starving. I ran to you, remember?"

"Of course. I understand." That lush body pressed close, her hands sliding under his arms to wrap up and over his shoulders.

He bit back a purr. His body was responding as if it knew hers, as if those dreams had been utterly real. He touched the backs of her thighs with his fingertips. "Jump."

She moved like they were one, wrapping her legs around his waist as he lunged to begin the climb, his claws slicing out to grip the smooth surface.

"Hold on tight." He could feel his body rubbing against hers with every movement. Her chest pushed into his back, a sweet, sensual pressure that he had no trouble enduring. Even through the leather-synth of her jacket, he could feel the heavy weight of those beautiful breasts he'd seen in his dreams and fantasized about for days. What would it take to tempt her enough to make dreams a reality?

Her legs tensed as he climbed higher, the heated core of her body cradled against the small of his back. It made him remember what they'd done in that last erotic dream. Smiling, he took a deep breath as he gripped the final branch. *Lord have mercy!*

Desire filled his nostrils, unleashing the beast that lived within. The panther batted at the scent, rolled it in his mouth, hungered for more of it. He might not be able to read minds but he could read bodies and Sascha's was screaming for his.

CHAPTER 10

He was fully erect by the time he landed on the leaf-strewn porch of his home. It was just as well that he hadn't tucked in the T-shirt. Sascha was hardly likely to be comforted by the sight of him primed and ready. He wasn't exactly comfortable with it himself. Perhaps she was unlike any other Psy he'd ever met but she was still Psy.

Still the enemy.

He'd promised his people that he'd allow no more of their women to be stolen, had taken an oath to see this through to the end, no matter what he had to do. "That wasn't so difficult, was it, darling?" He retracted his claws as Sascha slid off.

Her body pulled away from his as if she'd been burned. In spite of what he'd just reminded himself, he had to fight the urge to preen. This woman wanted him. Whether she knew it or not. "Come inside." Without turning to look at her, he opened the door and walked in.

Sascha was having trouble breathing. She continued to feel Lucas against the sensitive inner faces of her thighs, her muscles quickening in remembered sensation. She bit back a whimper—her mental walls were crumbling. Insanity beckoned. Image after image of incarceration at the Center shot through her mind, nightmare memories from an event that should've never taken place.

"No." She shoved everything she had into rebuilding those walls. Her fear of rehabilitation was so great that it momentarily dampened the heat between her legs. Only momentarily.

The instant she walked into Lucas's home, it shot through to inferno levels. She could see his silhouette behind a Japanese screen that looked to be separating the large room into living and sleeping areas. He was taking off his T-shirt and she couldn't help but watch. Her fingernails bit into her palms.

"Sascha? Do you mind starting the hot water? I'm going to take a shower to wash off the sweat from the run. Promise I'll be quick."

She was almost certain that he was deliberately trying to torment her. "Where is the control?" Her statement was very precise, because she was having trouble thinking past single words, her eyes riveted to his shadowy form.

"Straight ahead and to the left." His hands went to the top button of his jeans and his body began to turn to present a profile. She almost ran from the room. The section he'd directed her to was a small kitchen, the controls for the water on the wall.

His setup was understandably old-fashioned. She guessed it was powered by hidden eco-friendly generators. No changeling would choose any other method this deep in the wilderness. Pushing the appropriate button, she called out, "It's done."

"Thanks, darling."

She heard him moving and a few seconds later, the sound of falling water, so the shower had to be located off the sleeping area. Relieved to have a few minutes to calm herself down, she placed her hands to her cheeks and took a deep breath. The scent of man and forest infiltrated her mind like the most forbidden of drugs. She remembered the sharp glint of his claws as he'd climbed, and felt not fear, but a kind of awestruck wonder.

"Oh, God. Stop, Sascha, stop." She stared at the physical things around her in an effort to fight the repeating loop of pleasure and fear, sensation and cold terror. Even the threat of rehabilitation wasn't standing up against such intense proximity to Lucas.

The kitchen was small and compact, having a simple cooking/heating unit and very few other appliances. She noted a coffeemaker on the counter and moved to switch it on. Coffee wasn't something the Psy drank and though she'd tried it, it had never appealed to her. Since Lucas obviously liked it enough to have a high-tech machine, she started some before walking back to the living area.

It was wide and open, with several windows looking out into the forest. Given the fact that his lair had to be well protected, she guessed they were treated so as not to glimmer in the sun. Vines crawled along their surfaces, almost bringing the forest inside.

From the moistness in the air and the glimpse she'd had of a few water-loving plants she recognized, she guessed they were near a river, possibly close to one of the rare wetlands. Like most of his species, it appeared that the alpha of DarkRiver was adaptable to the extreme.

Looking away from the windows, she allowed herself to examine his living room. The light from the two motion-sensor lamps on the floor was soft, but then again, she thought, remembering those night-glow eyes, Lucas could see in the dark. The only other illumination came from a tiny red power light on the communication console set into the wall nearest the door. A closer look told her that it also functioned as a receiver for entertainment programs, though she had a feeling Lucas liked his entertainment far more physical . . . far more personal.

Flushing fever-hot, she moved away from the panel to look at the rest of the room. On the opposite side from the windows was a huge cushion, half of it propped against the wall, the other half on the floor, turning it into a defacto sofa. Lengthwise, it was more than enough for a leopard to stretch out on. Three smaller "sofas" were placed around the other walls.

A lot for one man but not for the alpha of DarkRiver. It was likely his packmates visited often. Only packmates? She shook her head. She wasn't that naïve. A man as sexual as Lucas would have more than his share of lovers. Lovers who were at home with their sexuality, open and wild enough to take him on. He had no need to seduce a Psy who'd never kissed a man in anything other than her dreams.

The shower shut off. Funnily enough, she was calmer. Throwing the cold water of reality over her fantasies had proven a far more effective counter to her hunger than any Psy trick. When she heard him moving into the sleeping area, she walked back to the kitchen. Another teasing shadow-play might undo everything.

The coffee wasn't done. "What would you like to eat?" she asked without shouting, cognizant of his superb hearing. "I can start it."

"Thanks. Why don't you heat up some of the pizza Rina left last night? It's in the cooler."

Her jaw set. Rina? Had she met that leopard? What did it matter if she had? So what if the other female had been in Lucas's home? Finding the cleverly camouflaged cooler, she grabbed several slices of pizza and put them in a special container before placing it on the heating unit.

The thought of Lucas with another woman coated her

with another icy layer of control. So much so that by the time the freshly washed scent of him invaded the air of the kitchen, she was back in the prison of her mind, back behind the walls she'd learned to put up before she could walk. "I'll wait for you in the living room," she told him, when she turned to find him facing her.

He let her pass with no trouble. "Thanks."

Lucas watched Sascha walk away, his eyes narrowed. Something had changed. Her body was stiff and if she hadn't been Psy, he'd have said she was angry. But her race were known to adopt stiff postures in their efforts to turn themselves into robots. The heating unit flicked off and he reached out to transfer the pizza onto a big plate.

Rina had brought too much. Even with two other soldiers there wolfing it down, they'd ended up with almost a whole pizza left over. The three had come over to talk to him about security for one of the safe houses but Rina had stayed behind to discuss Dorian. She was still young and seeing the sentinel almost lose it had shaken her.

Lucas picked up the plate and only then noticed that the coffee was ready. Sascha. She kept surprising him. Carrying the plate into the living room, he put it on a low table that sat in one corner of the room, before dragging the table to the cushion that Sascha had curled up against.

The cushions had been designed by Tara, a packmate. Meant to accommodate leopard bodies as well as human, there really was no way to sit stiffly in them.

Pleased by the liquid softness of her limbs, he smiled. "Grab a piece. I'll get the coffee."

"No coffee for me."

"Why?"

"I don't . . . require it."

"Water?"

"Thank you."

As he poured the coffee, he thought back over that small

hesitation. Had she been about to say that she didn't like the taste of coffee? Or was he trying to convince himself of things that didn't exist in order to justify this inappropriate attraction?

He was alpha, used to putting the pack above everything. This hunger for Sascha was a threat to that loyalty, a temptation that might lead to sleeping with the worst sort of enemy. But walking away wasn't an option—he'd never been a quitter and he was determined to find out what lay beneath that hard Psy shell.

All their lives might depend upon it.

Sascha was sitting in the same position when he returned. Putting her water and his coffee beside the pizza, he took a slice and deliberately collapsed on the same sofa she'd chosen, letting his body lie loosely against the cushion a scant couple of inches from hers. "Give it a try." He raised the slice to her mouth.

She hesitated and then took a small bite. "What flavor is this?"

He shrugged. "Mexican, I think." Taking a big bite, he watched her face as she analyzed the textures. Or was she savoring them? He raised it to her mouth again. "Bite."

Those eerie eyes seem to flash. "I'm not one of your pack to be given orders."

Temper, temper, he thought, the panther in him intrigued by that hint of fire. "Please."

After another small pause, she leaned forward and bit. This time she took more . . . and confirmed every one of his beliefs about her. Demolishing the rest of the piece, he picked up another one. She ate a good third.

"Enough?"

"Yes, thank you." She reached for her water. "Do you want your coffee?"

"Thanks." The mug was warm in his hands but it was the heat of her that he could feel most strongly. Her body was alive. Her body felt. Her body knew sensation. The crucial question was, was her mind strong enough to overpower her animal instincts?

They sat quietly until Sascha put down her water and turned to him. "Tell me about the murders."

A chill cooled the heat of his body. Getting rid of his own empty mug, he dropped his head against the cushion back. "We've tracked down seven confirmed victims in the past three years. Kylie was number eight. And Brenna, the SnowDancer who was taken, will be the ninth if we don't find her in time."

"So many?" It was a whisper.

"Yeah. But my gut says we haven't tagged all of his past kills—he's too good at this."

"Are you sure it's a man?"

He clenched his fists hard enough to hurt. "Yes."

"Why haven't you done more to track him down?"

"Kylie was murdered six months ago. At the time, we didn't know it was a serial and, given the clear evidence of Psy involvement, we thought Enforcement would quickly close the case. We gave them no problems regarding jurisdiction—we wanted blood but we didn't want war with the Psy.

"We were willing to settle for an Enforcement prosecution." It had nearly ripped the hearts out of them but they'd done it for the sake of their young. Dorian's rage hadn't been so great that he'd forgotten the vow he'd made simply by being born—to protect the vulnerable. "We understood that one monster didn't define a whole race. Even changelings sometimes spawn serial killers." Though they had them in the fewest numbers of the three races.

"Everyone believed the Council would launch a hunt on the PsyNet and hand over the culprit. With your psychic skills, there'd be no question of his guilt. Until then the

Council had done some questionable things, but no one thought they'd protect a killer."

Sascha's body seemed to curl up further, as if she were trying to hug herself. "What have you learned about him since you started searching?"

"He hunts widely. Of the kills we've tracked, the first two were in Nevada, the third in Oregon, the remaining four in Arizona. The last was Dorian's sister." He would never forget the coppery smell of innocent blood, the darkness of the splatters on the walls, the metallic stink of the Psy.

"He left bodies to find?"

He sat upright, arms crossed over bent knees, one hand grasping the wrist of the other in a punishing grip. "The bastard takes them, tortures them, and then returns them to some place that should've been safe."

"I don't understand." Sascha's voice was nearer, as if she'd moved forward when he had.

Looking over, he met those night-sky eyes head-on. "He delivers the killing blows in a place familiar to the women. Kylie's throat was slashed in her apartment."

Darkness crawled across Sascha's eyes, destroying the stars and almost succeeding in shocking him out of his fury. He'd heard that Psy eyes did that when they were expending huge amounts of Psy power but he'd never seen it happen. It was like watching the wings of the night close out the sun. The strange thing was, the hairs on the back of his neck weren't tingling in awareness. If Sascha wasn't using her powers, why were her eyes going midnight?

"He's very sure of himself," she said, shoving him back from fascination to fury.

"Of the other seven women," he continued, "one was murdered in her home, one at her place of work, another in her family crypt." Anger for each senseless death rippled through him. "The other four follow the same pattern."

Sascha wrapped her arms around her knees. The panther noticed the mirroring and filed it away. "Why didn't the other changeling groups do anything?"

"Several reasons, the major one being that this was buried so deep, no one had any idea it was a serial until we started digging."

"The other reasons?"

"A combination of the choice of victims and Enforcement complicity. The first woman wasn't part of a defined pack—her parents went to the authorities but got nowhere." He knew exactly why. "The second two belonged to fairly weak groups. None are dominant in their area and they simply didn't have the physical or strategic strength to push for answers when doors were slammed in their faces.

"The fourth was blamed on a rogue and since he was already slated for death by his pack, the case was termed to fall outside Enforcement jurisdiction and closed. The fifth and seventh were loners—there was no one left to fight for justice. The sixth victim was killed at the same time that a human serial killer was preying in the region and even her pack wasn't certain she hadn't been one of his victims. But when you set it beside the other Psy kills, there's no question it's the same predator."

"Then came Kylie."

"She was his first mistake." Lucas felt his claws pressing against the inside of his skin. "The second we put together the pattern and unearthed the other forgotten women, we started to hunt. We also got a warning out to every changeling group we could reach."

Sascha didn't speak. Not quite sure why he felt the need, he turned his body until he was facing her, one of his legs behind her, knee bent. The other he dropped loosely to the ground, crossed under the raised leg, before picking up her braid to play with the end.

He needed touch. Contrary to what Sascha believed, not just any touch would do. Usually only packmates were able to give him the peace he craved. Usually. "We're not weak," he began, pulling off the tie that kept her braid together.

She blinked and her body tensed but all she said was, "No, you're not."

Was she trying to be gentle with him? He looked into those infinite eyes and wished he could read her mind. "And we're not going to stop searching because the Psy want us to. Brenna *will* be saved and the killer *will* be executed. If DarkRiver is taken down, the SnowDancers will continue the fight. When they fall . . . there are others."

The world was changing and sooner or later, the Psy were going to come face-to-face with their worst nightmare—the relegation of their emotionless race to nothing more than a footnote in the history of man.

"How can you be absolutely certain it's a Psy?" she asked. "I won't betray my race on the basis of a suspicion."

Springy, silky curls began to overflow his hands as her braid started unraveling on its own. The panther was delighted by the texture and life in his hands. But it wasn't enough to make him forget blood and death. "I was with Dorian when he got the feeling that something was wrong. We must've arrived at Kylie's apartment on the killer's heels." What he'd seen there had been enough to make him believe in evil as a living, breathing entity. If Sascha wanted proof, he had it, seventy-nine precise pieces of it, all covered in blood and horror.

Those mysterious eyes looked at him with what he wanted to believe was sympathy. "That's why Dorian is so damaged. He thinks if he'd only been that much faster . . ."

No longer surprised at her understanding of the emotions that drove people, Lucas nodded. "When we got there, Kylie's body was warm to the touch but she was gone and so was the killer. However, he'd left behind a scent, one that's unmistakable to us."

He'd also left behind a faint psychic vibration in the air, something that Lucas alone had picked up. He knew the ability stemmed from the same sense that warned him when Psy power was being used. It wasn't something he was ready to share with his Psy, though he was almost certain that she was far more akin to him than she was to the people she called her own—almost wasn't good enough for an alpha.

"Is that the best evidence you have?"

He stopped playing with her curls. "He cut her. Precisely. Neatly. No mistakes. No hesitations. No cut deeper or shallower than the others. No cut shorter or longer. He cut her *exactly* seventy-nine times."

"Seventy-nine?"

"Just like in the last four kills." The Psy had been unable to bury that fact, because though the Arizona medical examiner was human, one of her older cousins was married to a changeling. They were a very close-knit extended family—something the Psy hadn't taken into account, crippled as they were by their inability to understand the bonds of blood. Dr. Cecily Montford had been so disturbed by the careless way her reports were being treated that she'd been more than willing to break confidentiality and talk to DarkRiver.

"Tell me, Sascha," he asked, not letting her look away, "can you think of any other race on the face of this planet with the control to do something that heinous and keep exactly to a set pattern?" His voice dropped an octave, the craving for vengeance bringing out the beast.

"He didn't make a single deviation in the length, depth, or width of those cuts across the five bodies we were able to get information on. He sliced them like they were lab rats. None of those cuts was fatal except the last."

Rage was powering him, making him push her in a way that he would've never pushed any other woman. He was used to protecting but Sascha's calm evaluation of the violent deaths of eight women—women who'd mattered, who'd been loved—had turned him savage. "Oh, and the autopsies showed that their minds were literally mush though their skulls hadn't been damaged. Who can do that aside from the Psy, Sascha? Who?"

She made a quick rising movement. He was faster. He trapped her with his body around hers, his leg at her back and his arms around her torso. "Where are you going?"

"You're letting emotion control you. Perhaps we should continue this when you're calmer."

The words sounded right, sounded like something a Psy would say, but he could hear an almost subvocal tremor, something no one but a changeling could've detected—a changeling who'd been marked as a Hunter since birth. Remorse thrust back the clawing anger of the beast.

"I'm sorry, kitten. That was uncalled for." He ran the hand on her back into her curls and to the nape of her neck. "I'm taking my anger out on you."

"It's understandable." She pushed at the arm holding her to him but not with enough force to make him think of it as a serious protest. "I represent the race you hold responsible for the death of your packmate and Dorian's hurt."

He ran his thumb against the warm skin of her nape, anchoring himself in the softness of her. The beast understood why she was able to do that for him but the man wasn't ready to face that truth. "The Psy *are* responsible."

"Perhaps the killer is Psy, but you have no proof of the Council being involved." Her hands clenched on his forearm.

The panther growled but the man knew enough not to point out the slip and risk shocking her back inside her mask. "They're the only body with the power to conceal something this bad. They have to know."

"No," she argued, staring at him with those beautiful, haunting eyes. "What possible reason could they have to hide a killer?"

"What's the basis of the Council's control of your people? What do they constantly point out to us changelings and humans?" He kept his tone consciously gentle, having no desire to hurt her again. But she had to face facts. And then she had to decide which side she was on.

"Nonviolence," she said at once. "The Psy have no violent crime compared to the other races."

"Supposedly." He shifted until she was almost cradled in the vee of his legs. "If people find out that that's a lie, your whole structure crumbles and the Council falls."

"My mother is Council." It was a whispered plea.

He'd almost forgotten. "I'm sorry, Sascha. She has to know."

She shook her head, silky curls tumbling everywhere. "No. She's powerful and ruthless, yes, but she's not evil."

CHAPTER 11

Evil. An interesting word choice from a Psy. "Nikita likes power. If the Council goes down, so does that power." He raised a hand and rubbed his knuckles along her cheek. "Think about it."

"I need time."

"You don't have long. He usually keeps them for seven days before killing them."

"Seven days of torture."

"Yes."

Silence descended over them. Even the forest outside had stopped whispering. It felt as if the whole world was holding its breath. He continued to caress her nape, her cheek, her chin. Her skin was as tempting as warm silk.

"You don't have skin privileges," she said, after what seemed like forever.

"What if I said I wanted them?" He didn't stop touching her, didn't stop gentling her as he would a changeling woman of whom he'd asked too much too soon. He'd taken a risk in telling her everything but it had had to be done. Sascha was their last chance.

"It's useless to have such privileges with the Psy. We can't return them." There was something defeated about her.

Lucas didn't like seeing her this way, hurt and bruised. Guilt squeezed his heart. It shouldn't have torn him up that he'd done this to her. Everything he did was for Pack. It was part of the price of being alpha. For the first time, he resented paying that price, resented having to hurt this woman.

He shifted an inch closer, deciding to let the panther's sensuality out to play in order to make it up to her. They'd discussed darkness and death, horror and evil. But that wasn't all he was, all she was. If he wanted to pull her out of the Psy armor she wore like a second skin, he'd have to tempt her with the beautiful side of emotion, rather than burying her in ugliness. "Was Dorian right?"

She finally turned her head to face him. "About what?"

"He said that sleeping with one of the Psy was like sleeping with a hunk of concrete."

"I wouldn't know." Her shoulders squared.

"Never slept with one of your brethren?"

"Why would I? Procreation, if desired, can be done far more efficiently using scientific methods." She sounded so prim it was a provocation.

"What about fun?"

"I'm Psy, remember? We don't have fun." A small pause. "In any case, I don't see the point of sex. It appears messy and completely impractical."

"Don't knock it till you've tried it, darling." He wanted to grin. Her stiff posture and oh-so-practical words were textbook Psy . . . as if she'd studied them.

"That's an unlikely possibility," she said, and sounded *almost* as if she believed. "I think it's time I left—it's after five." She glanced at her timepiece.

"A kiss," he whispered in her ear.

"What?" Her body stilled.

"I'm giving you a chance to try out some of that messy, purposeless interaction you don't understand." Taking her earlobe between his teeth, he bit down gently. The slight jerk of her body was unmistakable. Letting go, he cupped her cheek with one hand and turned her face toward his. "How about it?"

"I don't see why—"

"Think of it as an experiment." He ran his thumb over the softness of her lower lip, wanting to taste her more than he wanted to breathe. The urge to tease had turned into a craving to *take*. "You Psy like your experiments, don't you?"

She gave a slow nod. "Perhaps it'll help me understand why changelings and humans place so much emphasis on marriage and bonding."

He didn't give her a chance to change her mind. Bending his head, he ran his lips across hers in a quick, hot slide. Warm, soft, delicious, they invited him to return. When he did, he kept the kiss shallow—tugging at her lower lip, easing the hurt with his tongue, then suckling her upper lip. A soft, innately female moan silvered into the silence.

Heat seared him.

This was no block of concrete. He could feel the rise and fall of her breasts against his forearm, inviting his palm to go lower. For now, he satisfied himself with the pounding heartbeat he could feel in her neck, with the jagged breath she couldn't hide. The Psy could shut off emotion, but it was far harder to shut off the body's hunger for touch.

Sascha could see the edge of the cliff dropping away in front of her and she didn't care. Never in her life had she felt this much sensation, this much pleasure. Her fantasies were nothing compared to the reality of Lucas. The lazy greed with which he was kissing her was the most dangerous of temptations. His movements were so languorous, so subtle, so sensually slow that she'd opened her mouth to him before she knew it. Shocked at how far she'd come, she pulled back.

He didn't fight her withdrawal, watching her with those cat-green eyes tempered by arousal. "Enough experimenting, kitten?"

The endearment was straight out of her dreams. Terrified by her own reaction and by the realization she could see in his eyes, she said, "I'd like to return home." She knew she hadn't answered his question. She also knew that she couldn't say the words expected of a Psy without it being such a huge lie that she'd give herself away. The truth was, she hadn't had enough. Not by a long shot.

"All right." He leaned down and nipped at her lower lip with those sharp predatory teeth.

Marking her.

Sascha was home by eight a.m. Exhausted, she took a shower and started preparing for the day ahead. The first thing on the agenda was a meeting with her mother. Then she had to check on a couple of other family projects. After that she had to face Lucas again. Her face flushed as she tried to put her hair in order.

She couldn't forget the feel of his hands in her hair, the pleasure he'd taken from touching her. Yet it hadn't been the pleasure that had almost broken her. It had been the need she'd felt in him, the need for touch, for peace. It had captivated her that he'd found surcease in her, a Psy, one of the enemy.

Part of a race of killers.

Grim reality wiped away every trace of lingering pleasure. She couldn't accept his accusation, couldn't give up everything she believed in so easily. Perhaps she'd never fit in but the Psy were her people, all she had. Lucas had kissed her but he was a changeling and when push came to shove, he'd always choose his pack over her.

Wait for me outside.

The image of Lucas ordering her to leave, when Dorian had fragmented, merged with thoughts of him in bed with a woman called Rina. He'd never treated her as anything but an outsider, she thought, deliberately forgetting that visit to Tamsyn's home because it didn't fit, and she needed something to go right, something to make sense.

She needed to belong.

The second she turned against the Psy, she'd be saying good-bye not only to her life, but also to any hope she had of ever fitting in anywhere. Even if she somehow survived the anger of the Council, who'd take in a rogue Psy? Not Dark-River. She could still remember the hatred she'd glimpsed in Dorian's eyes as he'd accused her of being from a race of psychopaths.

Lucas had stood by Dorian while pushing her out—she'd been left on her own, once again an outsider. The leopards had come together for their packmate, but who'd come together for her when she'd found herself unconscious on the floor of her apartment? No one.

Because she was nothing but a tool.

Lucas had never hidden his nature. She'd known from the start that he'd utilize every advantage he had to get his way . . . even if it involved something as distasteful as kissing one of the stinking, metallic Psy. He was using her to gather information and the second she delivered, he'd be done with her.

Sharp pains stabbed her stomach but she stood her ground and forced herself to face the truth. As she'd always feared, the changelings had picked up on her flawed nature and were exploiting it to get what they wanted.

Lucas was exploiting it. Exploiting her.

"Stupid," she whispered, fighting tears. "I'm so stupid." How was it possible that the rest of her race repelled him, but she didn't? It wasn't. Only her pitiful need to be accepted, to be valued, had let her believe something so improbable. She'd been guilty of participating in her own deception.

It was time she stopped letting him blind her with emotion and the dangling threads of false hope and started thinking like a Psy. Maybe it wasn't too late to salvage her position, at least within the family. The first thing she had to do to ensure that was to tell Nikita everything she'd learned—she might never be a perfect cardinal, but she could be a perfect daughter. This was her chance to make a place for herself as something other than a mistake.

Humiliation and hurt combined to make a dangerous mixture. She wanted to make Lucas pay, wanted to wound him as he'd wounded her, shatter his dreams as he'd shattered hers. He'd taught her so much about his people. He shouldn't have. In the end, she was Psy.

And he was the enemy.

CHAPTER 12

Lucas knew something was wrong the instant Sascha walked onto the building site where he and his team were taking some initial measurements. They had to make sure everything looked normal on the surface—there was no need to tip off the Psy unnecessarily. To foster that impression, he was out here when he'd rather be hunting murderous human prey.

He watched Sascha park her car some distance from the others and walk to the eastern edge of the site, far from where they were working. Getting up from a crouch, he handed over his notepad to the woman next to him. "Hold the fort, Zara."

"What would you do without me?" The wildcat winked.

Smiling despite the fact that his gut was tight in anticipation of trouble, he headed after Sascha. It was a shock to come face-to-face with her only to realize that no trace remained of the woman who'd let him kiss her. Every nerve in him went stiff in rejection. Not of her. Of the mask she'd donned once again. She was hiding herself and that was unacceptable to both sides of his nature. He wanted nothing more than to force her to remove it . . . although he didn't understand why it made him so wildly furious.

"How long till construction begins?" she asked before he could speak.

"The plans will be complete in about a month. If you sign off on them, construction begins."

"Please keep me updated." There was a darkness to her eyes that set every one of his instincts on edge.

The panther's hackles rose. "What have you done?" he asked point-blank.

"I'm Psy, Lucas."

"Damn you." He grabbed her arm. She froze. "What the hell have you done?"

Her lips compressed to a fine white line. "I went to tell my mother everything."

The flames of betrayal spread like acid in his blood. "You bitch." He let go of her arm, disgusted.

"But I didn't." The words were so quiet he almost didn't hear them.

"What?"

"I couldn't tell her." Turning from him, she stared out at the trees that edged the lot. "Why not, Lucas? I'm Psy. My loyalty is theirs but I couldn't speak."

Relief kicked him so hard it was almost pain. "What have they done to earn your loyalty?" Mixed in with the relief was anger. Anger that she should've even considered betraying him.

"What have you?" She glanced over her shoulder.

"I trusted you." And he wasn't a man who trusted easily. "I figure that evens us out."

She averted her gaze. "I'm going to search the PsyNet for information. I'll give you what I have." There was something heartbreakingly lonely in the perfect tones of her voice, something that made him think she'd splinter into a thousand pieces if he spoke the wrong words.

"Sascha." He went to touch her shoulder, unable, in spite of his anger, to watch her suffer that way. It didn't occur to him to consider why it was so important that she not hurt. It just was.

"Don't." Moving away, she whispered, "I need to be something, even if that means I'm part of a race of killers. If I'm not Psy then what am I?"

Before he could respond, Zara called out his name. Giving her a wave, he said, "Who said the Psy can't be anything else?"

Sascha didn't speak again until Lucas was on the other side of the site. "Nature." The ragged whisper revealed the best-kept secret of their race. Like the rest of the Psy, she was dependent on the PsyNet for every breath she took. Cut off from it for much longer than a minute or two, she'd die a miserable death. And if her flaw were discovered, she'd be sentenced to living death through rehabilitation. Her only hope of survival was to become more Psy than the Psy, to become . . . unbreakable.

This morning she'd gone to Nikita with the full intention of giving her everything she had. Filled with confusion and a kind of blind anger at a fate that had shown her glory and then told her she couldn't have it, she'd convinced herself that if she betrayed DarkRiver, she'd redeem herself in Nikita's eyes, at last be the daughter her mother had always wanted.

Yet when she'd opened her mouth to speak, all that had come out had been a string of lies. Every single one of them had been told to protect the changelings, to protect Lucas. They'd come from a hidden part of her she'd never before seen, a bright, hard knot of fierce loyalty and utter determination. That part wouldn't let her do anything to hurt the panther who'd kissed her and smashed the glass walls of her existence into a million slivers.

It was then she'd realized that, for the first time in her life, she wanted something else even more than she wanted to belong. If only for a moment, if only for a second, she wanted to be loved.

What a futile, impossible dream for a Psy.

She would never have it, but she could at least help this race which knew *how* to love. Perhaps that would be enough to feed the need in her soul. Perhaps.

Lucas allowed Sascha to keep her distance as they finished the measurements, but he had no intention of letting her withdraw. He'd never been very good at following orders.

"Don't," she'd said when he'd tried to touch her. Not because she was one of the untouchable Psy but because she was something more—a woman who felt. If he hadn't been convinced of that after their kiss, he would've been left in no doubt after her confession. He hadn't forgiven her for even contemplating betrayal, but that didn't mean he was going to let her go.

He couldn't.

She was his. The idea of watching her walk away was simply not tolerable. He might've been blinkered to the facts before now, but the fire of his rage at the thought of her selling him out had ripped the blinkers from his eyes. The truth had hit him like a slap. As much as Sascha might react to him, he definitely reacted to *her*—physically, mentally, and sexually.

What she didn't know, because he'd been very careful not to let her agile mind figure it out, was that he didn't touch easily outside Pack. He hadn't been joking about skin privileges. Yes, he was more tactile than the Psy, but he didn't get affectionately intimate with those who were not his. Yet from the first, he'd found himself playing with her as he might play with a woman who'd aroused his most primitive instincts. Never had he treated her as the enemy deserved to be treated.

Part of him continued to resist the idea of what Sascha meant to him, really meant to him. That part had been tortured, broken, almost destroyed. It didn't want to open itself up, didn't want to permit a vulnerability that could lead to a harsher pain. Paradoxically, it was that same part which understood what this Psy was to him, and it was that same part which couldn't let her go.

Only one thing was certain—he was keeping her.

"Have you had lunch?" he asked at around one thirty, as they prepared to leave the site.

She continued heading to her car, parked several meters from the others. "I'm fine."

"You didn't answer my question." He could play this game just as well as his Psy.

"I have an energy bar in the car." Reaching her sleek vehicle, she went to open the door.

He stopped her by the simple expedient of putting his hand on hers.

"Don't," she said again, pulling away.

"Why not?"

She didn't answer but he saw a spark light those eyes. That temper of hers was flickering again, bringing her back to life. What he'd give to see her in full fury. "Come with me to Tammy's. She was asking about you." The healer had taken an unusually strong interest in Sascha.

"I don't think that would be wise." Her face was cool but he could hear the whispers of her soul, the panther in him attuned to every nuance of her body.

Leaning close, he whispered, "Don't worry—the cubs are off visiting family." In truth, they'd been spirited away to safety with the rest of DarkRiver's young. Something was going to break soon and the worst-case scenario equaled massive bloodshed. But for this one moment he allowed himself to play, aware that he was standing with the lone woman who might be able to stop the carnage. "Your boots are safe."

"I have no idea what you're talking about."

Grinning at the bold-faced lie, he tapped her cheek. "Zara's already taken my car back to the office. Keys?" He held out his hand.

She crossed her arms. "You have a short memory."

"Only for things I don't want to remember. Do you know the way?"

Her expression clearly said that that was a stupid question. "Get in."

Lucas let her give him the order, aware he'd won the first skirmish in their very private battle. However, it was a battle he could only continue if they won the much more dangerous war hanging over their heads.

Sascha waited until they were on their way to bring up the subject preying on her mind. "Have you learned more?"

Lucas didn't try to pretend he didn't know what she was talking about. His sudden fury was so pure and taut that she felt like she could reach out and touch it. What amazed her was that there was no confusion in that anger.

Lucas could think through his feelings, displaying a strength of will beyond anything she knew. She was barely skirting the edges of emotion and already it felt like a yawning abyss at her feet, ready to suck her in and spit her back out battered, bruised, and possibly dead.

"The SnowDancer he took is a twenty-year-old female.

Brenna was on the way to classes at a private school at the time she was taken. When she didn't arrive, a packmate in the same class sent out an alert."

"What was she studying?" She filed away the data—she'd need it to narrow down the search parameters in the Net. At the same time, she reached out with her psychic senses and soothed the jagged edges of his anger. It was done so instinctively that she was barely aware of it.

"Repair and maintenance of computronic systems, concentrating on communication consoles."

"Intelligent," she muttered.

"Yes, that's part of his pattern."

"When?"

"It must've been around noon because that was the time Brenna would've been on the path from where she was taken—she usually cut through a small park in her neighborhood."

"So someone could've picked up her habits?"

"Yes. But to abduct her in broad daylight speaks of extreme confidence. The park isn't large or particularly wooded. He could've been seen from several angles."

"Yet he wasn't." If he was Psy, then there were things he could've done to hide himself. "A Tk-Psy with the ability to teleport could've taken her out with him."

"Tk?"

"Telekinetic."

"How much power would that take?"

"More than most Psy have. I doubt it was done that way."

"Why?"

"Strong telekinetics can transport themselves easily but taking along another person is difficult, especially if they won't give you entry into their mind to ease the psychic transition."

She'd learned all this during elementary school, when

the different skills had still been in the same classes. Before the other cardinals had gone on to specialize and she'd been left alone to hone what pitiful skills she had, an embarrassment no one wanted to acknowledge.

"Could he have forced her mind open?" Lucas stretched out his legs and linked his arms around the back of the headrest. The lazy movement made her want to reach out and pet him . . . as she'd done in those forbidden dreams.

Clenching her hands on the wheel, she shook her head. "She's a changeling. That immediately doubles the difficulty, and even for a cardinal, forcing open a mind is already one of the most difficult of tasks. If you don't care about killing the victim, it can be done with a massive burst of power, but he wanted her alive." So he could torture her.

Sascha took a deep breath and forced herself to continue. "Plus to do that *and* teleport her would've taken enough power to lay him up for days. I haven't heard of any strong Psy in that condition. That sort of thing, a Psy flaming out, tends to create a buzz in the Net." She tapped the wheel. "He could've just planned it carefully and had a vehicle nearby. A lot of human serial killers function that way."

"That's what the SnowDancers think. They've found a witness who saw an unfamiliar large vehicle with muddied license plates." He rolled down his window as they entered a leafier part of the city. "Enforcement doesn't know. Except for the detectives working underground, this time nobody's even bothering to pretend to carry on an investigation."

The conceit of whoever it was who was controlling Enforcement stuck a spear into the bubble of hope Sascha had been carrying around that her people were innocent. "Were you able to identify the owner of the vehicle?"

"No."

"What was she wearing when she was taken?"

Lucas's scowl sounded in his voice. "Why do you need to know that?"

"The PsyNet is full of information. Anything that helps narrow things down might be useful." There was no way to explain the Net to those who hadn't experienced it. It was a mass of data and the only controlling factor was the influence of the NetMind, which tried to make order from chaos. An entity that had evolved into its own separate sentience, it wasn't *alive* but it thought in a way that took it beyond mere machinery.

"Blue jeans, white shirt, black sneakers."

She shot him a glance. "I didn't expect you to have that information at your fingertips."

"An alert's already gone out to every changeling clan in the region, friendly or not, warning of the killer's proximity and asking for assistance. This is Brenna's photo." He slid the glossy hard copy out from the pocket of his jacket but waited to hand it to her until she'd pulled up at a stoplight.

She took it with a feeling of inexplicable dread. The woman was laughing in the picture, her brown eyes brilliant with amusement, her head thrown back. Sunlight glinted off the pure blond strands of her straight hair and highlighted the curves of her body. She was short, perhaps five-four, but there was such life in her that she seemed to dwarf the two men in the photo with her.

"The males are her older brothers—Riley and Andrew," Lucas said when she handed back the picture. "According to the SnowDancer alpha, they're homicidal."

The light changed as she tried not to give in to the despair she'd felt from touching that photo. It was as if Brenna had reached out and pulled her into the hell she was undergoing. *Brenna.* A name. A face. A sentient being. "He wants to steal her life," she whispered.

"After torturing her."

"No, that's not what I mean." She turned down the leafy lane that would eventually lead to Tamsyn's home.

"What, then?"

"She appears so vibrant, so full of joy and *life*. He wants to take that from her, wants to keep it for himself."

Silence in the car.

"I don't know how I know that. I just do." She came to a stop outside the sprawling house she'd visited once before. "He must be driven by the most poisonous rage." She hadn't felt any such emotion in that odd, fleeting moment when she'd seemingly been sucked into Brenna's world, but what else could drive one being to so savage another?

"He doesn't know what rage is."

She turned to look at Lucas, not frightened by his open blood-hunger. There was something clean about it, something real. "No one who feels the dark things he must is going to be able to hide it forever. He's going to break sooner or later."

Lucas's eyes were hard green crystals. "For all our sakes it better be sooner. The clock is ticking."

Tamsyn was edgy. "I miss the cubs," she said to Lucas the second he walked in.

Hugging her, he tried to lend her some of his strength. Sascha stood quiet beside him but he felt the stirring at the base of his nape. It was, he realized, an almost constant feeling around her, so constant that he'd hardly been noticing. Something about Sascha gave off a low-level indication of Psy power in continual use.

Exactly what the heck was his Psy up to? Despite her unsuccessful attempt at betrayal, he wasn't immediately suspicious. The panther said that she was safe and the panther's instincts had never been wrong. Tamsyn took a deep breath and let go of him after several minutes.

"Better?" he asked, brushing her hair off her face. Every time he looked into those healer's eyes, his heart broke a little and then rejoined. She was a persistent reminder of the mother he'd lost but she was also a reminder of the goodness Shayla had been.

She nodded. "I made Nate go to work. Stupid." With that, she turned to head to her domain—the kitchen.

Sascha waited until Tammy was out of earshot. "If having the cubs away from her makes her this anxious, why did she let them go in the first place?"

"Overprotectiveness isn't good for predatory changelings." He'd been guilty of making that mistake, especially in the months after Kylie's death. His need to keep his people safe, to not lose anyone ever again, had threatened to suffocate them. He'd caught himself before he'd caused irreparable damage but it was a fault he had to guard against day in and day out.

"Tammy didn't appear overprotective. In fact she seemed very open to letting them explore by themselves."

"You've only seen her with them once." But she'd guessed correctly. Tammy was the one who'd ripped into him for his behavior toward the juveniles. However, he couldn't tell Sascha that. It was one thing to trust his instincts about her, quite another to place the lives of others' cubs in her hands. That was a trust she hadn't yet earned.

It was the right decision for an alpha but maybe it was also made because he was still fuming over the betrayal she'd contemplated. "What smells so good?" he asked, walking into the kitchen.

Tammy finished setting the places. "Chicken pot pie with strawberry tarts to follow."

"You didn't have to go to so much trouble," Sascha said, and though the words sounded stilted, Lucas knew the sentiment was genuine.

To his surprise, so did Tamsyn. She touched Sascha's

hand in fleeting reassurance. "Cooking relaxes me— maybe it's part of being a healer. If you don't help eat my efforts, Nate's going to start accusing me of trying to fatten him up."

Lucas pulled out a chair. Instead of taking it, Sascha went to the other side and pulled out her own. Stubborn woman. "You eating with us, Tammy?"

"Yup." She took off her apron and came to sit at the head of the table, Lucas to her right and Sascha to her left. "I feel strange sitting here—this is Nate's seat."

That was why Lucas hadn't taken it. He might be alpha but this was a packmate's home and in here, Nate believed that he was alpha. Tamsyn might disagree, Lucas thought with a hidden smile, but she let Nate think what he liked because she loved him.

As they began eating, the healer started talking. "I can't stop thinking about that poor girl—Brenna." She put down her fork. "He's probably hurting her right now. And we're sitting here doing nothing."

It was Sascha who said the right thing. "If you think so negatively you'll make it a self-fulfilling prophecy. Look past the anger and pain and think. Perhaps you'll discover a way to help her."

Tamsyn looked at her for a long moment. "You're more than you appear, aren't you, Sascha?"

"No, I'm not." Sascha stared at her food.

"The word is that the SnowDancers are skating the edge," Tamsyn commented, her eyes still on Sascha. "I heard her brothers had to be restrained until they came to their senses and stopped speaking about taking off Psy heads."

Neither of them mentioned Dorian. After his wild break-down, he'd been acting almost spookily normal. Everyone was afraid that he was going to snap when they least expected it.

"What did they hope to achieve?" Sascha raised her head to meet Lucas's gaze. "Two changelings against the entire Psy race? It would've been suicide."

"Logic and love don't necessarily coincide," he said, watching her eyes trace the clawlike lines on his face. Unlike many a nonchangeling, she'd never appeared put off by the violent-looking markings. He'd caught her staring at them as if fascinated more than once. Nor had he forgotten the way she'd caressed them in his dreams. "They were hurting because they couldn't protect their sister—their need to strike out is understandable."

Lucas appreciated their position as only someone who'd once been in that very place could. The years of waiting for his body to grow strong so he could claim vengeance had been torture of the most excruciating kind, slow and seemingly endless.

"What would Psy do in the same situation?" Tamsyn asked.

Sascha took long moments to answer. "There is no love in the Psy world, so logic would prevail." Her words were crisp but her eyes gave her away.

Somehow, he'd learned to read those night-sky eyes, learned to interpret the haunting sadness that flickered over them for barely a millisecond before she asked, "Tamsyn, may I use your home for a few hours this afternoon?"

Lucas pushed away his plate, excitement churning in his gut. Sascha was going to surf the PsyNet.

"Sure. People might drop by, though."

"I need a room where I won't be disturbed."

"You can use one of the upstairs guest rooms. Most visitors tend to hang around downstairs." Tamsyn rose to get the tarts. As she placed them on the table, the doorbell chimed. "I'll go see who that is."

Lucas touched Sascha's hand after Tammy had left. "You're going to try and search the Net?"

She nodded and slowly slid away her hand. "You can't be here."

"Why not?"

"Because your presence distracts me." The look on her face dared him to make anything of that.

The panther in him growled, smug. The man wasn't so easily appeased. "I'm not going to leave you unprotected."

"If I trip some silent alarm, you won't be able to protect me," she said, not skirting around the truth. "My mind would be jelly before you knew anything was wrong."

His jaw set. "Then you don't go in." The answer was instinctive—he wasn't even thinking of the lost SnowDancer.

"Don't worry. I'm only going to search the public archives. Nothing will happen." She looked over his shoulder as Tamsyn walked back into the room.

"I don't think you two have officially met," the healer commented. "Rina—Sascha. Rina is Kit's sister."

When Lucas turned, he saw Rina nod a wary hello to Sascha before the curvaceous blonde walked over to hug his neck from behind. Her cheek rubbed against his. Though Rina was a highly sexual female, her caress was asking for comfort. She'd never tried to come on to him, being young enough, now twenty-one, to have always treated him as her alpha rather than as an attractive male.

Moving his head, he kissed her on the lips, running his hand up her arm in a soothing gesture. It was a small thing but it helped her. She let go and sat in the chair beside him. Lucas glanced at Sascha to see how she'd handled the contact. Her face was expressionless, so much so that he knew she had to be hiding something pretty intense.

He bought his attention back to Rina. "What's wrong?"

"Kit's gone missing."

CHAPTER 13

"**What?**" The killer had never taken a male before.

"No, no, it's not like that," Rina protested. "He's just taken off on some joyriding trip to Big Sur with a couple of the other juveniles and I can't get in touch with them. I think it's Nico and Sarah with him."

"When did they leave?" A ban on nonauthorized travel had gone into effect early that morning.

"Before," Rina said, glancing at Sascha.

Normally the three kids' absence wouldn't be a cause for concern. Juveniles were notoriously wild, but Lucas suspected that Kit's sudden trip had to do with witnessing Dorian's collapse. He hero-worshipped the latent sentinel. "I'll track him down." The SnowDancer lieutenants who controlled those areas were usually reasonable, but these weren't ordinary times.

"Thanks, Lucas."

"Tamsyn, I'm going to head out with Rina." He stood and looked down at Sascha. "You staying?" He wasn't convinced of the safety of what she was planning to do but as

Rina had reminded him, more rested on this than his own desire to keep Sascha safe from harm. That didn't make it any easier to leave her—comprehension about her place in his life was starting to creep in, in spite of the barriers erected the day he'd lost everything.

"Yes." Night-sky eyes met his without blinking but refused to look at Rina.

Notwithstanding the bleak situation, it made him want to smile. "I'll catch up with you if I return before six. If not, leave a message with Tammy."

"All right. I hope you find Kit and the others."

"We will." They'd lost one of their young. It was more than enough.

Sascha stood in the guest bedroom trying to concentrate but all she could see was Lucas with Rina. Sensuality had poured from every molecule of the female, rich and heady and almost tangible. She'd felt as if she were drowning in it as she'd sat across from the two of them.

Then they'd kissed and she'd had another shock. Affection had whispered between them. Not passion, not hunger, not desire. Her mind was having trouble with the thought that Lucas's kiss hadn't caused Rina to burst into sexual flame.

A knock on the door startled her into a soundless gasp. "Yes?"

Tamsyn's smile appeared in the doorway. "I brought you a cup of hot chocolate. If you need anything else, let me know." She put the mug down on a bedside table. "I'll leave you in peace."

"Tamsyn?"

"Yes?" She paused with her hand on the doorknob.

"Can you explain something to me?" Sascha couldn't ask

Lucas. It would betray too much she wasn't ready to face. However, Tamysn had said she was a healer. Maybe that meant what was said between them would remain in confidence.

"The kiss?" Tamsyn raised a brow.

Sascha thought she hid her surprise well. "Yes."

"It's like when he kissed me the first time we met. He's alpha and each time he touches us, he reinforces the bonds of Pack. With the women, he's generally more affectionate." She rolled her eyes. "They're chauvinistic pigs but we love them. Anyway, as I was saying, that kiss wasn't sexual in any way. It was about . . . togetherness."

"What about with the men?" Sascha asked, the seeds of understanding blooming in her mind.

"They go for night runs, fight each other to test their skills, and occasionally get together to play poker or watch a game. It works." She gave a mystified shrug.

"So a kiss is nothing special to Lucas?" Her idiocy where this one male was concerned kept surprising her into hurt. He'd said it was an experiment. Perhaps he'd wanted to know what it was like to kiss a "hunk of concrete."

Tamsyn cocked her head to the side and gave Sascha a probing look. "Inside the pack, it's special because it tells us he cares for us, that he'll die for us."

Sascha nodded, feeling worse and worse.

"But outside the pack? The only women I've known Lucas to kiss outside the pack are the ones he wants in his bed." The door shut behind the grinning healer.

Sascha's cheeks flamed. Lucas wanted her in his bed. In spite of her vows to not let him reach her, she was aroused to fever pitch. Concentration went out the window. Dreams intertwined with reality and she remembered his kiss in the forest as she remembered his far more intimate kiss in her dreams.

It was the prosaic sound of an engine getting closer that brought back the world and reminded her what she was meant to be doing. Taking a deep breath, she sat down cross-legged on the floor and started to recite a mental exercise so demanding, it succeeded in driving everything else from her mind. Ready, she took the first step out into the Net.

The world opened.

In front of her was an endless starry sky. Each star was a mind, some strong, some weak. Her star was at the center of this universe because she was the entry point. The PsyNet was spread across the world but if she wanted find a particular mind, all she had to do was think of it and it would appear in her field of vision, something like a link on the human-changeling Internet. However, similarly to a link, she had to have a starting point—knowledge of what the mind felt like, looked like.

There was her mother's blazing star—a cool, pure brilliance. Over there were some of the Psy who worked in the Duncan empire. But she didn't want to speak to anyone today. What she was interested in were the dark spaces between minds, the spaces where information floated, controlled into order by the NetMind.

She allowed her consciousness to flow out, letting data filter through her as if she were doing nothing more than catching up on the news. The NetMind brushed past her and kept going, not alive, not dead, but sentient in a way the world had never known. Still young, it was the librarian of this vast archive.

It would've been easy to become sidetracked by the endless streams of data, but despite her free-floating appearance, she was being very choosy, her senses tuned to a fine point. This was about murder . . . and the greatest lie that had ever been perpetuated by a race upon its own kind.

* * *

Lucas returned a few minutes after five to find Sascha and Tamsyn standing in the yard.

"The juveniles?" the healer asked the second he got within earshot.

Sascha looked up, face drawn. "Are they all right?"

"They were already on their way back by the time I tracked down their whereabouts."

"They heard?" Tamsyn's relief was obvious.

Lucas saw Sascha frown as she realized that something was going on beneath the surface. It had been inevitable. She was too smart to miss much. "They were stopped by a SnowDancer patrol and told to haul ass back home."

"Were your packmates injured?"

He shook his head. "They treated the kids as if they were wolf pups." That was very unusual. When they'd first decided on a truce, Hawke had put out the word that the leopards were allies, but letting them pass without trouble and doing what the soldiers had done was something entirely different. Lucas had been alpha too long not to understand the implied message, but it was an offer he couldn't accept without considerable thought. "They'll be home by nightfall."

Tammy smiled. "I'll leave you two to catch up."

He waited for Sascha to ask what was going on but she shook her head. "Don't trust me." She rubbed at her eyes. "My mind is vulnerable as long as I'm uplinked to the Net."

He had far more faith in her skills than she had in herself, he thought. "What did you find?" They'd discuss her connection to the PsyNet another time.

"Nothing." Fatigue dulled her tone.

He moved close enough to caress her cheek with his knuckles. "It exhausted you."

She didn't pull away and when his hand dropped from her face to entangle with one of her hands, she curled her fingers around his. He had to stifle the panther's satisfied growl.

"There was nothing useful in the public files."

"But?" He could read the confusion, the bewilderment in her face. Whatever she'd learned had shaken her enough that she was no longer able to maintain her usual mask.

Ebony-dark eyes looked up at him before glancing away. "I felt the shadows of violence," she whispered. "Like someone had left behind a mental print in certain places."

"Could you use it to track them?"

"No." She shook her head. "The print is faint. Most Psy wouldn't even be able to detect it."

But she had, he thought, because she *felt*. Instead of making her confront something he was convinced of but she was clearly hiding from, he used his free hand to tuck an errant strand of hair behind her ear. "So the info's been buried deep?"

She nodded. "I'm going to try a few other things tonight."

He smelled fear in the air. "Will it be dangerous?"

"I'm a cardinal Psy."

"That's not an answer."

"It's all I have to give you." She pulled her hand from his.

Some time later, Lucas sat in the huge kitchen of their largest safe house, talking to Tamsyn and two of the most dangerous males in his pack. Dorian had fought his inexplicable handicap by skilling himself in human martial arts to such an extent that he could take down a fully grown leopard with his bare hands. Nate was perhaps even more lethal—he had cubs to protect.

"How many here?" Lucas asked.

"Fourteen maternal females, twenty cubs, eight juveniles, and six other soldiers aside from you three," Tamsyn said from the counter, where she was organizing medical supplies.

He turned to Dorian. "Is everyone accounted for?"

"Yes. Over half the children are already on their way to safe harbor."

"Let's start moving the remaining cubs and the vulnerable females tomorrow morning." The soldier females like Rina would remain behind. Many of them were far more deadly than the beta males. "Continue sprinkling the elders in among the evacuees." Their old ones would ensure DarkRiver's traditions were passed down no matter what.

"Why wait till tomorrow?" Nate leaned forward.

"If we move en masse, we might tip off the Psy that something's up."

"What about Sascha?" Dorian asked. "Is she going to help us?"

Lucas looked at the sentinel, trying to gauge whether he was really as calm as he sounded. Mere days ago, he'd been willing to gut Sascha where she stood. "She's trying but we have to plan for the worst-case scenario."

"That she fails and Brenna's body turns up." Nate shoved a hand through hair starting to show faint signs of gray. "If that happens, whatever Sascha might've found becomes a moot point."

Tamsyn walked over and put a hand on her mate's shoulder in silent support.

"I don't want that." Dorian's tone was as sharp as a blade. "I want the killer's head. Ripping out random Psy throats isn't going to be enough."

"No," Lucas agreed.

"I spoke to Riley and Andrew." Dorian's eyes were suddenly full of such anguish that it was a physical ache. "I convinced them to stay away from the Psy and give us time to find their sister. They listened to me." Unspoken was the terrible reason why.

Lucas didn't say anything about Dorian going into SnowDancer territory on his own. "Then we have a few days' grace. Let's get our people to safety and hope Sascha can find us the clue we need." His worry for her vied with his need to protect his pack. But he knew the choice wasn't his—she wasn't a woman who'd ever take orders from him.

"You trust her?" Nate asked.

"Yes." It was no longer a question. He *knew*.

The sentinel stared at him and then put his hand on the table, palm up. "Then I'm with you. For Pack."

Tamsyn wrapped her arms around her mate's neck, her eyes shining with agreement.

Dorian placed his hand on Nate's, in the same position. "For Pack."

Lucas put his over theirs, palm down. As their hands closed over his, his closed over theirs. "For Pack."

Sascha's fingers were trembling. She slipped her left hand unobtrusively into her pocket and met Enrique's gaze across the desk that separated them. He'd been waiting for her. Stalking her. The computers had informed her that her presence was required in Nikita's office the second she'd walked into the Duncan building.

Terrified that someone had picked up on the true purpose of her Net search, she'd entered to find Enrique sitting in her mother's chair, with Nikita standing beside him. It was a testament to the strength of her shields that not an ounce of her fear had leaked through. However, the trembling in her fingers was refusing to abate.

"Nikita tells me you haven't had much progress with getting information on the changelings." It was the most subtle of chastisements. Enrique wasn't used to waiting for anything or anyone.

"Nothing substantial," Sascha answered. She'd asked Lucas this afternoon what she could safely tell the other cardinal. It had betrayed that she'd been meant to be a spy but she'd known he had to have guessed that already. Like she'd told Enrique, changelings weren't stupid. Lucas hadn't berated her, simply given her what she needed.

"I did discover that they have the ability to change forms from childhood." That wasn't a secret—most of the Psy had just never bothered to look.

Enrique leaned forward. "Anything is useful."

"The only other fact you might find of use is that changeling family groups aren't as isolated as we believe." This was also information in the public domain. "When young alphas leave an established pack to start their own, they usually maintain friendly ties with their parent group."

"This is excellent, Sascha. You're the first Psy who's been this close to changelings for over a hundred years. Your cooperation will help us to substantially revise out-dated information."

If she didn't know better, she'd have thought Enrique was trying to fashion himself her mentor. At least he was no longer trying to fool her into believing there might be a place for her in the Council ranks.

"If that's all, sir, I have some matters to attend to," she said, frighteningly aware that the trembling in her left hand had been joined by twinges in her right. If she didn't get out of here soon, her physical deterioration would become impossible to hide.

"I may call on you later tonight—in case you recall something new." Enrique stood as she did.

She looked at Nikita. "Of course, sir. Mother." As she headed out, her eye fell on her foot and she saw that in her confusion this morning, she'd put on the boot Julian had chewed. Fear clawed at her.

"Sascha."

Turning, she tugged at the lapel of her jacket in an effort to hide the subtle trembling of her right hand. "Yes?"

"Your work will bring credit to the Duncan name." Enrique's shoulder was almost touching Nikita's as they stood side by side.

"You're doing well." Nikita nodded.

Suddenly, Sascha wondered how much of what her mother had told her earlier was true. Was Enrique really an ally who had to be kept pacified, or were the two of them in league for a far darker purpose? "Thank you."

This time they let her leave without interruption. The second she was outside the office, she slid her other hand into a pants pocket too. She wanted to head for her apartment but knew she couldn't—Enrique was unlikely to change his mind about seeking her out later. And if he saw her like this, she was as good as dead.

Her hands were trembling uncontrollably and she could no longer ignore the muscle spasms in her legs. Something had gone very wrong in the time since she'd spoken to Lucas. Barely able to think through the panic riding her, she got on the elevator and somehow found her way to her car without running into anyone. Her vision was beginning to blur by that stage and she could feel her heartbeat stopping and starting in a ragged rhythm that scared her.

She almost stumbled as she tried to open the door to her car. It felt as if her body was shutting down, system by necessary system. Fear bloomed a metallic taste in her throat. Then, in a bizarre twist, the urge to laugh almost overwhelmed her. Bare seconds after she closed the door behind her and pushed the button to tint the windows, sadness crashed into her.

Crying uncontrollably, she knew she was on the verge

of a major breakdown. The tears were gone as fast as they'd come and her body was suddenly melting in the throes of sensual pleasure. Then bang! She was hit with a load of guilt, of haunting loss. It gripped her throat and she thought she'd choke. A second later, it passed.

Nothing took its place.

Sascha forced herself to think in that fleeting moment of clarity. First, she reinforced her psychic shields. They'd stay up until she died, hiding her from the PsyNet. From her own people. Sorrow mixed with fear and the combination sparked a connection between the splintered neurons of her brain.

Leaning forward, she programmed a destination into the computer, a destination where no Psy would ever go. Then she left a message for her mother explaining her absence. She couldn't chance anyone instigating a search for her. Who knew what condition they'd find her in?

As she steered the car out of the garage, her vision narrowed to a mere pinprick in each eye. She was almost numb with terror but she managed to get the vehicle out onto the streets, where the automatic navigation systems could take over. The moment they did, she hugged her arms around herself and curled up on the seat.

Laughter bubbled out of her but she wasn't happy. Neither was she sad. She was both and she was more. She was angry. Insane. Satisfied. Hungry. Hurt. Glad. Amused. Aroused. Her entire body started to shake, her heartbeat a jackhammer against her ribs.

"Lucas," she whispered, not even aware that she was speaking. His image flared against her darkening sight but was immediately swallowed by the riot of emotion that crashed into her mind at the speed of light, destroying her ability to think. Pain short-circuited her nerve endings.

Her body arched as she screamed within the insulated confines of the car. Her screams were still reverberating in the vehicle when she lost consciousness, the car skimming smoothly along the streets.

The safe house was tense. Only the cubs were sleeping. All the maternal females were hyperaware, the soldiers and sentinels pumped with adrenaline. Lucas hadn't heard from Sascha since she'd left that afternoon and he was worried. His beast was prowling the corners of his mind, urging him to track her down. Something had to have gone wrong in her second attempt to surf the PsyNet.

He was standing outside the back door considering how to reach Sascha without tipping anyone off, when a huge white wolf prowled out from the woods behind the isolated property. Beside him, Rina's entire body went tight. "Friend or foe?" she whispered.

He met the wolf's icy blue gaze. "Go inside."

"Lucas."

"Inside." It was an alpha command.

Rina went but he felt both her frustration and her fear for him. After making sure she was safe, he trailed the wolf into the woods. It streaked off ahead of him and he let it go, following more slowly until the house was hidden from view. A few seconds later, a man dressed in a pair of faded jeans walked back toward him.

Hawke was muscular and he was lethal. A predator to the core. His eyes were the same icy blue whether he was in wolf or human form, his hair a thick silver-gold that had nothing to do with age. It echoed his pelt. Of all the changelings Lucas knew, it was Hawke who resembled his beast the most in humanity.

"What is it?" It had to be something pretty spectacular for the SnowDancer alpha to have left his people when they were so jumpy. Not only that, he'd come into the heart of DarkRiver territory, to a safe house, crossing an unspoken boundary.

"We found something on our land." His voice was low. "Our first instinct was to kill but since your scent is all over her, I thought you might be interested."

"Sascha." Lucas stared at Hawke. "A cardinal Psy?"

"Yes."

"Where is she?" A cold sweat threatened to break out over his entire body. He hadn't felt such terror since he'd been a boy watching his parents die. In their current mood, the wolves were likely to gut her while he spoke with Hawke.

"Not far." Hawke wasn't moving. "Who is she?"

Hawke didn't need to know that Sascha had been the possible leak Lucas had warned him about. "The one who might get us into the PsyNet." His beast was shoving at the walls of his mind, desperate to get to her.

Hawke's eyes watched Lucas without blinking. "If I find out you've lied to me, cat, all bets are off."

Lucas allowed a growl to roll up from his throat. "Don't threaten me on my own lands, wolf." He knew Hawke was dangerous but so was he and the other alpha couldn't be allowed to forget that. "Where is she?"

"Follow me." Hawke loped off. After several minutes of solid running that would've winded even other changelings, they stopped by a car parked at the end of a hidden lane.

Even from this far away Lucas could smell her. "You left her alone?"

"Would you rather I left her with my pack?" Hawke opened the back passenger-side door. "She's damn lucky it was Indigo who spotted her—the others would've executed her on sight."

Lucas saw Sascha's slumped form on the seat and felt fury arc through him. "What did you do to her?" Reaching inside, he lifted her in his arms. Her body was limp but she was breathing. Relief almost broke him and it was then that the last pieces of understanding shoved through to his conscious mind. Of course Sascha smelled of him—she was *his*.

"Nothing. She was found like this in her car." Hawke closed the door. "We hacked open the onboard computer— it was programmed to head into your forests until the engine ran out of power. She must've miscalculated. It crossed the border from your lands into mine before stopping."

"Thank you."

"Don't thank me. I'll kill her same as any other Psy if Brenna dies." Hawke's eyes held a cold promise.

Lucas stepped back with Sascha in his arms, admitting to himself that his loyalty now belonged to her. "She's never betrayed us. We'll fight to keep her safe." It was a declaration of intent. Touch Sascha and DarkRiver would rise against the SnowDancers, destroying the peace they'd worked so hard to achieve.

Hawke went still. "Mated to a Psy, panther?"

Lucas had only now realized the truth—he wasn't about to share it with a wolf. "Don't move against the Psy without talking to us."

Hawke stared at him for a long, icy moment. "Don't let me down. Brenna's been gone over thirty-six hours already. The single reason I'm letting you run this is because you have a head start. If DarkRiver fails, we take over."

"DarkRiver doesn't have a habit of failing."

The second he walked into the house with Sascha in his arms, things went to hell in a handbasket. Rina hissed and her claws popped out. Nate moved protectively to cover Tamsyn, who clearly didn't want to be protected. Even a recently returned Kit jumped to his feet.

Strangely enough, it was Dorian who came forward.

"What happened? Is she injured?" His concern was as clear as it was unexpected.

"Did the Psy hurt her?" Tamsyn said from around Nate, who was refusing to let her pass. She kicked him but he didn't move. "Let me go, Nate. She's my friend."

"She was found unconscious in SnowDancer lands." Lucas took her to the huge wooden table in the center of the kitchen and laid her down.

"And she's alive?" Kit asked, incredulous. "Why didn't they tear her to pieces?"

"I told them she might just be our entry into the PsyNet." Lucas wondered if despite Nate and Dorian's vows mere hours ago, he was going to have to fight his own pack to protect her. It would rip him apart. His loyalty had always been to Pack. Only ever to Pack. Until now.

"What happened to her boot?" Nate frowned. "It looks like most of mine."

"That's because Julian decided it tasted good." Tamsyn finally succeeded in getting out from behind him but it was because Nate had let her go. The healer walked over to the table and placed her hands over Sascha's body before closing her eyes. She didn't open them for several minutes. "I've never had a Psy patient so I don't quite know how to read her patterns. From what I can see, she's in a deep, deep sleep. It's almost like a coma."

"Will she wake?" The panther's desperation was turning into a kind of numbed pain. If he'd only understood who she was to him earlier, she might not have been hurt.

"I don't know."

"Could this have been an attack against her by the Psy?" Lucas looked at her lying there and suddenly realized how fragile she was. The Psy were physically much more delicate than changelings but they made up for it with the powers of their mind. Take that away and they were the most breakable of beings.

"It's possible but she's simply too different for me to make an accurate judgment." Tamsyn pushed back the tendrils of hair escaping Sascha's braid and looked at Lucas. "Why would they attack her and leave her alive?"

"Why would a Psy program her car to go into the most dangerous territory in the state?"

No one had any answers.

CHAPTER 14

Since the beds in the house were taken, it was decided to leave Sascha on the table where Tamsyn and the sentinels could keep an eye on her throughout the night. They found some blankets and placed them under her, along with a pillow for her head. Lucas covered her with a soft throw after removing her boots.

"Let her sleep." Tamsyn checked Sascha's pulse. "If she doesn't stir by tomorrow, then . . . I don't know what we'll do. Do we call the Psy? What if they're the ones who did this?" She shook her head and leaned against Nate. "Would Sascha want them to see her like this?"

Lucas didn't answer. He should've been concentrating on the safety of his pack but his attention was on the female lying before him. She was in a world he couldn't enter, a woman he couldn't protect. Just like he hadn't been able to protect another woman he'd loved.

Even after all this time, he couldn't remember his mother's laughter without remembering her screams. Young and weak, he'd watched her fall in a fury of claws and teeth, watched the brilliant light of her life splutter out. Vengeance had cooled the blazing anger inside him but Lucas knew the scars were for always, markers to the lost lives of his healer mother and sentinel father. Those scars had hardened him, but today he'd discovered that they couldn't protect against everything.

Sascha had somehow become firmly lodged inside him, a vibrant presence in the heart of hearts where only a mate could go. Now her light, too, was flickering in a storm he couldn't block, danger he couldn't even see. His helplessness devastated him. He was furious at fate for giving him a mate he couldn't keep safe. Perhaps that was why he'd been willfully blind to a truth the panther had known from the start—he hadn't wanted to suffer as he'd done once before, hadn't wanted to bleed his heart's blood.

"You will wake up," he ordered in a harsh whisper, his voice holding the rough edge of a growl. He had no intention of losing what he'd barely found.

Hours passed. They watched. They waited. Birds began to wake but no Psy swooped down on them. It appeared the SnowDancers had kept their word and that whatever had happened to Sascha, it hadn't been because the Council had learned she was helping them.

Nervous mothers started to relax but the soldiers remained on high alert. Just as the sky began to lighten, Sascha stirred. Lucas ordered everyone but Nate and Tamsyn out of the kitchen.

Her eyes opened and she stared up at the ceiling for several seconds before sitting up. "How did I get here?"

"The SnowDancers found you in their territory and I brought you here." He wanted to bare his teeth and mark her. Now that he understood, he had no desire to fight the primitive urges of his beast.

"What? I was supposed to stop in your lands." She went to push back her hair and froze. "You undid my braid."

"Yes." The single word was full of possessiveness.

She looked bewildered and it was the first time he'd ever seen any Psy look that way. "May I have some water?"

Tamsyn was already holding out a glass. Taking it from her, Sascha drank it down. "Thank you."

"You're welcome." Tamsyn took the glass back and her eyes met Lucas's. "Maybe I should check on the others."

"Yes."

Nate frowned but heard the message. A minute later, Lucas was alone in the kitchen with Sascha. Leaning forward, he did something he'd been aching to do since she'd woken. He lifted her up into his arms and sat down in a chair with her cradled in his embrace.

She froze. "What are you doing?"

"Holding you." He breathed in the scent of her, tangling one hand in the curls at her waist. "I thought you were dying. *You can't die.*"

As if she understood the anguish he'd gone through, she placed a slender hand hesitantly against his chest and tucked her head under his chin. "I think I was in a deep sleep state. My body is now functioning normally."

"What happened?"

"I don't know."

"I can smell a lie." He felt her tremble in his arms and every protective urge he had surged to the surface. "Speak to me, darling."

"I'll help you," she whispered. "I'll help you find the killer, give you everything I have."

There was a depth of conviction in her voice that hadn't been there earlier. "Why?"

"I have to be at my apartment by noon," she said, in place of an answer. "That was when I told Mother I'd be back from a trip to see an out-of-town architect with you."

"We'll get you there." He squeezed her tight, feeding the need in him, the need for her. "Tell me what happened. I'm not going to stop asking."

"I lost control of my body," she said softly. "I've been having problems for months. They always passed without major incident, but this time, it was like my entire system short-circuited. I headed for your lands because I thought I'd be safe from Psy eyes there."

"You need to be seen by a doctor."

"No." She shook her head. "No one can know that I'm starting to crack."

"It sounds like a physical problem, not a mental one."

"It isn't. I . . . felt things, Lucas. Things that drove me to unconsciousness. This is coming from my mind." Her hand clenched against his chest. "If they find out . . ."

He wasn't happy with her not seeing a doctor but knew he had little choice if she'd made up her mind—he'd never had reason to track down a doctor who'd treat Psy patients in confidence. It was something he was going to make it his business to find out. "How're you feeling now?"

"Fine. But I want to shower."

"All right." He continued to hold her. Her hunger for touch was so strong, it tore at him. "Sascha, I know you're not like other Psy." It was time to get the truth out into the open.

Her hand slapped over his mouth. "Don't *ever* say that out loud. Ever. If you have any . . . care for me, don't even think it." Fear vibrated in her voice. "If anyone overhears, it'll mean my death."

He kissed the palm of her hand and watched the night sky of her eyes darken in confusion. She jerked the hand away. "You'll have to talk about it soon."

"I know." She sat up, pushing away from him. "I'm breaking apart, but before I do, I'll help you."

"Breaking apart?"

"Madness." Her voice was so soft, he almost didn't catch the word. "I'm going insane. There's no more hiding from it—I might as well go down in a blaze of glory." Her eyes met his. "Will you promise me one thing?"

"What do you want?"

"When the madness breaks me, I want you to kill me. Quickly, cleanly, without mercy."

His heart stopped. "No."

"You must," she said, her tone urgent. "If you don't, they'll turn me into the walking dead. Promise."

He had no intention of killing her. But he could prevaricate as well as the next feline. "I'll kill you if you give in to insanity." No matter what her fears, there was no hint of mental sickness in her. None. He would've smelled the acrid scent of decay where he only smelled life and hope.

Sascha walked into the living room after her shower and came face-to-face with a leopard male she had every reason to fear. "Hello, Dorian."

He stared at her with those eyes of such pure blue it was impossible to believe the darkness that lurked within. "You did something to me." It wasn't an accusation but a statement of fact. The anger she'd expected was there, but it was a simmering shadow deep inside, not directed at her.

"I don't know what I did, if I did anything," she told him, her heart in her throat. She'd convinced herself that she'd imagined the entire incident, that it had been part of the encroaching madness. But what if . . . ?

Dorian touched her cheek with his fingertips. Not used to touch from anyone but Lucas, she flinched. His eyes narrowed and he dropped the hand. "No touching?"

"I'm not changeling." She knew it sounded cold but

how else could she explain? "Something so easy for you is . . . difficult for me."

To her surprise, he reached out to cup her face between his palms as he looked down into her eyes. "I want to see inside you," he said. "I want to see if you have a heart, a soul."

"I wish you could, too." She wasn't so sure herself. Had it been burned out of her during conditioning?

"Dorian." Lucas's voice came from her back, startling her. There was a thread of warning in his tone but he didn't interrupt. Not that it mattered. His power was in the air he breathed, in the scent of his skin. He was alpha and she was starting to understand what that really meant.

"I wasn't hurting you, was I, Sascha?" Dorian dropped his hands.

She felt his need, his anguish, his guilt. Taking a step forward, she put a hesitant hand on his shoulder. "You only hurt yourself." The knot of his pain was tight and growing tighter every day. She worried it would explode if he didn't start letting it go. "Stop it, Dorian. Stop punishing yourself for a monster's crime."

His lashes swept down and when his eyes opened again, he let her see the bloody edge of the fury that drove him. "Not until he's dead. Then we'll talk about it."

Sascha let go of his shoulder and turned to look at Lucas, a silent plea in her eyes. He shook his head. No one could help Dorian until he was willing.

"Ready to go?" Lucas asked.

She smoothed a hand over her suit, which Tamsyn had ironed for her, and nodded. "Yes." Fear crawled in from the corners of her mind. Enrique had likely left his spies around. He'd find her the second she walked back in. "I need to have something to give them since I was supposedly with you overnight. They'll expect me to have learned at least one fact."

Lucas walked closer and though he wasn't touching her,

she felt the pressure of his presence. It was as if her body knew his, as if it was reaching out to embrace him though they'd only ever kissed once. Looking into that savage face with its slashing marker, she wondered whether he could see into the torment of her heart.

"Can you stall?" He touched his finger to her cheek, running it down her neck before sliding his hand over her arm to link their fingers together.

Dorian moved to stand in front of them. "What are you talking about?"

"I'm supposed to be a spy," Sascha said, frayed enough to be blunt. "Part of my mission was to gather as much firsthand information about changelings as I could, and feed it to my mother and Councilor Enrique."

"How do we know you haven't been doing exactly that?" demanded a female voice from the doorway.

Sascha met Rina's hostile gaze. "You don't. You have no way of tracking the PsyNet."

The blonde came to a standstill, beside Dorian. "No lies, Psy?" Her eyes flicked nervously to Lucas even as she spoke.

Lucas's fingers tightened on Sascha's hand. "Are you questioning my judgment, Rina?"

"Are you sure you have any?" Rina's voice held defiance. "You brought a Psy into our safe house and you knew she was a mole!"

"Be quiet, Rina." Dorian's voice was harsh.

The other woman clenched her fists. "What? I'm not allowed to ask questions anymore?"

Lucas let go of Sascha's hand. "There's a fine line between asking questions and going too far."

"I have a right to know what's going on." Rina's eyes were trained on Lucas, no longer interested in Sascha. They all knew who the most dangerous person in the room was and he was concentrating solely on Rina.

"No, you don't." There was no mercy in Lucas's response. "You were made a soldier earlier this year. Your rank is so low you shouldn't even be part of this conversation."

Sascha was stunned by the flatness of that declaration. She'd never heard Lucas sound so autocratic, almost cruel. He'd clearly hit Rina where it hurt—her pride. As she watched, Dorian moved to flank his alpha. Rina was left alone on the other side.

"Lucas," Rina began, her voice shaky, "why are you being like this?"

"Because you've shown me that being soft on you was a mistake." He gripped her chin between his fingertips. "You haven't earned the right to speak to me like you just did. Do you understand?"

Rina's eyes welled up. For the first time, Sascha realized how young the female was, something her boldness had masked. Feeling sorry for her, she tried to move forward, but Lucas's furious glance stopped her in midstep. He turned back to look at Rina.

"You're a low-rank soldier," he repeated. "Your job is to follow orders. Dorian, where is Rina supposed to be?"

"Standing watch on the left side of the house with Barker." Dorian's tone was considerably harsher than Lucas's, a whip of vibrating anger.

"So you can't even follow orders." Lucas let go of the girl's chin. "Do you think we posted you there for fun?"

Mute, Rina shook her head. Sascha could feel waves of humiliation and shock coming off the girl. That alone told her neither of the men had ever before spoken to her like this. Unable to remain silent any longer, she said, "I think that's enough."

"Stay out of this." The markings on Lucas's face stood out in stark relief. "This is Pack business."

Her hurt at the clear exclusion was beyond proportion. "Do you usually rule by humiliation?"

"This isn't the perfect, clean world of the Psy. Cruelty is sometimes necessary." He looked back at Rina. "This isn't the first time you've disobeyed a direct order. You want to be independent that much, I'll let you walk away from Dark-River."

Rina shook her head. "No." It was a whisper.

"Then do the job you're supposed to." He glanced at Dorian. "She's under your command as of now. Don't sleep with her like Barker did. It's obviously affected his ability to treat her like a soldier."

"Don't worry. Spoiled little girls aren't my type."

Sascha saw the girl's face turn bright red and her lower lip start to tremble. "Stop it, both of you."

"Dorian, take Rina and close the door behind you."

Without a word, the other two leopards left. Sascha waited until the door was closed to speak her mind. "How could you do that to her? Nothing she said was bad enough to merit that ritual shredding of her pride."

"She questioned my authority." He reached out to touch her face but she pulled away. His jaw tightened.

"No one has the right to do that? You're protected from scrutiny?"

"There are men and women in this pack who've bled for me, who've followed orders to walk into dangerous territory without a single question. *They've* earned the right to say what they think about me." Anger flickered in the green of his eyes. "Vaughn, Clay, Mercy, Tammy, Dorian, Nate, Desiree, Cian, Jamie, and even that idiot Barker are some of the ones who have the right to question my decisions. Rina doesn't."

"Why?" She was still angry for the put-down he'd delivered to the girl. It felt too much like what people had done to her—not good enough to be a cardinal, not powerful enough, not anything enough to matter. "Aren't you supposed to be a family?"

"Families have hierarchy." He pulled her into his embrace with such speed that she couldn't escape. She froze, wondering if this was a good time to show him that she had a few tricks he didn't know about. "The safety of the entire family depends upon that hierarchy being followed."

His words made her think. "If she questions you and you let it go, then she might not do as you ask when it's necessary." Against her cheek his heart beat strong and powerful, another indication of his physical strength.

Some of the anger in his voice lessened. "Yes. Today, she walked off her watch. That could've meant death for some of us if anyone unfriendly was out there." He dropped his chin on her hair. "The newly mature males and females who are strong and independent enough to make good soldiers are also the hardest to control. If I let them have their way, they'd cause chaos."

"You were so harsh." She gave in to her own need and slipped her arms around the heat of his body. For the first time in her life, she didn't have to worry about revealing herself. Lucas *knew*. The wonderful thing was, he didn't think her flaw a flaw at all.

"I've treated Rina gently in the past because I thought it would harm her to do otherwise. But she's old enough to handle real discipline. If she can't, then she's not soldier material and we'll drop her rank."

The simple practicality shook her. "I guess you're not so different from the Psy—only the strong survive."

"No, Sascha darling." He ran his hand over her hair. "We're very different."

The endearment felt like another caress. "How?"

"We don't kick out our weak," he said. "We don't destroy those who are different. It's true that soldiers have high rank, but Tammy's rank is even higher, as high as a sentinel's. In some circumstances, she has the power to give the orders."

Sascha hadn't known that. "Sentinels?"

"My seconds in command."

"Dorian, Nate . . . Clay?" she guessed. There was a sense of power around the three men that set them apart. Even Dorian's pain didn't dim his internal strength.

"Yes. You haven't met Vaughn or Mercy yet."

"Are there other ranks?"

"Yes. For example, certain of the maternal females also hold extremely high rank, because without them, the soldiers would have no family to protect."

"I see." If she'd been born part of this race, she might not have been driven to madness.

"Our laws might seem harsh but we're not inhuman. We treasure every unique individual. We make room for difference."

And that was the one thing the Psy would never do.

CHAPTER 15

Lucas watched Sascha walk out to the yard. She was creating her mask of Psy uniformity even as she moved. And though it enraged his beast to see her shutting him out, he knew he had to let her protect herself her way. It rubbed him raw that he couldn't keep her safe, yet he was also proud of the strength in the fragile body of his mate.

"Rina?" he asked Dorian, who was standing on the verandah.

"She'll be fine."

"I was serious, Dorian. Don't sleep with her." Like many of the leopard females who'd recently achieved maturity, Rina was very sexual. Her scent was compelling to males and he couldn't fault Barker for falling. "The second you do, she'll try leading you around by the balls."

Dorian raised a brow. "And I meant what I said. She's too young and too soft."

Lucas looked at his friend. "Sascha's worried about you." So was he. Dorian was growing harder and harder to

reach, in spite of the way he'd recovered after they'd found
out about Brenna's abduction.

"I can take care of myself."

"You're Pack—you don't have to face the loss alone.
Kylie was ours, too." She'd been like Rina—a little wild, a
little rebellious, and utterly loved. That was why Lucas had
put Rina under the sentinel's control. Dorian might be a
hard taskmaster but he'd never do her any real harm.

"I need to feel his blood run from my teeth." Dorian
looked out to where Sascha stood by the car. "She doesn't
understand our need for vengeance."

"I think she understands a lot more than we give her
credit for." He'd seen a depth of compassion in those night-
sky eyes that he'd never felt from any other being. "I'll be
back in a few hours."

"I'll keep them safe."

Lucas dropped Sascha off around the corner from her
apartment. "How are you going to explain the absence of
your car?"

"I'll say it was stolen when I parked it near a changeling
area. I didn't bother filing a report because the area is populated by DarkRiver leopards and I decided the car's value
wasn't worth antagonizing you."

"They'll believe that?"

"Most of the Psy consider changelings to be a lower
species, so yes. I'll have a new car within a few hours." Her
crisp tones held no hint of the woman who'd wrapped her
arms around him. "Is there any information I can share
without making you vulnerable?"

He tapped the wheel with his finger. "I can't know what
they might use the information for."

"I'll stall."

"Is that safe?"

"I don't expect to be around long enough for them to get impatient. A couple more days might irritate Enrique but I can't see it escalating into anything major."

He caught the edge of something in her voice that he couldn't quite understand, but she was already opening the door. "Stay safe, Sascha darling."

For a second the mists fell from her eyes and he saw the real woman. "I wish I'd been born in another time, another place. Then maybe I could've escaped fate . . . maybe I could've been your darling."

She was gone before he could speak. He watched her walk down the street and turn the corner. She never looked back.

Enrique hadn't left Sascha a message the night before. He hadn't needed to. Once again he was waiting for her in her mother's office.

"Sascha," Nikita said from behind her desk, a certain hardness in her eyes. "I hope the amount of time you're spending on this project will prove justified."

It was an odd thing to say, especially since Nikita had been the one who'd first suggested that Sascha oversee every detail. "It's going along very smoothly, Mother. I believe changelings appreciate the personal touch."

"Very true." Enrique turned from the window to face her. "You appear to have a good handle on how they think."

Careful, Sascha told herself. She couldn't let them get suspicious about just what she knew and wasn't telling. "I'm not sure the praise is warranted, Councilor. I'm merely using well-known Psy techniques for dealing with their species. As I said, they're extremely wary about sharing any information with me."

"Are you saying you still haven't penetrated their

defenses?" It was almost a taunt and it came from Nikita.

Sascha's suspicions about Nikita and Enrique being a team grew stronger. "It's difficult. The leopards use emotions as their social glue." They could hardly fault her for being what they'd made her.

Enrique stared at her, cardinal eyes unblinking. "Unfortunately that's true." He looked at Nikita. "Perhaps we're putting undue importance on Sascha's ability to gather information."

We're.

So they were in it together, whatever it was. Instead of defending her skills, she let them make up their minds without interruption, as if the sly insult mattered nothing. Of course the insult was only in her mind. To Enrique it had probably been nothing more than a summation of her ability.

"Thank you, Sascha," Nikita said. "It appears this venture won't allow us to collect as much factual data as we'd hoped."

Sascha said her good-byes and left the office, a sick feeling in the pit of her stomach. Throughout everything, she'd been trying to ignore the fact that her mother might be assisting a killer escape justice, inventing fairy tales where Nikita somehow remained free from the rest of the Council. Seeing her with Enrique had slapped her awake. The Council was divided in some matters but when it came to the outside world, they were a solid wall.

If one knew, they all knew.

It was equally obvious that Sascha had been meant to be a mole from the start. Nikita had been the one to pursue a deal other Psy avoided and she'd been the one who'd suggested Sascha's ongoing involvement. Her earlier acquiescence to Sascha's reporting to her, rather than to Enrique, had likely been nothing more than a power play. What Sascha didn't know was what they'd hoped to learn.

She tried not to let her turbulent emotions filter through to the surface as she waited for the elevator. Nikita was her mother, the only mother she had. Her heart didn't want to accept that she was involved in something as dirty as covering a murderer's tracks.

A whisper of sound reached her ears the second before a heavy hand fell on her shoulder. If she hadn't been warned, she might've jumped and given away the game. Sliding smoothly out from under that hand like any normal Psy, she turned to face Enrique. "Was there something further, sir?"

"I find you to be an . . . unusual young woman." The Councilor's gaze didn't leave hers for a second.

At the word "unusual," Sascha's heart jumped into her throat. "I'm extremely ordinary, sir. As you know, my cardinal powers never developed." She confessed the truth she hated because it might be the one thing that would get him uninterested in her.

"Perhaps I can help you develop them." He smiled that cold, meaningless smile. "I'm sure Nikita would permit it."

Sascha felt a hole opening up beneath her feet. "I've been tested many times."

The elevator doors parted in a smooth swish at her back. Enrique glanced over her shoulder and took a small step back, his smile fading. "Latham."

"Councilor." The older Psy walked out and around Sascha. "I was told you'd be here."

"If there's nothing else, sir . . . ?" Sascha stepped backward into the elevator.

"We'll continue this later." Enrique's expression was bland but there was something piercing about the quality of his gaze.

She fought the urge to collapse as the doors closed, paranoid that every public space was monitored. The Councilor had detected something about her, something that had set him on her trail. He'd be relentless until he'd discovered exactly what it was that had set off his senses and then he'd show her no mercy. She'd seen his star on the PsyNet. There was no emotion there, no feeling, no flaw. Nothing but the coldest intelligence she'd ever glimpsed.

He was the most perfect product of Silence.

Lucas didn't head back to the safe house after dropping off Sascha. He had to give the appearance of normality. No one could suspect that the changelings were quietly preparing for possible war.

Leaving his car in the parking lot outside the DarkRiver building, he headed inside to see Zara. She had some things she wanted to talk to him about and he spent a good hour with her. Since she wasn't leopard, she'd been kept out of the loop. They'd protect her if it came to that, but there was no reason to pull her into the mess. Not yet.

Because of that, she was continuing on with her designs, unaware the buildings might never be erected. On the other hand, if they averted disaster by finding Brenna alive, this deal could become vitally important.

Despite those thoughts, his mind was almost fully focused on Sascha. Just what was she planning? There'd been something very determined in her gaze as she'd stepped out of his car, and he wasn't sure he'd liked the look of it. She was a stubborn female.

That didn't mean she wasn't breakable.

He knew she was going to put herself in danger and it infuriated him that he had no right to stop her. The beast in him growled, wanting those rights. The human half didn't disagree. He'd had it with trying to be civilized. Sascha Duncan was about to be marked.

"Lucas?"

He looked up to find Clay at the door. Excusing himself

from Zara, he walked with the sentinel until they were out of earshot. "What is it?"

"We might have a lead. One of the wolf juveniles broke the rules and went goofing off downtown—he's swearing up and down that he smelled Brenna's scent near a building."

Lucas's hackles rose. "Strong?" Surely the serial couldn't be keeping Brenna in the city.

"No. Weak. Like it had come off someone who'd been near her." He handed over the address to Lucas. "Since the building was a Psy one, the kid freaked out."

Lucas somehow knew what the piece of paper was going to say. "The Duncan HQ." Sascha was in there right now. His instincts screamed at him to go and get her out but he knew that drawing that kind of attention to her might get her killed. "Did he catch anything else?"

Clay shook his head.

Lucas looked at the piece of paper again. "If we combine the residents and the day staff, that building handles close to five hundred people daily. Add in the visitors and narrowing things down is going to be almost impossible." To be so close without being close enough had to be killing the wolves. It was gnawing at him, and Brenna wasn't part of his pack. "What did Hawke say?"

"His people are trying to get into the building's mainframe—those Psy high-rises record the IDs of everyone who enters or exits." The sentinel raised a brow. "Sascha could get that info without any problems."

"No. She'd leave a wide-open trail leading back to her." Lucas screwed up the piece of paper in his hand. "Anyone done a physical check?"

"Hawke went in." Clay's eyes said it all. "He didn't find a scent but he believes the juvenile. Kid's not the kind to make things up."

Staring at the computer panel built into a desk they were standing near, Lucas made a decision. "I'll work the computers, too." It'd give him something to do instead of standing by helplessly while Sascha put her life on the line. "Tell Hawke I'll let him know if I get anything."

Clay left without questioning Lucas's plan. Both of them believed in knowing the enemy. In the case of the Psy, that meant knowing computer systems inside out. The psychic race depended upon computers for everything. It was one of their only physical weaknesses.

But before doing anything else, both man and beast needed to make sure Sascha was safe. He pulled out his phone and punched in her code.

Her cool tones came on the line at once. "Mr. Hunter. What can I do for you?"

"You know the details I asked you to look over? Perhaps you'd better hold off on them."

"Why? Didn't you say you needed an answer ASAP?"

"We've had indications that there might be a leak in your team. We'd like to change certain elements to ensure commercial security." He didn't want her risking herself if the killer was nearby.

"I assure you, our security is foolproof." She wasn't backing down. "Please don't worry about your designs."

"It's in my nature to worry. Be careful." He wanted to reach through the phone and drag her to safety, wanted to keep her within the panther's protective embrace.

"Always."

He swore as the phone clicked off. Attempting to hack into the Duncan mainframe didn't make him forget what Sascha was doing, but it helped keep his mind busy. Unfortunately, he had a feeling that that was precisely what this was—busywork.

The answers to their questions weren't in any normal computer but in the inaccessible vaults of the PsyNet.

* * *

Sascha wondered if she'd understood Lucas correctly. Had he been warning her to back off because the killer might be in the Duncan building? It should've scared her but it didn't. Where she was going, physical distance mattered little and death could come far more swiftly than a murderer's slicing blade.

For the first time in her life, she was going to try to hack the PsyNet, quite possibly the biggest information archive in the world. Every Psy automatically linked into the PsyNet at the moment of birth. There was no way to escape it. However, because the Psy were viciously practical businesspeople, they were all taught how to put up firewalls to hold off unwanted intrusions.

The firewalls kept the gigantic PsyNet at bay by isolating the Psy's mind. However, all Psy fed data into the Net and some chose to live with complete openness to it. These individuals were considered extreme. It wasn't practical or efficient to live with information constantly filtering into your mind.

By the same token, tough firewalls were considered a sign of Psy strength. No one had raised a brow when, as a child, Sascha had begun building the strongest firewalls anyone had ever seen. As she'd grown, her firewalls had become ever more sophisticated.

It was the one thing she'd always excelled at, as if shielding skills had been imprinted upon her before birth. Other Psy had even come to her for training. She'd taught them many things but had kept back a few secrets, which, if discovered, might get her hauled before the Psy Council.

Though privacy was allowed and even encouraged, the NetMind was always aware of each and every individual in the Net. If a mind dropped out, the Psy was physically located and, in 100 percent of cases, was found to have either died or been damaged so badly that their mind had withdrawn as a prelude to death. Those were the only acceptable ways to leave.

Sascha hadn't figured out any other way. But she had discovered how to mask her presence, how to move within the Net without alerting the NetMind. As a child she'd played the mental game instinctively—perhaps she'd already known that one day she'd need to hide or lose her life. Back then she'd gone nowhere a child wouldn't go, so even if she'd been caught, no one would've thought to punish her. They would've simply put it down to a developing cardinal's somewhat erratic powers.

The older she'd grown, the better she'd become at "ghosting." The trick involved shadowing another mind, thereby gaining entrance to the mental rooms of information the shadowed mind had clearance for. No hacking of the shadowed mind was required.

Ever since she'd realized she was close to the edge, she'd been shadowing people who might have access to the sealed records of the Center. It had been an attempt to fight the nightmare she'd glimpsed in her childhood. She'd wanted to prove to herself that her child's mind had exaggerated the awfulness of the place. What she'd discovered had so horrified her, she'd started to look for minds who might know how to escape the Net and survive.

And had found nothing.

Tonight she was going to try to ghost a Council member. If she was found out, it would mean an automatic death sentence. The trick wasn't going to be easy, notwithstanding the fact that not all of the Councilors were cardinals.

Cardinals were often so cerebral, they cared nothing for politics. Conversely, some noncardinal Psy had extraordinary defensive and attacking qualities that made them as dangerous as the most highly trained cardinals. Every one of the Councillors fell into the lethal category.

Taking a deep breath, she put her communication console on mute and sat down cross-legged on her bed. Loneliness enclosed her in silence. After spending so much time with changelings, she felt lost at the absence of touch, of laughter, of contact.

She missed Lucas Hunter most of all.

Something flickered in her mind and she felt the brush of fur against her cheek, the whisper of trees in her mind, the scent of the wind in her nostrils. A second later, the moment was gone. Had it been a sensory memory or . . . ?

She shook her head. She couldn't afford to be distracted. Her panther was relying on her. They all were. A woman's life hung in the balance . . . and she was no longer so sure about the innate goodness of her people.

Closing her eyes, she went into her mind. The first thing she did was slip around her own firewall, leaving a vague ghost of her presence inside to fool the NetMind as to the current location of her consciousness. It was a simple ruse that had taken years to perfect.

She stood hidden in the shadow of her own mind. Lights stretched endlessly in every direction that she could see. Some were barely visible, marking the presence of lesser Psy, while others blazed so brightly they were miniature suns. The cardinals. She looked at her own light and wondered at its difference.

The variation had developed around puberty and she'd been good enough at multilayered shielding by then to hide it under a false shell. To the PsyNet, her star blazed the same as the other cardinals'. She alone knew what it really looked like—a rainbow of sparks that shot joyfully in every direction and then coalesced back into her mind. If she'd allowed it to spark without barriers, it would've infected the entire Net by now.

Turning away from the hidden beauty of her mind, she looked for her targets.

Nikita's star was easy to find, bound as she was to Sascha by lines of energy that told the story of their familial ties. Sascha had no intention of ghosting her mother. Not only was Nikita's mind too attuned to hers, she didn't think she could handle finding out that her mother was in league with those protecting a killer.

It was something no child should have to bear.

There were six other Councilors. An odd number to ensure that there would never be a hung vote. Marshall Hyde was the most cold-blooded man she'd ever met, his PsyNet star a pinwheel of cutting blades. He was a cardinal and had had over sixty years to refine his talent.

Tatiana Rika-Smythe's star was the softest light. She tested at 8.7 on the Gradient but that was deceptive. No one took a seat on the Council at such a young age without being ruthless in the way the Psy had patented.

Then there was Enrique. Deep in her soul, she shivered. There had been a personal touch to his recent interactions with her that couldn't be explained away by what she suspected him of being engaged in with Nikita. She wouldn't put it past him to lay a trap for her. His was one mind she wasn't going near.

Ming LeBon was another cardinal. Though less experienced than Marshall, he, too, had had almost thirty years over Sascha to hone his skills. It was rumored that Ming's particular specialty was mental combat.

Shoshanna and Henry Scott were both around 9.5 on the Gradient. The elegant and graceful Shoshanna was the public face of the Council, the one who appeared on broadcasts to the media and in newspaper articles. She looked fragile and harmless but could be as lethal as a viper.

Henry was her husband. They'd decided on a human-style marriage rather than a Psy reproduction contract in order to make themselves seem more sympathetic to the non-Psy news media. This wasn't common knowledge.

Nikita had told Sascha back when she'd still been grooming her child for a position in the Council networks, before they'd both accepted that Sascha's flaw was never going to fix itself.

Henry was her target. Though extremely powerful in his own right, he was clearly the beta member of the Shoshanna-Henry pairing. As such, he was the only Councilor who showed any submissive qualities. He was also easy to find on the Net, even if you'd never come into contact with him and had no idea of his mental signature.

It was part of the Councilors' jobs to be accessible to the populace they represented. In truth, the path to them was a minefield of assistants and guards. This would take work. Sascha began step-shadowing.

CHAPTER 16

She waited for a mind heading in the right direction to pass by—she couldn't move out herself or the NetMind would detect the anomaly of her presence in two places at once. When someone came close enough, she quickly took care of their simple alarms and merged into the edges of their consciousness, a shadow so fine, no one had ever detected her. She broke no moral law, exerted no mental influence. Her host was merely a vehicle to get her where she needed to go. From there, it was a game of luck and logic.

She shadowed one mind until it reached another that had permission to go further. It took her almost two hours to make it to Henry. Sticking to the consciousness of the assistant who'd brought her into the office, she began to gently circle around the edges of Henry's firewall, looking for traps and alarms.

Within two minutes she'd found three, all of which she could neutralize while ghosting. A double check confirmed her initial findings. Henry was one of the oldest members of the Council and his firewall reflected his complacency.

Sliding from the assistant when the man's consciousness passed close to Henry's, she merged into the Councilor's light, a speck of dirt so minute, it was impossible to see. It was fortunate for her that unlike most Psy, a portion of a Councilor's consciousness was always active on the Net, because of their need to keep up with the massive inflow of data.

From now on, she would go everywhere Henry ventured. If she was unlucky, he wouldn't leave his mental office. But he could just as well lead her into the sealed records of the Council chambers. The chambers existed solely on the PsyNet because the Council was scattered around the world. Enrique, Nikita, and Tatiana being in such close proximity had been sheer chance.

Henry suddenly moved. The acrid taste of fear bloomed on her tongue but it passed when he spent the next two hours sweeping through the part of the PsyNet that stored their race's history. She had no idea what he was looking for. This should've been a job for his assistants. Just as she was getting completely frustrated, she found him at the entrance to a vault she'd never known existed.

Inside were millions of memories and thoughts. Henry headed for his family's section of the vault. Temptation beckoned. Sascha knew it was a risk but this was a chance she couldn't miss—she'd always been told that her family's history had been corrupted by a rogue energy surge.

What if that, too, had been a lie?

Thankful that Henry had allowed his consciousness to spread in the vault, she drifted along the waves of his mind, riding swells until she reached the part that screamed with the Psy signature of her family.

Since she didn't know how long she'd be in here, she simply streamed through, siphoning data into her shadow-mind. She'd release and examine it once she was back behind the privacy of her own firewalls.

Unexpected movement.

Henry was leaving. She'd taken advantage of his absorption in his task to venture to the furthest edge of his consciousness. Now it was snapping back into a tight coil and if she didn't keep up, she'd be trapped here. Cut off from her mind for too long, her body would go into a coma from which she'd never recover.

Fear gnawed at the stomach of the woman on the bed but in the PsyNet, there was only a mind as calm as a pond. She barely managed to make it back before Henry went through the doors. After exiting, he charted a clear path to the darkest section of the Net, access to which was highly restricted. What she'd never expected as they cleared that section was the even darker core that lay within.

The Council chambers.

This was where it got tricky. If the other members were there, they might pick up what Henry hadn't. Nikita was the most dangerous. In the same manner that Sascha had recognized her family's signature in the vault, her mother would recognize hers if even the faintest hint of her mind emerged from the shadow of Henry's psyche.

However, Nikita had mentioned nothing about a meeting when they'd spoken. Sascha would've never instigated a ghosting otherwise. She told herself not to panic. Then they were through the final checkpoint and in the innermost core. Six other minds flared bright around them.

The Council was in session.

Taking desperate measures, Sascha forced herself to go under further than she'd ever before done, merging her consciousness with the outer layer of Henry's on a molecular level. Prolonging such a merge could mean the destruction of her psyche but there was no other option.

"Why are we here?" Crisp and young, the voice had to belong to Tatiana.

Though she was outside Henry's firewall and couldn't

hear what he was thinking, she *could* hear what he heard—the others' thoughts all had to pass through his firewall and, by extension, through her, to reach his mind. That was the genius of ghosting.

"Yes," Nikita said, "I had to pull out of something extremely important without notice."

"He's taken another changeling girl." Marshall's razor blade of a mind.

Buried so deep that she was no longer a person, Sascha recorded the conversation without processing it. Reaction was her enemy here.

"When?" Tatiana.

"Two and a half days ago. We did too good a job of telling our subordinates to bury any further cases—they didn't think we'd be interested in keeping up to date." Marshall's tone didn't change. "I stumbled onto the information during a conversation with one of my guards."

"This can't be allowed to continue." Nikita. "In spite of what some of you insist on thinking, the changelings aren't without power. DarkRiver hasn't forgotten their lost female—I wouldn't be surprised if they're already hunting. We'd better hope they don't grow impatient and decide one of us will do in lieu."

If Sascha had allowed herself to think, she might've been startled, having been unaware that Nikita had such a clear grasp of a truth most Psy ignored.

"What pack was it this time?" Enrique.

"The SnowDancers." Marshall.

"It's a wonder hundreds of us aren't already dead." Nikita. "Those wolves are vicious."

"They're only changelings." Ming's cool menace. "What can they do?"

"Don't be stupid." Nikita. "They know we have to get close to influence them—close enough to be vulnerable to their weaponry. The SnowDancers took out five Psy last year. The Net was never alerted that they were in any danger. They simply winked out of existence one after the other. Their bodies have never been found."

"Why didn't we make an example of them?" Henry.

"The Psy who got taken out were acting foolishly. They went alone into restricted territory open only to the wolves." Marshall's cold darkness. "We don't support fools."

"There's no mistake this killer is Psy?" Nikita.

"The NetMind has picked up traces of certain pathological traits within the patterns of a Psy mind. The traits peak during the week that he holds the women." Marshall. "There's been no success in tracking him."

"Only a very powerful psychic could hide himself so well." Nikita. "It has to be a cardinal or someone close to cardinal level, someone who has access to the highest levels of the PsyNet and can nudge the NetMind into looking the other way occasionally. Otherwise it would've picked up more than traces."

"We can't risk exposure." Tatiana. "He must be contained before he gives himself away."

"I agree. It's the only way to uphold the integrity of the PsyNet." Shoshanna. "What if he's a high-level Psy who's necessary to the functioning of the Net? We need to maintain the ratio of cardinal anchors. Too many of them have proven vulnerable to this particular side effect."

"If required, we leash him and keep him satisfied. We bring him the women he needs, women who won't be missed, women *not* from aggressive packs like DarkRiver or SnowDancer. And we ensure he's never discovered." Marshall. "As of now, we all devote a quarter of our minds to monitoring the NetMind—the second it picks up any hint of the applicable pathology, we track it back to him."

Applicable pathology? Something, which had once had a separate consciousness as a cardinal named Sascha, worried over the strange word choice.

"How do you know he won't choose to go underground until we give up?" Nikita. "If he's that good at hiding his tracks, he's going to be aware we're keeping watch."

"He hasn't killed the newest girl yet. I don't think he'll be able to stop himself from doing so." Marshall. "All our research on serial killing in the Psy populace supports the compulsion theory."

"How many others are operating at present?" Nikita. "The last data I received said fifty."

"Those are all the ones we're aware of. None are as much of a concern as our unknown—they aren't preying on high-visibility victims. Most are targeting other Psy, which makes our job considerably easier."

"What's being done about them?" Henry.

"They're being set up to be sentenced to rehabilitation for unrelated reasons. The ones we can't afford to lose are being provided for. Every one of them will be taken care of without alerting the PsyNet."

"But there will always be more."

"That is the nature of the Psy."

The meeting concluded without further discussion. Henry made his way back through the door and the outer core, Shoshanna by his side. They didn't speak until they were inside the walled rooms of their private vault.

"What do you think?" Henry asked.

"It's a reasonable outcome. We can take care of this matter without anyone knowing."

"The changelings are suspicious."

"Suspicion is worthless without proof. Nobody has uncovered even a single Psy serial killer since the first generation of Silence. We know how to keep our secrets." Shoshanna's energy flared. "Where were you?"

"In the history archives."

"Tagging?"

"Yes. You were right again—the indicators are present

in several members of the extended family, but it's the youngest boy who might become a cause for concern."

"Let's discuss it tonight." She left without a backward look.

Henry checked his calendar and began the return journey to the archives.

The part of him that was Sascha rose sluggishly to the surface, prodded awake by the recall of her earlier near-trapping in the vault. It took her precious seconds to realize her own consciousness. She'd come perilously close to losing herself in Henry. Detaching from him before he reached the vault was imperative but she had to separate as softly as she'd merged.

So she waited. They were almost to the vault when they passed a guard with a sloppy alarm system. She flowed from Henry to the guard's shadow. When the man completed his circular route and reached the outer level of the restricted zone, she flowed onto another guard. Step-shadowing her way back to her own mind took over three hours in real time because she was tired, exhausted by the extended immersion in another's consciousness.

At long last, she slipped back around her firewall and released the gathered information into her mind. It was like letting go of a data bomb loaded with shrapnel. Her eyes opened with a snap and she collapsed backward on the bed, her heart racing at a thousand beats per second. There was too much new information in her mind. She let it process while she lay there staring at the ceiling and thinking she was starving.

A look at her watch confirmed it was well past dinnertime. Groaning, she went to the console and checked for messages. There was one from Lucas. He looked very much like the predator he was, the lines on his face vivid against the golden heat of his skin. "Ms. Duncan. If you could spare some time this evening I'd like to discuss a matter to do with the design change. I'll be at our earlier meeting place." The message ended.

No one eavesdropping would've given it a second thought. Businesspeople left vague messages like that all the time. Only she saw the worry in those cat-green eyes, only she knew he'd called after she hadn't gotten back in touch within a reasonable amount of time, only she ached to go to him.

A glance in the mirror showed her appearance to be completely acceptable. No one looking at her would've guessed at the turmoil inside. Decision made, she went to the console to return the call but changed her mind. No use alerting anyone who was watching her as to her whereabouts. Her heart twisted at the thought of Lucas worrying but she knew he'd have told her to do exactly what she was doing.

She changed out of the relaxed clothing she'd been wearing and into a severe black pantsuit and white shirt. It was the uniform of the Psy and she couldn't afford to stand out. So armed, she walked out. And almost ran face-first into Enrique. If she hadn't spent a lifetime keeping secrets, the shock might've made her shell crack.

"Councilor. How can I help you?" She closed the door behind her. It was a subtle hint.

His dark eyes ran over her clothing. "A late meeting?"

"Yes." Meetings after nine weren't anything unusual.

"I'd like to talk to you. Now would be a good time." It was an order couched as a request.

"Mother wouldn't take it kindly if I missed this engagement." No matter how close Nikita and Enrique were over Council matters, Sascha's mother had no allies for whom she'd sacrifice money and power.

The white stars in his eyes flickered in a way she found disturbing. "Don't be too quick to turn down an offer of advancement."

She'd thought he'd given up holding out that lure to her. How stupid did he think she was? "What are you offering?" she asked instead of laughing in his face.

"That's what I want to discuss. We can do it in private in your quarters."

The hairs on her arms rose. It wasn't unknown for older Psy to poach talent from other families, but there was something fundamentally wrong about Enrique's offer. He was too eager to get her alone. And she was terrified she knew the reason why. "As I said, Councilor, I must decline." She glanced at her watch. "I need to be leaving if I'm to be on time."

He inclined his head and moved out of her way. "You'd do well to make time for me, Sascha. Most young cardinals would die to be in your position."

Death was exactly what she was afraid he was offering. "Sir." She kept her tone formal but the single word was a good-bye. She could feel his eyes on her back the entire length of the corridor. He knew something; he could obviously smell the flaw in her and was determined to expose it.

What she couldn't understand was why he was giving her so much attention at a time when the Council was concentrating on finding out the serial's identity. Was it possible he suspected her of being in league with the changelings?

As she entered the elevator and turned to face the closing doors, she saw him staring back at her across the distance. Belatedly, she remembered that Enrique was considered the best territorial strategician in the PsyNet.

He was a master at setting traps.

Lucas had almost scored grooves in the floor with his prowling. It was past ten at night—where was Sascha? If anyone had dared to harm her, he'd gut them with his bare claws. Someone moved behind him. "What is it, Nate?"

"Everyone's safe. Cubs, maternal females, and the elderly or injured have all been moved. I've told the sentinels, soldiers, and the older juveniles that the next alert means war."

Lucas had given that order after Sascha had woken from her unconscious state. "What's the mood of the pack?"

"No one's comfortable with a Psy being privy to our safe house but they'll back you whatever you decide." He put one hand on Lucas's shoulder. "You've earned their loyalty. They'll follow you into hell if you ask it."

Lucas turned and looked into the other man's face. "That's what I'm afraid of." At that moment, every instinct he had flared bright red. "She's here." Pushing past Nate, he ran out the back door just as Sascha's car came to a smooth stop behind the house.

She exited, looking as cold as a statue. Except he'd seen inside that stone mask. Aware that this area was safe from prying eyes, he went to her and hauled her into his arms. She stiffened and then hesitantly returned the hug. "I was very careful. No one followed me here."

"We can talk inside." He pulled away to tug her into the house—where he and his pack could keep her safe.

Dorian and Kit had run into the room as he'd exited and now they stood there with Tamsyn and Nate. Despite having seen Sascha before, all the males seemed shocked at the embrace they'd witnessed. Ignoring them for now, Lucas sat Sascha down in a chair, able to feel her tiredness.

To his surprise, she looked around for Tamsyn. "I'm sorry but I'm very hungry."

The healer grinned. "Then you've come to the right place. Let me get you something."

"Thank you." She turned back to him.

He'd taken a chair to her left and moved it so it faced her. "Dorian. Kit." The command was apparent. Following

Nate's lead, they took sentinel positions around the room. "Who's on the outside?"

"Clay, Mercy, and Barker. Rina and Vaughn are patrolling the outer perimeter." Now that the other safe houses were empty, the sentinels had gathered here.

"Kit. Go and replace Mercy."

The juvenile looked like he wanted to argue but he must've seen the implacability in Lucas's eyes. Without a word, he left. A minute later, Mercy entered and took his position. This was a matter for adults, not children, and no matter how grown up he looked, Kit was still considered a cub. He'd been allowed to stay behind but would never be asked to fight except as a last resort.

Taking Sascha's hand in his, he met her eyes. "Eat first."

Tamsyn put a plate of sandwiches in front of her. She refused to let go of his hand as she picked them up one by one and demolished them. The chocolate cookies went the same way, as did the glass of milk. There was such bliss on her face after each bite that he wondered what she'd do when he lavished real pleasure on her, something he had every intention of doing.

"More?" Tamsyn asked, clearing away the dishes.

"No. Thank you. I . . . like your food." Coming from a Psy, it was a wild declaration.

"My kitchen is always open."

Sascha looked like she wanted to smile but didn't quite know how to pull it off. "I hacked the PsyNet."

Everyone went silent.

"Tell us what that means, Sascha." His heart was breaking at the pain he could feel coming off her. The waves of sorrow were so deep, he wondered that they didn't kill her.

"I could never talk about it before," she said, reminding him of his earlier attempts to get her to share information.

"But now I can. I wonder if that means my mind's deteriorated so much that the blocks no longer hold."

"You just broke into the most secure information network in the world—your mind is fine." He frowned when she didn't seem to hear him.

"The PsyNet is like your Internet, except it's made up of minds, not computers," she said, instead of responding. "Most of it is public but there are hidden nodes of classified information. I obtained access to those restricted parts." It sounded so cool and practical but he knew it had to have been anything but.

"What would've happened if you'd been found?"

She met his eyes. "I would've been executed."

"You didn't tell us that." He was furious with her, so angry that he wanted to haul her to his lair and let the primitive in him take over. A growl threatened at the back of his throat.

"I didn't think it was relevant." She sounded so Psy that no one who hadn't been watching her eyes would've guessed at the depth of fear she must've experienced. "I learned more than we could've hoped for."

CHAPTER 17

"Who is it?" He hadn't forgotten her recklessness. They'd discuss it privately. And he'd teach his Psy that when it came to Pack, one member's life was very much relevant.

"They don't know the identity of the killer."

Dorian made a sound of anguish. A flare of Psy energy lit up Lucas's senses and when it flared back down, Dorian was calmer but no less frustrated.

"They've set a trap." She tightened her hand. "I could link into the PsyNet and shadow them until they know."

He narrowed his eyes. "How long?"

"Not very—the trap will spring the second he kills."

"That could take days. Can you survive being buried that long?" He was starting to get a glimmer of how the Net worked. "You're exhausted from what you did today and that was what—simply for a few hours?"

She flinched. "I'm strong enough. I'm a cardinal."

There was something broken about her statement but he

knew this wasn't the place to pursue it. He'd gentle the truth out of her in private.

"If we don't find her before she dies, the SnowDancers won't accept only the killer's blood in recompense." Dorian was staring at the back of Sascha's head as if he wanted to see through to her mind.

"I know." Sascha nodded. "I have an idea to expedite the process."

Lucas narrowed his eyes. "What?"

"The killer is a predator with very fixed needs—his women are all of a certain type and, according to the Council's research, he's compulsive. I think if we give him a wide-open target, he won't be able to resist going after it. And the trap will spring without Brenna's death."

"How do we set the trap when we don't know where he is?" Nate asked.

Lucas knew the answer. "You're going to be the bait, aren't you? The trap is going to be on the PsyNet."

"I'm not changeling but I'm flawed in a way that might negate that handicap. My mind appears to be able to . . . understand yours. We can use that to ensure the killer is attracted to me." Her voice remained strong though her hand was trembling. "With your help, I'll teach my mind to mimic changeling thought patterns. Once I'm in the Net, I'll drop my shields enough that he picks up the altered patterns."

"What happens next?"

"Because of his compulsive nature, I'm sure he'll attack me on the psychic plane, try to incapacitate me mentally so as to get a free pass to my physical body. Once I know who it is, I'll tell you."

"Then you'll fight for your life." His jaw was tight, his hand crushing hers.

"That's nonnegotiable," she whispered. "It's becoming almost impossible for me to hide myself in any case—you saw what the pressure did to me yesterday. I'd rather let the shields down in a controlled situation than chance having them collapse without warning."

"How are you going to make sure it's the killer who finds you first and not one of the others?" Tamsyn asked when Lucas remained silent. He knew the healer understood exactly what this was doing to him.

"I'll need a distraction big enough to draw the attention of most of the PsyNet. I haven't quite figured out how to do that yet but I'll think of something, even if it means setting off a psychic bomb of sorts." She took a deep breath and looked up.

"As well as giving me access to thought patterns I can mimic—ideally those of a female who fits the victim profile—one of you will have to allow me far enough into your mind that I can cloak myself in your . . . psychic scent. That person will also have to permit a psychic link during the entire plan's execution.

"The killer is attracted to changelings and, unlike the rest of the Psy, he'll recognize the presence of the scent before anyone else, especially if they're distracted by something else."

"Like waving fresh blood at a shark," Mercy commented from her position by the back door.

"Yes. There's something else." Sascha's eyes bled to darkness as Lucas watched and the panther knew she was hurting. It threatened to break him that he couldn't take away her pain. "Ever since Silence was instituted, the Psy have been proud of their lack of violence."

"Silence?" Tamsyn asked.

"A program to decondition young Psy to emotion. If we feel no rage, no jealousy, no love, then we won't kill. At least that was the rationale."

"Oh, my God," Tamsyn said. "They purposefully crippled their children."

"And they didn't solve the problem. According to what I learned today, there are fifty known serial killers circulating among the Psy population. It seems the Council has a policy of quietly taking care of them."

"Death?" Nate asked.

"Rehabilitation. It's death of the mind, completely wiping out the individual and most of the higher mental functions." Her eyes pleaded with Lucas to remember the promise he'd made to her. "But they're not caging all of them. Some of the serials are considered integral to the functioning of the PsyNet."

"I don't think I want to know," Tamsyn whispered.

"They provide victims for the indispensable ones, hide their trails, and ensure their kills don't make waves either in the PsyNet or the human-changeling world."

Lucas could see her fighting the urge to throw up. His beast wanted to pick her up and take her to safe harbor but her eyes said she hadn't finished. He was astounded by her strength—how could that fragile body hold so much courage, so much heart?

Dorian spit out a curse. "When they gave up their emotions, they gave up their humanity."

Sascha looked at the angry leopard. "I agree. I'm sorry your sister was stolen from you. If I could reverse your pain, I would. But I can't. All I can do is try to save another life."

Dorian's response surprised everyone in the room. "You're different, Sascha. I'm not so angry that I can't see the truth. You *feel*."

Sascha's laugh was so bittersweet, it ruffled Lucas's fur the wrong way. "My entire life, I've been terrified of those words. I always believed it would be one of the Council who discovered me. I never thought of it as a good thing . . . until I met you." She was looking at Lucas with eyes of ebony night, not a star in sight.

"Since I don't know when they'll realize my flaw and attempt to take me in, I'll need to get the information to you as soon as I get it. That's why I need a constant link to one of you. What I know, you'll know. You'll be cut free the second I drop out of the Net."

He knew she expected to be killed by the Council. "You're under our protection." The panther was so close to the surface his voice had dropped several octaves.

Nate, Dorian, Mercy, and Tamsyn voiced their agreement. Sascha had just earned the respect of some of the toughest leopards in DarkRiver. Once she was Pack, the others would follow their lead. And Lucas had no doubt that Sascha was going to become part of his pack.

Her face looked incredibly sad for a second. "No one escapes from the PsyNet." She glanced at the leopards around the room. "Thank you for showing me more life in a few days than I ever expected to experience. I won't go down easy—I want to *live*."

Lucas refused to let her say good-bye. "Who says no one ever escapes from the PsyNet? Has anybody ever tried?"

Her eyes widened. "No."

He shook his head. "Not as far as you know. If they're keeping quiet about serial killers, don't you think they'd bury the loss of any Psy out of the Net?"

"That won't work with me. I'm too visible. I couldn't disappear even if there was a way out. I'd have to change my identity and I can't." She pointed to her eyes. "No contact lenses made can hide these."

"I won't let them erase you. In any way." No one took one of Lucas's people without consequences. Kylie's death had never been forgotten and until vengeance was taken, it would remain a burning pain in his soul.

And his woman? If anyone so much as bruised her, he'd destroy them. He reached out to rub at the dark circles under her eyes. "You're exhausted. Even if we let you run this insane plan, you can't do it now."

"I'm afraid you're right. We still have a few days. This is the third night since he took Brenna." Her tone held the knowledge of the horror the SnowDancer had to be going through. "I wish I could recover quicker, but shadowing Henry drained me."

"Tamsyn?" He glanced at the healer.

"I've got her. Come on, honey." She touched Sascha's shoulder. "I'll make you up a room and find you something comfortable to sleep in."

Sascha stood and he felt the sharp rush of her disappointment. The vain cat in him preened, but the protective, possessive panther silently promised he'd make it up to her.

"Thank you. I should be fine by morning. Then we'll hunt." She didn't even seem to realize she'd used the words of a changeling . . . of a leopard.

He smiled. Sascha Duncan was no longer Psy, even if she refused to see that. Poor baby. He was going to enjoy educating her about living life as his mate.

Tamsyn closed the bedroom door before giving Sascha the cup of hot chocolate she'd whipped up. There was such an intense look on the woman's face that even without her strange ability to sense emotion, Sascha knew that whatever the healer had to tell her, it wouldn't be easy.

"I'm going to share something about Lucas with you that he never will—his need to protect you overwhelms every other instinct. It's not a choice he can make." Tamsyn's soft brown eyes were gentle but her tone held an edge of steel Sascha had never expected. "I'm telling you because I trust you."

Don't betray my trust.

She heard the unspoken words as clearly as if Tamsyn had opened her mouth and shaped them into sound. "Why tell me at all?"

"Because of what you said downstairs about needing an open mind when you go into the PsyNet." She frowned. "Sit down before you fall down. The last thing I need is Lucas after me for neglecting you."

Sascha sat. "What is it I need to know?" She put the drink on the bedside table.

Tamsyn sat down on the bed beside her and took a shaky breath. "When Lucas was barely thirteen, a small band of roaming leopards tried to infiltrate our territory. We weren't as strong back then and the ShadowWalkers thought they could destroy our power structure and install themselves as alpha." She sighed. "It's been done before—we might be more humane than the Psy but we're not perfect."

Sascha didn't interrupt, caught by the jagged shards of pain she could hear in Tamsyn's normally even tones.

"Lucas's mother was a healer, his father a sentinel." She smiled softly. "Sometimes I think that's why he allows me so much freedom in the pack."

Sascha had barely begun to give in to her hunger for touch, barely begun to understand that it was as essential to her as food, but she could feel Tamsyn's need like a second heartbeat. She put her hand over the other woman's. Tamsyn's fingers curled over hers.

"The ShadowWalkers couldn't get to our alpha pair so they decided to attack a sentinel and get information on our defenses. Lucas's family was on a run in the forests when they were surrounded. Afterward, we realized the original plan must've been to break Carlo by making him witness the rape and torture of his mate." Tamsyn's fingers threatened to crush Sascha's weaker bones.

She took another trembling breath. "But the ShadowWalkers underestimated Shayla. She was a healer but she was also a mother and she fought for the life of her child. The other leopards couldn't afford to lose Carlo but in the fighting, Shayla was killed."

"Tamsyn," Sascha began, alarmed by the depth of her anguish. It was so heavy, so old and potent, having matured over the years into pure sorrow.

"No, I can only do this once. After I leave this room, we'll never speak of it again." Her eyes asked for a promise, which Sascha gladly gave. "Lucas was so young, much weaker than the adult males who attacked them. He was easily contained when he tried to save his parents."

Sascha's heart hurt for the panther who was so possessive and protective. Now she understood his need to mark her, to hold her safe. "Was his father captured?"

"Yes. They took both Lucas and Carlo. Shayla's body was removed and buried deep where her scent wouldn't warn us. But it wasn't deep enough. We found her."

"How long?" How long had Lucas been in the hands of those merciless killers?

"Four days." Tamsyn's voice was haunted. "When we got to them, Carlo was so badly damaged that no one could save him. I was a trainee, a juvenile myself. Shayla had been our healer and she was gone. I burned myself out but I couldn't save him. It was as if his soul had flown with Shayla's." Tears streaked down her face.

"Tamsyn." Using the strange, inexplicable, wonderful part of her soul that could heal hearts, she gathered in the other woman's pain. As it settled in her, heavy and aching, Tamsyn's voice seemed to lighten.

"The last words Carlo said to us were, 'We didn't break.' That was when we realized Lucas must've survived. The ShadowWalkers had tried to hide him so they could retrieve him later—he was tied up in a cave not far from Carlo. Wh-when we found him, he had so many broken bones and bloody claw slashes on him that the only reason we recognized him was because of the Hunter marks." She touched her face as if stroking Lucas's mark. "His wrists and ankles were rubbed through to the bone from fighting the restraints."

Sascha felt a sob catch in her throat. "They tortured him to break Carlo?"

Tamsyn nodded. "They wanted what Carlo knew—the locations of our safe houses, the routes we run, our alpha pair's lair and defense grid."

"How did Lucas survive?"

"I don't know." Tamsyn sounded utterly bewildered. "They'd held back with his father because he was the important one, but with Lucas . . ." She shook her head. "It was as if he refused to die. Some people said he survived because he'd been born a Hunter and had strengths we didn't know about. I just think he wanted vengeance."

"The ShadowWalkers escaped?"

Tamsyn nodded. "We were strong enough to drive them off but not to track and take them down without leaving our young vulnerable. As a result, we lived under a kind of martial law for five years, never leaving the group, never making ourselves targets."

Her eyes met Sascha's. "When Lucas was only eighteen and still a juvenile by our standards, he went out one night with a pack of sentinels and some others. The sentinels had given him their loyalty the day they learned that despite the torture, he hadn't broken."

Sascha couldn't begin to imagine the strength of will it must've taken for Lucas to honor his loyalty to Pack. But he had.

"They went hunting every single adult male ShadowWalker." Blood fury threaded Tamsyn's normally gentle voice. "By the time they finished, the ShadowWalkers had ceased to exist and DarkRiver was a pack no one dared to threaten."

Sascha wasn't repulsed by the violence. It was far more palatable to her than the hypocrisy of the Psy, who let killers roam free while championing their peaceful image. At least the changelings were honest. At least they loved enough to hunger for vengeance. All the Psy hungered for was power.

"Five years later," Tamsyn said, wrenching Sascha out of her bleak thoughts, "Lachlan, our ruling alpha, stepped down in favor of Lucas. The sentinels vowed their blood oath without hesitation." She shook her head. "*He was only twenty-three.* Most leopards are barely mature at that age but Lucas was already tougher than any of the other males."

"He was honed in fire." Sascha thought of the pain that had created Lucas and mourned for the boy who'd never had a chance to be a youth. What must it have been like to grow up in the shadow of his parents' blood?

"Do you understand?" Tamsyn looked into Sascha's eyes.

"Yes." Tears fell in her most secret heart—she didn't yet know how to cry in the open.

The healer wasn't convinced. "The ShadowWalkers kept him tied up. They made him watch his father being tortured before turning on him. The things they did . . . Don't ask him to be the one who anchors you."

Don't ask him to watch you die while he stands helpless.

"He'll volunteer." Sascha knew what kind of a man Lucas was, what kind of a leader.

"Then stop him. Tell him he won't do. I'll take his place." Raw pain darkened Tamsyn's eyes.

Sascha nodded but they both knew that turning Lucas from his chosen path was an almost impossible task.

In spite of her mental exhaustion, she was lying awake in bed when she felt his presence nearby. A minute later, he pushed open the bedroom door and closed it behind him, treating her room as his territory.

She knew that to let him have his way would only reinforce his already autocratic tendencies, but she also knew that her chance of surviving her impending mental collapse, trap or no trap, was close to nil. Either she'd flame out or the Council's mercenaries would hunt her down after her shields failed.

Time was rushing out from between her desperately cupped hands—she didn't want to pretend not to adore him tonight. Quite simply, he was everything she'd ever dreamed of and never dared to touch.

In the soft darkness he was all masculine prowl as he got into bed beside her, lying atop the blankets while she lay below, barely dressed in an old T-shirt that Tamsyn had found. She'd given it to Sascha with an odd comment: "No other scent will pacify him."

He put one arm over her body. "I want to be naked under those sheets with you."

She felt herself blush and gloried in finally being able to just "be." Death was certain. She might as well enjoy the life she had left. "Is that how you usually woo prospective lovers?" She was teasing; this felt *right*, as if she'd been loving him forever.

He nuzzled at her neck, one hand moving up the sheet to clasp hers as it lay open beside her head. "Only women who already know my body inside out, who know my every desire, my every pleasure point. Only you."

Her heart threatened to stop beating. "What are you talking about?"

"You've loved me in my dreams, kitten. What about in reality?" He raised his head and those cat eyes glowed eerily.

For an instant, she was completely fascinated. "Do your eyes always do that in the dark?"

"No." Leaning down, he nipped at her lower lip, startling her . . . pleasuring her. "I just don't want to miss even an inch of your body." He tugged at the blanket.

She pulled it back up. "I'm not responsible for your dreams."

He spoke against her lips. "Do you know my favorite part?" Not waiting for her response, he said, "It was where you tasted me. I've never orgasmed so hard in my life. I was mad as hell to wake up and find myself alone."

Sascha couldn't breathe. It was suddenly far too hot. Pushing at the confining blanket, she shoved it down, helped along by Lucas. Too late she realized that her legs were now bare to her upper thighs. It didn't matter. Only the dreams mattered.

"How could you have seen my dreams?" she whispered. They'd been her most secret, most precious treasure. In those dreams she'd been who she might've been had she not lived the life of a Psy.

"You invited me in." He sat up above her with his knees on either side of her thighs. As she watched, dry-mouthed, he raised his black T-shirt over his head and threw it to the floor. "Do you know what I like?"

Without stopping to think, she scraped her nails down the hot steel of his abdomen. Hard. He purred and she froze. "I don't know how I did it—it wasn't intentional." She'd never have had the courage to taste him if she'd thought him real.

"You're a cardinal Psy." When she didn't continue to pet him, he raised her fingers and nibbled at them in playful warning. Her stomach filled with a thousand butterflies. Tugging her hand away, she tried to sit up. He wouldn't let her. "No, kitten. I like you like that." He braced himself on his palms beside her and sniffed at her neck like some great hunting beast.

Which was exactly what he was.

Then he did something utterly unexpected and mind-blowingly sensual. Giving her no warning, he moved his head and bit her nipple gently through the T-shirt. Her back arched. A scream threatened to rip from her throat. Instead of letting go, he sucked hard, making her mindless with lust. By the time he released her, his knees were on the inside of her thighs and he was slowly spreading her open.

"You smell of me," he growled against her throat, giving her a quick lick. "All over, you smell of me."

She moaned. "Wh-what?"

He pushed himself up above her and used the fingers of one hand to tug at the nipple he hadn't sucked. She had to fight herself not to reach out and pull down the zipper of his jeans, knowing precisely what he'd feel like in her palms. Hot, hard, silky smooth, and perfect.

CHAPTER 18

"This T-shirt is mine." He let go of her nipple and sat up again so he could run the palms of both hands along her torso to close over her breasts.

Her entire body was a heartbeat pounding in time to the pulse between her legs. "Why did Tamsyn give it to me?"

"Because you smell of me anyway." With another gentle squeeze, he released her breasts and ran his hands down to the edge of the T-shirt, pushing it up. "Even the damn wolves could smell me on you."

She knew she should protest the way he was acting but this was what she'd dreamed about, fantasized about. The only question was, was she going to survive the inferno she'd unleashed? A big male hand cupped her so boldly that she felt lights explode behind her eyes. He was rubbing at her with the heel of his palm, arousing her to fever pitch through the cotton of her panties.

"Where's the lace?" He paused in his caress.

"D-don't stop." It was a husky plea. Her reward was the renewal of his sensual movements.

His eyes glowed in the darkness and he was at once intensely beautiful and intensely wild. "In the dreams you wore lace panties."

"Psy don't have those kinds of garments." Hungry for more, she moved against him. He understood, changing his movement to a hard rotation that made her throat lock. For the next few seconds, she was completely insensitive to anything but the delirious onrush of sensation.

He thrust her over the edge with rough tenderness that tore a scream from her throat, her Psy mind no longer caring who was in the house, who was listening. She let the almost violent pleasure rip through her until she was damp, limp, and sated against his palm. When she opened her eyes, it was to find that he hadn't changed position.

Meeting her gaze, he removed his hand from between her legs, brought his palm to his mouth, and licked his fingers clean. It was the most erotic thing she'd ever seen. Her body quivered with aftershocks but something deeper was already awakening within.

"Feel better?" he asked.

"Yes." Her eye fell to the erection pushing against the zipper of his jeans.

"Are you going to do something about that?"

If she hadn't had those dreams, if she hadn't learned that he gave far more pleasure than he ever asked for, if she hadn't already tangled with his male demands and hunger, she might've balked.

Biting down on her lower lip, she ran a finger down the length of him.

"Stop teasing," he ordered, but made no move to halt her exploration.

"In my dreams," she whispered, accepting what she'd

known from the start. Those dreams had been far too vivid to have been figments of her own imagination. How could she have dreamed up the wild lover who'd shown her the ways of pleasure when she'd never known anyone like him? "In my dreams you told me you loved my mouth."

"I adore your mouth." He was braced on his hands by her head again. When he spoke it was against her lips and then he was kissing her with sensual enthusiasm that made her feel like she was his every fantasy come to life.

She couldn't break away, couldn't stop herself from grabbing onto his waist and digging her fingers into his flesh. He pushed his tongue into her mouth and she responded instinctively, tangling hers with his. His body was pure heat and sensation under her hands, the body of a male who'd never say no to touch.

"Skin privileges," she said when he let her breathe.

"We're way beyond skin privileges, darling." His smile was wicked as he sat back up to kneel between her spread thighs. Aware what he wanted, what he needed, she raised her hands to the button on his jeans and undid it. He hissed out a breath, his eyes appearing to glow even more brightly. When she tugged down the zipper, he growled in the back of his throat. "Careful."

"Always." The zipper was down. She could see the head of his erection pushing against the white fabric of his briefs. "You have to let me up."

He thought about it for a while, his fingers playing with her wet nipple through the soft cotton fabric. "I don't want to."

Her stomach clenched each time he plucked at the bud he'd sensitized to the extreme. "How can I . . . take you in my mouth if you don't?" In the glimmering darkness, the question was an erotic invitation she hadn't known she had the capacity to make.

He moved and it was so fast she barely caught it. Watching him stand beside the bed stripping off the rest of his clothing was a pleasure all on its own. There was no need for light, not when his skin seemed to shimmer with a fine layer of savage energy to her Psy senses. She was stunned by the dangerous beauty of him. When she sat up, his head whipped to pin her to the spot. "I don't want you to move." Alpha to the core, his order was arrogantly assured.

"But I want to move." To let him have his way at this point would equal disaster later.

He pounced with that stunning speed and she found herself flat on her back with his length pressed along her front. He'd clasped her wrists together and had them pinned above her head before she could gasp in a breath. "Now you're all mine." The comment held a hunting cat's pleasure at cornering his prey.

But this prey had claws. Reaching out with her mind, she wrapped mental hands around the erection that was nudging at her entrance. His body arched as a shout was torn from him. "What are you doing, kitten?"

"Playing," she said, using his word. The *feel* of him was everywhere, inside and outside. She wanted to taste him so badly, she ached. "Let me."

He leaned down and lapped at her nipple through the T-shirt, the gesture so feline that she was shocked into a moan. "I'm not feeling playful."

"Don't you want me to . . ." She used her mental hands to squeeze him tight, to show him what he could have.

He bit the side of her neck hard enough to mark but not hurt. "Stop that."

"Why?" At that moment it didn't occur to Sascha that she shouldn't have been able to connect to him so easily, that he was changeling and she was Psy and no Psy had ever been able to enter a changeling mind without effort. All she knew was that she was burning up for him.

He braced himself on his hands above her, setting her

free to grasp the hard length of his erection. He thrust into her hold, head thrown back, the tendons on his neck standing out in sharp relief. Not quite knowing how she knew what to do, she pushed up until she could slide her legs between the vee created by his kneeling thighs.

As he watched to see what she'd do next, she slithered her body down the bed until the hard evidence of his hunger was right above her. Holding onto his hips, she raised her head off the bed and took him inside her mouth.

His growl made every nerve in her body flicker with warning. But she didn't stop. She had skin privileges and she was going to take every advantage. He tasted better than her dreams, as rich and delectable as the most exquisite chocolate, as exotic as the panther he was.

Her neck was getting tired but she didn't want to let go. Pulling at his hips, she moved down but he refused to follow, sliding slowly out of her mouth and driving her to the edge of insanity.

Lucas, please. It was a wild plea from her mind to his.

"On the condition that you let me do the same." His voice was rough, hot, demanding. "No backing away."

You can do anything you like! she agreed without thought, so drunk on the overload of sensory pleasure that she was his slave.

He purred and did as she'd asked, moving his hips just enough to tease, to tempt. Craving him so badly that she could no longer function on any level but the physical, she sucked hard, squeezing her hands over the taut muscles of his buttocks. He groaned as she used her tongue to stroke the underside of his erection. She knew what he liked, had learned from the dreams that weren't dreams. Given free rein over his body, she used every skill she had to drive her wild lover to distraction.

"Harder, kitten." It was a hoarse whisper.

She complied, digging her nails into his flesh. The tiny

pleasure-pain made his muscles lock around her. Moaning deep in her throat, she poured everything she had into the loving, licking, sucking, *giving*.

He came for her in shuddering waves, a wordless growl emanating from his throat.

Maybe ten minutes later, Sascha realized she was still wearing the T-shirt. She tried to extricate herself from Lucas, who had her completely pinned to the bed, but he refused to move. He'd buried his face against her and now he licked out at her pulse, lazily tasting the salt on her.

She bit the side of his neck. "Lucas."

A low purr vibrated against her breasts, shocking sensation down her aroused body. Every nerve ending quivered in need so deep it hurt.

"I want to take off this T-shirt." It felt too hot, too confining. Even her panties were too much—she wanted to feel every inch of sweat-slick skin, every stroke of wild sensuality.

He rolled off her. His slitted eyes glowed a soft green in the darkness. They didn't leave her for an instant and the second she was naked, he pounced. Once again she found herself at his mercy. This time she was lying on her stomach, his hard length buried in the crease of her buttocks. "But you . . ."

He ran his fingernails up her side, making her entire body shiver. "I'm not human, Sascha. It takes more than a single round to leave me unable to perform." He nibbled at the shell of her ear.

"Oh."

"Now it's my turn." Those strong teeth scraped her shoulder and one of his hands slipped under her body to touch the damp curls between her thighs.

She made a soft noise that was so full of need she startled

herself. Lucas seemed to like it. Dipping lower, he rubbed at her, threatening to drive her to insanity.

Lucas. It was an intimate whisper.

"Raise your bottom for me," he said into her ear, lifting his body off hers.

Blushing, but unwilling to miss out on anything he wanted to show her, she bent her knees and pushed up. He moved the hand petting her curls to flatten over her stomach while his free hand stroked her bottom. She'd never felt more exposed, more vulnerable.

The hand on her bottom slipped down to the insides of her thighs and he pushed gently until she'd widened her stance. A throaty rumble sounded from behind her. Every muscle in her body tensed in anticipation.

"Your scent is like a drug to my senses." His voice was so rough she could barely understand him.

With another murmur that was more sound than words, he put one hand on her hip while the other continued to lie against her stomach and then he tasted her. A scream tore at her throat at the first slow lick. She could feel herself trembling and it was only the start.

Unhurried and careful, he lapped at her like a cat with a bowl of cream, intent on tasting every drop. Her entire body turned into liquid flame. She could barely breathe through the sensations, her face burning with heat that had nothing to do with embarrassment.

He moved the hand on her hip down to the inside of her thigh again. She let him widen her stance even more, let him use his fingers to spread her for a deeper taste, let him savor her until she saw stars. She just . . . let him. He took full advantage and she learned what it was like to be loved by an alpha panther who thought she belonged to him.

There was nothing tentative about his intimate kiss. Every touch screamed possession. The fingers on her thigh were hot and strong, holding her where he wanted her as his mouth ravaged her with a kind of rough tenderness she had no defense against.

She was almost insane with need when he nipped at her bottom with his teeth. "I'm sorry, kitten. I'm moving too fast but I want to be inside you."

Fast? He thought this was fast? What was Lucas's definition of slow? *I need you.* She was speaking to him on the most private of levels, not even thinking about what she was doing so easily.

She sensed him rise behind her, nerves taut with expectation. A soft scream escaped when he started to push into her. It felt like he was invading more than her body—he was going deep into her mind. And she wanted him deeper.

He surged forward in response to her silent urging. A sharp note of unexpected pain infiltrated her pleasure. "Wh-what? Lucas?"

"Shh. Never again." His lips kissed the line of her spine, distracting her with sensation. "You feel so good, darling, so hot and tight. Once isn't going to be enough."

The erotic whispers sent shivers racing across her skin. At the same time, the hand on her stomach pushed upward and she rose to press her back against his chest as he lay buried deep inside her. She felt the pulse of his heartbeat within her and it was exquisite, a carnal kiss unlike any other.

Reacting to instincts so old they had no name, she rotated her hips in a slow circle. His arm tightened against her stomach, enclosing her in pure muscle. The heat of his chest almost burned—it felt as if his body temperature was much higher than hers. One masculine hand rose to close over her breast, his fingers plucking at the nipple. Crying out, she moved again.

The hand on her breast slipped to clasp her hip. "Stop that."

She repeated the motion.

And felt the panther in Lucas take over. He pulled out almost all the way and then surged deep. Her body started to shake. Unable to remain still, she pushed back toward him.

His teeth closed over the curve of her neck, holding her in place as he drove them both to the edge. The hold wasn't painful, just so proprietary that she felt utterly possessed. It was a reminder that her lover wasn't human, wasn't Psy, wasn't controllable.

She adored him exactly as he was.

His hand slipped to the curls between her legs, finding the throbbing nub that she ached to have caressed. He knew perfectly how to rub, how to tease. Her scream came from deep inside her soul. In her passion, she reached back and scraped her nails down his biceps.

With a growl, he let go of her neck and began to move so hard and fast she could no longer meet him. Instead, she melted, accepting his hunger, his need, his *claim*, even as her body shattered into a thousand pieces, brilliant sparks of primitive color flashing before her eyes.

To her shock, Lucas pulled out of her. Before she could complain, he'd turned her in his arms and pulled her to sit with her legs around his hips. He was so deep inside her barely a breath later that she couldn't think.

"Open your eyes." A demand against her mouth.

She obeyed without thought. And met the glowing green of eyes gone utterly panther. "Why?"

"Fireworks," he whispered and took her lips in a kiss so hungry she felt consumed.

This time, his movements were deep and fast and unstoppable. She rode the storm, let him push her over again and again, let her wildness out to play. It was the most intimate, most dangerous, most wonderful dance of her life. When his muscular body shuddered in her arms and he let out a rough shout, she felt every feminine instinct she had moan in pleasure.

"Mine." That absolute statement was the last word he said in a long, long while.

They'd just finished breakfast when Lucas informed Sascha he was going to speak to Hawke, the SnowDancer alpha whom she'd never met, at least not while conscious. Vaughn and Mercy, who were also sitting at the table with them, looked up.

"You're on guard here," he told them. "I'm taking Clay and Dorian."

Sascha took a sip of tea and thought about what she was going to do. Returning home wasn't an option. Ever. After the night she'd spent in Lucas's arms, she could no longer keep up the pretence of being a normal Psy. Her shields were holding on the psychic plane but maintaining her mask in the real world had become impossible.

Then there was the fact that Lucas had marked her.

The second she'd walked into the kitchen, Tamsyn's eyes had gone to the bite mark on her neck. She'd thought the healer would be angry given what she'd told Sascha the day before. Instead, the other woman had grinned and said, "I bet you're starving."

So far no one had mentioned the screams. Or the long scratch marks on Lucas's arms. She'd nearly died when she'd come down to find him sitting at the table wearing a short-sleeved T-shirt. It was one thing to come apart in his embrace, quite another to have others bear witness to her utter surrender. At least he was putting on his black leather-synth jacket for the meeting with Hawke.

"Stay here," he ordered, though she'd made no move to leave. "You're not strong enough to hack the Net again even if we agree to your idiotic plan. Stay out of it. Rest."

He was right. Ghosting Henry had drained her more than she'd guessed. It would take at least one more day for her to recover enough to implement the plan. "I can only last another few days." The pressure inside her was intensifying minute by minute. "We have to act before then or they're going to find out about me and attempt containment."

Those cat-green eyes narrowed. "No one is going to contain you." He walked around to her side of the table and bent down to kiss her right in front of his people. It was no peck on the cheek. She gripped onto his waist and held on as he kissed her in a way that was blatantly sexual and possessive without end.

A minute later he was gone, leaving her starving for him. When she glanced at the two sentinels, she saw no reaction on their faces. Vaughn scared her. He wasn't cold and distant like Clay, but there was a prowling darkness behind his eyes that made her wonder just how close to the surface his beast was.

Mercy was a little more approachable but she couldn't get rid of the feeling that the sentinels wanted her gone. She couldn't blame them. She was part of a race guilty of helping the worst kind of scum. Who knew what she'd drag Lucas into?

"Are you here basically for my safety?" she asked, aware that there weren't any other vulnerable people in the house.

They nodded.

"Thank you." She put her hands on the table and made herself meet the male sentinel's eyes. "I know I'm not what Lucas needs but let me have him for a few more days. After that I won't be a problem." She refused to allow self-pity to destroy the magnificence of what she was experiencing, but what she'd said was fact.

The changelings didn't know the extent of the PsyNet. It had eyes and ears in every corner of the world, shadows within shadows. It was impossible to escape it physically even if her mind could somehow survive the mental separation.

Wherever she went, whatever she did, they'd hunt her down. They would've done so for any renegade because dissent undermined the Silence Protocol. However, her case would garner an extreme reaction—she was Nikita's daughter. Not only did she know too much, her defection would strike at the heart of the Council's image of invincibility.

Vaughn leaned forward, those strange almost goldcolored eyes focused completely on her. "If I'd thought you were going to harm Lucas, I would've ensured you never had the chance."

"So the fact I'm still breathing is a vote of confidence?" Sascha would not let him intimidate her, no matter that he made the hairs on the back of her neck stand up in primordial warning.

His lip quirked. "No."

Mercy put down her coffee cup. "Stop playing with her mind, Vaughn. I think she's been through enough."

"I think our Psy is a lot tougher than she looks, aren't you, Sascha?" Dark-gold eyes searched her face for something she couldn't even begin to guess at. She just knew that what was looking at her wasn't wholly civilized.

"I had to be to survive." Sascha held his gaze. "Even as a child, I knew that if they found out I was different, I'd be slated for rehabilitation—a kind of psychic brainwipe." To this day, she could hear the shuffling feet and mumbled whispers of the rehabilitated as they traversed the halls in the inner sanctum of the Center.

She should never have heard those sounds or seen the

nightmarish creatures who'd made them, but Nikita had taken her in one day when she'd been barely ten years old. She'd never forget her mother's words—"Don't ever be anything but perfect, Sascha. This is the result of failure."

Sascha had been a teenager before she'd understood why Nikita had gone that far. She had to have been aware of her child's flaw, had to have seen inside her mind before she was old enough to protect herself.

The harsh gesture had worked—to the outside world, Sascha had never been anything less than perfect. She'd even convinced Nikita that her flawed daughter had become a Psy to the absolute core. Until she'd started cracking apart.

"I can't believe they do that to their own people," Mercy muttered in disgust. "How can anyone choose to live like that? I'd prefer death."

Mercy's words had Sascha's throat closing up. "I need to ask you both a favor."

Vaughn raised a brow. He might have let her live but she knew he was withholding final judgment.

"If I get taken in when we put the plan into effect, if I get sent to the Center instead of being executed," she began, "I want you to kill me. I won't be able to do it myself because they'll lock my mind." A mental straitjacket that she knew would propel her into the final madness.

"That's Lucas's call," Mercy said, her tone pure steel. It was an indication that for all her beauty, she was a soldier first and a woman second.

"I don't want him to do it." Not anymore, not when she knew what it would cost him. "He shouldn't have to watch someone he cares for die." In Vaughn's eyes, she saw awareness of Lucas's past. "Even if you feel nothing for me, do it for him. He deserves better than to witness me being turned into a vegetable."

Vaughn stood and she thought he was rejecting her plea. But instead of leaving the room, he walked around to the back of her chair. Putting his hands on the wood, he leaned down until his lips touched her neck. She froze, feeling the power contained in that dangerous male body. He could snap her neck with one hand.

CHAPTER 19

"**You have skin** privileges," he said against her pulse, biting down very gently. "You're Pack."

It was the last thing she'd ever expected to hear.

Mercy closed her hand over Sascha's clenched fist. "We don't let Pack members die without a damn good fight."

Sascha felt tears burn at her eyes. "You don't understand!"

Vaughn nuzzled his way up her neck and bit her lightly on the ear before standing to his full height, his hands on her shoulders. "We understand you think the PsyNet is omnipotent. That's because it's all you've ever been taught." He moved around to lean against the table by her side. "But the rules have changed."

"What rules?" she said, feeling defeated by their refusal to see the truth. "They're just as powerful, just as deadly."

"But you aren't anything they've ever seen," Mercy said.

Sascha looked up into the other woman's face. "I'm only a broken Psy."

"Are you?" Vaughn ran the backs of his fingers down her cheek. Startled once again, she didn't know how to react. She'd seen the way the leopards touched each other but had never expected to be on the receiving end of such casual affection. Especially from the deadly sentinels. "Or are you something else entirely?"

A retort was on the tip of Sascha's tongue when she frowned and remembered those secret family files she'd retrieved but never examined. "I need to think," she muttered, already withdrawing into her mind.

Neither of the sentinels said a word. They simply ensured her protection while she sat there thumbing through pages and pages of mental data. Somewhere during that time, Tamsyn came into the kitchen and started baking cookies. With one corner of her mind, Sascha felt the healer's sorrow at having had to send Julian and Roman away. Lucas had shared the truth of their absence last night, trusting her more than she trusted herself. Tamsyn couldn't, wouldn't, go with her children—she was the healer and if blood was spilled, they'd need her.

Barely even thinking about it, Sascha gathered in Tamsyn's sharp sadness and took it inside her. As always, the emotions of others settled like rocks against her heart but she knew she could deal with it. Somehow, she had the power to neutralize those negative feelings.

She didn't know how long she'd been sitting there when she was startled out of her trancelike state by a kiss on the back of her neck. Only one male had the power to shatter her so completely. She blinked and turned to find Lucas behind her. He pulled her to her feet, his face set in harsh lines.

"What were you doing?" The simmering edge of his temper was visible in his eyes.

"Looking at some information I stole when I hacked the Net." Why was he angry?

His Hunter marks became vividly delineated. "I told you to stay put."

"I'm right here." Her own temper spiked. "What's the matter with you?"

His answer was a low growl that made every tiny hair on her body stand up.

Suddenly, she became aware of the others in the room. Vaughn, Mercy, and Tamsyn had now been joined by Dorian and Clay. Silent as the predators they were, the sentinels and the healer continued about their business, but she knew they were listening.

"Lucas," she said, intending on asking him to take this somewhere private.

"I specifically told you to stay out of the PsyNet." Fury coated every quiet word.

"I didn't go into it! I'm not completely brainless." She'd had enough. "Did you expect me to sit here . . . baking cookies while you were gone?" A twinge of amusement from somewhere in the room made her turn and say, "No offense intended, Tamsyn."

"I know, honey. You're not the cookie-baking type." The healer put some chocolate chips into a bowl.

"You were supposed to rest your mind. And don't tell me that whatever it was you were doing wasn't using up mental energy you don't have." Lucas gripped the back of her neck, pulling her toward him.

He was very careful with his strength but the dominance of the gesture wasn't lost on her. "Stop it." He might be alpha but she was a cardinal.

He didn't bother to answer, speaking to his sentinels instead. "Why the hell did you let her disobey my orders?"

She kicked out with her boot, catching Lucas on the shin. He didn't wince. "You'll pay for that." It was a silky warning.

And it made her explode. She might have been a failure

as a cardinal, but she had a little specialty not many people knew about. Reaching out with her mind, she *pushed* Lucas Hunter so hard, he was two feet from her before he could blink.

Everyone froze.

Sascha realized she'd just attacked the alpha of Dark-River. Too bad. He'd been acting like a complete Neanderthal. Meeting those eyes, which had gone more panther than human, she put her hands on her hips and tried to pretend the telekinetic effort hadn't worn her out.

"Still want to play?" It was a taunt she'd never have made before she'd started to spend so much time with changelings.

"Oh, yeah, kitten, I want to play." Lucas moved toward her in that lightning-fast way of his, his emotions a mix of exhilaration and challenge.

She was ready. Using her remaining strength, she jumped backward onto the table, the action almost catlike. Her Psy mind had watched the way the leopards moved and now it mimicked the beautifully smooth motion. Lucas's eyes widened as he found her halfway across the table. "You've been keeping secrets."

"Poor baby," she taunted.

He started to smile. "Come here."

"Are you going to behave?"

"No."

Her lips twitched. Feeling silly crouching on the table now that he was no longer chasing her, she jumped off to stand in front of him. His hand went to her neck again, holding her in a possessive grasp. Except this time, there was sensuality instead of anger in his touch. His kiss burned her through to her toes.

When he lifted his head, she took a few moments to catch her breath. "Have you heard of privacy?" she asked, aware of her skin turning scarlet. She could no longer curb the physical reactions of her body. That shield had burned out last night.

Tamsyn laughed. "Sorry, couldn't help overhearing."

Sascha batted at Lucas's hold until he let her go, content to prowl behind her as she walked to stand on the other side of the counter from Tamsyn. "What?"

The woman rolled her eyes. "DarkRiver males are damn possessive and complete exhibitionists during the mating dance."

Sascha ran through her dictionary of changeling termi-nology and could find no fit. "Mating dance?"

Mercy whistled. Dorian winced. Tamsyn suddenly got interested in her dough. Clay and Vaughn mysteriously dis-appeared. Behind her, Lucas's body was a hard wall of heat. "I think we need to discuss this upstairs."

"Oh, *now* you want to be alone?" she muttered.

He picked her up in his arms, shocking her into immo-bility. Before she could find the breath to complain, he was running up the stairs. A minute later, he dumped her on the bed and lay down beside her.

"Nuh-uh." She shook her head and tried to move away.

He threw a leg over hers. "Don't try any more tricks, kitten."

Just for that, she found another spurt of power and pushed his leg off her. A second later it was back.

"We're going to have to talk about this trick of yours," he said, sounding more amused than worried.

She narrowed her eyes. "I could turn your mind into mush if I wanted."

"But then who'd lick you to orgasm?"

Her entire body turned into a flame. "You can't say things like that!"

"Why not?" His hand parted the sides of her white shirt and it was only then that she realized he'd unbuttoned it.

Long fingers found her breast through her bra and plucked at her nipple.

"Lucas." It was more moan than word.

"The mating dance is what two leopards go through on their way to mating for life." He closed his hand over her breast and squeezed.

Her eyes flicked open, cold fear dousing the fire he'd stoked. "What happens if one half of a mated pair dies?"

"The survivor will never mate again." That possessive hand was pulling down the cup of her bra to rub lazily at her aroused flesh.

"No, Lucas." She tried to wiggle out from under him but he wouldn't let her. "You can't. I might not survive the week."

"You aren't going anywhere." He sounded more dominant than she'd ever before heard him sound, his eyes completely panther. "You belong to me."

They were words she'd waited for her whole life but she couldn't accept them. "Don't I get a choice?"

"You made it when you brought me into your dreams, into your mind." He nipped gently at her lower lip. "And you made it again when you let me into your body."

There was no way Sascha was going to leave Lucas without a mate for the rest of his life. "I won't cooperate."

"Sure you will." Moving his head, he sucked her nipple into his mouth.

Her fingers tunneled into the silky lushness of his hair. "Stop."

He murmured in pleasure and his other hand slipped down to cup her between her legs. Even through the material of her slacks, she felt the rough heat of his hold.

She tugged at his head and he lifted it only enough to give him room to move to her other breast. Instead of pushing down the cup, he licked her through it, one hand molding her stomach. It was impossible to think with this much sensation overloading her. But she had to speak, she had to make him understand. "You don't know me," she whispered.

He raised his head. "I know you inside out."

"No, Lucas. I'm not changeling—I'm Psy. My mind is who I am."

"Liar." He pinched one wet nipple.

Her entire body shuddered and for an instant she was nothing but a creature of the flesh.

"You're as much animal as me." It was a husky whisper against her ear. "As sexual, as hungry, as needy."

She shook her head, shaken by the power of his words, the addiction of his touch. "I could kill you with one thought."

He rubbed his jaw across the skin of her upper breasts. "Could you, kitten?"

That easily, he won their personal war. Lucas was more important to her than her own life. "Don't," she said. "Stop this before it's too late."

"No one can stop it. I'll kill anyone who tries."

Looking into those cat eyes, she was certain he meant every word. She was as certain that she had to stop him before he tied himself to a woman who was so deeply broken, she wasn't even sure she was Psy anymore.

A day later, Sascha sat in the living area of the safe house trying to think up arguments to convince Lucas of the soundness of her plan. The problem was, she hadn't figured out how to create the diversion that would give the killer a head start to scenting her. She'd spent the whole day trying to think of something and all she'd come up with was a crude "bomb."

If she couldn't work out anything else by tomorrow,

she'd have to use that—Brenna had suffered enough. At least neither Enrique nor Nikita had tried to contact her so far. She assumed that they were distracted by their own plan to catch the serial killer.

Lucas had been in and out throughout the day and she guessed that he'd been putting plans in place in case they weren't able to save the lost SnowDancer. Right now, he was standing by the window, staring out into the night. His skin glowed a burnished gold in the soft light of the lamps around the room.

"What information did you steal?" he asked, turning to look over his shoulder. He'd barely spoken to her that day but had touched her at every opportunity.

She remained curled up in the corner of the sofa, watching him as warily as a gazelle might watch a lion. Lucas wasn't human, wasn't Psy. He was a predator and he'd decided she was his. It was going to take everything she had to get away from him before she destroyed them both.

Even if Lucas didn't allow her to execute her plan, the Council's mercenaries would hunt her down on the PsyNet the second her failing shields revealed her flaw. Her firewalls were already starting to show the finest of hairline fractures. She might not be able to save herself but she would save Lucas. She *would not* sentence him to a life without a mate, no matter how much she ached for him to belong to her. "My family's history."

Someone walked into the room from the kitchen. Tamsyn's slender frame was followed by Nate's larger body. "Hope we're not interrupting."

"There's nothing to interrupt," Sascha said quickly, thankful for their presence. She needed a buffer between Lucas's demands and her own clawing desire to give in to them. "I was just telling Lucas I stole information about my family from the PsyNet."

Lucas shifted from his position by the window and

headed over to the sofa. His eyes tracked Nate's every move and Sascha felt a huge wave of almost dangerous possessiveness hit her. In a quiet moment while Lucas had been out, Tamsyn had shared that leopards were highly unstable at this stage of the mating dance and liable to attack anyone they saw as a threat.

She'd asked Sascha not to dispute Lucas's claim, warned her that fighting an alpha male during mating was simply not done. Sascha understood why Tamsyn had cautioned her but knew she couldn't follow the healer's advice, not if it meant a lifetime of loneliness for this male she adored. But she let him sit beside her on the sofa, let him put her feet on his thighs, let him massage her calves.

"Why would you need to steal information?" Nate frowned and took a seat as far from Sascha as possible. Tamsyn perched on his lap with her arm around his neck.

"Our family's physical records were destroyed during a fire at some stage in the past." Sascha had always been frustrated by that, had always felt like there was so much she didn't know. "The files on the PsyNet should've been our backup but we were told the Net information had been inexplicably corrupted."

Lucas's hand tightened on her calf, a silent signal to pay attention to him. "Was it?"

"No." She met his gaze. "It's all there, centuries of history." A rich archive that had been hidden from the very people who should've had access to it. What else did the Council keep from her people? What else was labeled restricted?

"What did you find out?" Tamsyn asked, curling up on Nate's lap. The movement was so catlike, so sensual, that Sascha was momentarily startled. The other woman's practical nature had almost blinded her to the fact that she, too, was a leopard.

"There was nothing really unusual until I went back to

my great-grandmother, Ai." Without conscious intent, she found she'd moved closer to Lucas until she was almost in his lap. One of his arms was stretched along the back of the sofa, while his other hand continued to stroke up and down her bent leg. "Her record was tagged with a red flag."

"Is that some kind of indexing system?" Nate was rubbing the back of Tamsyn's neck and his mate was almost limp in relaxation against him.

Sascha was struck by the trust evident between the two. No Psy would ever leave herself that vulnerable to a bigger male. Yet Tamsyn had without hesitation. And so had Sascha when she'd let Lucas love her as he pleased. These men might have the potential for the negative emotions that had driven her race to cripple their own children, but they also had the ability to care on a level the Psy would never experience.

"Not that I know of." She glanced away from the other couple to find Lucas's eyes looking at her so intently, she had the feeling he knew precisely what she'd been thinking. "My suspicion is that it's something Henry and Shoshanna Scott are doing on their own. I can't see my mother allowing them to go through our familial history."

A tree limb waved across the uncurtained window, casting shadows against the wall. And she became aware she was sitting in Lucas's lap, held to him by one arm while the other moved rhythmically over her outer thigh. She should've been frightened at her need for him, a need so deep it was overriding the powerful mental blocks she'd created to force herself to keep her distance. Instead, she wanted to rub up against his masculinity until heat and sensation were all she was.

"Kitten." The raw edges of possessiveness were gone from the husky murmur against her ear. It was as if her slow capitulation had calmed him. "Why the red flag?"

"I'm not sure but I think it had something to do with her

talents as a Psy." Laying her head against him, she shared the most terrifying thing. "After I saw that red flag, I went back through the more recent histories. There was a second flag."

No one spoke.

"It was on my record." Her mind snapped back to the way Enrique had been shadowing her. Someone knew or had guessed her flaw. That someone was watching her for any mistake. It was entirely likely that Enrique was playing both sides of the field, using Nikita and Henry to his own advantage.

"Do you have any idea why they might've singled you and Ai out?" The rough edge was back in his tone.

Sascha undid the top buttons of his shirt and slipped her hand inside to lie against the fury of his heartbeat. Almost immediately, she felt him pull his aggression back under control. It no longer startled her how she knew what to do to soothe her mate—it was part of the magic. "The terminology used back then was different. Ai was labeled an E-Psy. We no longer have that term in our lexicon."

Tamsyn frowned. "Was there any other information?"

"Ai was born in 1973. Silence went into effect in 1979, when she would've been six years old. Everyone under seven years of age was automatically enrolled into the Protocol." She couldn't imagine how that young girl must've felt at being taught to obliterate everything she'd learned to value.

"How many did they lose?" Tamsyn asked gently, her healer's mind seeing the problem.

"I don't know. The numbers are buried deep but everyone knows it was devastating. The transitional children had a very low survival rate."

Lucas's fingers stroked through her hair, which he'd undone while she'd been speaking. "But Ai survived."

"Yes. It was noted in her file that her mother, Mika, was

one of the strongest opponents of Silence. I thought at first that that was why Ai's file had been tagged but there were other odd things in there. Her designation was as an 8.3 E-Psy at birth but after she completed Silence, she was relegated to a 6.2 nonspecialized Psy." More had been destroyed than simply Ai's soul.

Sascha wept deep inside for the two women she'd never had the chance to know. What must it have done to Mika to watch the child she'd named Ai—which meant "love" in her language—be taught to devalue that very emotion?

"You've lost me." Tamsyn sat up within Nate's arms.

Sascha dragged her mind back from the horrors of the past. "Psy are classified according to our psychic strength and specialization. For example, my mother is a Gradient 9.1 Tp-Psy, which means her major talent lies in the area of telepathy. Like most Psy, she has several other skills, but in terms of strength, they all fall below 2 on the Gradient— our measuring system." She paused to ensure they understood.

"Go on," Tamsyn said.

"Then there are the Tk-Psy."

"Telekinetic," Nate guessed.

"Yes. We also have the M designation—Medical. The M-Psy can look inside a body and find the physical causes of illness. They're the specialty other races most commonly come into contact with. There are several other fields of talent. Telepaths are relatively common and tend to have other specialties within their telepathy."

Like her mother with her viral poisons and Ming LeBon's genius at mental combat. "Medical is midrange. Some rarer specialties include psychometry, the teleportation-capable telekinetics, and transmutation—the ability to force a physical object to change its shape. The most rare are the F-Psy."

Lucas's hand slipped under her shirt to lie against the skin of her back, hot and burning, a brand she had no desire to escape. She was having to fight herself as much as him in this shatteringly important decision. Not to mention the rest of the pack.

The leopards had closed ranks. No one would tell her what the final steps of the mating dance were so she could avoid taking them. She was their alpha's chosen mate and they weren't going to give her the chance to slip away. Even Vaughn had refused, though she'd tried to convince him it would save Lucas's life. Not one of them understood the power of the PsyNet. It could *not* be fought.

CHAPTER 20

"F-Psy," Lucas murmured. "Let me guess. Foresight?"

She nodded. "These days they're usually hired by businesses to forecast market trends, but I've heard that in the past, they often worked for Enforcement and local government in order to prevent murders and disasters."

If they hadn't succumbed to the lure of cold hard cash, forgetting the human emotions behind death and loss, perhaps Lucas's parents would still be alive. How could he not hate her people? Hate *her*?

"But no E-Psy," Tamsyn said.

"No." Sascha frowned. "It makes no sense. A specialty may be rare but it never disappears entirely."

"Did you check the classification system?" Lucas asked.

She nodded and decided not to mention that she'd had to make a quick visit to the PsyNet to do so. "It wasn't hidden. I guess they thought no one would ever care to look it up. Until Silence, E was an accepted designation. It disappeared soon after the Protocol went into effect and wasn't replaced in the classification charts." She made a frustrated sound. "But I don't know what it means!"

"What's your classification?" Nate asked.

It was the one question she didn't want to answer, the one question that showed her how useless she was. "I'm nonspecialized."

"But I know you're a telepath." Tamsyn frowned. "The cubs told me you talked to them."

Sascha smiled at the thought of Julian and Roman's mischievous welcome. "Telepathy is a base skill necessary for survival." Otherwise, the uplink to the Net couldn't be created or maintained. "All Psy have it to at least 1.0 on the Gradient. However, I have telepathy to approximately 3.5 on the Gradient, telekinetic powers to around 2.2, and whispers of some of the other powers to no real level."

"You're a cardinal." Lucas squeezed her tight, obviously seeing through the smile to the pain she'd tried to hide. "That means you have a great deal of power."

She shook her head. "No, it means I have the *potential* for a great deal of power. Cardinals are uniformly over 10.0 on the Gradient in their particular specialty—no one's been able to figure out a way to measure them past that. Not that measurement is necessary to figure out whether someone is a cardinal." Her eyes had marked her from birth.

"In my case the potential was never unlocked." Trying not to let them see how much it mattered to her, she shrugged. "According to Mother, it shouldn't have stopped me rising to the Council ranks but I think she meant to help me." Help by icily controlled murder. "Eventually she stopped mentioning that possibility. We both knew I'd never be powerful enough to survive at that level."

Tamsyn pushed off Nate and started to pace across the carpet. Her mate looked on, bemused. "I'm no Psy, Sascha, but I can feel your power same as I can feel Lucas's."

Sascha tipped her head to the side. "I'm not sure . . ."

"The Psy think we can't read them but some of us can." Tamsyn dropped the bombshell with a feline smile. "Ask Lucas."

She found him wearing that same smile. "Tell me."

"So demanding." It was a growl but there was mischief in his eyes. "Whenever you use Psy power, I know. Not only that, I can read spikes in Psy activity. And you, kitten, are no Gradient 3 in anything."

"Impossible." She scowled. "I've barely been using any Psy power since you've known me. What I have used, like when I pushed you telekinetically, has been very low level. You can't be reading the spikes right."

Leaning forward, he nipped her lower lip. "That was for the push."

She made a face. "Watch out or I'll use some of my transmutation powers—I have enough to turn your hair green." It was a bluff but she got to see Lucas's eyes narrow in warning as he debated whether she was serious.

"You have power," Tamsyn muttered, interrupting them. "Maybe you're an E-Psy like your great-grandmother. Maybe being an E-Psy is no longer allowed, so they categorize you as nonspecialized and bang it into you that you have no power to speak of. Tell someone a lie often enough and they'll start to believe it, even to the extent of handicapping themselves."

Sascha's eyes widened. "When I was a child undergoing training, the instructors always told me I had so much potential, and that it was such a pity it was blocked."

Lucas suddenly rose in a startlingly fast movement, destroying her train of thought.

"What—" She found her feet as he set her down.

"*Quiet.*" Nate's head jerked toward the front yard.

Lucas's body was a study in silent danger. "Where are Vaughn and Clay?"

"Out back." Nate prowled to stand beside Lucas. "Tammy, get Sascha out of here."

"I'm not leaving. This is my fight, too."

Lucas whipped her a blazing green look. "Actually it's not. That's the SnowDancers out there. *Tammy*."

The healer crossed the room and took Sascha's arm. "Come on. Lucas won't be able to concentrate if you're nearby." It was an almost inaudible whisper.

Sascha felt the protective fury in him and knew Tamsyn was right. Frustrated but unwilling to endanger him, she followed the other woman out of the living room and to one of the windowless upstairs bedrooms.

They encountered Dorian in the hallway, a sleek presence dressed head to toe in black. He put a finger to his lips and jerked his head for them to keep going. Sascha froze as she felt the lethal anger coming off him, so dangerous it threatened everything and everyone in its path.

"Come on." Tamsyn tugged at her arm.

Dorian scowled and motioned for her to go. Sascha forced herself to start moving again. The sentinel's deep anger wasn't something she could fix, not when he seemed determined to nurture it.

She turned to Tamsyn the second they were behind the solid wooden door of the bedroom. "How can you stand this? Being shut away safe while they might not be?"

"I'm the healer. It does no one any good if I die. I fight my battles after they've fought theirs." Intense emotion overlaid her every word.

"At least you get to fight. They should've let me help— I have enough Tk and Tp powers to cause some mayhem."

"There might not be any need for violence. The wolves have a pact with us." Tamsyn didn't sound too convinced of her own argument. "I've been thinking of something."

"What?" Sascha paced the room, feeling more like a caged animal than the cool, controlled Psy she was supposed to be. "That it's idiotic to be locked up here when we're fully capable of protecting ourselves?"

"If you go down, you make Lucas vulnerable." Tamsyn's words pleaded with her to think. "If the SnowDancers pick up that the mating dance is incomplete, they'll use you as a lever against him."

"Will they know if we don't tell them?"

Tamsyn paused. "I'm not sure. They're wolves, not cats. Their scent is very different from ours—they might assume you already belong to Lucas."

For some reason, that made Sascha smile. "How can you talk about belonging to someone so easily? I thought predatory changelings were independent by nature."

"Simple." Tamsyn walked over and took Sascha's hand. "Because Lucas belongs to you, too."

Sascha wanted to break the contact but she could feel the healer's need for touch, for Pack. Nate was down there facing off with the wolves, and despite the logic of her statements, Tamsyn was terrified. Not quite understanding how she knew what to do, she pulled the other woman into a hug. Tamsyn came without hesitation.

"How can you treat me like one of the pack?" Sascha asked, even as she stroked Tamsyn's thick fall of hair.

"You smell of Lucas, and I don't mean on a physical level. It's difficult to put into words." She pulled back from the embrace, as if she'd received what she needed to be strong again. "Our bodies and hearts recognize yours. We know you're one of us."

"But I'm not mated to Lucas yet," Sascha argued, feeling the noose slip about her neck. She couldn't, wouldn't, destroy these people who'd come to mean everything to her. If Lucas went down, DarkRiver would fragment. The pack might physically survive with the deadly sentinels at the helm, but they'd all be broken. She would not do that to them.

"You're so close as to make little to no difference." Tamsyn pushed her hair off her face and held up a hand when Sascha began to speak. "Don't ask me what the final steps are. I can't tell you. It's different for each couple . . ." She sighed. "But the male half of the pair usually has a better idea of what's needed—I guess it's nature's way of ensuring the more independent females can't avoid bonding."

"He'll never tell me." She sat down heavily on the floor, her head hanging between bent knees. "I'm coming apart at the seams and I refuse to take Lucas with me."

Tamsyn knelt in front of her. "That's not your choice to make. Mating isn't marriage. You can't divorce each other and you can't walk away once you've found one another."

Sascha met the other woman's compassionate gaze. "I'll destroy him." It was a painful whisper.

"Maybe. Or you might save him." Tamsyn smiled. "Without you, Lucas might've become too much his beast, too much the predator, cruel and without mercy."

"Never."

"He was christened in blood, Sascha. Don't ever forget that." Tamsyn sat down cross-legged in front of her. "Until he met you, do you know what he was like? Do you know where he was going? Day by day I watched him get more protective, more unbending and strict, especially with the kids, and there was nothing I could do."

Sascha was caught by the passion in the healer's voice.

"He's undoubtedly our alpha, someone we'd follow into hell and back if he asked it of us. But it takes more than an iron fist to rule, and he was starting to lose those other parts."

"He's so good with Kit," Sascha said, recalling all the times she'd seen him with the juvenile.

"Five months ago, not long after we lost Kylie, he banned Kit from solo runs."

"Why?"

"He didn't want the boy hurt." Tamsyn shook her head. "Kit has the scent of a future alpha—to have him always have a babysitter could've destroyed his development and turned him from us. Even more than the other juveniles, Kit needs the freedom to let his beast roam."

"You persuaded Lucas to change his mind?"

"No, Sascha. You did." She put a hand on Sascha's knee. "Kit was ready to rebel when Lucas quietly took him out for a run soon after he met you. When he came back, Kit wasn't with him."

"He let Kit go his own way?" Sascha knew it must've been one of the hardest things he'd ever done. Protecting his own was a compulsion with him. It was also something he couldn't indulge in—it would smother the very people he was trying to shelter from harm.

Tamsyn nodded. "You allow him to think, to see past his emotions."

"I think you're giving me too much credit. I can barely understand my own emotions."

"I think I know what an E-Psy is."

Sascha twisted her fingers together. "You think E stands for Emotion, don't you? I've already considered that but it makes no sense. Before Silence, all Psy felt emotion."

Tamsyn didn't answer her. "The changeling healers around the country have a sort of informal alliance," she said, in what seemed a complete change of topic. "We share our knowledge in spite of the fact that we might belong to enemy groups. The alphas don't even try to stop us. They know we're healers because we can't be anything else—we refuse to withhold information that could save a life."

"And the Psy call themselves enlightened," Sascha whispered, stunned by the humanity of these so-called animals. "We wouldn't give water to our enemy if he lay dying on our doorstep."

"*You* would, Sascha. You're Psy, too. Maybe, just maybe, there are more like you than you know."

"If you knew how much I hoped for that . . . I don't want to be alone, Tamsyn." Tears choked up her throat. "I don't want to die in cold silence."

Tamsyn shook her head. "You're never going to be alone again. You belong to us, to Pack." Her hand covered Sascha's. "Don't be afraid of letting go of the PsyNet. We'll catch you when you fall."

Sascha desperately wanted to tell her the truth but couldn't. If any of the leopards found out, they'd never allow her to set her plan in motion and it had to go ahead. If it didn't, the SnowDancers would declare war. In a war between the most lethal wolf and leopard packs in the country and the Psy, thousands would die, innocents and guilty alike.

Nobody could know the ultimate secret of the PsyNet. It wasn't only an information net, it was a life net. No one knew when it had been created, but theories abounded that it had come into existence on its own because Psy minds needed the feedback of other Psy minds.

Deprived of that feedback, they shut down and died. Even comatose Psy retained the PsyNet link, their bodies well aware of the requirement for the connection to ensure survival. The instant Sascha dropped out of the Net, she'd begin to slip into the final darkness.

"Thank you," she said to Tamsyn, hiding her fear.

The woman squeezed her hand. "The reason I told you about the healers alliance is that we pass on a lot of things through word of mouth. One of our oral stories is very interesting—it tells of healers of the mind. They disappeared from the stories almost a hundred years ago. Interesting timing, don't you think?"

Sascha stared. "Mind healers?"

"Yes. They could apparently take suffering and anger

from people, enabling them to see past the block emotion can often be. They could also heal those who'd been abused, violated, hurt in a thousand different ways. They bandaged up wounds that might otherwise have destroyed people." Tamsyn's eyes were intent. "They were adored because everything that they took from others, they put into themselves. They had the capacity to neutralize the burden, but it had to have hurt."

Sascha was so stunned, she was trembling. All those times she'd imagined taking away people's pain, all those times she'd felt the heavy rock of others' emotions sitting on her heart . . . none of it had been pretend. "They healed souls," she whispered, knowing Tamsyn was right.

The explanation fit. No wonder she was fracturing. Her cardinal powers had been brutally contained for twenty-six years, growing endlessly with no release. The pressure point had been reached.

"I think that's what you are, Sascha. A healer of souls."

A single tear streaked down Sascha's face. "They told me I was broken," she whispered. "They told me I was flawed." Because of their lies, she'd contained her light, her rainbow of stars, trapping the healing gifts of her mind. "They crippled me. And they had to have known!" Her mother certainly had to have understood her child's unusual mind. She was Council—she knew their history, what had to be hidden . . . what had to be destroyed.

"When they tried to get rid of violence," Tamsyn said, shifting over to sit beside Sascha, one arm around her shoulders, "they also got rid of one of their most precious gifts."

Lucas walked out to the front yard, Nate and Dorian by his side. Vaughn and Clay were hidden in the shadows and Mercy was prowling the treetops behind the SnowDancers.

Hawke stood in the yard flanked by two wolves Lucas knew to be his lieutenants. Indigo was a stunningly beautiful female with the cold eyes of a snow wolf. Tall and slender, she was undoubtedly deadly. Riley was a solid-looking male who appeared to move slow. It was an illusion. He could take down a fully grown wolf in about three seconds flat. Without changing form.

"Why are you here?" Lucas asked.

Hawke walked forward, leaving his lieutenants behind. Lucas did the same. Two alphas meeting in neutral territory. Except it wasn't. This was a DarkRiver safe house. The wolves shouldn't have set foot near it without a damn good reason. He'd accepted Hawke's previous intrusion because the alpha had come alone. Bringing others was a sign of aggression.

"We want to talk to your Psy," Hawke said without prelude.

Lucas felt fury ripple through him. "No."

"I trust you, cat, but I don't trust any of the Psy." Hawke's eyes held bloodlust. "I won't let the lives of my people hang in the hands of one of those creatures without meeting her for myself. This is the fourth day since Brenna was taken—we have only two days before he kills. And you're asking us to *wait*."

"If you trust me, why do you need to see her?"

"Wouldn't you do the same if the situations were reversed? What if it was Rina in the hands of that monster?" His entire face went unnaturally calm. "We're not here to pick a fight so you might want to tell the cat up in the trees to stay back."

Lucas wasn't surprised Hawke had picked up Mercy's scent—the man hadn't become alpha of a lethal pack by being weak. Neither had Lucas. "Mercy's not the one you should be worried about."

"Damn it to hell, Lucas. Don't break our alliance over a fucking, worthless Psy. They're nothing—"

Lucas slammed a fist into Hawke's jaw. Hard. The wolf went down. Growls echoed around the yard as sentinels and lieutenants crouched down for battle.

CHAPTER 21

Standing over the fallen wolf, Lucas forced himself not to bare his teeth. "She's mine. Think about that the next time you open your big mouth."

Getting up, Hawke slashed his hand down. Indigo and Riley straightened from their crouch. "Hell, Lucas. You could've told me you'd really mated to her." He rubbed at his bruised jaw and winced. "You have a right like a damn freight train."

"You shouldn't be here."

"I was the one who brought you your Psy safe and sound."

Lucas stared at the other alpha and even through the protective rage running through him, he knew Hawke was right. He did have a right to meet the woman he was being asked to entrust with the life of one of his people. Riley, too, must need assurance that his sister's life was in safe hands. "Do all your wolves know about this place?"

"No. Just like not all your leopards know the location of

our tunnels." It was a reminder that Lucas and his sentinels had tracked down the SnowDancers' main hideout.

Since the start, their alliance had been cool and distanced, two predators circling each other, not quite sure when the other would bite. It was time to take the next step, to build strength the Psy would truly fear. "I'm going to invite you into this home."

They'd always done their talking out in the open, away from their personal places. Though it had never been said, they both knew it was so that those places wouldn't be tainted by violence if blood was spilled. Theirs was a fragile trust and it was no longer enough. With his invitation, he'd not only accepted, but expanded, the offer that had been hinted at when Hawke's lieutenants had treated Dark-River juveniles as their own.

Ice-blue eyes looked at him without blinking. "That's a good deal of trust."

"Don't make me regret it." He held out his arm.

The other alpha clasped it at the elbow and they went toward each other in the hard embrace of two hunters. When they drew back, Lucas turned to head toward the safe house. Hawke followed with his lieutenants stalking behind him.

"Free passage," Hawke said as they walked. It was clear enough to be heard by the other changelings.

Lucas thought about the war that might break out, thought about the safety of his people. And then he thought about what they would want, what he had no right to deny them. They were predators but they were also human in a way the Psy would never be. "Free passage."

With those two simple words each, they'd turned their alliance into a blood bond. They'd given each other's packs free passage in all of their respective territories, the right to come and go without any of the current stipulations. But that wasn't the important part.

As of now, the wolves would come to the aid of the leopards and the leopards would die for the wolves.

No matter what the fight.

Once inside the house, the lieutenants and sentinels placed themselves in a protective circle, watching each other and their alphas. They might now be blood allies but complete trust would take time.

"Dorian." Lucas gave the other man the signal to fetch Sascha. Everything in him wanted to take care of it himself, wanted to protect her every step of the way. But he couldn't leave his people alone with the wolves, or betray his driving need, need which was this raw only at the final stage of mating.

Hawke couldn't be allowed to guess that the mating dance was incomplete. It wouldn't damage their alliance but it would probably make the other alpha back off from placing any faith in Sascha.

The beast wasn't convinced by the logical argument. It wanted Sascha. *Now*. It was taking too much of Lucas's will to fight the possessiveness of the panther. He didn't even trust the sentinels at this stage. It was part of the price he paid for being a leopard, an alpha, and a Hunter.

Nobody spoke until Sascha walked back into the room followed by Tamsyn, with Dorian shadowing their backs. Tammy didn't need to be here, to be vulnerable. Protecting one of their women was going to put enough pressure on the sentinels. Nate was clearly furious at his mate, his eyes narrowed in anger. Already, her presence was affecting their ability to defend.

"Tamsyn," Lucas said, walking over to pull Sascha to his side. "You need to leave." He rarely gave Tammy orders, knew he was too easy with her. He even knew why.

It wasn't because his mother had been a healer as many

people thought. No, it was because he'd seen the condition she'd been in after trying to save his father's life. She'd almost killed herself, given everything she'd had in that slender seventeen-year-old body. And when they'd found him, Lucas, she'd tried desperately to squeeze impossibly more from her worn-out soul.

However, right now, he couldn't afford to have her fight against him, couldn't afford to show any weakness. If she spoke up, he'd have to get very harsh and he didn't want to do that to Tammy. To his shock, Sascha was the one who spoke. "She needs to be here."

The SnowDancers raised their brows, but there was a kind of shadowed respect in their eyes. The rules were different for the mates of Pack alphas. No one wanted their alpha mated to a weak female.

"Why would that be?" Hawke turned to face them, his back to the mantel.

Lucas moved until Sascha and Tamsyn were both half-hidden by his body. "None of your business, wolf. You came to see Sascha. Here she is."

Sascha pushed at his back until he shifted enough that she could meet the wolf's gaze. It was as far as he was going to go.

"I know you don't trust me," she said. "I even know that you hate the Psy on a level that's so deep, it has no end."

Hawke's mouth tightened, his eyes going glacial.

"But you don't have to trust me in this—you have to trust Lucas."

Hawke snorted. "He's your mate. He's hardly likely to be unbiased."

Lucas waited for Sascha to dispute their mating, unable to do anything to warn her.

Her hand slipped around to lie against his stomach. The panther wanted to purr. "Do you really think he'd mate to someone who'd endanger his pack?"

"Yeah, wolf." Relief at her acceptance ran through Lucas like fire. "Just how much do you trust me?"

"How do you know she hasn't fucked with your mind?" It was a harsh question.

"Because you know as well as I do that the Psy can't hold on to our minds for longer than a few minutes." Lucas tracked Hawke's every movement, leaving Indigo and Riley to the sentinels. He had a feeling Riley was the more dangerous of the pair—like Dorian, he'd lost a sister to this killer. "She would've had to manipulate not only my mind but those of the sentinels as well."

"Psy never work alone." Hawke watched them both without blinking.

Sascha's hand clenched on Lucas's abdomen. "Psy also don't feel emotion." Stretching, she kissed the hard angle of Lucas's jaw from behind his shoulder. "Yet I feel so much, it's threatening to destroy me."

There was no arguing with her statement. She was sensually, beautifully female, her body's hunger for Lucas a siren song. The unmated males could no more ignore that than they could stop breathing.

Every instinct in him quivered, wanting to take her, right here, right now, and show everyone that she belonged to him. Fighting the animalistic urge merely served to heighten the craving, until the panther's fur rasped along the inside of his skin.

"Then those eyes of yours mean nothing." Hawke crossed his arms across his chest. "You're weaker than the ones we're fighting."

"You're calling emotion a weakness?" Tamsyn was trying to get past Dorian without success. Nate stared at her from across the room, obviously willing her to be silent, but the healer had never been good at following orders. "Emotion is what makes us strong!"

"She's not one of us," Hawke said. "Her strength comes

from feeling nothing. If she feels, it means she's damaged goods. We can't trust Brenna's life to a defective Psy who could crumble at any minute."

Lucas felt the panther's claws cut through his skin. "Be very careful what you say about my mate, Hawke. I'd hate to have to kill you." The warning lingered on the air.

Both of Sascha's arms wrapped around his middle. "Lucas, he's right. If I were weak, I'd be of no use."

"You're not weak." He held her hands flat against him, luxuriating in the public gesture of belonging. This Psy was his and he wasn't going to let her escape. Ever.

"No," she said, "I'm not. I'm a cardinal E-Psy."

Hawke's gaze reflected a bright flash of shock so deep, it couldn't be hidden.

"What do you know, wolf?" Lucas wondered what Sascha had learned that had enabled her to make that statement so confidently, but he wasn't going to ask her to explain in front of the SnowDancers.

"I want to see her face," the wolf demanded.

Lucas felt his muscles lock. Sascha's hand smoothed over his body as she drew back. "Let me, Lucas. This is my time to fight."

The anguish in her tone got through to him, cutting past the possessive beast to the man within. He let her move until she stood slightly in front of him, where he could quickly haul her behind his body. "You or your lieutenants even blink wrong and I'll slash you wide open." It wasn't a threat, just simple fact.

Hawke nodded. "Fair enough." Nobody played games with mates.

"What do you want to see?" Sascha tipped her head slightly to the side, her eyes on the wolf. He was feral in a way that even Dorian wasn't, his beast separated from his humanity by the thinnest of layers.

"I want you to prove you are what you say you are."

"Are you sure?" she asked softly.

Hawke's jaw could've been carved from stone. "Yes."

She took a breath and let her eyes flutter shut. As her senses expanded, she felt the full brunt of Lucas's possessive, dominant personality. He was pure strength, pure heart. But buried deep was an echo of the staggering pain suffered by the young boy he'd once been, an echo that now beat with a fierce need to protect. She felt his determination to keep her, too, but that was the one thing she could never allow. He'd already spent a childhood without parents—she would not condemn him to a lifetime without a mate.

Behind her panther, she could feel the dull anger that was Dorian, so wounded that she'd have to spend years to lighten his anguish. Except she didn't have years. Tamsyn was gentleness and joy, power and care. The soldiers of both groups gave off their own distinctive emotional scents. But it was Hawke that she was searching for and Hawke that she found.

The wolf's emotions struck cold terror into her heart. She'd never felt such pure, unadulterated rage. Dark and violent, it was a scar across his soul. Hawke could function, could rule, but this man would never love, not so long as he was blinded by the red veil of blood and death.

Sascha didn't know if he'd feel what she was doing, didn't know if he'd find his proof. What she did know was that she couldn't let him walk away without trying to heal the festering wounds in his soul. Like Dorian, he couldn't be healed overnight, but perhaps she could give him a moment's surcease.

She wrapped mental arms around him and drew away the anger, the violence. And gave back joy, laughter, pleasure. To her surprise, she felt him react to her like Lucas did. He jerked in shock and then started trying to push her out. He was no Psy but he was definitely saying *No!*

She withdrew at once.

When she opened her eyes, it was to find him staring at her as if she were a ghost. "I didn't think the empaths existed anymore." His voice was half wolf.

Empath.

It was the right word, the word that had been systematically destroyed from the Psy lexicon. "Neither did I," she whispered, letting her back rest against Lucas's front. His arms came around her and she swore she felt the ruffle of fur against the skin.

"Do you know how to attack using your powers?" Hawke's eyes lingered on her and Lucas's skin-to-skin contact.

"Nothing smooth," she told him, having thought about this upstairs. "But it'll keep me alive long enough to give you what you need to find Brenna."

Lucas's arms tightened across her shoulders. "I won't let her set the plan in motion unless we can pull her out of the Net safely."

Hawke shifted position. Sascha's eyes met his and her soul froze. He *knew*. Somehow, the alpha of the Snow-Dancers knew that she couldn't leave the PsyNet without facing death. Mutely, she pleaded with him to remain silent. If Lucas discovered the truth, he'd never let her go. *Never.*

And she needed to go, needed to wipe out a lifetime of failure by saving this one vibrant light before her own flickered out forever.

"Sorry, sweetcakes," Hawke raised his hands palms out, "but you're his mate. I'm not going to let you kill yourself and have Lucas out for my blood. In that kind of rage, I wouldn't want to take my chances against him."

Lucas's arms became manacles. "What's he talking about, Sascha?" It was a warning. She'd kept something from him and he wasn't happy about it. To Hawke, he said, "You can leave now. You got what you came for."

Hawke looked at them for another long moment before

nodding. "We have two more days if the killer sticks to his usual pattern. Protect your woman, panther." With that the wolves left, tracked out of DarkRiver territory by Mercy, Clay, and Vaughn.

Lucas didn't wait for the sentinels to return. "Nate, Dorian, secure the house."

"Lucas," Tamsyn began, "maybe you should—"

"Stay the hell out of this." Lucas's eyes met her shocked ones. He'd never spoken to Tammy like that. "Nate, if you want your mate to last the night, you'd better get her under control." He wasn't kidding. There was only so much he could take and Sascha's keeping a secret had pushed him over the edge.

I'm not going to let you kill yourself . . .

What did the wolf know that he didn't?

"Don't talk to Tammy like that," Sascha ordered.

"I'll talk to my pack however the hell I feel like. You don't get to have a voice until you explain yourself to me." Grabbing her hand, he began to haul her up the stairs.

A psychic blow hit his chest but he was expecting it and took it with a grunt. "You're not that powerful a Tk, kitten." He was in the grip of the panther's instincts and there was nothing civilized about them.

"Damn it, Lucas. Let me go!" She tried to pull her hand away and kicked out at his shin.

Fed up with her wriggling, he bent down, threw her over his shoulder in a fireman's carry, and ran up the stairs. Her weight was nothing to his changeling strength, her fists on his back mere caresses. She was yelling and screaming by the time he got her into the bedroom and locked the door.

When he put her down on the floor, she took a swing at him. Only his lightning-fast reflexes saved him from a black eye. He pinned her hands behind her back before she could try again. Furious eyes met his. The woman in his arms was pure fire and heat, as different from the Psy he'd first met as night was from day.

Desire sparked deep and low in his gut, brought to life by the stunning brilliance of her emotions. This was a fit mate, the panther in him growled. This female would never let herself be crushed by his demands and needs. She'd meet him more than halfway. And she'd fight to the death for him like his mother had fought for his father.

"If you don't let me go right now, I swear I'll knock you unconscious," she threatened. "I have enough Tk for a blow hard enough to rattle your thick skull."

"I'm not budging until you tell me what Hawke meant." The scent of her infiltrated his lungs, fuel to the inferno of his possessiveness.

"You don't need to know."

He swore. "How do you think that made me look down there? My own mate keeping secrets from me?"

She looked discomfited for an instant. "He shouldn't have known. Nobody should know."

"But he does and I have a right to. You're *mine*."

"Don't pull this alpha thing on me, Lucas. You're not my alpha!"

He had no desire to dominate her that way. "But I'm your mate." Leaning down, he nipped sharply at her jaw. Goose bumps appeared on the exposed skin of her neck. "I have certain rights."

"You're not my mate," she protested, but her voice was weak.

"Tell me, kitten. You know I'm not going to let it go however much you want me to."

Her eyes darkened, ebony spreading over the light. "Why?" she pleaded. "We can't let that girl die if I can save her. If I tell you everything, you'll try to stop me."

"You think I won't stop you right now?"

"You can't." Her eyes were almost pure black. "I can work the PsyNet from behind bars."

He used one hand to keep her wrists under control, still not sure she wouldn't go for his eyes like every other pissed-off female he knew. With the other, he clasped the back of her neck. "Yeah, but can you do it while unconscious?"

"You wouldn't." It was an outraged whisper.

"To keep you safe, I'd do worse things than knock you out."

Her eyes narrowed. "We're going to have to talk about this dominant streak of yours."

"It's not a streak. It's all of me." For her, he'd try to be reasonable occasionally. Except on this one point. "Are you going to talk or are you going to make me put you under? Do you know how much it'll hurt me to have to do that to you?"

Her entire body softened. He finally chanced letting her wrists go free. Instead of hitting out at him, she put them on his chest, palms down. *"Lucas."* Her eyes were pure black now, so dark that he could see nothing but his own reflection. "The PsyNet isn't a chosen part of our life," she began. "It isn't something that's forced on us either. It's necessary."

"Food and water are necessary," he said. "Why the Net?"

"My mind isn't built like yours—it needs to be fed by the electronic impulses of other Psy minds." She clenched her hands on his T-shirt.

The panther understood at the same moment as the man. "So once you expose yourself as bait and the Councilors pick up on your empathy, there's no way to get you out?" He was so furious he could barely speak.

CHAPTER 22

"There *never* was any way to get me out," she told him. "My shields are about to collapse. My plan won't change that future, it'll just speed up the process." When he remained silent, she tugged at the material under her hands. "I have to do this. I have to try to save Brenna." Her voice broke. "Let me die proud."

His entire body rejected the idea of her dying to save another. That other woman was only a name, an image. This was Sascha Duncan, his mate. "No."

Sascha jerked at the flatness of that sound. Lucas didn't even sound like he was considering it. "I'll never forgive myself if I let Brenna die."

"I don't care." Complete implacability.

"Hawke will come after you."

"No, he won't." His eyes were going panther. "Wolves mate for life, too. He knows I can't sacrifice you for his packmate. *She matters nothing to me.*" The eyes looking out at her were no longer human.

She tried to wrench herself from his embrace but he

wouldn't let her go. "You don't have the right to decide this."

"I have all sorts of rights over you."

"My mother, Lucas! My mother is hiding a killer. How do you think that makes me feel?" Shame was her constant companion.

"Nikita merely gave you half your genes," he retorted. "How has she ever been a mother to you? Don't punish yourself for her. She won't care."

Her head snapped at the blow. "I care."

"I care, too. About you."

So it went. They fought for most of the night. Sascha was tempted to put her plan into effect without his agreement. However, she knew it would be a senseless waste— there remained the need for a diversion.

A physical distraction could theoretically work if it was large scale, drawing the attention of the minds in San Francisco and the outlying areas. If DarkRiver and the Snow-Dancers worked together, they could create a multitude of events that coincided and confused.

Since the killer had to be nearby, given his habit of returning victims to a place they knew, it would probably be enough. The PsyNet was huge and endless but the physical location of a Psy did play a part in how quickly he or she could surf to another mind. It had to do with connections . . . links.

She was convinced their murderous prey would be compelled to come for her, bait that tantalized his savage needs and was available within such easy reach. All she needed was one glimpse. With her empathic gifts, she should be able to detect the ugliness of his rage almost immediately.

Her plan *could* work. Unfortunately, she needed the changelings to cooperate for it to do so. But Lucas wasn't budging. Without his agreement, she knew no one would help her. Even the wolves would stand back, though it was their packmate's life on the line.

She fought her panther with every ounce of will she had.

And she failed.

Well before dawn the next morning, Hawke rang to say the SnowDancers could provide the needed distraction.

"How?" Lucas asked, not really caring. As long as Sascha had to die for the plan to succeed, it wasn't going ahead. Right now he couldn't think about what else she'd revealed—*My shields are about to collapse.* He'd allow nothing to speed up the process, not until they'd worked out a way to protect her from the Council.

A small pause. "I think you'd better come over. Bring your Psy with you."

Lucas knew exactly where Hawke's den was. Just as he knew it was guarded around the clock by wolves who wouldn't hesitate to go for his throat. "Free passage," he reminded Hawke.

"Don't insult me, cat. I don't break my vows. Be here as soon as you can—the pack is getting restless. If we aren't going to move on the PsyNet, I'm going to give the order to take down all the high-ranking Psy we can.

"We've already got people in place near the residences of every one of the Councilors, no matter where they happen to live. Somebody will talk if you make enough of them bleed." He hung up.

"What did Hawke have to say?" a sleepy voice asked.

Lucas turned to find Sascha sitting up in bed behind him. He wanted to lie, to protect, but they'd gone beyond that. "He says he can provide a diversion."

Sascha frowned. "That's the weakest part of the plan," she muttered. "With a physical distraction, there's always the chance that it might not take away enough Psy minds to give the killer a head start. I wonder what Hawke's going to suggest."

He wanted to shake her. The weakest part of the plan was the one her life hinged on. "Get dressed. We're going to Hawke's place."

Fifteen minutes later, they gathered downstairs. He told Nate and Mercy to remain behind to guard the safe house.

Tamsyn frowned. "It's only me left here now. Why don't you let me come along and then you don't have to leave two sentinels behind."

"You're our healer." Lucas touched her cheek. He'd been harsh with her the night before. "We need you safe so you can patch us up if anything goes wrong."

Her jaw set but she didn't argue, hugging him tight instead. "Be safe."

Hawke's den was located deep in the Sierra Nevada, almost at subalpine level. Lucas drove up the nearly invisible track in his four-wheel drive, cursing as branches scraped along the sides.

"If it was only you and your pack, you could've run with them," Sascha said, her eyes staring out at the gray early-morning light. Darkness had fled in the time it had taken them to drive this far.

"If it was only me and my pack, we'd never have had a chance to save the girl at all."

Her organizer chimed unexpectedly into the small silence. She checked the message. "It's Mother. I'll ignore it. If she asks, I'll tell her I forgot to take it with me."

"Enrique?"

"I have a feeling he's too busy with keeping track of the NetMind's search for the killer." She leaned forward and squinted. "I can't see them."

"Of course not. That's their job." Vaughn and Clay were racing beside them as they drove into Hawke's territory, having left their vehicle a couple of miles back. They were fully capable of infiltrating the SnowDancer den and had done it before with Lucas by their side. Dorian had driven in ahead of them, dumped his vehicle, and taken to the trees. He'd already called in on a secure line to tell them he was situated above the den.

"Is that the house?" Sascha pointed to the barely visible walls of a large lodge, half-hidden by the trunks of the firs that lined the slope leading up to the clearing.

"No." He grinned at the wolves' cunning. "But it's sure fooled a lot of would-be attackers."

"It's a front? It looks so real."

"It is real. It's just not their hideout." Circling around the house, he stopped the car. "Stay inside until I'm beside you."

For once, she didn't argue. "This is your world, Lucas. I'm a novice."

He cupped her cheek in a fleeting caress before exiting the car and walking around to her door. No wolf would take him in the back. In the same way, Dorian would never shoot at an unarmed wolf from his position in the canopy. They were animals but both packs had a kind of honor most of the Psy would never understand. If it came to a fight, it would be face-to-face, hands against hands, claws against claws, not a sniper's bullet.

Still, he wasn't going to take chances with his mate's life. He scented the air to ensure Vaughn and Clay were with him. As he'd expected, their scents had been joined by those of several wolves. None were venturing too close. Good. He pulled open Sascha's door and she stepped out.

He shut the door. "Stay behind me." Already, he was placing his body in front of hers.

"I can feel five emotional signatures I don't know," she whispered, real soft.

His brows raised. "I didn't know you could do that."

"I've been practicing." She sounded almost proud of herself, as though she was getting past the fear that she was "flawed." "Vaughn and Clay are circling us, one in front, one behind."

"Let's go." He started to walk into the forest, which appeared to go on endlessly, the dark green firs so close together they blotted out the sun. They walked for five minutes before he found the rutted path half-hidden by carefully strewn forest debris.

"Usually," he told Sascha, "if you got this far, there'd be a welcoming committee awaiting you. Nobody's ever found a single bone of the missing." The predator in him appreciated the efficiency.

"Do you think they eat them?"

He grinned at her gory attempt at a joke. "Nah. Even wolves have higher standards than to feed on human carrion."

Her hand rose to his shoulder. Something taut in him relaxed. His mate was starting to trust him on a level so deep she was completely unaware of it.

Thirty minutes later, they finally reached the end of the winding path, only to find themselves up against the craggy stone face of a mountain that seemed to reach for the sky. It looked like the path simply stopped, an illusion that had protected the SnowDancers for years.

"Open up, Hawke." He allowed his voice to carry. Leopards and wolves were their solitary audience.

A few seconds later, the bottom of the mountain magically started to crack open. The "door" slid back just far enough to allow them to enter. Lucas could feel Sascha's fascination at the structure but waited until they were inside to speak. The door closed behind them without any hint that it had ever been open.

Sascha's gasp echoed off the stone walls as lights came on all around them, illuminating a long tunnel beautifully paved with river stones. Paintings graced every surface, the artist having used the rock of the tunnel as a canvas. The scenes were of the wild, of wolves running, of the different faces of the forest. There was something hypnotically beautiful about the images. Beautiful and dangerous.

"Welcome." Hawke stepped out of the shadows and raised a brow. "Should I let your sentinels in?"

"No need." Lucas smiled. Vaughn and Clay were already inside. Dorian was to remain on the outside.

Hawke's eyes betrayed nothing but Lucas knew the other alpha was pissed that his people had managed to get inside . . . again. "Care to share?"

"Everyone needs secrets. Don't tell me you can't get into our safe houses."

Hawke scowled. "What about mutual trust?"

Sascha laughed and both men turned to look at her, their beasts fascinated by the purity of the sound. It was, Lucas realized, the first time he'd ever heard her laugh. The possessive need in him tightened to the most aching kind of tenderness. She meant more to him than she'd ever know. If she died, so would his heart.

"You're like two wild animals who aren't quite sure you believe the other's offer of peace. I wonder how long you'll circle around each other before you decide." She shook her head, those eerie eyes sparkling with feminine amusement. At that moment she was everything the beast in him craved, woman and passion, laughter and play, sensuality and hunger.

Lucas felt Hawke take a deep breath. When he looked back at the wolf, he read a simple message on his face: If she weren't yours . . .

"But she is," Lucas said, one predator to another, one alpha to another.

Sascha, who was staring at one of the paintings, didn't hear. "These are lovely, Hawke." She turned to him. "Is the artist one of your pack?"

Hawke's face seemed to harden till it was as unfeeling as the rock upon which the paint had been laid. "She was." He jerked his head behind him. "Let's go."

Troubled eyes met Lucas's when he went to take Sascha's hand. He shook his head—he knew nothing of the artist.

"They live underground?" Sascha asked after they'd been walking for five minutes, going steadily deeper.

"Some of them. This functions as their Pack headquarters." Before the SnowDancers had become as feared as they now were, group after group had tried to find the hideout in order to take them down. They'd all failed. Until DarkRiver. Lucas and his sentinels had not only found the den, they'd infiltrated it. Their sole purpose had been to leave behind a simple message.

Don't hurt us and we won't hurt you. DR.

A day later, a response had been found in Lucas's lair.

Agreed. SD.

Sometimes it was good being an animal. In the world of the Psy and even in the human world, such negotiations could've taken months. In the years following that initial contact, they'd started to edge warily toward a more workable relationship. But that simple rule remained—don't hurt us and we won't hurt you.

Hawke turned right ahead of them.

"What's on the left?" Sascha asked, looking down that corridor.

"Homes." When they'd first breached the tunnels, Dark-River had ensured the SnowDancers knew that they'd been near the homes of their pups and had left without doing harm. There was no clearer indication of friendship.

A few minutes later, they came to another fork. The corridors went off in several different directions. Ahead, they could see rooms opening up and people walking about. Hawke took them through the rightmost corridor and stopped in front of a closed door.

Beside him, Lucas felt Sascha's whole body go quiet. "Hawke," she said, an odd note in her voice. "What can I feel behind that door?"

Those icy eyes met theirs. "You'll see." Pushing open the door, he walked in.

Lucas went in ahead of Sascha, every one of his senses primed for trouble. Vaughn and Clay were already nearby, having taken human form and put on stolen clothing to throw the wolves off their scent. It would be hard getting out if something happened. Hard, but not impossible. Otherwise Lucas would've never brought his mate here.

However, what awaited them in the room wasn't anything he could've prepared for. Five people of varying ages sat around a large circular table. They didn't smell like wolf. Then one of them raised her head and night-sky eyes met his. "Christ!" He let Sascha enter but left the door open.

Sascha knew who the five people were the instant she saw them—Nikita had told her the details of the case. "The Lauren family," she whispered. She'd never known the ages of the five Psy who'd disappeared into SnowDancer territory, had never expected any of them to be children, because even after everything she'd learned, she hadn't been ready to admit that her own people would so callously turn their backs on the most innocent of the innocent.

The oldest two were males, one dark blond, the other

with hair the color of rich chocolate. Both had human eyes. The fair-haired male looked to be around forty, but the other was nearer Sascha's age. Then there was a teenage girl with deep red hair and the eyes of a cardinal Psy. She sat protectively next to a young boy who had the same hair and the same eyes. Last, a girl of about ten sat between the two older males. She had strawberry blonde hair and the feel of a powerful Psy. Her eyes were a pale green.

"How?" How had they survived being cut off from the Net? How had they survived at all?

"We're not cold-blooded murderers, Sascha." Hawke's voice was ice. "Not like the Psy." He sat down and Sascha let Lucas nudge her into a seat, too.

The teenager's head shot up and Sascha swore she felt a spike of temper. "You're making generalizations again. That's the same as saying all wolves are vicious."

Instead of getting angry, Hawke seemed to relax a fraction. "Sascha Duncan, meet Sienna Lauren. Next to her is her brother, Toby." He gestured to the two older males.

The blond one stood, his bearing as erect as a soldier's. "I'm Walker Lauren. Sienna and Toby are the children of my deceased sister. This is my daughter, Marlee." He nodded to the girl who sat beside him. A small hand slipped into his and his fingers curled around it.

"I'm Judd Lauren," the dark-haired man said after Walker sat down. "Walker's brother."

"I don't understand." Sascha could barely think through the riot of questions in her mind. "You're listed as dead on the Net." And the NetMind did not make mistakes.

"As far as the Net is concerned, we are," Walker answered.

In spite of the way he'd accepted Marlee's touch, she could feel nothing from him. Nothing. The same with Judd Lauren. The youngest two, Marlee and Toby, were definitely giving off emotion but Sienna was harder to read. "Are you all E-Psy?"

Sienna shook her head. "What's an E-Psy?"

Walker threw her a sharp look. "Sienna."

The teenager sat back, her mouth shut. Sascha knew that the two males had to be worried that Sascha would betray them, linked as she was to the Net.

"Why did you come into SnowDancer territory? You had to know it was courting death."

Walker and Judd glanced at each other and when Walker spoke, she knew he spoke for all of them. "We defected."

Her shock had her reaching for Lucas's hand, clasping it tight as it sat on the table. "What?"

"The entire family was slated for rehabilitation after our sister committed suicide." Walker's calm tone gave away nothing but Sascha could feel pain and anguish coming off Marlee and Toby.

Instinctively, she did what she could to soothe them. Sienna's eyes widened. "What are you doing, Sascha?"

Walker and Judd froze, looking at Sascha as one would eye a poisonous snake. Judd turned to Hawke. "You promised us she was safe." The words were razor sharp.

"She is." The pale eyes of a wolf met Sascha's. "Tell them what you were doing, sweetheart."

Lucas bristled. "Watch it, wolf."

Hawke's smile was slow and very satisfied. Next to him, Sienna sat up absolutely straight in her chair, looking from the two alphas back to Sascha.

"I'm sorry," Sascha apologized, ignoring the byplay between the males. "My control over my powers is still a little erratic. I'm an E-Psy, an empath."

Walker leaned forward. "There's no such thing as an E designation."

"There used to be before Silence," she told him. "E-Psy

are healers of the mind. We're supposed to help people who are drowning under the weight of emotion, but I guess our existence was a roadblock to the implementation of the Protocol." So they'd been quietly destroyed. Despite everything she knew about her race, that admission of ultimate betrayal felt like a knife cut to the soul.

"I think we need to talk," Walker said.

"Yes." She felt Lucas's beast awaken, his possessive instincts disliking the idea of her alone with the other male. "I think we *all* need to talk more."

Walker took the hint. "Of course."

She thought back to what they'd been speaking about. "Why was the whole family sentenced to the Center?" She looked at the innocent faces of the children and wondered what kind of a cruel mind could deprive them of their personalities before they'd even had a chance to develop. She wasn't naïve enough to think that the Lauren children had been the first to be so condemned, but nothing she'd seen thus far had prepared her for this new horror.

"My mother took her life in a most unusual fashion for a Psy—a cardinal Psy," Sienna said, ignoring Walker's look. "She stripped herself naked and teleported off Golden Gate Bridge, screaming that she was finally free."

CHAPTER 23

Sascha looked into the young cardinal's eyes and wanted to tell her to let the anger and pain out. Damming it up behind a wall of silence would only equal a slow death. She'd learned that the hard way.

"We'd also had several . . . incidents in the past. The Council decided they needed to 'purge' our family tree of undesirable traits." Judd's eyes went to Marlee. "Nonbiological members of the family were given the choice to renounce any relationship or undergo rehabilitation."

Sascha read between the lines and what she heard was so heartbreaking she couldn't speak. Marlee's biological mother had forsaken her child, handed her over for torture. The staggering nature of the betrayal was something no one with a human or changeling heart would ever understand. And Sascha's heart was no longer Psy, if it had ever been.

"How can you be alive?" Lucas raised her hand to his lips for a gentle kiss. She knew it wasn't a territorial marking—it was simply a changeling gesture of affection for a mate, something he hadn't even thought about. But all the Psy in the room noticed. And wondered. "According to Sascha, once you're cut off from the Net, you lose the feedback needed to function."

"That's what we thought," Walker began. "When we decided to defect, we came to the SnowDancers because of their reputation with the Psy. They're thought of as brutal animals who kill without conscience. However, we'd researched them during the time the Council allowed us to wrap up our affairs. We knew they wouldn't destroy Toby and Marlee on sight."

Sascha frowned. "I don't think the little ones need to be here for this." Their fear was very real and very scary.

"That's what I told them," Hawke said, a tic at the corner of his mouth. "We don't talk about this kind of stuff in front of pups."

"You expect us to leave them to your tender care?" Judd asked.

"Sienna, take the kids and go," Hawke ordered.

Surprising Sascha, the clearly headstrong teenager stood and took Toby's hand. "Marlee, come here."

The girl looked to her father. Finally, Walker nodded. Marlee almost ran to Sienna's other side and slipped her hand into the redhead's free one. The young ones had obviously become used to touch in the months they'd been here and, Sascha guessed, the older Psy were trying to learn to accept those touches for the children's sake. No normal Psy would've ever allowed care for another to influence them, but the Laurens were hardly normal.

"I'm doing this for Toby and Marlee, not you." The defiant words were directed at Hawke.

The alpha gave her a mock-salute. "Heaven forbid you do anything because I asked you to."

"I deserve to know what's going on." Sienna looked at her uncles. "I'm not a child."

"Stay in contact." Walker's tone revealed nothing of what he thought of Sienna's going over to the "dark side" and obeying Hawke's command.

No one spoke until the door had closed behind Sienna and the kids. Then they talked of death.

"So you expected to die," Sascha said.

"Of course." Walker nodded. "But we wanted to give Toby and Marlee a chance. They're young enough to learn to live a new way, their minds still plastic. We hoped that they might survive the necessary cutoff from the Net, somehow be able to find new pathways in their brain. It wasn't much of a chance but it was more than they'd have had otherwise."

"Sienna?"

"She was sixteen at the time." Walker's eyes were so coldly clinical that it startled Sascha to realize they were the same pale green as Marlee's. "We worked on the assumption that the wolves would see her as a threat and eliminate her."

"Yet you brought her in?" Lucas's voice was a whip. "You took a juvenile into almost certain death?"

If Sascha didn't know better, she'd have thought that Judd's jaw set in anger. "We had no choice," the younger male said. "Sienna would rather have died than be rehabilitated. If we hadn't taken her, she would've followed us on her own."

Sascha stroked Lucas with the secret part of her mind, which she was finally learning to understand. "They're right," she said. "Rehabilitation is worse than death, worse than anything you can imagine."

Lucas allowed her to soothe him, allowed her to surround him in affection. "Why didn't you kill them?" he asked Hawke.

"We're not idiots—it was obvious they'd come expecting death-by-changeling." His hand was a fist on the table.

"We captured them with the intention of collecting a ransom."

"Then we told him it was the Council that would pay the ransom and why," Judd said. "It left him in a bad position. He couldn't have five Net-linked Psy in his territory and since he has a conscience, he couldn't simply execute us or hand us over to be rehabilitated. He told us to cut the link."

"We'd always known that any of us who survived the SnowDancers would have to do that in any case to ensure our safety," Walker added. "Once the Council figured out we'd escaped, they would've used the Net link to exterminate us. No one defects from the Psy."

Judd looked straight at Sascha and she realized that he was quite unbelievably handsome in the perfect way of the Psy. "Sienna was the one who thought of it." His bearing was as formal as his brother's.

"Of what?" Sascha was fascinated by the Laurens. It was clear that the two youngest were indeed starting to adapt, their minds able to integrate with the changeling way of life. Equally, Judd and Walker remained locked in their Psy world, having lived the lie for too long.

Unlike her, the two males didn't have the very nature of their powers forcing them to face up to their emotions. Then there was Sienna, caught in the middle. At sixteen she would've been almost fully conditioned, ready to function as a cog in the Psy machine.

"Of a familial PsyNet," Walker said, meeting her gaze. "She proposed that we start to drop out of the Net one after the other, with only milliseconds between each drop."

"As if we were butchering them." Hawke's eyes were the chill blue of Arctic ice. Sascha fought the urge to reach out to him—he'd likely bite her hand off. The woman who took on this wolf would have to be either very brave or very stupid.

"Exactly." Walker nodded. "It also made it impossible

for anyone to get a lock on us. The second we dropped out, we linked our mind to another member of the family. The first to drop out had to be someone powerful enough to anchor the link, someone who could survive the initial separation and isolation."

"Sienna?" Sascha asked.

"No. She's cardinal but she didn't have enough control over her powers. Judd did it." Walker looked at his brother. "I was the last to drop out—I had to guide the kids out."

Sascha guessed that Judd had to be just below cardinal level to have taken on the job as anchor. "It worked?" Her heart was in her throat.

"Yes. We created a closed circle that constantly feeds upon the energy generated inside the loop."

Excitement and hope burst inside her. "Can . . ."

Walker started to speak before she could get the desperate question out. "No, Sascha. I'm sorry." The words were gentler than she'd expected from one of the Psy. "For the loop to function, we had to lock it shut. With three immature minds, it takes everything Judd and I have to keep it going. Until Sienna is old enough to help, we're the ones controlling Marlee's and Toby's instinctive attempts to rejoin the PsyNet."

"The second you open the loop," she whispered, "they're going to try to relink."

Walker nodded. "They can't help it. It's something we're born with—this need to be part of the Net. The two of us are old and powerful enough to control the instinct but even Sienna continues to have trouble. We can't take the risk of opening the loop to let you in and losing them."

"I understand."

Lucas shifted beside her. "Protecting your young comes first." There was no accusation in his voice and she knew he'd have made the same choice. But she could also feel his frustration, his need to protect *her*. If it ever came down to it, she understood that her mate would have no trouble sacrificing every single one of the Laurens to save her. It was almost terrifying to be adored that much. Almost.

The other two Psy looked at him. "Yes."

"But," Judd said, "we *can* provide the distraction you need. Sienna and I are both telepaths with a number of . . . unusual abilities. We've figured out a way to sneak back into the Net through the mind of a weak Psy.

"We intend to feed our powers through that individual's uplink and scramble a couple of the major lines of communication. It's going to be fairly rough—secondhand sabotage depends upon the Gradient of the mind being used, and our guy's scarcely 4.5."

Sascha knew they were talking about mind control, something that was both illegal and immoral. "If you do that, we're no better than them."

Judd looked across at Hawke and back to her. "We're only going to use the link to the Net. Neither of us has any interest in scanning the drug-addled mind of our volunteer. It's your choice."

Sascha struggled with the ethics of breaking one rule to uphold another; Brenna's life against the invasion of a mind. What decided her were the painful shadows she glimpsed around Hawke. He was dying each second his packmate was held in enemy hands, the alpha heart of him shredded by the twin talons of guilt and grief.

"Volunteer?"

"Money talks. He doesn't even care what he's volunteering for." Hawke nodded at Judd to continue.

"The break will be minute—we can't risk anyone tracing us through the other's mind. It's the same reason none of us can play your role. The instant they even suspect we're alive, they'll hunt us down."

"A minute break should be enough. The flow-on effects will ripple through the Net for some time," Sascha said, frowning in thought. "The killer should detect the changeling nature of my psychic scent before everyone else calms down and starts to wonder what's wrong with me.

"Even then, they probably won't immediately understand—most Psy have never seen inside a changeling mind. There's no reason it shouldn't work." Unless everything went to hell and the first ones to become aware of her were the Councilors.

Her hand tightened on Lucas's, fear a tight knot in her stomach. She didn't want to die, didn't want to leave this man she'd discovered after twenty-six years of loneliness. But neither could she steal an extra few days to love him with Brenna's death weighing down her conscience. Her mother was part of the horror and she had to save at least one life.

Even if no one could save her own.

The unfairness of it threatened to make her shatter—how dare she be shown this glory only to have it snatched from her grasp? Except, of course, the glory had never been meant to be hers. Fed by the poison of Silence, her mind's collapse had begun long before she'd met her panther.

"Kitten." Lucas's voice was a purr against her ear. "Stop hurting." Before she could comment, he did something that mere days ago would've shocked her utterly. Pushing back his chair, he lifted her into his lap. The casual display of strength reminded her of the differences between them, the surprises, the things she'd never get a chance to fully explore.

Having no desire to fight the embrace, she put her head against his shoulder and breathed in his scent. Lucas might try to stop her but she knew she was going to go through with this. Death was certain—it was just a case of how she'd make her final exit. So for now she'd live her life to the emotional zenith. She'd touch and laugh and be publicly held.

"Though we're the wrong gender to appeal to the killer, Walker and I have both tried to think of a way we could implement your plan, since we're already out of the Net," Judd said, watching the way she lay trustingly in Lucas's arms. "Unfortunately, it'd involve letting them know that at least one of us is alive."

"Which would make them suspicious about the deaths of the others," Sascha completed. "I understand, Judd. Don't feel guilty about putting the lives of the children first. I'd do the same."

"The Psy don't feel guilt." Judd's eyes were cool.

Despite the urgency of the situation, she wanted to smile. "Of course not."

Lucas kissed the tip of her nose and the gesture was so playful, she could do nothing to hide her smile any longer.

"My Psy does." Laughter flickered in his eyes but his arms held her tight.

Hawke looked at the two of them. "And we're not going to lose her."

Lucas locked gazes with the wolf. Sascha didn't understand the depths to which predatory changelings would go to protect their mates, didn't understand that she *owned* him in a way no one else ever would. "No, we're not."

"They refuse to believe I can't survive outside the PsyNet." Sascha shook her head. "Tell them."

"She's correct," Walker said. "She needs to have another psychic net in place to link to when she drops out. If she doesn't, she'll die of a kind of psychic starvation in a matter of minutes."

"Even if we could somehow figure out a way to get her out of the Net, she'd be a prisoner like Toby and Sienna." Judd pointed to her eyes. "We can alter our appearance and go out into the world, but you can't hide cardinal eyes."

"She won't be hiding." Lucas had no intention of burying

Sascha in any way—she'd spent too much of her life buried already. "My mate is going to stand by my side."

"The Council will find a way to kill her." Walker's tone was matter-of-fact.

"Leave them to us," Hawke said. It was clear he was talking about both DarkRiver and the SnowDancers. "Your job is to help us figure out how to keep Sascha alive outside the PsyNet."

A deep silence spread over the room. Lucas stroked Sascha's back and thought about how to scare the Council so badly that no one would ever dare touch her. They might not feel emotion but everyone was afraid to die.

Judd's eyes unfocused in front of him. A moment later, Walker's did the same. Lucas felt the hairs on the back of his neck rise and knew the two were telepathing intensely. As if aware of his discomfort, Sascha snuggled closer, wrapping her arms around his neck. He let his body feel her soft weight, her heat, her *life*, and gloried in having found his mate. No way in hell was he going to lose her.

"There's a possibility," Walker said.

Everyone looked at the eldest Psy.

"Sienna's been trying to convince us that our minds simply need feedback, not necessarily Psy feedback."

"The problem is, there's no way to test that without dropping out of the Net." Judd looked like he was continuing to argue with Sienna even as he spoke to them.

Sascha's forehead wrinkled. "How would I get the feedback without linking with Psy minds?"

"You'd link with changeling minds. For reasons we'll explain, we don't think human minds would work."

Lucas squeezed Sascha so tight that she protested. "Sorry, kitten," he muttered, his concentration on Walker Lauren. "Can that be done?"

"No, of course not." Sascha sat up, tucking behind her

ear a strand of hair that had come loose from her plait. "How could a link be held without Tp power on both sides? All Psy are born with telepathy to a minimal level."

Lucas's beast scented a kind of raw desperation in her that told him she was hiding something. "Let them talk, Sascha."

"Why?" she cried. "So they can sell us lies?"

"Shh." He ran the knuckles of his hand down her cheek. "Are you so eager to leave me?" How could she not want to fight for every day they could have together?

Pain fractured the beauty of her eyes. With a ragged sob, she dropped her face into her hands. "I can't handle being given hope only to lose it."

He wished he could take the hurt from her, wished he were the empath, not his vulnerable mate.

"Sienna is convinced it'll work." Walker's pale green eyes followed the motion of Lucas's hand as he rubbed the back of Sascha's neck. "She thinks the way two mates bond equals a kind of psychic link. That mating link should keep Sascha alive when she drops out of the PsyNet."

Sascha's head jerked up. "Don't you think I haven't thought of that?"

"What?" Lucas growled. "Why didn't you tell me?" The panther wanted to bare its fangs in fury.

"Ask them why." She was more furious than he'd ever seen her. "Because a single mind can't supply the feedback I need without killing itself. To use a link with you in any way is sentencing you to a slow death with me."

"Yes," Walker said. "Our familial net functions the same way as the PsyNet but on a smaller scale—the feedback somehow accumulates. However, we're all Psy and we all supply the Net as well as feeding from it, which we believe creates the multiplication effect.

"In your case, there would be no such effect. To make

up the deficit, you'd have to link with others in your mate's pack. With three or four minds, there'd be a pool of background feedback—spare energy every mind produces. You wouldn't be actively draining anyone."

"Impossible." Sascha was leaning forward, palms braced on the table. "I agree the connection between mates is almost psychic, but that bond doesn't exist for me with anyone else. How do I mate with more than one leopard?"

"You don't," Lucas snapped before he could stop himself. "You belong to me. End of story."

She narrowed her eyes at him. "I know that, your highness, but I was pointing out the impossibility of what Walker is suggesting. There's no way for me to link with anyone outside of you."

Lucas's beast hated the thought of her linked to anyone other than him, but he realized that if it would keep her alive, he'd share her. It would tear him to pieces but he'd do it. It was the first time he'd understood the depth of his own feelings.

"Any other ideas?" Hawke asked.

Silence.

The wolf stood. "Prepare for war."

Sascha argued with him every inch of the drive home. "You're going to let hundreds die because you want to keep me alive for a few extra days?"

"An hour of your life is worth more than a thousand people to me."

"What about Julian and Roman? What about Kit? What about Rina? Are you willing to lose them?"

He felt the questions like kicks to the heart. "They won't die."

"Like hell they won't!" The use of profanity told him

how far he'd pushed her. "If the Council decides to eliminate your pack, every single one of you *will* be eliminated, even if it takes them years."

"So you want me to lie back and let you kill yourself?" His words were so angry, her head snapped back as if he'd hit her.

"No. I want you to help me save someone's life. I want you to give me back my pride."

He scowled. "When did you lose it?"

"When I found out my mother was aiding and abetting murderers." It was a brutally honest statement.

He tried to grasp her hand. She tore it away. "No! I won't let you do this."

"You need us to cooperate for your plan to work," he pointed out. "No one is going to go behind my back to help you." They knew he'd gut them, tear them into such small strips that nothing would remain. He wasn't alpha because he played nice when his people were threatened. And his woman? He'd lay waste to the world for her.

"Maybe I don't," she whispered. "Maybe I'll try it without one of you. My shields are failing one by one—exposure is inevitable. They'll come after me within days and when they do, I'll have to drop out of the Net anyway, to escape rehabilitation."

And he knew. "You're going to do it with or without my help." He brought the vehicle to a stop in the front yard of the safe house.

CHAPTER 24

"**What would you** do in my place?" Her eyes were pure black when he looked at her. "What would honor demand?"

"You're my mate. Honor means nothing."

She opened the door and got out. He sat inside until she came around to his side and opened the door. Her hands were warm and alive on his face. "Liar," she whispered. "Honor means everything. Otherwise, we're exactly like them."

Getting out, he wrapped his arms tight around her trembling form. "I'll do it." He wondered if she understood that he'd just torn out his heart and laid it at her feet.

She shook her head. "I can't hurt you like that."

"No dice, kitten. I'll anchor you and, afterward, you'll psychically reach out for me. No more fighting our mating. Your reluctance is the only thing holding it back—the second you try to link, the bond should snap into place."

Pushing off him hard enough to break his hold, she said, "No."

"Yes."

"What will happen to DarkRiver without you? Have you thought of that?" She was shaking her head, eyes ebony night. "You're not going to last longer than a couple of months if I link with you in any way—I'll suck you dry. *Don't ask me to destroy you.*"

"Vaughn's strong enough to take over until Kit comes of age." There was no choice to be made.

"No, Lucas. No." Her entire body was shaking.

"It's the only way I'll allow you to go in." He let her hear the steel in his voice, let her remember his threat to incapacitate her. There was nothing civilized in him where Sascha was concerned. "Promise me."

She shook her head mutely.

"Promise me, kitten."

Turning, she ran from him. He let her go into the house. Then he waited until Vaughn slipped out of the woods to stand before him. "She's right. DarkRiver needs you."

"And I need her." Lucas had watched one woman he loved die. He couldn't do it again. "If I survive her, I'll be as good as dead anyway."

Aware she hadn't fully recovered from shadowing Henry, Sascha decided to put the plan into effect the following night. It would give her time to carefully examine the thought patterns she'd be mimicking. Rina had volunteered to allow Sascha to scan her patterns, as it had become clear that the young soldier fit the victim profile.

Those were the logical reasons but the truth was, no matter how selfish it made her, she wanted one more night with her lover. In bed, in the darkness, she was the one who reached for him.

He was wild and angry and she felt his withheld fury. But his hands were unbearably tender, his touch a kind of devotion she'd never dreamed of. She fell asleep in his arms, safe and protected. Which was why when the dream began, she couldn't quite believe the horror.

"Help me!" It was a scream from the core of a woman's consciousness. "Please help me!"

Broken by the raw suffering she could hear, Sascha tried to soothe her. The woman retreated from her as if she'd been burned. "No!"

"Let me help you," Sascha begged, tears streaming inside her mind for this woman whose face she couldn't see.

"You're Psy." That voice was full of rage but agony throbbed endlessly beneath the surface.

"I'm not like him." She sent out subtle waves of healing. The emotions that washed back up to her echoed with so much suffering, she ached. She kept taking it and it kept coming. "You're unbelievably strong."

"I cried." The defiance was gone from the whisper. It was as if she had to trust Sascha, the solitary voice in the darkness. "I begged him to stop."

Sascha tried to fix the tattered shreds of the woman's pride. "You survived and you kept him from your mind. You didn't break. That's what's important."

"I don't know how much longer I can do this."

"We're coming for you. Survive for us."

"You're not Pack. You smell like the cats."

"We're all one against the enemy." The depth of damage in the young girl's psyche staggered her. That she'd managed to keep the killer from her innermost mind was a testament to her incredible strength of will. "We're coming, Brenna. We're coming."

"Hurry." The voice was fading. "Please hurry."

Sascha woke as morning was breaking and knew they couldn't wait any longer. "Now," she told Lucas, finding him in the living room with Hawke, his lieutenants, and two other males. It didn't surprise her to see the wolves there—both alphas were preparing to rise against the Psy. "We have to do it now. We can't leave Brenna with him any longer." Her tone was on this side of hysterical.

Lucas ordered everyone out. Nobody spoke a word as they filed out and closed the door behind them. Nobody but Hawke. "What time should I tell the Laurens?"

Sascha reached for her timepiece as he reached for his. "Five minutes from now."

"I'll call Judd."

She nodded.

"We'll keep you safe, sweetheart." He touched her face and left.

Hope was a dangerous commodity and she couldn't indulge in it. Her eyes met Lucas's as she walked across the room to face him. "It doesn't have to be you," she said one more time, begging him.

"It has to be me. I'm yours." His kiss held his heart.

It broke hers.

"Let's start," she whispered, unable to bear this any longer. If she thought about what she was going to do, she might never do it, might leave Brenna to be tortured and murdered, her mind raped and then discarded. That she'd even consider such a thing made her fear for her soul.

She felt Lucas's mind welcome hers. Though he wasn't a Psy, it felt almost like shields dropping. She didn't need to go completely inside to gain what she needed. Instead, she made a superficial link that would allow her to feed him information and smell of him on a psychic level.

That scent would bolster the impression of a changeling mind that she was going to create using the glimpse she'd had of Rina's thought patterns. Their minds worked differently enough from those of the Psy that no one would ever mistake one for the other. However, it might be possible to fool the killer long enough for Sascha to get a fix on him.

"Don't expose yourself unnecessarily."

Sascha nodded. One way or another, she'd have to drop out of the Net, but she wanted to get out without revealing the entire scope of her empathic mind. It would keep others like her safe . . . if there were any others like her. "If he's drawn to this bait enough that he ventures close, I won't have to. But if he's wary, I might have to give him a more interesting victim."

Lucas's eyes flashed with denial but he didn't try to tell her not to do it. Her alpha male was finally learning that she couldn't be ordered around. "Come back to me, Sascha. Promise me you'll initiate the link."

Brenna's screams echoed in her mind, urging haste. "I promise." Leaning forward, she brushed her lips against his, wishing for just another hour, another minute, another lifetime. "Thank you for teaching me how to live."

His hand clasped the back of her neck, those Hunter's eyes violent with the animal's hunger for her. "If you want to thank me, stay alive. Keep your promise."

Initiate the link.

Sascha forced herself to nod. "We should start." She led him to the sofa. Lucas sat down, legs sprawled along its length. Without argument, she crawled up to lie with her head against his chest, putting her arms around his muscular frame.

She could hear his heart, his life, through the soft cotton of his gray T-shirt. How could he condemn her to steal that from him? How could he force his pack to go on without their leader? She wasn't worth the sacrifice, a woman born of a race who'd lost their humanity a hundred years ago.

"Ready?" A gentle hand smoothed over her unbound hair.

She'd never be ready to kill them both. Only, the alternative was much worse. "Yes. Judd and Sienna will be setting off the distraction in a minute." Taking a deep breath, she closed her eyes and found him.

Lucas's flame was pure heat, pure light. He'd trusted his mind to her but she didn't go in, couldn't face what she might see. His emotions for her might destroy her. Instead, she gently merged into the upper layer until her thought patterns began to echo his in a subtle way that didn't change them but altered their psychic *feel*.

Letting Lucas's heartbeat soothe her, she opened her mind's eye. She was still behind her shields, still protected. If she wanted, she could pull back without betraying anything.

Brenna's screams reverberated in her mind.

No, she could never pull back. First, she checked that the truth of her healing, rainbow-bright mind was hidden deep. Then she manufactured a flaw in her shields, something that looked natural. In a way, her plan was blindingly simple . . . *if* you were a cardinal E-Psy forced into becoming a genius of multilayered shields, and *if* you were able to link with and so easily mimic changeling minds.

She'd realized sometime last night that her ability to touch changeling minds was part of her gift, because the nature of empathy made it impossible for one to turn evil and do harm to an open mind. When they'd crushed the development of empaths, the Psy had destroyed the growth of their conscience.

"This one's for us," she said within her soul. It was for all those E-Psy who'd died tortured deaths in the transitional phase, all those who'd gone insane under Silence, and all those who'd buried their gifts so deep they thought they were broken.

After a lifetime of feeling as if she'd failed at being Psy, she was winning at being everything she was capable of being. And if the changelings alone ever knew of her victory, then that was good enough for her. More than good enough. Because they *remembered*. Unlike the Psy, they didn't systematically erase those who didn't "fit."

Using the flaw she'd created, she allowed vague tendrils of her Lucas-influenced thought patterns to filter through. She shaped the outgoing whispers based on Rina's mind. Rebellious, headstrong, loyal, independent, and sensual, these were the traits of the women the killer had taken. The altered blend of her psychic signature was very carefully tailored to appeal to him.

Most Psy would have no idea what was unusual about it. Some might notice but they'd see her cardinal star and put it down to some odd talent. Only a Psy who'd ripped open a changeling mind would recognize this scent for what it was.

Fifty known operators.

Sascha refused to let herself think about failure. She had to trust in fate and the killer's hunger for this particular breed of prey.

As the thought patterns filtered through, she slipped out a hidden doorway built into her outer shield and into the starry night of the PsyNet. It was the same trick she used while ghosting. But this was even more dangerous.

Today, her mind was trapped inside her shields, because it needed to maintain the contact with Lucas and feed the false illusion. When she went ghosting, she left behind an illusion mind, while her consciousness, her self, traveled the Net. In a sense, she split herself into body and mind.

A variation on the same thing occurred when she "met" someone on the PsyNet. Because she usually needed to continue functioning on the physical level, she sent out a roaming piece of herself. For the time it was on the Net, that piece acted as a separate individual apart from her, almost as if she'd copied herself. There was vulnerability there on account of the underlying connection to her inner mind, but it was so low most Psy never worried about it.

The part of her on the outside today was connected directly to the core of her mind. She couldn't use a roaming piece of herself because the NetMind would pick it up and so would other Psy. To create the illusion that she wasn't in the Net at all, she had to be outside but fully connected to the core. However, if someone took control of her here, they'd have unhindered access to her brain—mind control on the most intimate level.

However, she couldn't worry about that possibility—she had too much else choking up her throat. Already, the currents of the Net were spreading her bait. All she had to do was wait and watch. Hidden against her own mind, her presence was almost impossible to detect. This was such a dangerous maneuver that most Psy would never think to look for it, but she had to be outside her shields to see the killer's mental face.

Even if she didn't recognize him, she'd have enough to ID him from the PsyNet databases. So long as the rainbow of her true mind stayed hidden, she'd be able to use the resources of the Net.

Two curious high-Gradient minds passed close by but didn't stop. She heard parts of their conversation, which they weren't bothering to shield. The word "cardinal" featured prominently. The flaw she'd created was unique but not so overwhelmingly a bad fit that normal Psy would question it. She'd counted on their arrogance, which led them to think changelings harmless and thus not worth studying as you would an enemy.

Her nerves relaxed a fraction at the small success. The temptation to go back and wipe away her shields until she could touch Lucas's mind in a psychic kiss was almost overwhelming. She needed touch and she knew her lover wouldn't mind the caress despite his independent nature.

He belonged to her as much as she belonged to him.

However, to expose him that way would be sheer selfishness. An intruding Psy could harm him through her if her shields cracked. And Lucas couldn't die. She wouldn't allow it.

Something pinged on her outermost shields, which weren't actually shields but warning beacons, one of her secret creations. Excitement mounting, she watched. Oh hell! Why hadn't she realized that she'd inevitably draw this one mind?

Sascha.

Mother. I'm sorry I haven't responded to your call—I've been very busy. She answered using the mental pathways of telepathy, as if she wasn't actually present on the Net. Hopefully, her mother was too preoccupied by the hunt for the killer and the Laurens' distraction to quiz her about exactly what she'd been up to.

One of your shields has a fracture. Fix it before people try to take advantage and sneak in viruses.

Of course Nikita would worry about viruses. *Thank you.*

There's something odd about your patterns. Perhaps a visit to Medical is in order.

Fear and betrayal gripped Sascha around the throat. Nikita had to know what was wrong with her daughter, had to have seen her before she'd been old enough to conceal her mind. Yet she was giving advice that could lead to Sascha's exposure. Did she suspect how far her offspring had gone from the accepted Psy path?

Are you sure that's necessary? she asked. *It appears to be a minor problem.*

As the head of the Duncan household, I received a notice from Medical noting your lack of physical examinations since you reached adulthood. Nikita's tone didn't change but Sascha thought she heard a thread of warning. *It might be politic to get a scan done before they pull you up for a random check.*

Her relief was almost crushing. Whatever else she

might be doing, at least Nikita wasn't trying to serve her daughter up to the authorities. It wasn't much but it was something. *I'll do it as soon as possible.*

You haven't reported on the DarkRiver project for a couple of—She paused. *I have to go. Something's just gone wrong with two of the main information relay points. Things are already becoming gridlocked.* With that, Nikita's mind was gone as quickly as it had appeared.

Sascha felt the information backing up on the Net and breathed a sigh of relief. Sienna and Judd had come through. Every Psy surfing the Net in this location would be streaming toward those points, looking to fix the damage before it cascaded into chaos.

Likely, they'd already fixed it, but the backlog would take hours to clear. In the tumult, her odd signature would hopefully gain no real attention . . . except from one very dangerous Psy.

These things were thought by the hidden part of her that was a fountaining rainbow inside unbreakable walls. Outside those walls, she was cool and remote, protecting herself from disclosure even when most people, including Psy, would've considered themselves safe.

A whisper of violence swept by her. Every one of her senses screamed and she felt the rough edge of a growl in the back of her throat. Lucas's personality was alpha, too strong. It shouldn't have been coming through this clearly but it was and she had to use it. Thinking quickly, she merged the anger into the tendrils of thought going out into the Net. These women would have the capacity for anger. Anger was a kind of passion.

Her race had tried to delete anger, rage, hate, but they hadn't understood that anger could spring from deep love, the most complete need to protect. Lucas was furious because she was putting herself at risk, enraged at the thought of her being hurt. There was nothing evil about those emotions. They were so pure they burned.

Unlike the emotions now coming slowly closer. This violence was sly, cunning in the way of jackals or vultures. Most Psy probably never understood why this outwardly "normal" mind made them slightly uncomfortable, because most Psy no longer had the ability to recognize evil, even if it stood right in front of them. What a perfect hiding ground for a killer, Sascha realized.

The scent of rotting malevolence abruptly stopped approaching and then disappeared altogether. She frowned. Had the murderer been scared off? A second later, she felt another familiar presence and almost cursed. Enrique's cardinal blaze was obvious a mile away. No wonder the killer had run.

She wanted to scream in frustration. Something deep within her flexed its claws and it felt good. Right at that instant, she itched to tear into Enrique's interfering arrogance, arrogance that might cost Brenna her life.

He didn't contact her when he reached her, not seeing her presence on the Net. Instead, he examined the manufactured flaw with the utmost care. Sascha wondered whether he even understood what he was looking at.

She'd have suspected him for the murderer, except that she knew there was no emotion in Enrique. None. Even for the Psy, he was the coldest creature she'd ever met. Nothing in her empathy reacted to him. That, she realized at last, was why he'd constantly rubbed her raw.

Her mother was cold, but Sascha's senses had always picked up a low-level emotional feedback from her, as they did from other Psy. Her race might've buried their emotions but they were there. In Enrique's case, there was nothing to indicate he'd ever had the capacity to feel.

"Sascha." A polite telepathic page.

She became the mask. "Sir."

"Your shield is fractured."

"Thank you, sir. I've already begun repairing it. It isn't anything major." So why had the Councilor bothered to tell her about it? Her mother, she could understand. Nikita had a vested interest in ensuring Sascha's secret never got out—it would undermine her own position.

Which made Sascha wonder why she'd been allowed to live in the first place. Wouldn't it have been simpler to terminate her once it had been discovered that she was flawed? Or were not even the Psy capable of killing their young? Then she remembered Marlee and Toby and that hope collapsed.

"You have some very unusual thought patterns."

CHAPTER 25

"Some of my talents are rather unusual, sir." That told him nothing. Her hidden talents could include a degree of foresight she didn't want competitors to know about or a hundred other things.

"I always knew you were an interesting woman, but I never guessed you were so perfect."

In the dark velvet night of the PsyNet, Sascha felt shivers crawl along her nerves. *Perfect.* What was she perfect for? "A high compliment." She couldn't move. Enrique's power was everywhere—he'd surrounded her as stealthily as a hunting leopard.

"I thought you were like me," he said, his tone shifting to something so polite it was a mockery. "But you're something else altogether."

If she hadn't intended to drop out of the Net, she would've panicked at the way his shields had spread to encompass her star. Because this was a trap. Nikita had taught her this variation long ago. Sometimes it paid to have a mother whose power lay in murder and poison.

Enrique believed her to be telepathing. Once he'd finished encircling her star, he'd lure her out into the PsyNet. The instant she emerged, he'd lock a shield around the partial "self" she'd send out to meet with him. For the first milliseconds after a Psy manifested on the psychic plane, he or she was vulnerable. It took that long for the mobile firewalls to rise. Almost no one had the power to spring a trap in that infinitesimal amount of time.

However, Enrique was no ordinary Psy—he could possibly pull it off. If he succeeded, he'd cut off the roaming part of her psyche from the rest. A successful capture was one of the more brutal ways to paralyze the physical body of a Psy. If the paralysis was maintained too long, the underlying connection between self and mind snapped, the two parts of the psyche unable to survive the separation.

The result was death and the absorption of that roaming part of the victim's consciousness into the vastness of the PsyNet. Some theorized that that was how the NetMind had begun—with the lost minds of Psy who'd been ambushed or otherwise lost in the dark skies of the Net.

"I'm not sure what you mean, sir."

"I think it's time we discussed this, Sascha." He was everywhere. Cold and focused like the finest of lasers.

"I'm in a meeting."

"Cancel it." The walls around her began to constrict.

"Mother has given me instructions to close this deal." This was bad, very bad. What she couldn't understand was why Enrique was coming after her.

There was nothing overtly "wrong" about the patterns she was leaking. The traces were both very faint and came from a deep part of the changeling consciousness that Psy couldn't usually access, not without ripping open minds. Only a Psy who'd done that would understand what it was that he was seeing.

"I'm tired of waiting for you to make time. Unless you want to find yourself pulled up before the Council, I want to see you. *Now*."

"On what basis would you call me before the Council?" She filled her mental tone with the confidence of someone who'd been born a cardinal, someone whose mother was a Councilor.

"You're not pure, Sascha. You think like *them*." It was an accusation that held supreme confidence. "Like the animals you work so well with."

Caught utterly off guard, she almost gave herself away. She'd never known Enrique to have any contact with changelings. How did he recognize the taint in her mental signature? "I'm sure you're mistaken."

"I've been in their minds. I know exactly what they look like." His mental trap was almost solid. There was no way she would've been able to break out if she'd planned on doing so. Enrique was stronger than she'd ever guessed, possibly the strongest cardinal in the Net.

"How?" Confusion and desperation were taking their toll. Murder sprang from rage, fury, jealousy. Enrique didn't feel anything, so how could he be the violence that had stolen so many lives?

"The Council likes to know the enemy. We've been using volunteers to study their mental patterns." He pushed at the flaw in her mind as one would poke at a wound.

It hurt. "Sir, what are you doing?"

"I don't like waiting, Sascha."

But he liked talking, she thought. "I'm tying up the meeting. If I leave suddenly, it'll negate everything we've achieved to date. I didn't realize the Council was running such research."

"Call it a private interest. Their women make the best subjects—there's something perfect about them."

I never guessed you were so perfect.

"They're weak," she said, prodding him on. "They feel. It's the Psy who are perfect."

Enrique's energy whirled cold and menacing around her as she started to inch back toward the hidden doorway into her mind. She had to get inside before she dropped out of the PsyNet. If Enrique succeeded in infiltrating her defenses, he'd destroy Lucas along with her. No, she thought, furious. Her mate would *not* die.

A whisper of the forest in her mind. The panther hidden deep within her was pleased by her thoughts but its attention was fixed on Enrique, on the threat to its mate. Claws slid out and she felt her fingertips tingle.

"Psy have to suppress emotion in order to survive, but changelings thrive without breaking under the pressure. I'd say that makes them the stronger species." He paused and she froze her creeping progress. "Are you almost done?"

"Yes, sir." She made her voice hold the faintest thread of fear, let him pick up the emotion.

The walls of his mind went blue like the deepest oceanic ice. It was frighteningly beautiful. "Sascha, Sascha," he whispered. "You're truly extraordinary."

She didn't respond, every ounce of concentration focused on getting back into her mind. His comments had her convinced he was the killer one second and confused the next. How could he be the serial? How? Those women had been torn part, annihilated from the mind out. Enrique was a man who didn't feel any negative emotion. Not rage. Not anger. Not hatred.

Was he simply out for her because she was flawed? Had he driven away the real murderer, the one who'd infected the Net with traces of violence? Disappointment tightened her gut. She couldn't fail, couldn't let the need for revenge plunge DarkRiver and the SnowDancers into war. They were her people now.

"You're even more perfect than the changeling women."

"Who were these women?" she asked, nearly to the doorway. "I'd like to speak to them as well. The leopards tell me nothing."

"I'm afraid the experiments were a little taxing. They don't like to let Psy into their minds. I had to damage them in order to gain an in-depth understanding."

Horror stopped her in midstep. "You killed them?"

Lucas lunged at the walls of her mind, wanting to go for Enrique's throat.

"Lab animals often die."

If she'd been in her physical body, she would've thrown up then and there. It was crystal clear that Enrique was happy to tell her everything—his only audience—because he thought he had her trapped. He was closing around her like a giant pincer.

"There's pressure on my mind." She could start to feel it but it wasn't dangerous, not yet.

"I'm at the end of my patience. Either you speak to me or I execute you. I assure you, the Council would back me fully for dealing with a defective Psy."

It was the word "defective" that got her moving again. She wasn't defective and the changelings weren't lab animals. They were the most beautiful, most alive, most passionate beings she'd ever met. But before she broke away, she had to make sure she had the right evil, the right killer. "Why seventy-nine?" she asked softly.

"Nineteen seventy-nine, Sascha, 1979. It's my little way of celebrating what I see as the true birth of our race." He paused. "How did you know about that?" The crushing walls of his mind came to a standstill.

She used that moment to push through the hidden door

and lock it behind her. Something slammed into it a second later—Enrique's mind trying to shove into hers, destroy hers. Cracks appeared in the already fragmented shields around the doorway.

"Very clever, Sascha," he said. "How long have you been hiding out here?"

She didn't answer, trying to patch up the door enough that she could run into the second layer of her shields. Even so close to him, her senses picked up nothing of the deep-seated rage she'd expected from the murderer. Enrique didn't feel. And yet he killed.

You're a race of psychopaths!

Dorian's accusation ripped open from some forgotten pocket of memory.

No conscience, no heart, no feelings! How else do you define psychopath?

The true horror of Silence hit her so hard, her inner walls shook. But there was no time to think. Enrique was close to breaking through. Slamming a temporary block on the door to her mind, she ran through the second layer of shields just as the block on the outer shields shattered.

He was inside her mind.

His power crashed into her, shocking pain into every synapse. Shaking, she threw everything she had into her inner shields and went even deeper, until she was behind a third layer. Enrique couldn't violate these so easily. They were the natural walls of the mind—the walls he'd ripped open in the changeling women he'd taken. She had no doubt he'd tear her apart, too, if she gave him the time.

Fed by adrenaline, she found her mental link to the PsyNet. Even Enrique's trap couldn't cut that link. It went too deep, was too instinctive. She touched the lifeline for the last time and whispered, "Good-bye."

Enrique hit her with another shockwave of pain and at that exact instant, she sliced the link into two. Everything stopped for her. Her mind was silent. Alone. There were no stars in the darkness, nothing but emptiness.

Death opened its arms.

She screamed awake in Lucas's hold. Excruciating agony cramped every nerve in her body and she could feel her mind desperately trying to re-create the link. Forcing herself to think despite the red-hot torture sparking through her, she cauterized the wound and shut down the instinctive reaching. It hurt. Like being shot point-blank in the face.

The agony was everywhere. Her skin felt as if it was being flayed off her. Her mind screamed and screamed, gasping for the feedback it needed to survive. She clawed at Lucas's chest, unable to breathe. Claustrophobia closed around her, the darkness pressing down deeper than Enrique's attempts at crushing her mind. She was going to choke to death. Alone. She was so alone.

Alone. Dark. Black. Cold.

Lucas was terrified by what he saw in Sascha's eyes. All the stars had disappeared in a blink when she'd opened her eyes and now there was such deep ebony in the depths, he thought he could see eternity.

"Sascha!" He shook her, ignoring the others who'd run into the room at the sound of her screams. It didn't occur to him that he knew the killer's name, that he could start the hunt for vengeance. Only she mattered. "Sascha!" She didn't respond. It was as if she couldn't see him.

He wasn't Psy. He couldn't get into her mind. But he could anchor her another way. Wrapping one hand around her nape, he pulled her close and kissed her. Hard. Without mercy. It was a brutal, savage, possessive kiss and it held every emotion he felt for her. He poured it all into her mouth, calling her back with touch. Her clawlike grip eased but she clung to him, wrapping her arms and legs around him as if she wanted to crawl into his soul.

Alone. So alone.

It was as if he heard the words in his mind. Had she linked? Had she followed through on her promise? Was that why he could feel the load of darkness pressing down on her? He pushed it back with heat and fire and emotion, squeezing her body close.

When he broke the kiss so she could breathe, she whimpered, "No, no, no, no." He pressed his lips against hers once again. The darkness was no longer so heavy but it wasn't disappearing. Why not? She was linked to him. She wasn't alone. Not anymore. Never again.

The next time the kiss broke, she took a deep breath and said, "It's Councilor Santano Enrique. He feels nothing. Doesn't know about you. Thinks I'm just flawed." It came out in a staccato rush—as if she were spitting things out before they were forever lost.

Lucas looked at Hawke, who'd been first into the room. "Go. Dorian. Vaughn." His eyes locked with the jaguar's. Vaughn gave a slight nod. He understood his job—to protect Dorian from his own rage. Lucas couldn't go with them, not with his mate growing alarmingly weak in his arms.

Hawke's eyes slid to Sascha, who was starting to draw shallow breaths that sounded like fatal whispers. "What's wrong with her?" He held his arm out to stop Brenna's two brothers from leaving the room in pursuit of their quarry. It was an indication of his power that they paused though their eyes had gone wolf.

"She's dying." Tamsyn pushed between the males to touch Sascha's cheek.

Sascha jerked. "Enrique lives in . . . uh . . ." Her teeth began to chatter.

"We have the address." Hawke's face was a study in the most chilling fury. "I'll take care of him." The words were directed at Lucas.

It was time to trust the wolf.

"Complete the plan." They'd hatched it between them early this morning. It was designed to keep Sascha safe . . . forever. "Go." He was entrusting Hawke with his mate's life. The plan had called for Lucas to ensure this part of their strategy was implemented, but not for anything would he leave Sascha.

"Your Psy belongs to us, too. We won't fail her." Hawke moved and the four wolves in the room, along with Dorian and Vaughn, streamed out with him.

Tamsyn dropped a throw around Sascha's shaking body. "I don't understand. Your mind should be feeding hers."

Lucas suddenly understood. "You haven't tried to initiate a link, have you?" Terror and fury combined to chill his heart.

Sascha smiled and shook her head. "You have to live."

"You promised!" he yelled, driven beyond patience, beyond anything but demand and need. His mate couldn't die.

Those beautiful eyes were fading. "I'm sorry."

"No! No!" He cradled her in his arms, his voice shaking. "Link, damn you! Link!"

Her hand rose to lie against his heartbeat. "Love you." A single tear fell from eyes gone charcoal gray.

"Tammy! Do something!"

The healer was trembling, her eyes wet. "I can't, Lucas. She has to . . ."

"Do it, Sascha!" he ordered, crushing her to him. *"Don't you leave me."*

She gasped and the fingers on his chest curled. But she didn't reach out to his mind, didn't take the step that would complete the mating dance.

"If you don't, I'll start taking out the Councilors," he threatened. "They'll hunt me down and kill me anyway."

But his mate was beyond hearing. Her eyes drifted shut and her face smoothed out as her shivers faded.

"No!" His scream was of purest rage. "I won't let you die! You're mine and damn if I'm ever going to let you go. You're mine. *Mine*." The panther clawed to the surface and let out a roar that was nothing human.

That was when he felt it. The bond between them snapping taut. The panther recognized the bond, though it had never before felt it. It calmed him enough to let Lucas think, holding fast even as Sascha's heartbeat stuttered. Lucas closed his eyes and *fed* her. He didn't know what he was doing, just knew that as long as the bond stayed strong, Sascha would live.

A minute later, her eyes fluttered open again. The deathly gray was being replaced by dark ebony. "Lucas? What's happening?"

"You're going to live." It was nonnegotiable.

He felt her search for and find the link. Felt her try to cut it—his heart stopped—but it wasn't something she could influence. This link wasn't Psy. It was changeling and it was unbreakable. The cat began to smile—her safety was no longer out of his grasp.

"You can't," she whispered. "Stop doing what you're doing. You're giving me your lifeforce. It's worse than if I simply accepted the bond and let it keep me alive."

"Then accept, because I'm not going to stop." He poured even more of himself into her.

Futility darkened her expression. "Damn you for being so stubborn!"

"Accept."

Her shoulders fell. She shot back along that bond, dropping the barriers she'd erected in an effort to prevent their mating. Suddenly, she was a rainbow inside him, a sparkling fountain of such beauty that he felt blessed to have been allowed to see her. For one instant, their minds were one and he saw how desperately, how wildly, how unreasonably she loved him—enough to break a promise, to choose death so he could live.

She saw how much her panther adored her, how his heart beat for her alone, how life would turn into death after she was gone. The beast was angry at her for attempting to deny him his mate, and the man was beyond angry, but beneath the anger was hunger, need, *love*. Such intense, furious love that it had no beginning and no end.

She pulled back with a gasp, allowing their two minds to separate, allowing them to think private thoughts once more. Somehow, Lucas knew that if he should ever ask, she'd open to him again. She was his and he was hers. They had under-the-skin privileges.

Those dark eyes looked up at him. Tears streamed down her face. "I've killed you. I've killed you. I've killed you!"

Sascha knew Lucas was enraged with her but she was too mad to care. How could he have forced her into this? It didn't matter that the mating bond wasn't controllable. As far as she was concerned, if he'd accepted her choice, if he'd let her go, it wouldn't have come into being. Even now, she was sucking his life away so she could be healthy and strong. Her life at the price of his. Damn him!

Ten hours had passed since the plan had been successfully executed. Depleted by his attempt at trapping her, Enrique's powers hadn't been strong enough to withstand the changelings. Improbably, he'd kept Brenna caged in his large soundproofed apartment, safe because no Psy could feel her pain. She was alive. The SnowDancers and DarkRiver's soldiers had also ensured Sascha's safety. No one was going to be hunting her or the changelings.

"We took what was due us," Hawke told her in the living room of the safe house. His gaze included Dorian. "And we left them a message. Should anything ever happen to you, we'll go after each and every one of the Council, no matter who it was that set the dogs on you. What we did to Enrique will seem like a picnic."

"How can you be sure that'll keep them contained?" Sascha knew the Council too well.

"The message we left," Hawke said, his eyes pure blue flame. "It was stapled to Enrique's tongue. Tatiana Rika-Smythe got the tongue in a velvet jewelry box inside her bedroom. Nikita got the remainder of the head."

She couldn't breathe. She tried to speak but nothing came out. Hawke continued his bloody narrative.

"The Councilors outside the immediate area have been promised personal delivery of a piece of Enrique—I'm thinking we'll leave the gifts on their pillows."

Sascha felt her gorge rise. She gripped Lucas's hand. "How could you . . . ?"

"We did nothing to him he didn't do to our women," Dorian gritted out. "We did less—he raped their minds!"

She looked at him, felt his anguish—anguish that vengeance hadn't calmed—and knew he needed her to accept what he'd done. She was his alpha's mate and for the first time, she saw what that entailed. Not quite sure what she was doing, she crossed the room and took his face in her hands. He stilled. When she brushed her lips over his, a sigh seemed to ripple through his body.

CHAPTER 26

Lucas didn't growl, didn't act territorial. She was his and this was part of what the pack would need from her. Touch. Love. Affection. Sometimes the best way to give affection to the strongest males was with a simple kiss. They'd accept that when they might reject words of care. How she knew that was a mystery to her.

As she drew back, she felt a stab in her heart. Dorian was looking at her as if she belonged, as if he was sure of her, as if she was Pack. She was. For the next couple of months. Until she dragged Lucas down with her into unconsciousness and death.

"That's not everything," Hawke said, when she turned to him again. "We made sure they knew we're aware of violence in the Psy populace. Enrique confessed quite prettily on camera. Liked to talk."

"They can't have that getting out." Sascha watched her mate walk toward her and felt something low and hot in her tighten. Anger was no barrier against the passion he could arouse in her. "Silence would be deemed a failure."

"Maybe that would be a good thing," Tamsyn said.

"Only if there's something to take its place. To spread this information without having any way to manage the fallout would be irresponsible." She shook her head.

"This big a shockwave could cripple thousands of innocents. When something happens on the psychic plane, it has physical effects." She knew that too well. Nothing had prepared her for the agony she'd suffered.

Lucas walked around to her back and hugged her against him. "I wonder how they'll explain your presence out of the Net?"

"We suggested they tell people a difference in her mind made her susceptible to mating with a changeling and that was how she dropped out." Hawke shrugged. "Doesn't matter to us so long as they don't touch her."

"It's going to shake things up regardless of how they do it." Lucas's arms were solid muscle around her. Nothing had ever felt as good.

Sascha knew the leopards and wolves had achieved the impossible—they'd leashed the Council. It was a bittersweet victory.

The wolves asked Sascha to come to their hideout three days later, bare minutes after she'd finished speaking with Nikita. Her mother had informed her that she'd been officially cut off from the Duncan family group.

"You're no longer Psy. Your mind is too flawed. It couldn't even hold on to the link with the PsyNet. Obviously, you were never meant to be a part of it."

So that was how the Council was spinning it. "No, Mother. I'm perfect."

Nikita didn't blink. "The deal with DarkRiver—we'd like it to continue. Lucas Hunter's odd . . . connection with you is why we allowed you to leave the Net. One flawed

Psy wasn't worth destroying business ties with the cats and the wolves."

Sascha got the message. Business was something every Psy could understand. "We have no problem honoring the deal." Then she ended the call and let herself cry.

Lucas held her and when the wolves sent for her, he didn't try to stop her from doing what she had to do.

"Brenna's dying," Hawke said the second they entered the tunnels.

Sascha thought of the incredibly powerful will she'd touched once in the darkness. "No." She refused to let that light go out. "Take me to her."

Brenna lay in a soft bed covered by a cerulean blue blanket. Tamsyn and another woman, who Sascha assumed was the SnowDancer healer, stood talking quietly in one corner of the bedroom. Tammy's eyes pleaded with her to do something.

Making a silent promise, Sascha looked back at Brenna. Her hair had been cut brutally short, as if someone had tried to rob her of her femininity. Bruises covered her face and ringed her neck, but Sascha didn't see all that. What she saw was the flickering candle of Brenna's mind.

She cupped her healer's hands around that flame. *Don't give up now, Brenna.*

Silence.

You know me. I won't hurt you.

You lied. A whispery accusation.

When?

You said Pack would come for me. Pain and betrayal. *But I'm alone.*

Sascha blinked and looked to Hawke. "Was she conscious when you found her?"

"No. The human medics said they couldn't do anything for her so we brought her home." Human medics because none of them trusted the M-Psy anymore.

"She doesn't know she's home. Talk to her. Touch her."

The wolf didn't argue. Walking to the bed, he began to caress Brenna's bruised face with disarming gentleness, reminding her of nothing so much as a father with his child. Brenna's two brothers moved to join him, one taking her hand, the other kneeling down beside the bed to stroke her spiky hair. There was something heartbreaking about seeing three predatory males, used to protecting their women, trying to be strong while their souls were being torn to pieces.

Inside the darkness of Brenna's mind, Sascha whispered, *You're home, Brenna.*

It's a lie.

Can't you feel them? Hawke, Riley, Andrew . . . they're here and they're waiting for you.

A silence so full of terrified hope that Sascha shivered.

They found you. They avenged your honor. She was mated to an alpha Hunter. She knew the value of vengeance, the importance of honor, the power of loyalty. *Don't make them wait any longer—I think their hearts are going to break.*

I can't bear any more. Tears sounded in every word. *What if this is a dream, you're a dream, and I wake to him? I might never escape again and I'm so tired.*

Sascha thought about who Brenna had been before Enrique, about who she still was deep in her soul. She thought of Rina and Mercy, of their will, their pride. *You have so much heart it humbles me and you fought a brave fight. If you want to slip into the last sleep, no one will judge you. You've earned your peace.*

I don't want to die.

Then choose to live. Sascha wasn't playing games. She'd told the absolute truth—Brenna had earned her right to die. *We miss you.*

Who are you?

I'm Sascha, mate to Lucas Hunter and a healer of DarkRiver. She was no longer a woman who belonged nowhere, no longer part of a race that would've punished her for her gift. Pride shimmered in her tone. Accepted, more than accepted by her new family, she'd never mourn who she'd once been.

Sascha, I'm broken.

So was I, Brenna. She reached out and hugged the girl's floundering spirit. *What is broken can be healed.*

Help me. The voice was resolute, that flickering flame settling to a slender column of purity. *I won't give in to death. Help me wake up to reality . . . whatever that might be.*

Pride for the young woman's courage mixed with anguish for the pain she'd suffered, but Sascha let her feel only the pride. *I'm here.* Slowly, she guided Brenna's broken mind through the shreds of her spirit.

Can this ever be fixed? Brenna asked, aware of the extent of the damage that had been done to her.

I was born to heal you. And if it took every second of the remainder of her time on this Earth, she *would* heal Brenna.

Take me home, Sascha.

Sascha opened her eyes perhaps an hour after she'd spoken to Hawke, and found herself sitting on the bed beside Brenna, her hand in the young woman's. She had no recollection of moving there, or of clasping her other hand with Lucas's. Brenna's brothers and Hawke surrounded the bed, touching their packmate wherever they could.

"Wake up, Brenna." Sascha brushed a gentle kiss on her forehead. As she sat back up, the girl's eyelids fluttered and then opened. Wary eyes met Sascha's. With a smile, Sascha said, "Hey, sleepyhead."

Brenna blinked. One of her brothers choked back a cry and pushed in front of Sascha to cup his sister's face with hands that were consciously gentle. "Bren? God damn it, Bren, you had us worried to death."

Over the top of Riley's head, Sascha met brown eyes filled with so much joy it was almost blinding. She got off the bed and let Lucas hold her. Now it was time for the wolves to heal Brenna, to cover her in their love and affection. Sascha would return to help her repair her mind and soul, but for today, this was enough.

"Let's go home," she said to Lucas.

He ran his knuckles down her cheek and dropped a kiss on her nose. "Still mad, Sascha darling?"

"Yes." Her hug was fierce. She lived with guilt every day of her life for condemning him to death.

A week later, she picked up Julian and rubbed his belly. The little cub growled and asked for more. Laughing, she gave him what he wanted. Tammy was out of town for the day and when she'd asked Sascha to look after the cubs, she'd jumped at the chance. They'd turned up at Lucas's lair as two adorable boys in blue jeans and T-shirts, but minutes later, she'd found two cubs chewing on her boots.

"You look like you're enjoying yourself," Lucas said from the doorway, a strained smile on his face.

She knew the reason for the strain. It was her. She was so angry with him for what he'd done and he felt it. How could he not? He was bonded with her. She watched him pick up Roman and let the cub claw playfully at his T-shirted chest, and knew she had to give up the anger.

How long did they have left? One month, maybe two. Her man was extraordinary and he knew how to love, how to feel, how to fight for his mate with every emotion he had in him. If he hadn't fought so hard, if he hadn't forced her hand, he wouldn't be the man she adored so hopelessly.

"I love you, Lucas," she whispered.

His eyes turned cat-green. "No more claws, kitten?"

She shook her head. "I'm so glad for you."

He looked like he wanted to walk over and kiss her till she begged for mercy. Except they had two squirming cubs in their arms. Looking at each other, they started to laugh. Started to live.

That night, she asked him to change for her. Without a word, he stripped off his clothing and the world turned into a multicolored shimmer. It was so beautiful, she felt her heart stop. She blinked and when she opened her eyes, a huge hunting cat lay on the bed beside her.

Despite the fact that she knew this was Lucas, she was a little scared. But not enough to miss the chance. Holding her breath, she ran her fingers through his silky black fur. There was nothing she could compare the sensation to. Bonded as they were, she'd felt him run, felt his joy in the wind and the forests, felt the panther just . . . be. But never had she touched the animal in him so intimately.

When he made a sound that was incredibly close to a purr, she started to laugh. "You like being petted whether you're in human or panther form."

The panther snapped his teeth at her and, under her hands, light shimmered. Heart in her throat, she remained perfectly immobile until Lucas lay naked beside her, the exotic tattoo on his upper arm a reminder of the wildness within. "Wow."

"Of course. I'm the most beautiful creature you've ever seen." A smug smile.

Laughing, she let him tease her, let him teach her how to grasp the moment, how to love without fear or guilt, how to just *be*.

"Something's wrong," she said to him a month later.

He put his hand on her breast under the sheet and threw

one leg over hers. "What?" His voice was a purr in the darkness.

Already, her body was heating up for his. "I've never felt better. You're the same. Every single physical symptom I had is gone and I don't think they're going to reappear."

"That's a problem?" His amusement was obvious. On her breast, his hand moved in easy circles.

She let her senses surrender, melting for him. "I'm serious. You shouldn't be able to keep my mind . . . fed, and function so well yourself."

He stopped caressing her and slid his hand down to her ribs. She knew he'd heard the seriousness in her tone. "Do you think it's the calm before the storm?"

"No. It should be a gradual drain." She stared up at the ceiling, where leaves crawled across the space. Lucas had no problem with the forest taking over his home and she was starting to accept it, too, though she did get the occasional urge to make everything spotless. "Will you mind if I go searching in our minds?" It was the first time she'd asked for that since that initial moment of utter unity.

"You know everything there is to know, kitten."

"I'm not sorry Tammy told me," she said, mutinous. They'd finally talked about his family several days ago and she'd held her Hunter as he remembered. Those wounds were scars but not the kind that twisted—his scars had a place on his soul. They were a marker of those he'd lost.

He growled against her neck and rubbed the stubble of his beard on her sensitive skin. "I didn't think so. The two of you are too damn close." There was no anger in him. "Search."

Taking a deep breath, she closed her eyes and unconsciously shifted her body until she was almost covered by him. Body and mind in tune. When she opened her mind's eye on the psychic level and peeked out, she didn't see the starry plane she was used to. Nor did she see empty darkness. Instead, she saw a web. At the center of the web was Lucas's light, so bright it was like a cardinal's but somehow more pure, more intense, hot instead of cold.

His light was being showered upon by rainbow-colored sparks and she knew that was her. She wanted to smile. She was doing what she'd always said she would if set free—infecting everyone around her. However, she now understood that the rainbow sparks healed. It was their lack in the PsyNet that had turned the Psy so cruel, so unable to see right from wrong.

Every part of the web glimmered with color.

Web.

"How can there be a web with only two?" she said out loud.

Lucas nuzzled her neck and ran his hands down her body, keeping her anchored with nothing but touch. She stroked her own hands down the heated silk of his back as she followed the strands of the web.

At the end of one filament blazed a light somehow feminine in feel, and yet, it also held hints of martial strength. At the end of another two were solid masculine stars, brilliant enough to burn.

One of those masculine stars had another strand of the web tracing out from it. At the end of *that* was a gentle, beautiful flame that spoke of purest love. Amazingly, that light had two small glowing beacons tracing from it. The strands from those two linked back to the male star.

Another strand led from Lucas to a light that was bruised and battered, but slowly being healed by the rainbows that crept in when the mind wasn't looking. And the last light, it was somehow unique, golden and wild, pure like Lucas's but tantalizingly different.

"You're connected to five others," she whispered.

"Of course," he muttered against her neck. "The sentinels take a blood oath."

Shock had her eyes snapping wide open. Mercy, a soldier female. Clay and Nate, pure strength. It was Nate's line that was joined by another's—Tamsyn, his mate. Dorian, broken but healing. Vaughn, jaguar not leopard. She searched more carefully for her own cardinal star.

There she was, enclosed *within* Lucas's light, the rainbow showers bursting through him to the outside. It didn't hurt him. In fact, it seemed to make him stronger, as if she were repairing the tiniest of fissures. It didn't mean he didn't feel negative emotions, only that he was able to see past them.

"Lucas," she said, pushing at his shoulders until he got up and looked down at her with those hunting-cat eyes.

"What's wrong?" His body tensed.

"Nothing," she whispered, starting to shudder. "Nothing. Everything's perfect!"

"Kitten, you're scaring me." He leaned down to kiss her. "What did you see?"

"You're part of a network, Lucas. The feedback you give me is bolstered by the sentinels and Tamsyn."

He thought for a moment. "The blood oath links the sentinels to me on a psychic level?"

"Somehow," Sascha said. "I don't understand how— nobody has ever seen this before—the Psy don't know changelings can link this way." Part of her wanted to share the exciting discovery, but a bigger part of her wanted to keep it secret, a weapon unlike any other. "You didn't know?"

"No. I knew the sentinels gave me their loyalty but we're not Psy."

"You have Psy potential. Everyone does. Don't forget—

we all started with the same basic material." She frowned. "Sienna Lauren was right."

"Why is Tamsyn in the net?" Lucas asked, and then answered his own question. "She's linked to Nate through the mating bond. The cubs?"

"They're there, too."

"Why aren't parents and siblings?"

"I'm guessing but I'd say that parents aren't because those are bonds we break as we grow older. We love but we're no longer as intertwined. The cubs will likely drop out as they age." She frowned. "Maybe sibling bonds aren't strong enough? From what I see, it's only mating bonds and the blood oath that work."

"I can understand that. Mating is psychic on some level. The blood oath—well, I guess there's a reason it's been passed down through the centuries."

She looked again at the web and her hands clenched on Lucas's biceps. "The Laurens were wrong on one point."

"What?"

"This is amazing! Though I'm the solitary Psy, there *is* a multiplication effect. Our web is bursting with energy." She couldn't work out how but now she had a lifetime to figure it out.

They were both quiet for a long while.

"Sascha, what does this mean?"

"We're safe," she whispered, barely believing it. "Seven adult minds are feeding the web . . . giving me what I need. It's more than enough."

Lucas clasped her to his chest, rolling over on his back. "Are you sure?"

"Yes." She kissed his chest, his neck, his chin. "Yes! Thank you for being so damn stubborn."

He didn't return the caresses, holding her so tightly she

could barely breathe. "You almost killed yourself for no reason."

"No, Lucas." She squeezed him back. "I lived because of you. That's how I'll always remember it."

"It's going to take me a long time to forgive you."

Sascha wanted to cry in joy. "We've got forever."

EPILOGUE

They held a meeting of the sentinels and Tamsyn later that week. The leopards were sprawled around the living room of their lair, some seated, some standing.

"So you can come into our minds?" Mercy asked.

"Only if you let me. I'd never walk in uninvited—I can't." Sascha knew she was talking to the most independent members of DarkRiver. They would hate to be vulnerable on any level.

"But I know you're doing something to me," Dorian said quietly. "I wondered what it was. It feels like before . . . when I wanted to go for your throat."

"I'm sorry, Dorian. That's not something I can help."

Amazingly, the sentinel gave her a slow smile. "I can handle being kissed by you."

She wanted to blush. "It's not like that."

"A hug, then." He shrugged. "It feels good."

The others frowned. Clay said, "I don't feel any different."

Sascha wondered how to say this but Dorian beat her to

it. "Because you don't need patching up, Clay. Right, Sascha?"

She sighed. "I think you're a menace but yes, Dorian's a little bit more battered than the rest of you. Once he's up and running, my empathic gifts won't really affect him, like they don't really do anything to you." The sparks healed, but on the most subconscious of levels. Dorian was only feeling them because he was so hurt.

Lucas squeezed her shoulders as she stood in front of him by the short hallway that led to the kitchen area. "We're giving you a choice. Sascha says she can cut some of you free from the web without doing damage."

"Tell me, Sascha," Tamsyn said, "is it easy to slip in and out of our minds?"

"No. Every mind has a natural shield. On the PsyNet, the only open minds belonged to the exhibitionists. All of you are shut up tight. To go in without your consent, I'd have to rip you apart."

"And kill us." Vaughn's eyes were almost glowing.

"Yes." She wouldn't lie to them, wouldn't tell them they weren't vulnerable to her. "Remember, I'm an empath. Causing you pain would double back on me."

"When I took the blood oath," Vaughn said, "I vowed to lay my life down for Lucas. As his mate, you have that same promise."

She'd expected the loner, the jaguar, to balk. "Are you sure?"

"Yes, Sascha darling." He prowled over to stand in front of her, tall and beautiful and dangerous. She gasped as he brushed his lips over hers. "My life is yours." Then he was gone, a golden blur as he leaped off the porch.

Shaken by the commitment, Sascha leaned backward into Lucas. Her eyes followed Dorian as he stood and walked over.

"I've been yours since the day you first took my pain."

Dorian picked up her hand and kissed her fingertips, before leaving the same way as Vaughn.

Mercy uncurled from her cushion and came to stand in front of Sascha. Her stunning face was serious but there was a smile in her eyes. "Think you could find out some male secrets for me?"

Sascha smiled. "The only male I know that intimately is this one." She turned to steal a kiss from Lucas. "And his secrets are mine."

Laughing, Mercy hugged her. "I'm a sentinel. I vowed to stick by Lucas to death. If he trusts you, so do I. I'll see you later—I'm going to catch up with Dorian."

Clay, the most distant sentinel, the one who never touched her, was the one Sascha had feared most would choose to be cut from the web. She didn't know what effect it would have on him, and had discussed it with Lucas. They'd decided to wait for the decisions before borrowing trouble.

Now the dark-skinned man came to stand in front of her. "My mind is not someplace you want to be," he said quietly.

She felt his coolness, felt his control, wondered what lay behind it. "I'll only come in if I'm invited."

He touched her cheek and she knew he'd accepted. Moments later, he was gone. Nate and Tamsyn were the only ones left. The healer was grinning. "You know I'll never say no, and Nate's so dedicated, I think he loves our alpha more than me."

"I resent that," Nate grumbled. "I might love football more than you, but definitely not Lucas's ugly mug."

Sascha laughed at their joking, fully aware they were crazy for each other. The web spoke for itself. It was bursting with light, with rainbows, with love. "The Web of Stars," she whispered.

"Is that what it looks like?" Lucas's voice was a rough purr in her ear.

"Yes." The starry plane of the PsyNet was barren compared to the Web of Stars, a cacophony of color and emotion, a web created not by need alone but by choice. Choices of loyalty, choices of love, choices of emotion. "I've got so much to learn." Her powers were growing, changing, *becoming*.

"We have a lifetime."

Turning, she wrapped her arms around him and threw back her head as he picked her up to spin her around. Her laughter sparkled along the Web of Stars, flickering joy that affected every mind within it. It was small and barely aware, but at that moment, the Web was far, far stronger than the PsyNet could ever hope to be.

Turn the page for a sneak peak at the second novel
in the Psy-Changeling series, *Visions of Heat*

Faith NightStar of the PsyClan NightStar was aware she was considered the most powerful F-Psy of her generation. At only twenty-four years of age, she'd already made more money than most Psy did in their entire lifetimes. But then again, she'd been working since she was three years old, since she'd found her voice. It had taken her longer than most children, but that was to be expected—she was a cardinal F-Psy of extraordinary ability.

It wouldn't have surprised anyone if she'd never spoken.

That was why the F-Psy belonged to PsyClans, which took care of everything the foreseers couldn't, from investing their millions to checking their medical status and ensuring they didn't starve. The F-Psy weren't very good at practical things like that. They forgot. Even after more than a century of forecasting business trends rather than murders and accidents, disasters and wars, they forgot.

Faith had been forgetting a lot of things lately. For example, she'd forgotten to eat three days in a row. That was when NightStar employees had intervened, alerted by the sophisticated Tec 3 computer which ran the house. Three days was the allowable window—sometimes, F-Psy went into trances. If that had been the case, they would've put her on a drip and left her to it. "Thank you," she said, directing her words to the head M-Psy. "I'll be fine now."

Xi Yun nodded. "Finish the entire meal. It contains the exact number of calories you need."

"Of course." She watched him leave, preceded by his staff. In his hand was a small medical kit that she knew contained both chemicals designed to shock her awake out of a catatonic trance or knock her down from a manic state. Neither had been required today. She'd simply forgotten to eat.

After consuming all the nutritional bars and energy drinks he'd left behind, she sat back down in the large reclining chair where she usually spent the majority of her time. Designed to double as a bed, it was uplinked to the Tec 3 and fed it a constant stream of data about her vital functions. An M-Psy stood on alert should she need medical attention any time of day or night. That wasn't normal procedure even for the F designation, but Faith was no ordinary F-Psy.

She was the best.

Every prediction Faith ever made, if not purposefully circumvented, came true. That was why she was worth untold millions. Possibly even billions. NightStar considered her their most prized asset. Like any asset, she was kept in the best condition for optimum functionality. And like any asset, should she prove defective, she'd be overhauled and used for parts.

Faith's eyes blinked open at that furtive thought. She stared up at the pale green of the ceiling and fought to bring her heart-rate down. If she didn't, the M-Psy might decide to pay her a return visit and she didn't want anyone to see her right now. She wasn't sure what her eyes would reveal. Sometimes, even the night-sky eyes of a cardinal Psy told secrets that were better kept within.

"Parts," she whispered out loud. Her statement was being recorded of course. The F-Psy occasionally made predictions during trance states. No one wanted to miss a word. Perhaps that was why those of her designation preferred to keep their silence when they could.

Used for parts.

It seemed an illogical statement but the more she thought about it, the more she realized that once again, her abilities had told her of a future she could never have imagined. Most defective Psy were rehabilitated, their minds swept clean by a psychic brainwipe that left them functioning on the level of menial laborers, but not the F-Psy. They were too rare, too valuable, too unique.

If she went insane beyond acceptable levels, the levels where she could still make predictions, the M-Psy would see to it that she met with an accident that left her brain unharmed. And then they'd use that flawed brain for scientific experimentation, subject it to analysis. Everyone wanted to know what made the F-Psy tick. Of all the Psy designations, they were the least explored, the most shadowed—it was difficult to find experimental subjects when their occurrence in the population was barely above 1 percent.

Faith dug her hands into the thick red fabric of the chair, hyperaware of her breath beginning to grow jagged. The reaction hadn't yet proceeded to a point where M-Psy intervention would be deemed necessary, as F-Psy displayed some unusual behavior during visions, but she couldn't chance her overload turning into a mental cascade.

Even as she attempted to temper her physical body, her mind flashed with images of her brain on a set of scientific scales while cold Psy eyes examined it from every angle. She knew the images were nonsensical. Nothing like that would ever happen in a lab. Her consciousness was simply trying to make sense of something that made no sense. Just like the dreams that had been plaguing her sleep for the past two weeks.

At first, it had been nothing more than a vague foreshadowing, a darkness that pushed at her mind. She'd thought it might herald an oncoming vision—a market crash or a sudden business failure, but day after day, that darkness had grown to crushing proportions without showing her anything concrete. And she'd *felt*. Though she'd never before felt anything, in those dreams she'd been drenched in fear, suffocated by the weight of terror.

It was as well that she'd long ago demanded her bedroom be free of any and all monitoring devices. Something in her had known what was coming. Something in her always knew. But this time, she hadn't been able to make sense of the raw ugliness of a rage which had almost cut off her breath. The first dreams had felt like someone was choking her, choking her until terror was all she was.

Last night had been different. Last night, she hadn't woken as the hands closed about her throat. No matter how hard she'd tried, she hadn't been able to break free of the horror, hadn't been able to anchor herself in reality.

Last night, she had died.

Vaughn D'Angelo jumped down from the branch he'd been padding along and landed gracefully on the forest floor. In the silvery light that had turned darkness into twilight, his orange-black coat should've shone like a spotlight, but he was invisible, a jaguar who knew how to use the shadows of the night to hide and conceal. No one ever saw Vaughn when he didn't want to be seen.

Above him, the moon hung like a bright disk in the sky, visible even through the thick canopy. For long moments, he stood and watched it through the dark filigree of reaching branches. Both man and beast were drawn to the glimmering beauty, though neither could've said why. It didn't matter. Tonight the jaguar was in charge, and it simply accepted what the man would have been tempted to think about.

A whisper of scent in the breeze had him lifting his nose into the air. *Pack.* A second later, he identified the scent as that of Clay, one of the other sentinels. Then it was gone, as if the leopard male had realized Vaughn had already claimed this range. Opening his mouth, Vaughn let out a soft growl and stretched his powerful feline body. His lethally sharp canines gleamed in the moonlight, but tonight he wasn't out to hunt and capture prey, to deliver merciful death with a single crushing bite.

Tonight, he wanted to run.

His loping gait could cover vast distances and usually, he preferred to run deep into the forests that sprawled over most of California. But today he found himself heading toward the populated lake city of Tahoe. It wasn't hard to walk among the humans and Psy even in his cat form. He wasn't a sentinel for show—he could infiltrate even the most well-guarded citadels without giving himself away.

However, this time he didn't actually enter the city proper, drawn to something unexpected on the fringe. Set back only a few meters from the dark green spread of the forest, the small compound was protected by electrified fences and motion-sensor cameras among other things. The house within was hidden behind several layers of vegetation and possibly another fence but he knew it lay inside. What surprised him was that he smelled the metallic stink of the Psy around the entire compound.

Interesting.

The Psy preferred to live surrounded by skyscrapers and cities. Yet deep within that compound was a Psy, and whoever that person was, they were being protected by others of their kind. Rarely did a non-Council Psy qualify for such a privilege. Curiosity aroused, he prowled around the entire perimeter, out of range of the monitoring devices. It took him less than ten minutes to discover a way in—the Psy race's sense of arrogance had led them, once again, to disregard the animals with whom they shared the Earth.

Or perhaps, the man thought within the beast, the Psy just didn't understand the capabilities of the other races. To them, the changelings and humans were nothing because they couldn't do the things the Psy could with their minds. They'd forgotten that it was the mind which moved the body, and animals were very, very good at using their bodies.

Climbing onto a tree branch that would lead him over the first fence and into the compound, the cat's heart beat in anticipation. But even the jaguar knew he couldn't do this. He had no reason to go in there and put himself in danger. Danger didn't bother either man or beast, but the cat's curiosity was held back by a deeper emotion—loyalty.

Vaughn was a DarkRiver sentinel and that duty overcame every other emotion, every other need. Later tonight, he was supposed to be guarding Sascha Duncan, his alpha's mate, while Lucas attended a meeting at the Snow-Dancer den. Vaughn knew Sascha had agreed to stay behind reluctantly and only because she'd known Lucas could travel faster without her. And Lucas had only gone because he'd trusted his sentinels to keep her safe.

With a last lingering look into the guarded compound, Vaughn backed down the branch, leaped to the ground, and started to head toward Lucas's lair. He hadn't forgotten and he hadn't given up. The mystery of a Psy living so close to changeling territory would be solved. No one escaped the jaguar once he was on their trail.

* * *

Faith stared out the kitchen window, and though only darkness looked back at her, she couldn't shake the feeling of being stalked. Something very dangerous circled the fences that kept her isolated from the outside world. Shivering, she wrapped her arms around herself. And froze. She was Psy—why was she reacting like this? Was it the dark visions? Were they affecting her mental shields? Dropping her arms through sheer strength of will, she went to turn from the window.

And found she couldn't.

Instead, she pressed forward, lifting one hand to press against the glass, as if she could reach outside. *Outside.* It was a world she hardly knew. She'd always lived inside walls, had had to live inside them. On the outside, the threat of psychic disintegration was a continuous drumbeat in her head, a pounding echo she couldn't block. On the outside, emotions hit at her from every angle and she saw things that were inhuman and vicious and painful. On the outside, she was breakable. It was far safer to live behind walls.

Except now the walls were cracking. Now things were getting in and she couldn't escape them. She knew that as certainly as she knew she couldn't escape whatever it was that prowled the edges of her property. The predator hunting her wouldn't rest until he had her in his claws. She should've been afraid. But of course, she was Psy. She felt no fear. Except when she slept. That was when she felt so much, she worried that her PsyNet shields would crack, revealing her to the Council. It had gotten to the point where she didn't want to fall sleep. What if she died again and this time it was for real?

The communication console chimed into the endless silence that was her life. This late at night, it was an unexpected interruption—the M-Psy had prescribed certain hours of sleep for her.

She looked away from the window at last. As she walked, a sense of impending disaster seemed to cloak her, a sinister knowing that lay somewhere in the shadowlands between a true foretelling and the merest inkling of what might be. This, too, was new, this heavy awareness of something hovering maliciously in the wings, just waiting for her guard to slip.

Schooling her face to show nothing of her internal confusion, she pressed the answer key on the touchpad. The face that appeared onscreen was not one she'd anticipated. "Father."

Anthony Kyriakus was the head of her family. Before she'd officially reached adulthood at twenty, he'd shared custody of her with Zanna Liskowski, with whom he'd formed a fertilization contract twenty-five years ago. They'd both had a say in her upbringing, though her childhood had been nothing anyone would ever label as such. At three years after birth, she'd been removed from their care, with their full cooperation, and placed in a controlled environment where her ability could be fully trained and utilized.

And where the encroaching tendrils of madness could be kept at bay.

"Faith. I have some unfortunate news concerning our family."

"Yes?" Her heart was suddenly a sledgehammer. She pushed all her strength toward containing the reaction. Not only was it unusual, it was the harbinger of a potential vision. And she couldn't have a vision right now. Not the kind of vision she'd been having lately.

"Your sibling, Marine, is deceased."

Her mind went blank. "Marine?" Marine was her younger sister, a sister she'd never really known but had kept an eye on from afar. A cardinal telepath, Marine had already climbed high in the family's interests. "How? Was is a physical abnormality?"

"Fortunately not."

Fortunately, because it meant that Faith was in no danger. Though having two of the rare cardinals had made NightStar a line of considerable power, it was indisputable that Faith was the biggest NightStar asset. She was the one who brought in enough income and work to place the entire PsyClan above the masses. Only Faith's health was truly important—Marine's death was a mere inconvenience. So cold, so brutally cold, Faith thought, though she knew she was as cold. It was a matter of survival. "An accident?"

"She was murdered."

The blank that had been her mind buzzed with white noise, but she refused to listen. "Murder? A human or a changeling?" Because the Psy had no killers, hadn't had them for a hundred years, ever since the implementation of the Silence Protocol. Silence had wiped violence, hate, rage, anger, jealousy, and envy from the Psy. The side effect had been the loss of all their other emotions.

"We don't know which. Enforcement is investigating. Get some rest." He nodded in a sharp physical period.

"Wait."

"Yes?"

She forced herself to ask. "What was the mode of murder?"

Anthony didn't even blink as he said, "Manual strangulation."

Love ♥ Romantic and 👄 Sexy novels?

Snuggle up with a Vampire..

Love Bites

LYNSAY SANDS

Etienne Argeneau can turn one human into a vampire in his lifetime - an honour his kind usually reserve for their life mates, to let their love live forever. But when Rachel Garrett, a beautiful coroner, saves his life at the cost of her own, Etienne has a choice to make. He can save her life in turn, and thus doom himself to an eternity alone, or he can watch his saviour die.

Have you fallen in love with **Love Bites?** Then why not continue the romance with: **Single White Vampire** and **Tall, Dark & Hungry**

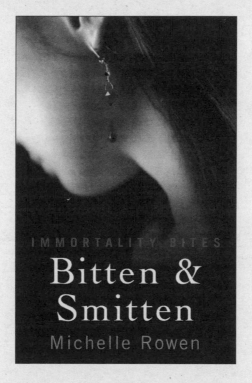

Love 😊 Funny and ❤ Romantic novels?

Be bitten by a vampire

CHLOE NEILL

SOME GIRLS BITE

A CHICAGOLAND VAMPIRES NOVEL

Merit thought graduate school sucked – that is, until she met some real bloodsuckers. After being attacked by a rogue vampire Merit is rescued by Ethan 'Lord o' the Manor' Sullivan who decides the best way to save her life was to take it. Now she's traded her thesis for surviving the Chicago nightlife as she navigates feuding vampire houses and the impossibly charming Ethan.

Enjoyed Some Girls Bite?
Then sink your teeth into Merit`s next adventure: Friday Night Bites

For more Urban Fantasy visit www.orionbooks.co.uk/urbanfantasy
for the latest news, updates and giveaways!

Nalini Singh was born in Fiji and raised in New Zealand. She spent three years living and working in Japan, and travelling around Asia before returning to New Zealand.

She has worked as a lawyer, a librarian, a candy factory general hand, a bank temp and an English teacher, not necessarily in that order.

Learn more about her and her novels at:
www.nalinisingh.com